ICE NEVER F

ICE NEVER F

A NOVEL BY

GIL ORLOVITZ

Tough Poets Press
Arlington, Massachusetts

Cover design by Ethan Orlovitz and Rick Schober.

Back cover photo by Victor Laredo,
used with permission from his estate.

ISBN 978-0-578-48266-8

This edition published with permission from
the Estate of Gil Orlovitz in April 2019 by:

Tough Poets Press
49 Churchill Avenue, Floor 2
Arlington, Massachusetts 02476
U.S.A.

www.toughpoets.com

For my son,
Guy-Max

At once, changes

Looking into the louring cloud, Aarons ear a thunderous vibration on the pale round fat ear I am angry with you God says. Pale round fat gray green

Eyes. Pale round fat

Hands. Fat round pale

Torso, and

Thighs, and

Skull I am angry with Aaron Emanuel thunders Adonai, Name of Names, the Face upon the waters of Aaron.

The small slugcurrents of his body

Here is an example, Lee thicks through cornedbeef slabs in the stupendous red white yellow black kitchen of the Naroyan familys Victorian mansion at Old York Road and Lindley Avenue, southeast corner

honesttogod I was raped Daniel Naroyan yells

to Daniel listening respectfully, I love the man Lee, I realize this is a shocking thing to reveal in a letter, Daniel writes, of a human organism a slime-mould who lacks a cellular wall. It could be true of Danny as well as of my uncle Aaron. Not of Danny in the physical sense, though he too is short, round, but wrought up in muscle, as though his muscles are hammers, not his nerves; Danny punches forward, and is chopped at; he never retreats to be axed, sliced, slashed. Still, experiencing him, I feel no armored sense in him.

Alls open, Uncle Aaron sees no gigantic sign on the concrete silos containing the anthracite reading LEVI COAL COMPANY, one two three four five lightgray cylinders like unique organpipes all quite even under the darkergray louring cloud over the Philadelphia Reading Coal and Iron freightyards paralleling Bodine Street in Kensington I have to punish you

What do you mean hes angry with you hes got to punish you. Levi

Emanuel patient. Still, he smiles sarcastically.

Glancing away, there is no eye Aaron can meet, there is no body he can rest upon, there is no hand he can touch, there is no object he can tarry at, no lingering at what pale within his pallor; if limited the traverse of his neck, the tallow torso bears the turn; if the torso strains no more at twist, the legs veer, the toes tremble in the gloomy voluminous shoes three sizes larger than his feet; he backs away, he sidles, his fingers permeate the hollow squares between the iron network that stretches from dusty linoleumed floor to the ceiling to form the cramped office on the one side and the narrow corridor on the other from which through larger periodical openings in the grillwork at the end of the day pace the sooty independent truckmen shoving fistfuls of green currency and silver and copper coin, but their percentage is in pennies, a half a cent a bag of charcoal sold in the round of grocerystores made from sunrise to sunset, a cent maybe on a bag of hardcoal

Levi what the hell am I gonna give my daughter when she grows up to get married if you dont have some rachmoniss on me now, three dollars and twentythree and a half cents my account says I should get more, all right Ill throw away the half a cent, give it to the synagogue, Hymie Krause of the fine thin convex nose, a double for Disraeli in a gray workshirt and an old army overcoat that hangs on him an underdeveloped scarecrow, What the hell didya say, you know goddamn right Im hard of hearing, hah? Big Bernie of the elephantine flat feet and the gigantically generous grin pokes at him, Ah the fuck with your hard of hearing, whatsa matter look at my feet I got corns I got bunions you hear me complaining, of course you couldnt hear me, watch him, Levi, Big Bernie bawls the hawing warning through the iron network, its an act, he cries in his schnapps.

Dave's youngest son limps to the television set and his oldest son squints through thick glasses, and the son in between is dead in between of leukemia of Alaska of Texas of California of a sprint from Pennsylvania Jeez I saw Big Bernie the other day over in East Los Angeles, same as he always was with his big flat feet yeh and that floppy grin of his his feet are still hurtin him

You and your goddamn feet whatsa matter with my head I got headaches and I got sinus everything wrong with the head I got and Im deaf yet. You know what, Levi? Hymie suddenly becomes friend to friend, I think maybe its that accident I had lets see I was just fourteen then yeh. A horse kicked me in the head, waddya know remember my helper Izzy? Yeh, hes a bigtimer now in Hollywood. Funny? Was he, funny? Im tellin ya the minute he got on the truck it was nothin but laughs so wheres my three dollars and twentythree cents? Whats the matter with Chief Aaron over there?

Sure it was this house, right here in Redondo Beach, in that chair, the one youre sitting in, Lee, Sue shrillnasals, sucking Dave into the accusation while Martin the eldest child squints quietly at television and Gregg the youngest with the clubfoot peers at his mother placidly, betraying nothing, thats where Phil died, little by little, day by day, I watched him fade away, teletransvision by transtelefusion, naw, there nothin you can do about leukemia, hiccoughing, thats why I didnt want to come back here.

75th Street, Staten Island, 23rd Street, Jennifer Hazlit finally SKF BALL BEARINGS Lee the sight of the freight could be the ocean beyond Provincetown of the iridescent harbor from the breakwater of rocks that Sy Tarassoff paints. Watercolors

A hoof is left in the head. Pow! The vibrations never stop. A certain punishment for not having actually felt the kick in the first place. Pow! Hoof as billiardball. Cannon, as with Aaron. Vibrations never, as with Herman Tarassoff, Sy's father, and punishment to the heart which is all over, the circulatory system carries the decree to all the physiological categories. Nobody feels the kick. Except the horse that kicks, and

Where does the horse go? rages sombrely the watercolorist along the Roosevelt Boulevard, greenlined and talltreed, the doubledirectioned center highway U.S. Number One coming into Philadelphia flanked by wide verdant strips for some ten miles themselves flanked by two additional one-way highways on either side proceeding east and west, past farmland and the transmitter for radio station WCAU, past seafood and hotdog casual one-storey wooden structures at the terminating circle on the eastern end—we are leaving the Pennsylvania State Hospital For The Insane behind at Byberry—and thus reversing through yellow meadow, courses for smashing golfballs into drives exclusively, fresh middleclass slum housing developments, two-storey brick homes one against the other with no land between or behind but simply iron poles and cord on the concrete tilt behind the garage for hanging the wash and the steep or shallow stinging green lawn in front all the way to Oxford Circle where a synagogue and medium cathedral adjoin and the avenues spoking beyond offer cemeteries of the major religions and a modest city park, though the description is not complete without pointing out that Barry and Selma Handler are moving with their shaggy behemoth collie into one of the newlybuilts since Barry decides, after seven years of psychoanalysis, to partnership his father in the latter's leathergoods business although that therapized son insists on retaining as friends communists and fellowtravellers, pow! Rachel and Levi Emanuel, parents of Lee and David, reside, on the other hand, between A Street and B Street on the Roosevelt Boulevard, at Number 236, just east of Rising Sun Avenue, in a considerably older dwelling, nonmortgaged, clear, although the night is sombre and Sy's rage clotted as he and Lee stop for a car racing by the corner of B and Roosevelt where, in a house that persists in appearing suspiciously private, a revolting faction splintering off from the parent congregation at D Street has set up its Hebrew quarters The hell with painting today Sy declares, turning from the fence separating him, Lee and Sam Abrams on Commercial Street from the Provincetown Harbor, the wind blowing white and blue, Its a little rough for a canoe, but lets take one out anyhow. You game?

Sam smiles his easy toothless smile and shows the open palms of his shoulders.

Sure, Lee says. The wind darkly trowels the waters, the unseen horses kicking the goyim should only have my headaches Hymie insists to Levi, who frowns Why do you have to bring them into it, they say the same things about you, but does that mean you have to make matters worse? My father is a very tolerant man, Lee tells others proudly, pow! Then why doesnt he give you more? Look at all he gave Dave, Rena complains bitterly and nakedly in the narrow bathroom at 3892 Frankford Avenue where Lee studiously leans into the mirror squinting at the lean darkblue features and delighting in poppissing a whitehead at the ragged dullpink target of a nipple jouncing in the slatefoam reflection of his wife's torso in the shower hovering at his neck and luxuriating in the tinge of elation diffused over his forehead as he cautiously compels the recessed minuscule viscid white jet from a blackhead onto the spotted splotched gleaming black hair;

been squeezed and pressed time upon time; whiteandblackheads forming at exactly the same location this year as last, tomorrow as yesterday, thirteen as at twentyseven or thirtyfive or sixteen, a calculated system of waste disposal synchronized with the pleasure function, Did you realize that he grins, turning and backwarding against the sink

theres another sink downstairs

theres a wide meaty rump of a Rena sitting on the porcelain in the dark usually reserved for dishes

Doctor Newman has a chuckle seizure. Its bent, he says to Rena. Its positively bent. How long have you been having intercourse on

the penis that spurts white viscid sperm. Now its entirely possible that this too is a waste disposal unit located on the forehead

No no no its impossible to reproduce the color areas in great art with fidelity. I dont agree with Malraux, Lee sprawls in the 804 Marley Road residence. The Lesbians upstairs are making an unconscionable racket, one blonde heavyfootedly pursuing the lightfooted dark Italian in consequence of an advertisement placed by Rena in the PHILADELPHIA INQUIRER to rent the upstairs apartment. Hes altogether ridiculous; he hasnt a single fresh insight into the plastic arts—you might just as well try to depict a Beethoven sonata verbally. Lonnie Mahan the Rendezvous celebrity sputters crooked teeth. Doctor Saul Reed, pediatrician, stutters through dense spectacles; his wife in saucer mask listens in enthralled agony. Daniel Naroyan imagines his peasant father running from City Hall to their house in West Philadelphia, terrified lest night fall and he lose his way

and the doors of Marley Road stand with their ears to their citizens

there goes Rena Emanuel with a thin short dark man

(Rick Russo)

but Lees in New York

whats Rena doing with a dark short thin man while Lees in New York

with a little puppy on a leash

they always make sure to walk only at night

weve known Lee since he was a kid

we know his family

we know Rachel

Levi

David

mother and father belong to the Congregation Brith Mikveh

where Lee is barmitzvahd
and confirmed
and gets up to talk brilliantly after the Friday Night Services
the short thin dark man looks Italian yet
what a shame for the parents
shame
shame
somebody is punished in blood
POW!

Its not the goddamn weather thats so bad Sam baritonally wails in the stem of the canoe but the wake of that goddamn Boston ferryboat. Lee fatalistically giggles in the middle. Disgustedly Sy suggests they make for the wharf pilings so they can change positions and Lee paddle for awhile from the bow, Youve been a passenger in the lap of luxury since we took her out, sitting there like a crooked vagina Doctor Newman was it unnatural the way I was sitting up there on the sink with my legs up? Well what led you to do it in the first place? We had nowhere else to go, Doctor, we couldnt do it in the livingroom we were afraid my mother might burst in. Wasnt it cold on your rump sitting up there on the porcelain? It was so cold I always gave a little yelp when I sat on it, I had to get warmed up first on my buttocks before Id let Lee put it in I dont understand my sisterin-law Frances decorating the kitchen in crimson, crimson lace curtains, crimson walls and ceiling, crimson kitchentabletop, yellow and crimson plaid linoleum floor, crimson wall cabinets, crimson

Wait a minute you idiot Sam yells as Sy extends his arm to grab one of the pilings theyre covered with barnacles and he abruptly rudderpaddles off on a veer, Lee stressing his body to the opposite side to keep them from capsizing, but not soon enough for Sy to withdraw his arm from a gentle brush with the barnacles that slash him wrist up forearm up the inside of the elbow up as far as the bicep, scythes of blood fanning down in streams.

Impossible to observe any blood in Sam's corpse underneath the paintings of his exhibition debut on 57th Street sponsored by the Abington Square Society. All the blood is in the paintings.

In Rena's vagina, too.

On the phone Doctor Lobov, the Goldsteins alternate family physician, advises Lee to give her up. In the voice of doom he says, Oil and water just dont mix. Let her go, Lee, let her go. The details are just too sordid, believe me. I treated her directly after

Sam doesnt eat. Well, an occasional hotdog maybe, Sy says placidly in his studio at Third Avenue and Thirtyfourth Street. Im tellin you he doesnt eat hardly that, rotund Nina wife number one with the wildly broken mask of face squeals.

Have you heard from Jennifer, Sy inquires in gentle nasty placidity. Sam serenely tugs at his pipe in the shack whose rear abuts the overgrown sanddune clotted with scrubby vegetation. Chief Aaron listens intently in his Girard Avenue walkup, the pale slugs of fat toes crawling around toward the flopping tongues of his outsize army shoes BOOM BOOM BOOM the greenhorn listens to the big guns BOOM BOOM BOOM Lithuania is spat across the Atlantic thousands upon thousands of miles away BOOM BOOM BOOM the guns blow Aaron's insides straight across the Atlantic to Lithuania

the snow is twelve feet deep

the Greek Orthodox church is smitten gold in the proning sun and Levi Emanuel gallops bareback on the horse toward the little town of N'muxt boasting three hundred and twentynine souls

galloping hooves in Hymie Krause's skull, through the blackheads and the whiteheads of the brain, theres a waste to be done across the aristocratic physiognomy

jolly redfaced Herman Tarassoff drives Sy and Lee and Al Gordon through the Jersey marshland over the Pulaski Skyway toward New York into the dusk. Lowkey lavender autumns the Raritan River. Early ice blues wharf and water indentation. The Skyway ramps to the Chrysler Building silverspire, throatlow lavender on the twilightslate. Crisscross blacksteel buttressing lowthroats over the river below, early icefloe, dim whitecow floating, an idling tug, a still man mooding from the deck, the redfruit brakelights of a hundred thousand cars ascending toward the Manhattan skyline in the humthrumthroated traffic, jolly Herman silent now, redface a glimmer in the rearview mirror, Sy and Lee and Al humbled in the early cold in the blanket over their thighs in the backseat, stalesmoked, duskeyed, ethyl and late autumn wind, the tower of the Empire State Building moored to the curving icefloe of the freshlyquartered moon, some dead bright silver thing dangled over the human structures, faintly gold the moon, faintly old, this is my father who paints too, on black velvet, for the commercial houses, peacocks and chinese pagodas to be hung on the middleclass walls when black velvet is in vogue, my father the interior decorator, pokerplaying till the fabulous peacocks scream from the middleclass night and swilling a fifth of Old Grandad with his cronies sitting by while an ailing Riva his sallowfaced wife whines from upstairs quietly ever so quietly as deuce and king high the wig of the heart is blown off

past Lithuania

past the BOOM BOOM BOOM

and the heart, baldheaded, cannot stand the shame

Im glad he died quietly, Sy says on the other side of B Street

No, I havent. Jennifer said she loved me in the letter she wrote me when I first got to Provincetown. I think Ive written her at least ten times. Did you see her?

Once, I think, in the Heel, with Guy Schonfeld.

Sam's corpse placidly puffs on the pipe on the floor at the bottom of the gallery his paintings hang in. Lee's belly, toothless, exhibits a gallery of ulcers, grinning in pain from the smoke of Sam's pipe, stinging. Blithely reeling a roulade, Rena pokes her face away from the piano toward the long lean Lee flatbacked on the sofa, My father had a whole nest of ulcers.

certainly I remember him, was introduced, hes an instructor in sociology at Penn State. You saw him with Jennifer?

Thats right.

God said its punishment. Aaron he said, I dont want you should eat. Im telling you I saw him plain as your face, in the Yard, up in the cloud. He was angry. He was very angry, Levi. The pale round fat gray green cherub shuffles to Lee, my nephew, look, its my nephew, I dont see my nephew very often, Youre in New York now Lee, hah? So what are you doing in New York? smiles Chief of the Cherubim Aaron.

Im writing plays, uncle.

Plays, plays, I know plays, its for people they should act in. Thats right, isnt it Lee? You saw him with Jennifer?

Yes, uncle.

So, Chief Aaron, you got everything under control in the Yard? The baggers got my truck loaded yet? Hymie jabs the cherub. Widegreeneyed, Aaron misplaces his smile, searches for it behind Hymie, around Levi's feet, toward the weighing scales. Levi made me the Superintendent of the Coal Yard. I got to see everything should be going right. The baggers shouldnt loaf. That big nigger Eddie Jackson is a troublemaker, some head loader he is. And that smart nigger Cal Lacefield, hes got too many things to say altogether. Levi whos the superintendent Cal Lacefield or me, because its snowing, the truckdrivers in the Yard are ignoring him as he shoutmumbles Load at Number Three, get off the scales momsarum the filthfaced neighbourhood kids shriek around the corner and race jumping up the steps skipping two and skipping three, hover at the rail shooting snowballs at Aaron standing and floating down there in the Yard in his giantsized flapping army overcoat cursing the filthfaces on their way to the pedestrian bridge that arcs over the freightyard tracks and sidings, the freight locomotive with its single pale yellow round jellyfish in the slateclouded day pushing a coalcar nutcoal peacoal stovecoal into the Yard where under the tinroofed shed the hotcold sweating Negros chuting anthracite into the heavyduty paper sacks

You ask me to be honest with you. You ask for the truth.

Thats all Im asking, Levi sits in his easychair under the brocaded lamp. Thats all I want my sons to be, is honest. Just tell me the truth.

Lee diametric across the livingroom, in another fat easychair where in the late afternoons alone against the dark wall the sweeping headlights of the passing traffic on the Roosevelt Boulevard endlessly flash

not even between the long fine sweep of Christine Novak's legs can Aaron detect his smile, youngest child of Rebeccah and Simon Emanuel, woolcarder of N'Muxt, Lithuania, not even among the reverberating field pieces at Camp Meade, this is where my Uncle Aaron Lee surveys the endless rows of gray barracks the first day after induction trying not to register the short stocky curlyblackhaired Kentuckian under the covers of the cot next to him slyly peering beneath the covers as he strokes his penis as he would a puppy Ah sho hated to leave that little ol galah got me down theah an if she ain heah ah guess this is the nex bes thing as can do, ain that right Lee, now look at that theah thing perkin itself up thinkin of mah little ol gal, you-all like to see how its coming up Lee?

No.

The seven children of Rebeccah and Simon Emanuel all contribute to finance the eighth child, Aaron, into the retail drygoods business after he is mustered out of the army following the Armistice. They rent a store for him at 4th and Master Streets in South Philadelphia. There is a butcher shop on one side and a funeral parlor on the other. The mortician is a widower who marries a glossybreasted Italian girl who, whenever her husband is called away to the graves, can be seen in her best black attire rushing past Aaron's shop into the butcher's where, delegating the cleaver to his assistant, the butcher hustles the mortician's wife into the back room and, as the refrigerator door can be heard slammed by the assistant as he reaches for frozenly bleeding shoulders and flanks and rumps, the butcher booms into the mortician's wife open grave

POW

with a little mustache of a smile Aaron hands the wrapped pair of mens socks to the customer.

filthfaced neighborhood boys pellmell past the shop upsetting some of counters piled with merchandise on the pavement in front of the shop-window shoelaces striped socks mens striped silk shirts bvds slantstriped ties selling for a nickel the patrons of the roumanian restaurant idly looking up from their gefullte fish across the narrow cobblestoned street, Fourth Street, the Number Seven trolleycar of the PHILADELPHIA RAPID TRANSIT, the PRT as it is intimately though with some rancor referred to, clanging by ironrumped and weathergreenbeaten, the motorman's black heel of the blackshod foot digging at the metal plug protruding from the floor to produce the clang, digging, digging, the refrigerator door slamming, the filthfaced boys pellmell past the shrugging cop on the beat, past the yellow firehydrant, a bloodstained truckman hefting a quarter of steer onto his redsplotched whitesmocked shoulder and staggering with it into the alleyway toward the rear entrance of the roumanian restaurant, the hearse leading the funeral procession honking at the traffic on both sides of the trolleycar,

let the dead man through

let the dead man through

the butcher in the back room thudding the mortician's wife open grave

let jesuschrist rest the dead man let sylvana the mortician's wife rest the live man

heel and

CLANG

the Kentuckian Wanna see him like a little ol puppy

POW

what do I owe you for the socks the customer says

the lithuanian guns go off in the italian butcher's back room

Im the youngest of eight brothers and sisters says Aaron

what do I owe you for the socks

Im the youngest of eight brothers and sisters i dont understand american yet somebody with stripes on his sleeve is telling me to do something papa Ill be a good woolcarder wont I

the guns are filled with water, three thousand miles of water

what do I owe you for the socks

I dont want to be in the army I didnt want to come to america its only because the whole familys in america

christine novak such a beautiful blonde polack only with such pimples on her face otherwise like the lithuanian christian girls

ulcers

Im sorry shes dead, pop

Lee what are such pimples called on the face

acne

so what causes it in Aaron I want to know did I want to come to america? neither did I, Levi says, its only because the family wants me to come, Im going to the university in Riga, I got a scholarship, one scholarship after another in the cheders, my father is proud of me, nobody asks me to card the wool so what causes it in Aaron who do you think is supporting him you think the rest of the family cares so much I brought him into the yard I pay for the room on Girard Avenue, me and Ben, Ben is the only other one who gives a damn

what do I owe you for the socks

the deadly razorcunted barnacles fan blood down Sy's arm If I keep living with you Ill kill you, Rena's blackpowdered hazel eyes stare at Lee on the top floor of the 75th Street walkup, I think you should know that, she says

interesting to know that somebody knows the notebook of Sam Abrams reads but what if you think nobody knows. What then? The cats in my studio know as much as anybody meticulously avoiding the empty beerbottles. They know Ill get them milk. And I do. Ill go without food for myself to get them milk. I have six cats, prowling amid the canvasses. I dont think Im a great painter. One thing I know: I like painting. Another thing: Ill live till I die—but painting. Doing nothing else. Its too hard to do other things. Its easy to paint. I do only whats easy. Its too painful to do things that are hard to do. And if I go without eating in order to go without pain, thats all right. Because to eat I would have to do things that are hard. And if little by little I die, thats all right, if it happens while I do the easy thing, the painting. An acquaintance of mine by the name of Lee Emanuel told me about his Uncle Aaron, a very interesting

No I wont contribute any money to help publish Sam Abrams' notebooks. I dont think theyre worth anything, Lee yells at Sy's friend, a nonobjective artist by the name of Bill Sachs, a slim swarthy young man with the expression of a misunderstood demon fanatically vehement on the superiority of Vivaldi over Bach. Edith flinches.

Round plaid scotch illegitimate Laura Ingersoll in her billowing peasant skirt all of seventeen years of plump age stands outside the Provincetown bus station near the Boston steamer wharf, the blood running from the barnacles, waiting with Lee to see him off on the late summer day late in the summer, the wind gusting at her skirt, the graycap clouds low on the wharf, the silvercap waves on their broomsticks in the bay

I dont see why you cant stay overnight another night, Lee, she says.

Ive got to get back to Philadelphia.

Somebody waiting for you?

No.

Well then, she says.

Ive got to get back.

I wish you didnt have to, Laura says, the round blue eyes in the round confection face, her lips firming in annoyance as her hands strive to keep her skirt low against the wind.

So do I.

Youll write me.

Yes.

Ill be going to New York so I can come see you in Philadelphia, she says.

Will you really?

Yes. Yes. I love you. But you dont love me, do you?

I do love you.

No you dont. I can tell. Maybe I dont love you either. Its just another summer romance. I feel bitter. I think I might cry.

I might too, Lee says. Laura smiles.

Even though theres a girl in Philadelphia? she says.

There isnt any there.

Oh go on. There must be three or four.

No there arent.

You being truthful, Lee?

Yes.

I think I love you very much, oh very much, Lee. They kiss very hard. The bus comes. Lee boards it. He takes a seat. Laura waves. Her skirt goes high in the wind. She has tears on her face as she tries to keep waving and her skirt down as the bus pulls out of the station with Lee looking back at Laura and her naked legs on the verge of plumpness

what do I owe you

You take the socks, Aaron nods at the customer.

Yes but what do I owe you. Was it fifteen cents or twenty, you told me but I forgot

You dont owe me nothing.

Big Bernie of the elephantine flat feet shambles his hulk through the Levi Coal Company office door and flattens his massive mitts against the iron cage. Hymies dead, he says, his big nose brooding down into the trough of his mouth. I just came from the Krauses. He died halfpast two. Im tellin ya, from the horse's kick he died, like he told us, when he was a kid.

How do you know, Levi says, his face grimacing.

Whaddya mean how do I know, Levi? They looked into his head. An autopsy they made, the thieves! They looked and they found a growth, a tumor, the size of a peach, thats how I know.

What the hell am I gonna give my daughter when she grows up to get married

to get married when she grows up

my daughter what the hell

am I gonna give

Headaches is a world?

Loving Lee in a distant way, playing with the smile on his own face as he would with a kitten though he never owns a kitten or a pet of any kind, fondling the smile in a corner of his face now and then, as if he must apologise for the smile if he finds it at all, loving Lee we say in a distant way, as if the temperature of love is too high to handle, surprised at the love, its not seen too often, seen as often as Aaron sees Lee, his nephew, his brother Levi's son, brother Levi, theres a surprise too, though there are other brothers and sisters Ben and Bella and Fanny and Jeremiah and Sadie and Dora and Naomi but only Ben visits him, loving perhaps not Lee in himself but the presence of the young man, a shy paternity in Aaron that is not done, no woman done by Aaron at all in his pale fat virginity, a lowkey dispersion of love all over his body, the love impossible to focus, as if Aaron cannot round it up as he looks for it as it scurries this way and that, therefore he musnt disturb the filthcaked Girard Avenue walkup he lives in because love is fear-possessed and though it may never become visible to Aaron nevertheless it is present, invisible because actually he must not look upon it, love actually then at last the Adonai, the Unutterable, the sexless God himself routed from the Old Testament, dirtcovered and thereby arrayed in gray cloud louring over Aaron's skull, with the face of anger capitalized, cloud indeed all that Aaron can gaze directly upon

the truckman with the thin aristocratic face of a disraeli but with the corner of the mouth twisted so as to point directly up and into the cannonading within the skull contrives no more to accumulate the quarter of a cent per bag in the coffin

thats nice youre writing plays, Aaron says to Lee. Someday youll be famous.

Yeh. Heavily grunts Levi.

Whats the matter with you you shouldnt believe in your own son, Hymie Krause scolds him. What kinda father are you anyway, hah?

Hurry up with the cash already, Big Bernie maudlins, Im dying on my feet.

Its a sure thing you aint gonna die with your boots on, Hymie taunts him. You aint even gonna die with your feet on.

Here take the socks, Aaron thrusts them on the customer. Dont pay me. Its free. To another slackjawed customer examining his wet shoes on the rainy pavement, Here take the shirt, please dont give me any money, its for free. You like this dress? he asks the woman. Fine. Take. It dont cost a thing. Im giving it away. Im giving all my stock away. The stock didnt cost me nothing so why should I charge for it?

What the fucks it matter how you die, Gene Hertzog rattles the office door behind him as he squats himself in, ears flapping, his burntred face with a diabolic mickeymouse expression, snakelipped, Lissen Levi when am I gonna get my money I cant stick around this godforsaken place all night, Ill never get home, theres four inches of snow out there already fuhchrissake, whatll my wife think, my hernias way up my ass by now

Shut up, Levi yells, you think Christine aint got ears

Pipe down, runt, Big Bernie lumbers his voice out

Hertzog dont worry me any, Levi, Christine's vast gray eyes snap up from her double entries.

Sam Abrams at the first one-man show of his paintings expires of a heart failure directly traceable to malnutrition,

but he has ten thousand dollars posted to his savings account. Ten thousand. But he doesnt stop his noneating habit. The cats are on the prowl for milk. They claw the canvasses trying to find milk. Theres no garbage in Sam's studio but the canvasses. The cats prowl and spit and meow and all they find is art. Not great art, even. The cats cant be blamed. Hes got ten thousand dollars. Why doesnt he start eating? Sam for christ's sake what good will pickles do you. Its very simple, Sam writes in his notebooks, the heart has been transferred to the belly. And you dont stuff the heart with food. That would be dangerous. I dont want to take chances. The heart must be kept clean, toothless, and we can see his heart naked on his gums as he smiles sweetly, innocently, guilelessly, my friend Lee tells me about his Uncle Aaron whom I understand perfectly, hes taken up lodgings here, hes my Uncle Homunculus, all the vital organs have been transferred to the belly. The brain and the whole nervous system now live in the belly. My prick lives in my belly. And not one of them is fed. Only cats can scream for food, and spit, and be unfaithful, and slam themselves against my body yowling for food, and I feed them, because theyre outside, and you can feed the outside animals, this is permissible, but the inside you must starve, and you can only pinpoint purity

by centering all your organs in your belly so you can feel the force of the necessity of denial PRICKING PRICKING PRICKING

Lee jabs an icepick at the discarded glass washboard standing atilt in the small black trashdrum against the whitewashed garage wall. We look curiously at the little boy, then the garage, and then the summer just outside the garage in the little backyard. We note a few other matters: his mother is gone for the afternoon; his father is working at the Yard; his brother is newly married and running his own coalyard financed by Levi;

Georgiana, the Emanuel's Negro girl who does the washing, ironing and housecleaning

Cal Lacefield suddenly laughs white scars delivering stovecoal to replenish the Emanuel's bin got to through an alleyway running the length of the house in the autumn the chute on an oblique from the rear of the truck down to the cellarwindow the flying black lumps slide and jostle and careen with scraping roar and swerves off his lumpy cap to reveal the cinnamon crown of his cranium to Georgiana piling the white scars into her guffaw dark as she rakes the rusty lawn of its autumn leaves, all muscular dipping sheer belly in and buttocks out five feet six inches of her with shakefist tits iglooing from her chest

the only one in the house. The backyard grass is a churn of green

the prayingmantis silently hissing defies the gartersnake

on the castiron fence demarcating the adjacent yard the profuse brambles pricklepicket the red roses. Streamers of honeysuckle spiral, shoot, shimmy, loop and spurt up the brick wall of the back of the garage over the tiny square window up trellis and rainspout to reach the roof, there teetering, imminent acrobats in a purr of breeze, the dense sweet effusion of civetsaccharine, a bladderthurible slowly swung in an imminent relief of osmotic dispersion by the breezepurr purring, a smellfilm molding whatever wave within or without, neargurgitantly sick drifting into the open door of the garage where the boy with honeysucked mouth and the flaring nostrils of the icepick stabs at the glass washboard in a studious fury. A fat little boy with black hair glinted oilblue and the ruddy flesh of Levi and big brown

hes got bedroom eyes, smirks Donna Zion, his cousin from across the Boulevard

and small rose ears that mug out a little from his skull

dimly sometimes in the bedroom night he hears Rachel and Levi talk of Aaron he may soon be leaving the Veterans Hospital hell feel better thinking hes superintendent in the Yard hell feel better

be a lot happier

naturally we wont give him any real responsibility

its a trick

why does this have to be played on him

Levi why dont you bring the boy to the Yard sometimes, Aaron worriedly counselinquires of his brother, He should be learning the business,

Ill teach him

YOULL TEACH HIM YOULL TEACH HIM

YOU?

why not?

Go back into the Yard, Levi thunders, for god's sake dont bother me youre needed outside Im telling you, Im in here, Levi, your brother, you recognize your brother, dont you

Levi certainly I rec

So leave me alone already

Aaron goes, shoulders under a tent, I was only trying to

Shut up the drivers are waiting, we get a good season, its cold and it has to snow IT HAS TO SNOW so I got three trucks stuck on the street i cant deliver

I CANT DELIVER LEAVE ME IN PEACE FOR GOD'S SAKE AARON

Waddya hafta shout at Chief Aaron for? Hymie Krause says to Levi. Your own flesh. What can he know? Waddya want from him? He means well. Your own brother

Levi is abashed. Flushes. What am I yelling for he says to himself.

Oilslick patches the garage, from the drip of the father's Buick, poppa always buys a Buick, trades it in, year after year, for the new model, the Buick is downtown at the Yard, parked on a small vacant lot opposite the office next to the runted two-storey houses of squeezed Bodine Street with its proliferating poor in Irish and Pole and Bohunk and German and Italian

Capish italian? it means do you know Italian Levi genially speaks from his square ruddy face down to the boy in the whiteenameled kitchen with the table of the one rickety leg

The praying mantis strikes, grips the garter snake thrashing in the churn of the green grass, the bared brittleness of the praying mantis Lee watched for twenty minutes, his testicles tightening, his penis swelling, grabbing the icepick from the little shed containing the massive refrigerator adjoining the kitchen serviced by Tom Shannon the square-chunked pinkfaced iceman loud and bluff bearing the ponderous silver-gray aluminumstreaked icechunk on his pianoshoulders winter and summer blackstained with melt his gray shirt Is it to be ten or fifteen pounds this mornin Mrs Emanuel who girlygiggles in reply

races into the garage and methodically jabs jabs jabs the discarded glass washboard, the icesweat sticking his blue rayon shortsleeve shirt against his bellfed body, gasoline and oil and honeysuckle and swirling gartersnake and snapclawed praying mantis and thrashing green grass and iglootitted Georgiana in the pale gray green slugs of his nose mucously swelling

(There is no doubt about the fact that the genitals, in order to be blown clean, often as not take up lodging in the nostrils.)

REEKSKRUNKSKRAAAK the glass splays glittering shards, Lee blurtbodies, neckskids, spinescreams, skull pulls the stretched ladders of the throat, no slicesplinter blading him but one slim seer of a hissing needlerasp across the back of the little finger of his right hand, a slip of slit a chit shy of the bone. Still. Crouch. Lee. Looks.

A sigh of a silence.

Dusk scarlet the blood pumps out.

Pumps.

Pumps.

Pumps.

Bulge of the blood, and a spurtsplurge, and a recession. Bulge of the, and a spurtspl, and a reces

Pumps. Scarletdusk against blackstained icesweated blue rayon chest. He doesnt lose his spine. He wraps a fist around the little finger. Sticky. He can feel the bulgepump, the recessional splurge. He feels as if his heart his testicles his penis are all splurged out of the little finger. Theres a block a chunk a fifteen pound slab of clotted air plunked down inside his throat. First he walks out of the garage. The gartersnake is dead. Lee smells no sweet. Then he trots into the house. Georgiana he calls, Georgiana.

Whats the matter boy.

I think I cut myself.

Oh mygod boy.

What do you think I should do.

Here now lemme wrap that in a hankachiff

reddening.

reddening the fine wrinkled white

reddening

he looks at it, curious, fear not knowing what to do. fear looks around. fear looks in his balls. fear looks in his eyes. fear searches the belly, the thighs, the neck, the bowels. no, not there. where must fear go now. it feels strange. fear feels like a stranger in the boy. fear becomes panicstricken. the boy doesnt know what to do with his fear. his fear pleads. all right. take it easy. wait a second, okay, okay

now you just get yourself to the drugstore the druggistman hell fix it up

will he?

sure he will.

the druggistll take care of it?

sure he will.

reddening. the whole handkerchief sodden with crimson.

all right.

he trots. thru the garage. across Ruscomb Street. theres a crazyguy a few houses down the section of Ruscomb street still a dirtroad rutted west one block to A Street. down to Rockland Street, at the corner of B and Rockland the druggist

youre lucky, lee, you nearly hit the bone.

will i be okay?

sure. look its almost stopped bleeding. you clot quick.

oh.

Im gonna bandage it very tight, Lee. its a clean wound. its deep and it could be sewn but i dont think its necessary.

okay, the boy says.

it might leave a little scar, the druggist shrugs. thats all. you wont mind.

no i wont mind. so Im allright, huh?

sure you are. youll be fine.

thanks a lot.

thats all right, the druggist smiles.

it scared me a little because it was coming out so fast, but it didnt scare me too much, Lee looks up at the druggist behind the counter in the rear, where past him the little vestshaped swinging door he could see the old upright piano of a typewriter for the prescriptions one piece of paper in there a label partly written the shelves stacked with Latin names and

i think you were pretty calm, the druggist says.

trotting

but what is he going to tell his mother

Yeh my mother has a weak heart, Sy says disgustedly.

High up on the bank of the Rocky River in the deep pine woods of South Carolina Lee trails as the last man in a company of thirty socalled volunteer swimmers on a mission for the armored infantry regiment of the 3rd Armored Division during summer maneuvers preceding the North African invasion. After a thirtyfive mile forced march, the volunteers must swim across the Rocky River with full field packs and rifles and establish a position on the opposite bank. Sweating from the midsummer heat, almost as intense now at dawn as it will be at noon, near exhaustion from the last twisted scrabble and scramble through dense underbrush and shredding bramble to reach the ridge overlooking the river, his rifle sling rubbing his shoulder raw through his drenched fatigues, and his fullfield pack heavy as two twentyfive pound charcoal bags, Lee hears a rending soprano scream and momentarily halts.

Passing Dr Jonah Silver's house, between B and C Streets, Lee automatically notes that the Brith Mikveh's rabbi is quietly reading in the light of the glassshaded table lamp on the enclosed porch. Dr Silver's goatee rhythmically nods over the book. There are the pale plump cheeks and the faintly mongoloid large shining brown eyes and the fine straight black hair brushed to one side. His limp white hand reaches up to stroke the goatee. The mouth is small but voluptuous and very red. Compounded fatalism and anxiety harass the features. Lee idly wonders where Mrs Silver, the rebbetzin, taller than her husband by at least a head, lantern-jawed, slackmouthed, adenoidalvoiced—can be. Dr Silver is first assigned to Brith Mikveh when the organizers of the synagogue select him upon graduation from the seminary; the house of worship is only a two-storey residence on the corner of B and Ruscomb, an empty lot adjacent, where Lee and the other children throw snowballs after Hebrew School in the winter twilight

Funny thing, Sy says at his side.

Eh?

I can feel the barnacles slashing down the inside of my forearm. I can feel the sting, Sy says moodily.

The blood drips slowly into the green water.

Why should I remember the barnacles bringing blood to my arm at Provincetown when my father's just died?

I dont know, Lee says.

They were just barnacles. We were having a time.

I know.

My arm stings. Why is that?

I dont know.

Why dont you know? You know a lot of other things.

I just dont know, Lee says calmly.

Im sorry, Im not mad at you, Sy says.

I know.

More than anything else in the world I didnt want my father to die. Sy's voice is cumbrous. The maple trees lining the Boulevard are sluggishly shadowed. I care more about his death than I would about my mother's. I loved him, Lee. You remember him.

Yes.

He laughed more than any other guy I know. He was a very witty man.

Yes.

He always had a joke.

Thats right.

He was so jolly, my father.

Yes.

Its damn nice of you to walk with me.

Sure.

I had to walk with somebody. I had to talk to somebody. I couldnt think of anybody but you I could talk to.

Its all right, Sy.

I wish I could remember more about my father. All of a sudden all I can remember is my father laughing with a red face. Beet red, Lee.

Why didnt you stop by Danny's?

Naroyan? Hed chatter. I couldnt stand chatter now. Dannys like a magpie. Its not that I dont like Naroyan. But right now I couldnt be with him.

The green blue spring night through the maples. Incessantly the headlights white and the rearlights red east and west through the greenblue, a district called Feltonville in Philadelphia. Sys from Logan, fifteen blocks away, on a street called Wellens Avenue.

Christ lets get past Eli Berman's fast, Sy says. Eli Berman with the crazy grin, with the giggle that always sounds as if its coming through mucous. Why is his head always tilted to one side? He looks like a storm-trooper with weak glasses. He laughs like a girl. Hes a lousy painter, he doesnt even know how lousy he is, hes got an obsession with red. Almost exclusively a red palette

Wheres Lee Mrs Emanuel? Is Lee at home? Gee youre looking well Mrs Emanuel. Will Lee be home later dya think? Tell him to call me when he gets home, Eli grins fatuously, his skull tilted, his weak glasses misted, his thin body quivering Hows Mr Emanuel? He certainly works hard doesnt he? Your Lee is certainly one wonderful boy let me tell you Mrs Emanuel youre looking younger than ever, go ahead laugh Mrs Emanuel I like to hear you laugh you sound just like a young girl are you sure Lee isnt home, now dont tell me youre hiding him? Youre not, are you, he laughs in high register peering through misted glasses from the enclosed porch into the living room, his shoulders stooped, Lee youre not busy upstairs are you, youll tell him I was here wont you Mrs Emanuel thank thank thank you

A few strolling couples nose to nose returning from the second show at the Feltonville Theater, the neighborhood movie house. Otherwise the Boulevard pavements are empty under the maples. Sy Tarassoff's magnificently semitic nose turns down its nostrils over the upper lip. A half a head shorter than Lee, who is a liltle more than six feet, Sy turns his triangular face toward him. The broad brow is augmented by a receding hairline. The pointed tiny chin with the sharp underthrust is accentuated by the thick mustache on the curt space between the upper lip and the base of the nostrils.

He means well, Lee temporizes.

Who? Sy demands, pugnacious.

Eli Berman.

Ah I stopped thinking about him, Sy sniffs in disdain. Then, he is baffled, worried, chiding. Whered the horse go?

What are you talking about.

The horse that kicked my father's heart in. The heart had to be kicked in before hed die. Whered the horse go? How could he kick anybody who laughed? I dont understand, Lee.

Hows your mother?

Shes at my aunt's. Shell be all right. Sy tosses her aside, cryptically. Shes just gone from sitting up in one bed to sitting up in another, with her weak heart. Tachycardia. Sometimes it races, sometimes it slows down too much. Shell live a long time. Shes always upstairs in bed. Not my father. Hes downstairs, downstairs, playing poker, telling the latest jokes. Whered the horse go in the exclusively red palette? I mean, you scrape your arm against barnacles on the pier and they cut you like scalpels while youre having a decent time. Black little barnacles. Were you jealous?

Of what?

That I dated Laura Ingersoll that week?

Lee shrugs. Ahead the Boulevard suddenly squeezes a waspwaist where it bridges over Shit Creek. I made up with her, Lee says, after you left. She made the overture, out on the rocks, the breakwater. The sprained ankle ruse.

Why the hell didnt you tell me youd been seeing her?

Lee is silent. The traffic squeezes in over the bridge. The creek stinks, used for garbage and factory waste. The stink leans solitarily over the thick stone rail where the two young men halt for awhile, joining the stink. Beyond the banks of the creek the blue green spring night is a stupefyingly deep quarry. Lee smokes a cigarette. Sy takes out his pipe. You ought to try a pipe, Sy says.

Im impatient.

Ah Im just baiting you. I didnt give a damn for Laura. She was young and sweet and all that. I figured you and Jennifer . . . Have you seen her at all lately?

No.

You dont mind my talking about her, Im trying to forget my father a little while. Just a little while.

I dont mind.

Something had to kick his heart in. Sy carefully stuffs his pipe, then a long match in flaring light, pulsing, gouges the pits of his nostrils as the pipe bowl glows in an exclusively red palette. Lee traces the scar on his right little finger. A boy jabs at a discarded glass washboard in a garage.

The lousy black little barnacles, Sy spits, then slowly puffs on the pipe. Its a little cold for a spring night.

You want to walk back?

Not yet. What kicks a man's heart in? If not a horse, what? He made other people laugh. I take after my father, Sy says, frowning, his nose practically touching his chin. I wouldnt miss anybody else. But Ill miss him. You sure you dont mind my talking to you ?

No.

The headlights of the passing cars sweep over them. Like the blank wall in the livingroom I like to watch when Im by myself, Lee thinks. But wheres the child that watches the wall? Your remembering the barnacles slashing your arm is an inept symbol, Lee says. Youre provided with an inadequate pain. Youre sleepy, youre feeling dull, sluggish, cumbersome, heavy. The memory tries to quicken your grief.

Maybe youre right, Sy says dully.

But it doesnt quite work. Its only remotely tantalizing. The blood drips slowly into the green water. Theres not much blood. The wound is superficial, after all. It looks serious, but it isnt. Lee's heart penetrates thumping drum and stays inside. His skull feels thickly light. The head-lights slash at them through the bluegreen night, cooling rapidly, the chill rising slowly through their feet.

Maybe youre right. Sy is sunken in his own chill. Sam Abrams lies at their feet. Sy kicks at him, idly. Idly, Lee turns over the toothlessfaced body that idly smokes a pipe. His bluegreen paintings are suspended from the Philadelphia nightsky. Mild Sam Abrams. Sams so plastic, Sy says, malleable, you can do anything with him, he wont argue, he wont fight, all the horses of the world can stomp him, kick in his guts, smash in his face, pound his heart to a pulp

the symbol isnt working. (the major defect of man in his world. Up to a point, they function. Up to a point, they convey. Up to point they

)What goods a symbol, Lee thinks, if it cant make me feel any grief for Herman Tarassoff, his heart inside the drum as the drum is thumped, the heart resisting, thats why it gets inside, the sound so immense that it cannot involve the heart at all, I should feel as if Sy's father is my father, I want to feel grief

There are tears in Lee Emanuel's eyes. Ive got another father, he exults. Not only mine. Two now. One live, one dead. Perhaps I can acquire more fathers. There should be no limit, my pier covered with barnacle fathers slashing down my entire body till all my blood is gone due to the cutting fathers. I got to scratch my whole body against an indefinite barnacle multitude of fathers, because sons itch with too much blood, were too rich with the accumulations of the past fatherhoods, so that we must shed this blood, doesnt my own father drink an irradiated chemical to thin out his own blood? Isnt his own heart too violent from never having poured out any blood? Thats why hes had his two heartattacks, and the diabetes, he never let his blood out for his own father or grandfather he never talks about them at all, he never tells me any stories about them simply that his father cards wool and makes trips and hardly ever sees him in N'Muxt, what the hell does my father expect, but its Sy whos slashed, not me, and thats terribly unfair, I hate Sy for his valid grief, or at least his potential for grieving even though he isnt capable of it now with the lights scraping against the sharp blank wall, I want to see something come out of the wall, thats why I stare at it so intently, I want a transformation to take place in my loneliness up there on the wall that Sam Abrams paints. Ah, you see. Sam paints my blank walls. Sam is the traffic along the Boulevard. Sam autos east and west, with no idea of where hes going except to rub up against the walls of all the unknown solitary people watching them

Im very cold, Sy. Come on, Ill walk you back.

Merely nods, Sy does, bows

You got to eat, Aaron.

God forbids me, Levi. He is angry with me his pale round fat gray green

Eyes. Pale round fat

Hands. Fat round pale

Torso, and

Thighs, and

Is determined. Intractable. Stubbornsweet. As a fat white ant crawling, or a black one, ponderous in the gut. The brothers and sisters assemble in his Girard Avenue walkup, a chair and a table and an army cot and a wooden icebox and piles of ancient newspapers, a Shit Creek stink, a rope used for a belt around Aaron's middle, the dripping obese barrel of the virginal man turning full circle in the gunnysack pants at the powwow of Ben Emanuel and Bella Zion and Sadie Schwartz and Levi Emanuel, who sit watching the bare thick fatpadded ankles of Aaron wading in the oleaginous army shoes, I could run out and get something so maybe you could have some tea, Aaron suggests vaguely, worried a little that nobody is eating or drinking and worried

a little

that his brothers and sisters seem concerned, his body padding around the room without moving on the skeletal structure, as if his flesh so ballooned, on impulse at any time, he could float without motion, his mouth tripping ever so slightly over a tiny object of a smile, three pairs of graygreenblue eyes

squarefaced thickbodied bulgebiceped Levi his hair blanching;

longrectanglefaced Bella with her mouth trimmed of any curve on a boneinspired body, but a cunning sweetness fanning out from the lips, her hair altogether gray;

shorterrectanglefaced Ben of waxed pointed mustache, guileless irony masking him, the Yiddish boulevardier.

And one pair of snapping chipperglinting black eyes

his sister Sadie, the oldest of the lot, back nearly bent in two, the partial cripple hobbling here and there around the city in cold weather and in hot, early and late, her hair still gleamingly black with a white thread here and there, the belle of N'Muxt

all fixed on Aaron. Ben hunched on a corner of the table, Levi in the chair, the sisters on the cot.

Well Aaron, Bella the sweet reasoner, for whom any problem at all a solution may be found, the mothersister, the whip encased in sugar

Lee and Rena stealthily slip into the upstairs room of the house in Atlantic City, astonished to find Aunt Bella sitting upright in a white wicker chair, flesh white as the wicker, the trimmed mouth more trimmed and utterly bloodless, the graybluegreen eyes reluctant to veer from the open window looking out over the ocean, her body hardly a trapped thing in the nightgown, the nurse hovering at the bed, Aunt Bella hovering over her own body and rinsing her brain incessantly over the oncoming combers of the Atlantic, rinsing, rinsing, clean white gray blue green, a bloodless season in the summertime

Its not we dont believe in God, Bella says to Aaron

Bella?

Yes, Aaron.

Bella.

Yes.

Bella.

Yes, Aaron.

A tentative recognition, a comber coming upon the shore, but as swiftly receding

Bella?

But coming in again.

Its good to see you, Aaron says. I cant understand you shouldnt come more often. You know Im ashamed I cant visit the family myself but the family can come here

Bella. My clothes. You know. Im not dressed.

Who cares if youre dressed, Bella says.

I dont want to go out, Aaron apologises. Except where Im needed, like at Levi's Yard.

We need you there, Levi says. All the truckers are asking for you, Hymie, Gene Hertzog, Big Bernie

Tell them Ill be there, Ill be there, Aaron nods seriously, very gravely, They should wait for me, tell them Ill be back, they shouldnt try to put anything over on you, Ill be back to supervise.

Snapping, cracking her back in two, digging her lips all the way into her mouth so that they touch her teeth, worshiping forward, she never misses a synagogue service, she hobbles along Roosevelt Boulevard like a turtle rockingchair, fiercely bent on attaining Brith Mikveh, where she must pray, vengefully, there goes Sadie Schwartz, nothing stops her, her nose flaring, widening as she pulls in her mouth, her arthritic joints snapping and creaking, whos well, what do you mean how am i feeling, look and see how Im feeling, but I manage, a person has to manage, I cant stick in the house, I take the Number 50 trolley every morning to the drygoods store, what do you mean I should retire, I give a ten thousand dowry to each of my daughters, what have I got left, I still got to work,

So why dont you eat and get some strength back, she snaps at Aaron, so you can be the superintendent again, hah?

Oh stop, Sadie, Ben sneers, you cant talk to him that way, whats the matter with you

God loves you, Aaron, Bella is the sweetly startled one, gently reproving, malice the last thing she could possibly be accused of, all humans complete children to her, sane or insane, male or female, though she can hardly bare to keep sitting on the cot, cleanliness her greatest virtue and yet very much crawled into here, her skin putting out feelers for any sudden materialization of vermin, So why should he want to tell you stop eating. Come have supper with us on the Boulevard

How could I have supper, Im not dressed, and its such a long trip, aint it a long trip? Aaron is vague. Besides, Bella?

Yes.

Besides, I couldnt break the law God tells me.

But Aaron, Bella insists with the softest of philosophic tones, endearing, Aaron darling, suppose, God forbid, you keep on not eating, hah? Just suppose.

What what?

Just suppose.

Bella, Levi says, Im telling you this is no good. Ridiculous so many of the family should be here. Im telling you we cant do anything.

Just suppose, Aaron.

Bella.

Aaron darling if God forbid you dont eat from now on you could starve. You dont want to starve. From this you could die.

What are you talking Bella, Aaron pads over to her, patting her, God wont let me die, what are you talking?

Ben stands abruptly, fingering his mustache, twirling it, his fingers a spring, his body a touch and spring, his mustache a twitch, his long fingers bunched in but the index finger springing out, Look here, Levi, better we should finish this somewhere else?

On the second floor flat of the apartment house on the south side of 75th Street between Columbus Avenue and Central Park West Lee's eyes swerve past the crossed sabres on the wall. He can with some misgivings fancy himself a target. To the naked body of Gia Antonelli lying on the bed beneath the crossed sabres, memento of the days when her husband is a fencing instructor. Now her husband sells foreign cars and suffers from a heart ailment as well. Gia herself displays some five feet six inches of creamy meat; childless, though thirtyone years of age; with great helpings of tit heaped up to Lee's mouth sucking on the darkclouded nipples; the ribridge permitting the belly to slide down to a sucked waist; high on the forehead of Gia Antonelli's groin a thick twisted mass of shining coarse black curls slickly scoop at the squirming pink scallops on which Lee's finger scrapes, but these barnacles bring no blood from his flesh; low on Gia's forehead the hairline supports profuse whorls of charcoal black tresses. The woman, her long sabrecurved legs with their veins still whitely masked drawn up and splayed

Get it over with, Lee. I really dont know when hes coming back

At the Veterans Hospital on the outskirts of Philadelphia, the moment he is admitted, Aaron displays a wide rottentoothed grin.

Cant you get it up, Lee?

Im trying. It takes a little while. I dont like the situation of being rushed.

Well then forget about it now.

I dont want to, Gia. Lee sweats at the uncrossed sabres. Frantically he sucks at the nipples, chews the breasts. The woman is too beautiful, something he doesnt want to admit. Gia is the most beautiful woman he has ever been naked with; with the faintest suggestion of a humped nose; a nudge of a chin; the stuporous stupid cuntaleptic faintly bulging whitegleaming black eyes. Hes got to get an erection, hes got to make the damn thing come up, the praying mantis must devour the gartersnake, and he tries to insert his abashed bulge. If he can only get the damn thing in, itll grow

You happy now, Aaron, Levi asks his superintendent lying on the white hospital bed.

Aaron nods happily if he can only make his prick become a forearm to be slashed by a pink barnacle he doesnt give a damn, scrape it, scrape it, scrape it damn it till the blood will come

I dont want to anymore, Lee, Im scared. Please stop.

No

the hell with the praying mantis and the gartersnake, the baby contemplates the crawling fat black ants on the white cement path curving toward the house under the arbor at 7th and Berks Street Rachel Emanuel complains proudly that Lee talks to anybody on the corner whos waiting for the trolley

Please stop

No itll be big in a minute Aaron's sabre of a smile is without wound the fencing has been hung up the smile is a trophy it can hurt nobody

Im scared hell come in Lee I think youre a sadist

No, Gia Ben flicks at his mustache, the Yiddish boulevardier is sad Now youre in the hospital Aaron I see youre eating again my uncle Aaron Lee tells Gia in the Museum Restaurant on the southeast corner of 77th Street and Columbus Avenue his belly like my exwife Rena's father's used to be is a nest of ulcers theyre bleeding the belly scraped against too many barnacles in his life theres a forearm shoving against the pier with the gentlest of motions nothing really should happen its with astonishment that Sy draws his arm away to find the wound fanning blood into the choppy green waters a helluva day to go out in a canoe even with the gentlest motion something is slashed

dont cry so hard Lee

the ulcers are bleeding Gia

the ulcers are bleeding my father says the doctors told him Aaron maybe has a week to live

FUCK FUCK FUCK

I CANT I CANT I CANT

he never hurt anybody why does a horse have to go kick him in the head hes always telling jokes hes a merry man

a merry man

now the ants crawling across the white sabre pathway Lee regards contemplatively at the end of winter its still too cold for him to be sitting on the pavement he lowers his head so his big brown eyes can more minutely study the crawling creatures fat and black crawling with their shining burdens up the white belly her hair grows as far up as her navel

stop it Lee Im frightened please

please

please how come youre eating now Aaron Ben bobs his head up and down

cherubic pale round fat gray green white slugcrawl of a face of sweetboy fiftysix years of age upon the neat white hospital of the earth perfectly arranged now in the oblong room with the starched nurses darting in and out no gray louring cloud that Sam Abrams can hang from the ceiling

God aint angry with me anymore is

Smiling,

IT WONT GET HARD GODDAMN IT IT WONT GET HARD GIA

WILL YOU GET UP AND GET DRESSED PLEASE IM BEGGING YOU LEE IM BEGGING YOU

ALL RIGHT GODDAMN IT ALL

I think hes dead, Levi, Ben says, his waxed mustache pooped. His waxed mustache melts a little. A piece of melted wax drops on Aaron's grinning face.

Yeh, Levi says, ponderous, staring down dryeyed at his dead brother, the youngest of the family, the fat pale slug crawling down Lee's path.

No, Ben says, he died happy.

Sure, Levi says. Very happy, he says, with ponderous sarcasm.

Its possible, Ben says, he was happy.

Yes, Levi says. La commedia e finita, he tells his son Lee. One of Levi's favorite expressions. La commedia e

Good old Oedipus, Daniel Naroyan writes, he should have never blinded himself; if he had any sense he would have merely sat under a palm tree and contemplated his Id. Or better still, he should have gone queer, and like Socrates, chased after the Athenian athletes, just to teach the Id a lesson . . . damn if HE was a motherfucker . . . Im forty now, tired, half bitter, half sweet. Yes, I will continue to tinker away at my clavier . . . loving the little tinkle tones and caressing the chords of the tonic and dominant triads. But I am, like other hapless artists both behind and ahead of my time. For in me is the old . . . and everyone wants the new, so I must wait until more searching and loving eyes will turn to me, seeing the new in the old . . . And besides, I can always ply my Bach, who is Daddy to me now, that God and master to whom all art owes timeless allegiance and within whose folds there is eternal peace and a kind of final resting place. Sebastian Bach! Rock! Friend! Rampart! Love and greetings to you all, Daniel. P.S. Vale Toscanini. Art and fire.

So. So heres a little boy. His name is Lee Emanuel. A long path of hard pavement curves like a sabre to the threestorey frame house over an enormous lawn. The front of the house is shaded by a great poplar tree, and vines and creepers overhang the roof of the front porch. Theres a little swing for Lee and theres a rockinghorse. One morning at the back of the house a photographer appears with a pony, and Lee is swung into the saddle, his body packed in a hive of clothing. Its a white pony with brown patches. Lee looks straight at the photographer who bundles his head under a black cloth attached to a black box with silver trimmings and a glistening silvercollared eye. The photographer squeezes a black bulb and Lee falls

onto the sabrepath where hived in packed wool he sits staring at crawling black curls emerging from between the cement blocks. Fat tiny black curls straightening out and curling and pulling little bits of things. He shouldnt be sitting on the pavement, because its still cold, and spring

is still a little ways off. His mother doesnt know. Shes in the house
what will he tell mother
huh?
whats a mother?

besides, its worse than that even, because hes sitting under an arbor that is shaded from the sun, with all that trelliswork. A fat little boy, the fat holding his nose up, and his chin, and his brown eyes widening and expanding all over his face because the tiny black curls are crawling all over his retina, not saying a word, simply busy at their hauling snips of straw and tits of breadcrumb and guileless brain. Levi Emanuel, riding bareback on the galloping horse toward N'Muxt, sees the minaret of Greek Orthodox church smitten gold in the setting sun for the first time and it seems to him that the Christian Devil, Satan himself, has come to rest in his redgold wings upon the minaret. The question occurs to him: how is a good Jewish boy permitted to see the Christian Devil? Terrified, he spurs the horse: he must reach home before night falls. Someday he will ask his grandfather the question, the grandfather who is the Chief Rabbi of Lithuania, if grandfather lives

mother isnt home shes visiting Moyamensing Prison in the breakfast room furnished in middleclass imitation Chinese-Hindu marooncolored buddhas thick glasstopped oblong table over which is suspended a small chandelier at the bottom of which is a glass ball cut prismatically a long maroon cabinet that Lee faces when he eats curiously examining the tiny metal vases underneath MADE IN INDIA MADE IN CHINA and a bacchanalian painting on cloth on the wall depicting a group of Spanish men gazing lasciviously on a Spanish peasant girl bulging her breasts and lofting a tambourine against a spurious Moorish architectured background lets eat now Lee urges his mother lets eat now all right Lee dad called to say hes going to be late and Lee is overjoyed

because the tiny fat black curls have transparencies extended on either side of them Lee his overmouthjoyed openness sitting with his legs tucked in on the sabrepath underneath the arbor dustygreen in the dusk the path still retaining mother will have nothing to say the warmth of the bluegreen spring day no I never see a devil on a minaret the little fat black curls are crawling are sprung with silverblue transparencies from their bodies now and flying oh theyre flying a chubby Lee arm curling the gentlest of fists into the dustygreen dusk curling the gentlest of faces at

the ants oh theyre flying they just now crawling in the chill now oh theyre
not that you want to catch any of them not really as they float cumbrously
about your tentative fist and tentative face simply that you want to tell
them as your lips begin to edge upward upward as the start of a flight till
out of your mouth comes flying a laughter because you approve, thats
what it is after all, you approve and you want to pat the heads of the flying
ants because they dont have to crawl all the time, oh no, they can fly too,
too, too, and it is the last of winter and the first of spring flying

    flying

    flying

    not crying crying as Levi is in the maroondark breakfast room Chris-
tine Novak dead at threethirty in the morning. Lee sits at the maroon
glasstopped telephone table, thirtyone years of age Christine, for thirteen
years secretary and cashier of the Levi Coal Company, alternately crying
and smiling Levi

    hes taking it hard, Rachel says to Lee. After all why shouldnt he? She
was the best worker he ever had in the office. She was there in the morning when the office opened six oclock, and she only went home when Levi
was ready to go home. Pinchworried, dressed in black, with a brief black
veil, Rachel tells Lee on the enclosed porch that shes late, that his Uncle
Victor, her brother, must be waiting for her impatiently, He looks so bad,
Victor does, her glistening eyes screwing up, hes so yellow, that prisonlife
doesnt agree with him, this should teach you, Lee, its the worst thing in
life you should be in jail I cant tell you how awful it is, Lee, when those
big iron doors

    oh mamma mamma mamma pudgy Rachel Emanual scurrying
down the Boulevard to catch the Number Fifty trolley along Rising Sun
Avenue scurrying in her black clothes

    so ashamed oh mamma

    shes so ashamed

    scurrying under her brief black veil day after day after day in the
quartzflung sunlight and in the rain Levi takes time off from the business
to drive her down to Moyamensing to Victor her brother

    you musnt tell anybody, Rachel begs Lee. Im so ashamed the neigh-
bors should know. Its in the papers. If anybody asks you you hear you
dont know anything about it, Rachel pleads

    Im telling you, Lee, Levi stands bullshouldered against the long white oblong entrance to the kitchen, Lee making marks on the telephone book. Not from jaundice, not from pneumonia did Christine Novak die. It just took her three days. Tuesday night she was taken to the hospital. Friday morning she died. She didnt want to live, Im telling you the true story, Lee, yes, Levi alternately smiles and fights his tears. Lee feels sick. Mamma is visiting his Uncle Victor in prison and his father tells him about Christine because

Even your mother dont know the true story, Levi says, you shouldnt tell her, you understand?

Yes, I understand. The new french phone. Not the oldfashioned hook&receiver upright piano telephone but the new babygrand talk& listen instrument all in one black piece the alleyway like a shallow v tilted to one side runs by the window, one side of the house because of how the lot is sold has a crook in it. Next door a gray slab of a threestorey wall unbroken by any windows where the Forstens live, mother, father, daughter and soninlaw, Hungarians. Old man Forsten a retired master carpenter, moderately wealthy on realestate, a long nail of a man still wearing a celluloid collar twice his neck size and a dark sweater buttoned down the front summer and winter, with sprinklebrown eyes, old Mrs Forsten a jolly cow, each summer theyre off to Wildwood New Jersey, old Forsten three hundred and fifty years of age and not getting any younger with dark redleather skin pulled tight around a jagged adamsapple

Rachel commiserates with Gertrude the Forstens' daughter over the backyard fence the Monday wash flapping smartly in the chapped autumn breeze, carrotcolored Gertrude's hair in bright curlers a long nail of a woman like her father and a stiffcorseted nose and tiny sprinklebrown eyes Im tellin ya Mrs Emanuel she says her skinny elbows and redsplotched hands resting on the iron rail

i woke up in the hospital and saw my daughter I just cried and cried, Gertrude says, sniffling, the curlers springing out of her eyes

we dont have a girl I do all the ironing the washing the housecleaning my husband just makes a fair living as a housepainter yknow even though he works fairly steady for the Navy Yard my parents wont give us a cent well why should they were living here rent free aint we Mrs Emanuel

I just lay in that there hospital thinkin my goodness what a tragedy what a tragedy I just couldnt look Mrs Emanuel Im tellinya I couldnt bear to look

the wind rattling the monday wash the sheets whipping whitely their tips touching the bare honeysuckle vines on the garage Levi's long winter underwear out of the mothballs Georgianas not such a good laundress but my how she can iron Rachel admires brightly then complaining I have such trouble with the colored girls each one you have theres something wrong with them. Rachel waves her hand deprecatingly and shakes her head and purses her lips, You just cant trust them, each time one of them leaves would you believe it somethings missing I can understand how you feel Gertrude

Well Mrs Emanuel when I saw my baby's right hand I just blacked out then and there two fingers missing altogether and another just not there from the second joint I thought it was a curse God visited on me

Oh thats just not true, Rachel waves her hand, dismissing that cause entirely and laughing merrily, Its an unfortunate accident, she thrills at Gertrude in her high girlvoice Youll get over it and the babyll grow up to be a beautiful girl you just mark my word. Curiously, then, The doctorsll be able to do something about it, wont they? Rachel thinks it would be a horrible tragedy if they couldnt and she would have to pity Gertrude Forsten that much more, not that Rachel minds, she would positively enjoy pitying her more, Youll see there wont be a child wholl even notice the missing fingers, Rachel chuckles, trying to make the chuckle appear to be something Gertrude should join in with, because that will make her feel much better, Rachel assumes

Oh yeh the doctors told me when she gets older shell be able to wear plastic fingers but they dont want to fit her now because, well you know, shes growing

yknow I didnt even want to nurse my baby, Gertrude wrinkles her narrow brow Levi's brow, square and high, the irongray hairs dulling the original blond, rarely wrinkles I really dont want my father to tell me the story but Lee wants deliciously to share Levi's agony he simply wishes the itching around the upper inside part of his left thigh would stop. The little white scales with their red centers might come from his masturbating against that area; still, the inside part of his right thigh is affected too and he never rubs his penis against that. Doctor Newman's ointment isnt having any success at all, it simply makes the whole area greasy and messy and altogether disgusting. No wonder Lee is going to have to give up Valerie Moses, that tall girl with the heartshaped face from D Street

Theyre nice ones, Valerie.

I dont like them, theyre too small. Lee presses her against the dark vestibule wall, next to the brass umbrella stand, One guy said theyre like peaches.

I like peaches, Lee says.

Anyhow the nipples are big, Valerie boasts. You like big nipples, Lee? Sure.

Rub them some more. Harder, Lee. I dont mind if you rub them as hard as you can.

Christine Novak didnt want to live. She drank like a fish, Lee.

Lets try it, Valerie.

Oh I dont think we can standing up, Lee. Its just impossible. You got anything on?

Uhhuh.

Well lets try. Gee, that feels good.

Can you spread your legs a little more?

Thats as far as theyll go. Gee, honey, you just cant get it up there with me standing like this. Look Ill tell you what.

What?

My mother wont be here Sunday afternoon we could use the upstairs bedroom.

I dont know about Sunday, Valerie, I think theres a family ceremony of some kind. Ill give you a call.

Okay. Try and make it, huh?

Lee sees himself undressing before Valerie and her looking at the hammock he wears around his testicles so that the ringworm infection wont spread to them, or being repelled by the ointment on his thighs and groin. Even if he wipes off the stuff and doesnt wear the hammock, shes sure to notice the flaky pustules and not want to get near him at all and he knows it will be impossible for him to make the phonecall

She kept a bottle in her desk drawer, Levi says to his son pityingly. Every time my back was turned or she didnt think anybody was looking she took out a little paper cup and poured bourbon into it, thats what she drank, all because Lee, Levi says with deadly seriousness, she was in love with a man who had a wife who wouldnt give him a divorce, a man already with three children, can you imagine? I knew the man personally and I knew his wife. You never saw such a mean woman like his wife. Tears roll down Levi's open square broad face on either side of the fine straight nose on the fair skin. Lee judges his father a liar. He believes his father is talking about himself and Christine. Theres no need for his father to tell him the story—why does he have to relate it to Lee and warn him not to pass it on to his mother? Look at his father smiling now, smiling sweetly and pityingly at Lee, as if he has unburdened himself. But of course the story may or may not be true of Levi. Lee quite understands his own desire to condemn his father, sweepingly, mercilessly; he wants both to condemn and affirm his father's right to take a mistress if that is what he has chosen. Lee likes the idea. With his desire to condemn the desire to be enormously tolerant is parallel. Condemnation and tolerance coexistent in a single feeling is a unique sensation. Mingled with it is an outpouring of love in Lee toward his father: Levi confides in him. How else is the love toward his father possible if the latter doesnt confide in him? By such logic, then, Levi's story is a concealment of the truth of the essential confidence. Certainly, then, because Lee must love his father, he must conclude infidelity on the part of Levi. Wonderful bastard Lee shouts inside of himself, his groin itching insanely, hes got to scratch it, he cant call Valerie, the little red microscopic ants are crawling under his skin near his genitals: he wishes they would sprout wings and fly off, the ants of course, he chuckles to himself, not the genitals—how will the poor things look flying around without the rest of the man? Trylon and perispheres, the symbol of the New York World Fair all alone, without any Fair Male to be proud of. It is possible that he can love Harry Ring as well? Harry Ring bears a superficial resemblance to Levi, but also to Bruno Canova—as much as Lee can determine from the photograph published in The Evening Bulletin. There, will be no end to the biceps of this world, Lee heavily reflects heavily mounting to the second floor

Goodnight, mom, he calls to his mother with the thinning dyed black hair, the fine whiteness of her skullflesh showing through as she lies on the overstuffed livingroom sofa faintly snoring, her kimona partly open revealing the nylons curving up her still lovely legs as long as the varicose veins are concealed, her shapeless breasts floating vaguely all over her chest as if they have been torn loose from their moorings, the nylons secured to the corset, her mouth open and the gold fillings reflecting the light of the readinglamp brokennecked over the powerfully snoring Levi asprawl in the easychair, THE JEWISH FORWARD its pages askew humped on the carpet beneath, his biceps practically the size of Lees thighs extending like stubby cannon from his shortsleeved summershirt, the big GILBERT ELECTRIC CLOCK like a sideview of a lioness on the mantelpiece over the fireplace used now only for a brass opentopped box filled with glass coals glowing from artificial illumination underneath and flanked by purely ornamental brass coalbucket and andirons and poker and a small aluminum pitcher to one side that Rachel decides makes a pretty and effective contrast chimes KLOONG KLOONG KLOONG KLOONG KLOONG KLOONG KLOONG KLOONG KLOONG KLOONG KLOONG post meridian

each night Aunt Bella visits from across the Boulevard and hears the clock chiming she interrupts herself or anybody else who happens to be talking and painfully stretches a grin across bloodless lips and remarks Aha! the clock strikes the truth

is there is no end to the biceps of this world. Goodnight, Lee, his mother calls back, not bothering to open her eyes but smiling sleepily I got such a headache one of my worst ones I guess I should go to bed now if I dont I wont sleep all night Rachel complains, Levi, she calls, and his only reply is a snore,

Levi

what What WHAT he starts forward from the easychair

you know what time it is her voice nags

oh for gods sakes let me alone, he sags back

Goodnight, pop.

Goodnight, Lee, his father alters his tone with incredible suddenness into gentleness, Goodnight, goodnight

Gazing down at his mother and father from the head of the stairs, Lee knows his father's biceps neither whip nor batter him, though many times he wants his father to fling him from one end of the room to the other rather than hear once again the too gentle voice, the wise remonstrance, the patient understanding, the scholarly but never condescending interrogation. Levi explodes in anger at his sons in his business office, rarely at home. The radio is still playing, the clock is a little fast, Ben Bernie is signing off the air with his orchestra in the background grinding out its sentimental sorrow, And so, Goodnight, Au Revoir, Toodle-oo, Pleasant Dree-ams and God Bless You as Lee walks to the rear of the second floor through the narrow carpeted corridor with its single shaded window past his study to his bedroom recently repainted in chocolate brown, his mother's choice, on the canvas paneling of the walls, the ceiling an unrelieved brown while the walls carry out Rachel's idea of variation to the painter, namely, a series of chocolate brown whorls made by spiraling the paintbrush, so that some areas of the whorls are light brown, Lee hoping he will be asleep by the time his mother and father retire and his mother begins to nag Levi. There is no end to the biceps of this world, Lee pulls the defective chain for the bathroom light, a defective yellow light barely managing to seep through the dark. Sitting on the ivorypatinaed toiletseat, Lee massages his penis a moment, then decides to hell with it, lets it droop, wipes his anus, curiously regarding the chocolate brown smears tinged with streaks of blood from the harsh toiletpaper his mother prefers, exactly the color of his room. He stands, pulls up his shorts and leans into the bodylength mirror straining forward from the wall to the right of the toilet. The mirror is here and there reticulated and through the years has produced a strange remotely green undertone, as though it has been subjected to thousands upon thousands of fathoms deep oceanwater. Lee pities the insufficient width of his shoulders. They are not nearly so wide as his father's nor half so bulky as his brother David's. Still, he assuages his sense of deficiency by remarking to himself how sharply his torso cuts in at the waist so that in the illusory proportions his shoulders fly out to either side most esthetically. His legs are long and shapely, he admits. But his arms. He is abashed. The forearms are sticks while the biceps are mere implications of muscle. He flexes his arms. The biceps, at least, show an approach to power. He desires Levi's biceps. He wants his father's prick for his very own. It is a big horseprick his father has. Lee sees him piss before dinner sometimes as he passes by the bathroom. Levi's is a thick muscular prick, more than an echo of his biceps. It is thick and long, even while unerect. And all he sees his father do with it is piss. Lee would like to see his father use it on and in Christine Novak. Thats where it belongs. Not in Rachel. Who wants to fuck Rachel? Not Levi. Not Lee. Not David. Nobody. Poor mamma. Mamma is the chairlady of the Brith Mikveh Sisterhood. Mamma raises money for the synagogue. She speaks authoritatively. Lee sees her photograph in the Brith Mikveh Yearbook right at the front just after the pictures of the rabbi and the president of the congregation. She has two pages, one for her picture, and one for Words Of Greeting To The Congregation For The Coming Year, may you prosper, be healthy, and in behalf of the other ladies and myself, Lee how do you spell behalf? I used to be a good speller, the best in my highschool class she cheerily tells Lee on the porch in the jingling yellowbright sunlight shining through the spotlessly clean windowpanes over the geraniums and the rubberplants the Roosevelt Boulevard after the snow blacklaned and whitecolumned, the frost hugging the corner of the panes, There goes Lila Kastrow the dentist's wife, Rachel stations herself behind the rubberplant so that shes effectively concealed from outside view. Lilas out in all kinds of weather. Look how shes bringing soup to her mother. Isnt it a shame she still has that awful limp from the automobile accident thats why I keep telling you Lee you should watch when you cross the Boulevard its so dangerous didnt Lila get hit that way right when she was almost on the pavement going home you have to have eyes in the back of your head, his mother counsels him, scolding now, You never look where youre going, Lee, Ive told you a thousand times if Ive told you once, Rachel's soft brown eyes sparkling at her son, admonishing him with the index finger, You hear me? You watch careful when you cross streets, hah? Poor poor Lila, Rachel shakes her head from side to side, I can feel it myself—see see see! Rachel peeks through the rubberplant like a woodpecker, a young woman yet, still in her prime, such a lovely girl, I remember yet when she married Milton Kastrow when he was studying dentistry yet at the University of Pennsylvania, would you believe it Lee he had to come all the way from New York to study here, he graduated from Columbia, sure why not, why not shouldnt heve married Lila shes a good girl a pretty girl raised real nice by her parents, look at her now, drawn in the face, limping through the snow, one leg is shorter than the other, my god I can feel the pain right here shes going through Im so sorry for her you have no idea, but like I was telling you Lee I got good grades in high school let me tell you, I was no dummy, Rachel wrinkles her low forehead, laughing at herself now, blushing like a girl, Of course, she giggles, Im getting a little forgetful now, my mind isnt what it used to be

Oh, mother, certainly it

No. No it isnt. Youd be surprised what slips my mind, you get older, his mother whines, broods

Mother why dont you go out?

I dont want to. I dont feel well.

Youll feel better if you do.

Id have to get dressed and farputzed I dont have the energy like I used to.

The air would do you good.

Lee I just dont have the same desire. The ladies from the Sisterhood keep calling me I should come to a luncheon here, I should go to a dinner there, but I just dont have the same desire, his mother lifts her shoulders and lolls her head to one side like a rag doll.

You see the ladies like you, they want you to come out.

I know I know I know but my joints hurt and I got such a headache and my bunions are bothering me and I got to make supper and I wouldnt get home in time and you know how Dad likes his supper on time even if he calls up hell be at the barber or hell be late he has to wait for a truck

He will be at the barber. He has to wait for a late truck. Mother, mother, mother.

You know, Lee.

Yes.

Ever since Victor.

Lee doesnt want to sleep. He doesnt want to dream of Grampop Joshua, Victor Nathanson's father and Rachel's. There will be no end to the biceps of this world, Lee pronounces offhandedly to Danny Naroyan in the late summer night on the Naroyan veranda overlooking the wide lawn, the thick shrubbery, the massive trees and Old York Road. Two blocks away the hum of the traffic up and down North Broad Street. Cutting diametrically across Broad Street at Lindley Avenue is a PENNSYL-VANIA RAILROAD passenger train and freight bridge, bearing the crack expresses between Philadelphia and New York. Once every half hour earlier in the day the expresses thunder by. Now, perhaps once an hour. Coming from the West, from Pittsburgh, Chicago, Des Moines. Glancing out of one side of the veranda Lee cannot escape the GENERAL OUTDOOR ADVERTISING billboard GOODRICH RUBBER TIRES garishly colored under thousandwatted electric bulbs. Danny pushes himself back and forth on the swing. Lee steadily oscillates in an ancient wicker rocker. A cocker spaniel stares adoringly up at Danny, his head and tail wagging as Danny swings, Danny periodically squealing endearing terms at the spaniel. Theres no reality but power, Lee says in a luxuriously fatalistic voice. A gravidly whipped dull orange moon hangs like an immeasurably ancient infant in the starslitted sky, wrinklemoon, as an insideout flesh ballooned and puffed with a whole damn mountain of rock, about to spill, crash, sluice its piebald guts over Goodrich Rubber Tires.

Even a dead moon has power

Like Bruno Canova.

What? Danny wedges at Lee. That names familiar.

Think you saw it in the newspaper, did you? Lee sarcasms.

Well? Danny quiets the dog, whining. Rachelspaniel, barking at the Sisterhood. What? More power in brotherhood, Lee, Danny stoutly, Certainly, what do you mean, Dannys off in a rush of syllables, Marxism teaches the doctrine

AAAAAH. Somebody from the RCA plant in Camdens going to, jesus I see all kinds of bended knees

Well. Now youve met Rena

Marx? Bruno Canova. Both sit in the museums of power. Not that my uncles guilty. Christ I dont know. Maybe Im a little proud. What the hell, I am proud: Murder, Marx, Hamlet, Bruno Canova, Victor Nathanson, Powers all there is. The moon. The summer night. The illegitimacy of Laura Ingersoll. Harry Ring. Levi Emanuel. Dave Emanuel

Even Beethoven's last message, Danny interposes.

Last Message, those, theyre fulla organized bravado.

Alle Menschen

Should Be Brothers

Scourging the world, Danny, Lee roars. Marx, from his museum, the big carbuncles on his ass, Dictatorship of the Proletariat, christ, would Christ have shifted whole populations, were they puppets on the end of the Cross adangle, eh? Bruno Canova spins a Marx, all of them wielding death from the inscrutable buddhistics of a Stalin, did you know weve got representations of Buddha in our maroon breakfast room on the cabinet, Lee laughs helplessly smelling the orange moonlight hanging from the boughs of the majoustic elms, ythink my mother has any idea

She supposed to have an idea, Lee? Arent you being just a trifle harsh

ALL ABOARD FOR NEW YORK NEW YORK EXPRESS straight into the maroon moon squashed on the summer night

Power comes out of hate, Lee says, grasping the veranda's wooden column

Youre not going to shake it
shave the groin
desamsonized
delilah cut off his
Trouble was Samson couldnt satisfy Delilah, thats all, and Danny
flies out in all directions, bouncing up and down on the veranda, making
the moonlight fly like orange catfur, his belly morsecoding gagagiggles
Not out of love. Oh, theres a degree, as with Roosevelt, who thinks
himself a kind of satanic Christ ymightsay, but what the hell this is a
Hudson Squire full of gracious mothers and wives. THEY HAVE TO PULL
DOWN THE SUN AND THE MOON AND THE STARS WITH THEM, Lee turns
heeheeheevoiced to Danny, theyre in a hurry to change
oil to motion
radical to orthodox and orthodox back to radical again and virgins
to pregnancy and cut out the mother's child from her womb to make her
rusty virgin again
and fantasies into the outside real so the outside real can make fantasy again
and the death of sleep into the murder of the sleep of victims into
brief life so as to cut them down again into long death this is the power
this is the power
Lee
Ah?
Lee, calm down.
Calm down calm down calm down
I dont want to go down again to the calm down nor dream again Lee
sinking into the waters, the corporal's grip of deathcharged fist around
Lee's wrist
Its late, Lee, put out the light, you think electricity grows on trees,
hah? Rachel nags down the hallway.
The boy flicks off the light in the chocolatebrown room. AND JAM
BACK UP INTO THE HEAVENS THE STAR THE MOON AND THE SUN, like
the crazy paperhanger from Vienna hanging his paper fantasies jamming
them up the assskies of the German multitudes his screwsmos up into
their bowels with his salute
HEIL HITLER
HEIL HITLER

HEIL HITLER.

Flikker sits, knees drawn up, on the broad open windowsill of Lee's room on the second storey of 119 West 75th Street, midway between Columbus and Amsterdam. East in the startling silver night the tip of the Chrysler Building. The overage boy that is Flikker has a wizened withal in sweetness smile. His back is against the windowjamb; hes half Lee's height. Lee sprawls on the cot's greasy coverlet of dullred and dimorange stripe, longitudinal. A cockroach crawls on the wall above the desk opposite. In the apartment directly opposite across the street a young woman in panties and bra sits reading a newspaper opposite a fat man in undershirt and shorts. Through the cardboard wall against which Lee's desk stands can be clearly heard the voices of the adjacent apartment. The unseen woman snivels, Im going back to mother right now, she whines. Well fuchrissake gawhead, Im sickntired uh you talkin about it an not doin nothin about it so gawhead, willya WILLYA the unseen man snarls.

Finsh the beer, Flikker says.

Obligingly Lee tilts the can.

Two sensitive fairies pout down the street. The Puerto Ricans lounging on the outside steps of the brownstones laugh at them goodnaturedly and increase the volume of the samba, interrupting each other with sprays of stacatto spanish.

Lee's room is long narrow and highceilinged. It is the size of two commodious closets placed end to end. The rent is eight dollars and fifty cents a week. If he is too lazy to go up to the toilet on the next floor, he pisses here in the sink.

I put twentyfive bucks on Stevenson, Lee announces.

Against Ike? Flikker says incredulously.

Sure.

Youre not serious about the possibility of Stevensons winning, Flikker hunches over.

Certainly I am.

If I thought you were serious I might risk a bet on Adlai myself. What makes you think hes got a chance?

Lee lights a cigarette. Three packs a day. Smokes them through a cigaretteholder containing a filter. Black and silver holder in his teeth. Denicotea the brand name. Lee swears by it. No longer suffers from a severe attack of bronchitis twice a year. But of course realizes hes got a fair chance of ultimately dying of cancer. The thought of death does not at the moment particularly terrify him though he thinks about death at least once a day. He feels the scar on the little finger of his right hand. He visualizes the blood spurting, GLOOMP

GLOOMP

GLOOMP

He sees a small boy gulping

Theres a moment of absolute emotionlessness. A moment of void is possible directly after an accident occurs. No anger, no love, no hate, no regret, no desire, no hunger, no fear. Only void. A boy staring at the gloomping blood. Then, perhaps, incredulity. But before the not believing is the registration of the bleeding finger. But it is a mechanical registration. As if the body must make certain that particular seen events are at their occurrence precisely recorded.

Of course the shock can kill the body, Lee dryly observes.

By reason of the accuracy being intolerable to the body, Flikker adds.

The body can tolerate anything but death and accuracy, Lee says.

Flikker's smile is a straight line across big somewhat projecting teeth.

Simply that the voters at large rarely change their party allegiances during a time of general prosperity.

Flikker looks down at a swaying Puerto Rican maiden on the sidewalk. Theres a war in Korea, Lee. The people may believe that Eisenhower can get the boys home quicker than Adlai.

You think the mothers and fathers want their boys home?

Dont they?

Its possible the parents think they want their boys home. Lee grins.

That alone could win the election for Ike.

True.

Flikker swings his legs into the room over the radiator. His lank hair is the color of brown wrappingpaper falling over a narrow brow. His agate eyes hunch over Lee's long body. All right, he says, how do you conclude these mothers and fathers only think they want their boys home?

Arent they supposed to think that way? Lee is very mild. You see, Im betting on Adlai anyhow. I choose to think the voters wont feel so guilty as to think theyve got to get their male children back home. I choose to think the voters will feel it doesnt really matter who the president of the United States is, and that they might just as well keep the Democrats in. At bottom, of course, it doesnt matter to the voters. And right theres the major trouble that will probably elect Ike: the voters wont be honest: theyll decide that it does matter whos elected. The tradition of something mattering to people is a very powerful one, dont you think? I guess its the mother to whom the illusion is the most powerful: she thinks she wants her boy back to propagate his kind, or rather, her kind. Which is partly true, I suppose, Lee scatters his ashes on the ancient parquet floor. But if shed really get to be conscious that such a desire is the least individual part of her, she might go ahead and vote for Stevenson. Not that the mammas who will vote for Adlai will be conscious of that, because they too will just as righteously feel that Stevenson will return their boys with greater rapidity. All the mothers dishonestly tell themselves that if men must fight they might just as well do it on home grounds, where mother has more of a chance of keeping an eye on them. To top it off, Ike will doubtlessly be elected because more people are making money and they figure the Republicans are more experienced in handling prosperous voters.

Donald Schwartz, Aunt Sadie's son, he of the bulging gazelle eyes and Lincolnian nose, an assistant district attorney by way of appointment from the Philadelphia Republican Administration, hayfever and asthma sufferer, is close to oil tears as he opens the Emanuels' porch door because of yesterday's death of Franklin Delano Roosevelt. I voted for Roosevelt, says he in a greasy melancholy, because he was the only friend the Jews ever had. He was a real friend of the Jews, he nods gravely at Levi and Rachel and Lee.

Flikker wrinkles his brow. Im afraid the Republicans will come into power.

Thats nothing to be afraid of, Lee shrugs. The woman next door is weeping. Ah shutup, the man next door growls. The idea of power is a fallacy. Power implies that given two forces one is stronger or greater or more magnetic. Lee pushes himself up from the bed, plucks a kleenex, steps over to the wall over his desk, scoops the cockroach into the kleenex, crushes it, wads the kleenex, flips it into the wastebasket. Such is not the case.

What did your demonstration with the cockroach imply?

Oh. Why, change.

Obviously, however, you had the power to change a situation. One moment the cockroach was alive; the next, dead.

No, no. Lee is patiently and patently superior. You incorrectly described the event. What if I were to say that the cockroach, because of the meanings it holds for me, because of its power—if you insist on using the word—by reason of what I was taught about it by my mother—to repel me, Lee stands over Flikker's bowed head, and because of the path it chose to take, without its probably being aware of me at all—theres the sheer marvel of it right there—led me to surrender a position of comfort on the cot, inspired revulsion, and drove me to kill it. Certainly the ridiculously obvious must now have occurred to you, that insects as a class of animals undoubtedly because of their power have long posed and continue to pose a threat to the vertebrates, otherwise we would not be taking the radical measures we do in order to extirpate them. We haven't eliminated them. Should I infer, then, that they possess more power? On the allegedly more sublime scale of politics, where men believe they are alone involved, we speak of power plays and the like. Lee chuckles. Nothing could be less true. They are, very complexly, positional changes. No one matter is strong, no one matter is weak. Strength and weakness are simply terms in the difficult attempt to describe the slipperiness of event

The young woman in panties and bra without lifting her eyes from the newspaper in response to a movement of the fat man's lips rises and sits down again on the fat man's thigh. The fat man continues to peer out of the window. She is reading the New York Times.

Its just because were not married you treat me like this.

Aw go home to yer mother, youve threatened me enough times. Go home awready.

I bet thats just what youd like me to do so you could have some of your women up here. All you men are alike. Well if you think Im gonna give you such an opportunity all I can tell you is you are very much mistaken.

oh jesus christ
dont you jesuschrist me
will ya let up awready
Ill let up when Im good and ready
whats takin you so long
in my own good time
you never hadda good time

you never knew how to give me one Hubert

I got to go martha Ill be late at the restaurant

dont stop in for no drink on your way back

ah jesus

dont call me now Im not gonna rush down to no first floor and answer the phone

well dont call me

you afraid

no Im not afraid but the managers pretty irritated

well tell the bastard off

I might at that Martha I might

and on your way out tell the landlord about that Lee next door he has women there all hours

aw whatsa matter with you Martha

well i dont hafta sit and take all the sounds they make Im a respectable woman

keep your voice down hell hear you

i dont care if he does and bring back a bottle

youve had enough awready

Ill be the judge of that

okay okay

goodnight darling

goodnight dear

between Trieste and Haifa on the Mediterranean in the hot dawn of a glassy day Harry Ring moves out of a hatchway of an Irgun ship transporting five hundred Jews, men women and children, to the Promised Land. He resembles my father. Really not that much, but enough. My father's face is square, Harry's a triangle. My father's face is kind, sometimes angry, but never cruel. Harry's is sometimes cruel. My father walks erect. Harry walks like an ape. My father's eyes are graygreen blue but theyre there. Harry's have the same colors but as though theyve been washed so many times that the colors have faded: he seems blind. My father is tall. Harry is shorter than I am, shorter than my father. My father has fine wellshaped legs. Harry's are spindly, crooked, bowed. My father's shoulders are, but Harry's only seem: he removes his coat and the shoulders vanish and theres no muscle in the bicep. But his eyes are acid though blind. He can talk Yiddish with my father. He has an authoritative ease. I love and I fear Harry Ring sees the Jews even crowded onto the deck are still asleep. Except for one old man, a Rabbi, a venerable, a sage, a wise man, a man who is Godfearing, eightyseven years of age, a Chassid, a Teacher. This man, this Rabbi, he is awake. The Mediterranean is a long low vast blue swell. The Jews lie limp in bundles of body on deck, many stripped to the waist, many of them in shorts and dungarees. Not so the Rabbi. He is caparisoned in black gabardine. A skullcap sits on his head, a yarmulke. A white tallith, bordered a light yellow, the praying-shawl, curves about his neck. Like my father he is a tall man but thinner. He faces Jerusalem because the tvillim are strapped to one wrist and to the forehead: they are small black boxes containing the Ten Commandments in minuscule: the Rabbi is concluding his morning prayers on the deck of the ship bound for Haifa, up the long blue swell of the Mediterranean down which the wide blue sky slides, the Rabbi of white hair and the long sharp beak and the scissoring blue eyes. Harry respectfully approaches the Wise One. The first sister whom Levi approaches upon his coming to America is Bella Zion in her husband Sidney's drygoods store on North Fifth Street between Erie and Allegheny. Brother and sister sit at the oak roundtable in the livingroom behind the long narrow store, scissor, tapemeasure and pincushion on the counter. An oak victrola is the one luxury of the livingroom. It is open; a record by Caruso is on the turntable; another called Cohen At The Picnic, a recent acquisition, lies on the roundtable. Bella's straight blond hair is drawn severely back from her forehead and gathered up behind in a tight knot. Sidney Zion waits upon a customer in the store which one goes to from the livingroom by descending two steps. Levi can glimpse the man from time to time at an angle: a short fat man of round face and spectacles forever slipping down on his nose, a rich baritone speaking voice, a little too obsequious at times perhaps, a little too animated now and then, but one suspects only to compensate and perhaps atone for long sad silences in company. A kind sweet man in the essence is Sidney Zion, his angers, when rarely they occur, easily siphoned off. Sidney would give you the money if you asked him, Bella says to her brother, but I dont want him to; it would be a hardship; whats first is first, Donna and Russell come first. Levi is temperate, his objection is a gentle one. He reminds Bella that this is not what Sadie and Dora and Jeremiah, four sisters and a brother firmly established in business, wrote in the letters to him in N'Muxt, in Lithuania.

You wanted me to come to America, he says most judiciously to Bella.

You pleaded with me in the letters. All of you. I was the only one left in the old country. Did I want to come?

Whats fair is fair, whats true is true, Levi. No, you didnt want to come. Bella doesnt avoid his eye. The corners of her lips are turned up, very neatly. A smile is always about to bubble on Bella's face. Sometimes she laughs but it is never a bubble: it is high and hearty.

I was content to stay in Lithuania. I wrote you back I didnt want to come. I had a scholarship to the University of Riga. I was ready to study for the law.

Its the truth, Bella nods.

Sidney Zion climbs the high slanted castered ladder to seek an extra large size of blue jeans for the customer

you can take as many of the Merriwell series as you like, Lee, Russell says kindly, lightboned and lithe, poutlipped and wavyhaired, with long blond lashes as Lee catches a glimpse of the nude photos that Carl Emanuel, Uncle Jeremiah's youngest son, dark and crinklelaughing, is surreptitiously showing Russell. Youre too young for this kind of thing, Russ says to Lee, and dont tell your mother. Oh I wont I wont Lee promises

christ I never even had a chance to see Laura naked. I couldve. The night before I left Provincetown. I couldve stayed the rest of the week. Regret is a disaster. I couldve loved her. We couldve had an affair between Philadelphia and New York, oh not that Idve had the money, but she couldve come to see me, Jennifers all done. One thing done and regret for another

I couldve

the truth. Yes. So?

What should I say Levi?

Flowers on the Zions' livingroom wallpaper, faded red roses on white. What is to be done with faded red roses on white wallpaper Levi chews in his mind, in the midst of a single emergency. Levi is mild, considerate, judicious, politic, yes, all of these things to his sister Bella. He doesnt lose his temper with her. Hes all of sixteen, an offer of a scholarship to the University of Riga in his pocket, the concepts of the Law, Lee, I want you to be a lawyer

No.

A doctor, Rachel says. I always wanted a son of mine to be a doctor.

No.

Youre listened to with respect at the congregation, Levi smiles sweetly, entreating, Ill support you all through school, you wont have to worry about a thing, Ill open an office for you, youll make a fine lawyer, what are your objections, be reasonable, you know Im always open to reason, his son, pain of his loins

No.

Temperate, judicious, considerate, eventempered to his beloved sister Bella, the one hes closest to, The whole family promised they would support me while I went to college and law school, thats how you got me to come to America, you know that, Bella, dont you, what are you telling me now, I dont understand, Bella. But even, sweet, a tiny kick of a smile, judicious, politic Levi as his voice descends slowly down the ladder like Sidney, carefully, perhaps breathing a little hard, but no more than that, considerate of his customer.

Yes, Levi. But you know who has most of the cash in the family.

Sadie.

Yes.

Go see Sadie. Spray and wave petrify at odd angles: white scallions heaped atop the chinese dewspotted configurations of lettuce and the sun is coned into carrot and squeezed into orange and the sun setting blurts on apple and pales at lemon in the pouted dusk of vermilion grape guillotined seed and syrrup onto the elbowed hipped loopshoved pavement of 4th Street near Bainbridge the pushcarts all well and hale and hearty and creaking under the tonnage of wristflopping slithering fish and vegetables and fruit and sticky yellow raincoats, to fist, up finger, cross palm, test, weigh, pull, is it worth a quarter no haggle it down two cents lemme look at the unfinished pants mister you think itll fit

TAKE A CHANCE WHAT COULD YOU LOSE Sadie take a chance what could you

what are you talking about Levi, Sadie's fingers rapidly counting the handkerchiefs, sorting the scarves, ALL RIGHT bittering to a thousandcushioned fortyyearoldwoman waddlecrushed in the rasping grasping searching headhunting IM LOOKING FOR A COLOR GRAY SEVENTEEN CUSTOMERS ARE AHEAD OF YOU LADY, look Levi, yawning her scrawning neck to avoid three fish splashing on the scale on the adjacent pushcart WATCH HOW YOU SLAP DOWN THE FISH MYER DANNENBERG, talk to Micah, no dont talk to Micah it wont do you any good Micah smiling benignly as a buddhist stalin Micah stolidly standing at one end of the pushcart puffing on his cigarillos You want a cigarillo Levi? Its possible youre a little young to smoke a cigarillo but Im telling you they last longer than a cigarette and they aint so strong as a cigar I smoke them all the time MICAH WAIT ON THE LADY, bitter, grasping, black shrew the belle of N'Muxt hunched and brittlebent over the merchandise MY MERCHANDISE WHAT ARE YOU TALKING LEVI no whats the use talking where its quiet talk here

talk anywhere

talk in the autumn or winter or spring what difference does it make DONT SHOVE MISTER

sure you couldve stayed in N'Muxt sure we all promised you we would give a share but right now we cant do it Im pregnant already the third time ah she could wring Micah's neck

Micah Micah with the cigarillo benign yes very benign he pushed me in a third time look look at him so proud what does he do YES its true CAPITAL he gave me, his mother and father gave HIM, so well help you too Levi, well start you in a business whats the matter youre too proud to go to nightschool HAH?

you got to live. first.

you got to make a living. first thing.

you got to eat. first.

you got to have a roof over your head. first thing.

THEN YOU CAN STUDY

sure Im sorry Im sorry who shouldnt be sorry were all sorry Bella is sorry

Jeremiah is sorry JUST KEEP YOUR DIRTY FILTHY FINGERS OFF THE MERCHANDISE YOU SNOTTY KID YOU

NO LEVI WE DIDNT CARE WE HAD TO LIE SO YOU WOULD COME OVER HERE MAYBE YOURE TOO YOUNG WITH ALL YOUR TORAH IN THE HEAD TO UNDERSTAND WHATS HAPPENING IN EUROPE BETTER WE THOUGHT WE SHOULD LIE TO YOU SO YOU WOULD COME OVER AT LEAST YOU COULD LIVE IN THE UNITED STATES OF AMERICA AND NOT DIE LIKE A JEW DOG IN LITHUANIA

crying.

Levi is crying.

in the middle of the pavement on Fourth Street near Bainbridge the young Levi in the grasping shoving shouting multitude is crying himself shoved against the plateglass window of a shoe shop no thats too tight mister

give her a bigger size shes a child I dont want she should ruin her feet crying

sadie wont look up her big belly rammed against the pushcart wheel her arm stretching ten million feet across the army pants and the corduroys looking for a doily for a customer what are you going to do for her diningroomtable she wants a doily

thats right Alice stand up and walk around in the shoe see how it feels

it hurts mommy its still too tight

Levi pushes out his belly to push out his throat so his neck muscles swell so he can with all his chest and belly and throat might MASS BACK THE TEARS HOLD THEM BACK STOP THEM NOBODYS GOING TO SEE ME CRYING

opening his mouth WIDE YAWNING, and, shutting, it, YAWN, STUFF, THE, AIR, BACK his skullbones pounding

and if america gets into a war

get married

get children

what will Aaron do. The youngest. I never knew my family, Lee, you see. I. I, was busy, studying. Under orange glow. OLD GILBERT CLOCK, to wind. Rachel winds. Each eight days. I was exempt. I didnt card the wool. Everybody helped in the business. Ben, Bella, Fanny, Jeremiah, Sadie, Dora, Naomi, even little Aaron. But in cheder I was the smart one. Yes. The Five Books of Moses I knew by heart. So, at school, mostly. Who had time for the family. Eat, they gave me. Bed, they gave me. Six feet deep the snow outside. We took the animals inside. The chickens. The cow. The horse. Near the stove we put them. Why should the animals die in the cold and the snow? They were our animals. They were part of the family. More than I was, maybe. But I cant forgive them. I wont forgive them. A lie they didnt have to tell me, no, Lee. That much with my sisters and brothers I wont get over. That much I hate.

In the mildness and gentleness of Levi's graygreen blue eyes Lee cant sleep. He wants to be as big as his father. The chest of drawers near his bed magnifies. His head feels like a sack of booming featheriness. He raises a finger in front of his eyes: it looks puffed, gigantic, feels it weighs forty tons but with the sensation of floatingness, airy.

Down the slanted monorail the elevator drops.

Rena? Danny is cagey. For one thing, Lee, shes one of the most vivid girls Ive ever met. Well, here it is, Lee.

Here it is is a tiny oldfashioned church organ with foot bellows. Me and my brother carried it all the way up to the attic. Up here youd never believe theres a tailorshop downstairs. You ought to have heard my brother curse. He doesnt know from nothing about music. What the hell dya want with an old church organ Danny he yelled at me. Oh Danny Danny my pop muttered, dont forget deliver couple dresses Mrs Mahoney.

The attic is dark and cool on the summer evening. Danny switches on the little light over the music and leans forward over Bach's Little Preludes and Fugues with his bulbous nose and the sharply concerned green eyes. Of the round head and the start of the loss of the lightcolored hair, rubbing the top of his skull furiously from time to time. Steadily he pumps the bellows with his feet. The ornate mahogany with the dim gloss from the many hands. Danny's bending round shoulders. He must crowd himself forward to push the bellows, so short are his legs.

My mother just looked at me and shook her head, Danny giggles in his basso. They cant understand why I want to be a musician, and being a composer means absolutely nothing to them. The only reason they ever bought me a piano was because they couldnt stop me pounding on the radiator. When I was about five Id pound on the radiator, Lee, with a hammer, and make a kind of childish melody, you know, on each of the metal fins because they made different tones. You think they appreciate good music? Dont be silly. Oh sure they like to go to the big Armenian gettogethers and dance—theyll dance the whole night, to the Armenian folksongs—Danny mimics the music with nasal sliding twangs in a minor key—all the folksongs are alike, Lee, the Jewish, the Armenian, the Gypsy, the Arabian, the Turkish—all in the minor key, they all wail or jabber. Im very popular. They think Im great when I play the Armenian stuff. They listen and dance to me the whole night.

Theres something I dont understand. About my father.

Sure.

Lee leans forward in the stiffbacked chair. Danny's green eyes dwell on him, blinking, the dynamic owl. Lee's shoulders hunch; the music-stand lights pulls out his chin; he stuffs and tangles his legs under the chair; a tousle of blueblack hair shivers over one long black eyebrow; the other eyebrows sardonically up: he spends many hours exercising that eyebrow's muscle so that it will diabolically arch

My father tells me his brothers and sisters promised him if he came to America theyd support his higher education. He says they went back on their promise.

So?

Well I think hes leaving something out. Because he had a scholarship in the old country. He told me the only reason he came here was because they promised him he could go to a university. Their going back on their word was pretty monstrous, and I sort of dont believe they would, because all they had to do was let him stay in Lithuania and continue his schooling.

Lee for God's sake its pretty obvious, Danny's impatient, turning back to the organ score. They got him here on the only pretext they could, because their main purpose obviously was to save his life. They knew he was taking a chance on his life by staying there.

Lee spreads his arms in front of him, vehement. All right, Danny, so why didnt he tell me that? What objection could he have against admitting to me his family lied to him so hed have a better chance to survive?

Danny shuts the organ score, giving a basso chuckle. He pulls his legs up on the stool, knees against his barrel chest. Lee when I first took notice of you at Olney High you were asking the political science teacher a long articulate question.

Lee, embarrassed, smiles, brushes the comment aside.

What do you want from me, Lee? I dont know the answer about your father. But I wouldnt judge him harshly. All things considered, hes a sweet man, he understands a great deal, he wants only the best for you.

I know I know.

I hope so.

Lee stands in the dark cool summer evening attic. There is a rumble from the Philadelphia-New York Express. You think he doesnt want me to know he hates them not for having betrayed him but for having possibly saved his life?

Flikker runs his finger over the long shelves of books in the second-floor apartment of a ramshackle house on West Third Street, two blocks away from New York University. I must apologize for all the volumes on the various religions of the world. They are not mine, Lee; theyre my roommate's: he dabbles in God. He flimsily lights a cigarette in the stuffy cabbage odors. It sounds like a question of values, I mean your father.

He was careful, then, to select what he thought I should hate.

Betrayal of a promise is much easier for an adolescent to comprehend and hate than a hatred of one's relations because they presumed to save your fathers life.

He didnt want me to know that he hated life.

Subtler than that, Lee. He didnt want you to know that his relatives were able to select a position which resulted in his hating life when it might have been a position from which he might have hated it anyway. That paradox was too much for him to look at with any equanimity. He certainly didnt want to pass on to you the feeling that he couldnt cope with a paradox. He was at the mercy of the consideration that had they not attempted to bring him over to this country and put his life therefore into possible jeopardy from that particular nonaction, from that particular position of noninterference, mind you, he might have hated them even more. The contemplation of that kind of hatred, perhaps overwhelming in its dimensions, was not to be borne. Really, he had to be grateful that they saved him from a possibly profounder hatred. Such gratitude cannot be admitted; it must immediately be made palatable; the palatability to him and to you was the lesser hatred issuing from the betrayal. It also served the purpose of putting you on his side; otherwise, you might have aligned yourself with his brothers and sisters. Lee, a man needs somebody besides himself on his side in order to die through the long years. Because, you see, he had been afraid once—in Europe—of dying suddenly all by himself. Nobody had compelled him to answer the pleas of his brothers and sisters by coming to America on the basis of their promise. In Europe he had a scholarship in his pocket. In America he had a promise. He chose a promise because he felt it meant longer life; he rejected a scholarship, because it might have meant death—and he was enraged at his brothers and sisters because they had penetrated to his weakness out of love, you understand? Out of love, Lee, they exposed his weakness. How many of us can stand it when a person who loves us exposes our weakness—and, worse, when we immensely respond to the very exposure by rushing into the arms of those who love us? Your father could have used the exposure by redoubling his energy and going to nightschool to study the law. But he couldnt: his family had shown him, out of love, that he had little courage. They knew he had little courage, and were afraid for him—that had he had to remain in Europe he mightve become an abject, lowly man. Instead, they rescued him from such abjection. That must be true, because his abjectness stayed with him: he didnt have the courage to go to lawschool at night, like many men from Europe whod emigrated here had.

Maybe he didnt have the courage to prove to them he did have courage by going to nightschool, because that would have proved beyond a shadow of a doubt that his brothers and sisters could be more than right, that what could be done in Europe could certainly be done in the United States—this wouldve taken the play and the choice away from him altogether. So. So, he chooses to die a long time in the coal business. And—and he wanted me to join him, to die in the same way, this would have altogether justified his behaviour. Christ I can hear him saying to me—saying—Lee, Lee, I built up the business—who did I build it up for? One son becomes a baseball player. I built a business. Look at the silos. Five concrete silos, Lee. I dont want to give it to a stranger. Its for my son

he dabbles in God

not the Rabbi aboard the Irgun ship. With clean silverwhite fingernails the Chassid tenderly replaces the prayingshawl and the tvillim in the blue and yellow velvet carrying pouch. No mortal soul is awake on deck in the sliding blue and yellow of the Mediterranean Sea and the Mediterranean Sky but this Wise Man and the deferential Harry Ring on his monkey legs. The old man is a Polish Jew. The young man is an American Jew. Below, the engines pound anciently, like many old horses galloping in a circle to turn the great wheel. It is an old ship making an old journey across a sea crossed and recrossed without number; and flies, in the accident of things and flags, the Brazilian flag, though here on deck the flag might just as well be the Chassid's white beard, frisky as a child in the nimble morning breeze, Laura Ingersoll's peasant skirt, a fresh calf springing from his face as a nose

Good morning, Chassid, Harry respectfully tenders his voice in a you will forgive my mockery in the smile, meaning only I am alert as a lover to the passing of my self.

A good morning to you, my son, says the Chassid in all gravity. The tall Wise Man folds his arms across his spare body. The scissoring blue eyes are laid upon the table.

I am impressed, Harry says, that you pray to God before the other Jews awake. I am impressed that you pray alone.

It is my presumption, my son, that the Almighty created the Universe alone, and hears us all as one voice. In my arrogance, I would make one voice. The scissoring blue eyes are taken once again into their sockets. The thin strong whiteyellow hands with their silverwhite fingernails grasp the deck rail. The white spray flies as a beard from his face is it possible that the story Laura tells of her illegitimacy is a fantasy Lee wonders. Each man deserves at least one arrogance, Harry defers his brow into frown, hunching with forearms flat against the rail.

The order of merit is the Lord's, vouchsafes the Chassid.

You are full of joy, doubtless, that at last as an old man you will soon reach the Promised Land. Harry no longer is alert as a lover to the passing of his self. He is a frame of gray flint against the bluegreen Mediterranean. There are mean and shrugging passages in his mind. The swartburnt Rena billows her hips on the New Jersey sand, and with Levi's money buys Harry a roundtrip ticket from New York to Fort Worth, Texas, where Lee is stationed at an army airfield; on the face of it Harry wishes to intercede for a man writing a letter to Rena in which he richly describes the memorable performance of Alla Nazimova in Mourning Becomes Electra as Christine in a green velvet gown. Lee has a tormenting case of prickly heat in the dry rashweather of summer Texas

The Chassid does not nod. He merely inclines his mouth. I am full of happiness, my son, that I will live on the land where God dwells.

The damnation of innocence pervades Harry Ring. We are classic too early in the morning; true, it is to such a time that the classic belongs; but the lean white tapering column of this beard is too much so; I would tweak the Greek in the Hebrew Man; puddle purity with my squalid East Side Yiddishism; the bluegold Mediterranean is as false to me as any place could possibly be; the Greeks are dead; the Jew survives, more so in Harry Ring than in the Chassid: Lee understands that, but he doesnt want to embrace me; he may embrace me through his wife, the whore, the ChildWhore; I destroy her for him, she wants nothing more than to roll the red carpet out from between her legs, Harry slaps the deckrail in abrupt mirth. Does God dwell in the Land of Israel? Harry nudges the

Chassid with the palethrust chin of his vacant eyes.

Should He not?

No sprawled soul wakes on the decks. We will bring all of our selves sleeping to the Promised Land, castouts from the Exterminatory. Vengeance upon the Teuton, that no man shall tell us apart. Bubbles of tickle ascend from the deck through Harry Ring's monkey limbs. Once more the world is a wonder; no more does meanness stalk his interior; he feels kind and merry; the journey from Trieste to Haifa is a lark, a saucy nonsense, a potpourri of gladsome sun and sleeping Jewry and a sprightly Chassid at his side I do not say that He should not dwell in Eretz Yisroel. I simply ask, Is that His abode?

The Chassid's blue scissors snip at Harry Ring. You are a Jew from America?

Yes, Rabbi.

I thought all Jews from America are tall people.

As a child I was born on the East Side in New York. My mother and father were very poor. I did not eat well.

Does that explain it?

No it does not. The explanation of my inferior stature is that I was always looking for things upon the earth.

The abode of God, my son, is in man's heart.

Then there is no necessity for you to journey to Jerusalem.

That is true. And there is no necessity for you to help any Jew reach Jerusalem, my son.

Harry Ring bends at his knees and slaps them, an antique clown. Sometimes he so abounds in the utter abolition of the tragic that gurgles goggle in him as in an infant, as if hiccuping uncontrollably at the acrobats of laughter leaping from organ to organ.

And the Old Jew says, I did not mean to wound you, young man.

Precipitately, Harry shrugs with a single shoulder. He is composed and genuflects with the back of his hand at the necks of knuckle. I will be very honest with you, Chassid.

Just—honest, my son. The white beard takes a swipe at a passing gust.

This illegal movement of the Jews to Palestine benefits me. Otherwise I would be a soldier in the American army.

You avoid military duty to undergo a greater danger?

I would go mad if I did not constantly seek to undergo the greater danger at all times, Chassid. Does God dwell in my heart, oh Wise Man?

The Jews begin to stir on the deck. They yawn, they scratch, they belch, they glance uncertainly at the young man and the Seer holding forth blackly against the sun.

I will be honest, says the Rabbi.

Honesty is not incumbent upon the Chassid, Harry says. Truth is too much for a young man, he protests. You must make certain of a man's age before you dare to be honest with him. Triumphantly, then, Although I have stated I am young you cannot be certain of my age or whether it is ready for you. I will say flatly I am not ready for you; flatly that I must look upon you as a Figure, as someone Impersonal, a Representative, if you will. I am not ready for you as a person to be hooked to me. Also, you are too old to be my friend. I am meagre in your presence. You are a tall old Jew with God abiding in your heart, standing on a deck on which you may be murdered by the British before you reach port. The murder of a Figure will make me bellow in fury; the murder of a man I love will make me inept with grief. Love disembowels a man. When I look upon myself I am weak with lassitude, motionless, incompetent, therefore I choose not to regard myself. I am meagre in my own Presence. I am a Figure to myself

It cannot matter to me, if truth be known, if I reach Jerusalem or no, the Chassid pronounces. Neither will you bellow in fury nor be prostrate in grief. There is something lesser that you must have of me, as you must have of all men

Too subtle, too subtle, too subtle, Harry Ring flutters his hand and moves away, Too subtle, Chassid

God is an Invalid in your heart, my son

Ah

an Invalid

You need not go on.

He is Jesus Christ in your heart, my son

Harry halts. His cheek flickers in the sun. Some Jews go to the toilet. Mothers pull out their teats and slap them into the puckers of infants. Harry is apologetic. I am a Jew, he murmurs.

You are fearful of your Old Man, your Chassid, as Christ was. Very suitable.

You are an evil man, Chassid.

You do not understand God at all, do you, my son? As Christ never understood his Father.

Did He understand his Son?

Will you speak of understanding when you speak of fathers? The scissoring blue eyes gouge the blue air. The old Jew is a slim pillar on the deck, his yellowwhite hands lifting the buoyancies of the golden morning. The transported Jews avoid these two, the monkeylike younger, and the arch of slim stalwart honeybearded white that is the elder. What a poor bumbling idiot is the son who asks that his father understand him, says the Chassid. Such a son has no sons in him!

Harry pats the Chassid's shoulder and grins crookedly. Go to Jerusalem. Thats a good man, go you to Jerusalem, yes, yes, you do that, Rabbi, go, go, as Harry backs away, I am wanted in the ancient engineroom, but go to Jerusalem, I beg you

survive

well just dont stand there, Lee, come help me, Ive twisted my ankle, plump Laura Ingersoll twists her plumpness, pretty sixteen yearold putty, pleading, the White Rock Girl loses her gossamer wings somewhere as she leans over the jagged slab of the manifold slabs of the Provincetown Breakwater leading out to the spit of sand and the lighthouse where Sy and Sam and Lee go buckbathing of a salty gullscreaming day, at least Sam and Sy do, lean Lee stops short of removing his undershorts lest the ringworm infection be observed, offering the excuse to the others that he doesnt feel quite free to dangle his balls and swing his prick like a shillalegh, Sam blushflushing under the orangerine sun Let the boy keep his modesty and Sy crying Its his privy privilege as all three loop their bodies into the crystalshock shove of the cobracombers whitegreening into the shore, red blood hissing into the ice, breasting high as the eyekite can overtumble into the blorangerine hammock of the sun, the jagjammerjumble of the spoolsprawl skull and the buckling buttock and the tangle of torso with wet and weed and one's own bodyown in the drift of downdrown humming in the emeralding but neckspitting to scoop the air, scruff it down the throat, lambasting the flat flanks of the sea, slapsprank and fistburst, what do you mean Sams dead, not here, or no not here my liege elegiac in the Pacific comedown from Atlanticround, not here Redondo smacking of Provincetown, same salt I mean, same sea and same me I swear zounds and godsblood, what toothless Sam in neverneverland heres not the dirt nor the shovel nor the despicable spade, come Sy come Sam seasigh with me, alls true alls fair alls soft as flab-bySam all tears gone this is oceania for Sam and the swing of us, bare gums grinning as he sucks the wind, no toothpick in my toothless heart here for Sam, I cite Laura and I cite Sy insists the Lee, is Sam the gull or the lighthouse or the rock, no not one of the three but he says the swim is good, gasping like a tremble, quick to his pipe and fiddler puff in the impossible sheer and now astretch in the sand and no harm done because I put him down, I wave my heart, I summon the wand of wave to walk and talk and bend and blurt and baffle and squirm, this is he, this is my immortal self in Sam and Rena and Harry and Sy and Danny and Saul, hey Sam! Hey Lee! my ankle hurts says she in the trough of the rock, round smearplea of a phiz with a flummeragony drizzling from her eyes in the spumepounded dark, dim white slits of sea toughtendrilling over blackrockjag and serpentsiphoning back into the stingy stygian, not a moon for all the invocations and incandleations of crestondom for the guessing girl toward boy Im glad Sys gone, I hardly saw you for two whole weeks Lee, my ankles hurting, will you please help me, come back Lee, Im not angry, I never will be, I twisted my ankle conventionally, its a paltry little joke but its all I could think of in the dark and with you going with your brow like a boulder over your eyes Lee, come back because the waves are high and Im all alone and I cant see a thing and Im wet and Im cold and Im soaked through and through Lee and I love you enough to make pretexts and lies and sillygirl strategems and Ill never be an actress, its just not in me, Lee. He slitherslips on a rock and lands slaplaughing by her miseryside and kisses her through and through and through.

I think I should take you home, youre wet and cold, Lee says.

No, I want to stay awhile, Laura says in a limited simulation of bliss.

Thats a very convincing kiss the young man has, Jennifer mock opines, twisting in the ascent of the steep stairway to give Lee the defer-ential nod while he stands, minimally shaking, at the bottom looking up at the lowslung calves of extomboy Miss Hazlitt whose face nonetheless partakes of certain Nordic hollowcheeked characteristics, complete with shoulderlength ash tresses and British flatchestedness; two attributes of the girl alone repel him: redrimmed eyelids and the granulation thereon, the latter inevitably reminiscent of the white flaky scales of the fungus growing near his testicles. But Jennifer's acerb wit craftily controls her own marred masculine beauty.

Touching, wheres Jennifer, Laura wheres. But whos the question asked of in the touching, who touched? The personalized anonymity a blinding crutch staggers bluewhite through the lowering cloud Laura touches Lee's bicep, the twisttoll of a femininity astride with finger on his muscle, her freckles blue in the white bluecalcined litterlightning, thunder following in the epic burden, as Jennifer never holds, entreats nor can be aided, the fishjawed boulder leaping caught on the lightningline, the crutchcast from the high on the retina a bulletchatter eyehooves along the iced horseshoe of the Provincetown Harbor, the angular curve, the Jennifer flatheel along the sand, warpwharved, spanishcombs of pierpilings whirling the shadows on the plumpfest of Laura, askew on the boulder, a transient terror to the boy pining for power, Uncle Aaron a specific truth upon Lee's waters sweeping both Jennifer and Laura away, the Godboom as boom as anything, where does the touch of the erotic specific go, Come challenge me blurts out the inside raging jealousy of Lee biting the cobblestoned streets of Philadelphia receiving Jennifer's flatheels, let the thunder and the lightning destroy, I will consume another's flesh tenfold as Aaron tenfold abstention, I will rage, I will be envious, churned though it is to the storm outside, I will eat as Jennifer is being eaten, though I do not consume Laura enveloping Jennifer, Jennifers elsewhere as Lauras here, though there is at the same time the sense of the bottomless as I run my finger along Laura's thigh, forgetting neither Laura nor Jennifer but knowing that the lightning I extrude is myself allparamount while burned to this bluewhite powder, must, must, must be, shall be one with the impersonality of the storm itself and thus minimize earthly connexions and wounding permanences, preferring the macroscopic to the binding cutting barnacles, no letters, busy at Hedgerow a postcard says, Jennifer too at a theatre in the hills of Rose Valley, a summer at this, a summer at that, befitting a member of Temple University's socalled X Group composed of the high I.Q. graduates of the Philadelphia highschools for one fouryear experimentation, said William to Mary it aint necessary itll be all right if you wear a pessary plink plank plink plank—plunk Jennifer punching it out at the piano in music and painting and acting and writing, Wonderfully funny Jennifer, delightful Jennifer, more verses Jennifer to meet Guy Schonfeld the druggist's son at one in the morning after finishing with Lee, Guy the man she must marry, income, status and one baby if you please, no more, for the popular professor's wife at Penn State must entertain the students as she catches sight of Lee at Temple during an audition of the Templayers, Ah now theres fine material for Hedgerow till the divorce from Guy is final and she marries a ballbearing magnate with a stately mansion in Jenkintown and therein with no further childbearing encumbrances is the toast of the American officers of the Second World War stationed in the precincts of Quakertown, the granulation on the eyelids more massive than ever before, the red rims puffed, the Nordic countenance chapped sardonic iron, pitted with sneer and urbane snarl to run a fashion show on the Westinghouse television outlet on Walnut Street, my father a retired merchant that Lee and Guy know as one of the janitors of Temple University, Jennifer climb a tree, Jennifer skipbalancing along a backyard rail, boybaiting Jennifer in all the mornings and afternoons she spends with Lee in the musicroom of the Logan Square Library, on the library roof overlooking the center of the city with its massively soft limestone rail looking out over Benjamin Franklin Parkway and the greenscummed howitzerbreasted stonewomen and horses of the fountain between the library and the Benjamin Franklin Museum with the frail primitive biplane exhibited in front, do you ever notice the statue of Billy Penn atop City Hall from this angle as he holds hat in hand from here it appears as a penis in hand to shake the last drops over the pigeoninfested courtyard, the pneumococcibearers as the City Council accuse them, we must be rid of the pigeons and starlings, the debate raging pro and con in The Philadelphia Evening Bulletin and The Philadelphia Record and The Philadelphia Inquirer and The Philadelphia Daily News and in the City Council itself, while to the right hand at the end of the Parkway at the outer limits of Fairmount Park we have the Philadelphia Museum of Art, sometimes referred to as the Greek Garage, at a cost of some thirtytwo millions of dollars, half of which is modestly estimated as graft, not to mention the tunnel under the Schuylkill River constructed for rapid underground transit and then mysteriously abandoned for obscure generalizations but actually because it is discovered after completion that the grade approach to the tunnel is prohibitively steep so that the poor greenrumped trolleycars could never make the descent without courting imminent catastrophe NIAGARA FALLS in its sudden billionspumed epiphany upon plump little Lee encircles the Provincetown nightheavens in the same violetblack burdenpour I will extract a confession from Jennifer in the Arch Street Station of the Subway, not that he doesnt have the confession already

    not that he doesnt have the confession now

    now

    in the arching ass and the entreating puffball face of Laura Ingersoll. There might be confession if he remains celibate at Provincetown, we use celibacy of course in the looser sense, the boys still a pioneer on the vaginal fringes, the outlands of nubile anatomies, to be whipped by some male statuary in the storm, peer upon me, regard my fearless form, damn all things and particularly all men in the reverberant storm, I stand leanly virile in the fulminating night confronting the blasts of Uncle Aaron's God, wipe me off the grace of the earth, turn Levi to nothingness for his Christine Novak and his elder son David for the one hundred and fifty thousand dollars he loses, kill Victor Nathanson, make Lee grovel before Rena because he cannot deracinate the face of Harry Ring before his very eyes in all his waking hours for the sake of Rena and the unforgiveable malingering in the Army of the United States, punish Gertrude Forsten's child by plucking out the fingers from her hand, smash Lee for holding up to scorn the very existence of Adonai

    the Lord God Almighty

    as a child

    a question

    to Levi

    for masturbation

    for fungus around the groin

    for figuratively pissing on Rena

    and Edith Parker

    for the liar Lee

    liar for twentythree years

    why does he try to save a man from drowning

    BUCKLE THE AXIS OF THE EARTH ITSELF so that we as adolescents shall not cringe with every turn I AM FOULLY BETRAYED all children believe themselves betrayed as the child state of Israel must think itself betrayed among the parent nations

    STRIKE JOSHUA NATHANSON DEAD. Dead to my dreams, grandfather of the amber glasses of tea, that we

    survive

that was an awful storm last night wasnt it Lee?

Yes.

Everythings so calm now.

The spiders are out too, Lee says. Look in the crevices. Did you ever look in them?

Oh I dont want to. They make me shudder, Please dont talk about spiders.

All right.

Leaving the front door of the house at 236 East Roosevelt Boulevard at approximately eightfourtyfive in the morning, Lee Emanuel, calling out a solong mom to Rachel Emanuel, goes down the seamed cement steps in fear. Reaching the pavement, observing white chalky streaks on the bark of the maple trees, he turns left and proceeds west, past the Emanuel's feeble snowball bush and their nextdoor neighbors the Kasters, German Jews, Mister Kaster a wholesale butcher with two sons assisting him in the business, one jolly rosefaced and stupid, the other sallow sneering and canny. Lee waves a good morning to Mr and Mrs Diebele, a childless couple residing in the house adjacent to the Kasters; the Diebeles are white, sanguine and Protestant and the only Christians in a block of Jews. Mister Diebele is taking leave of his wife to attend to building&loan business which consumes some of the time being spent in retirement; he does not permit his entire day to be allotted to business; on the contrary, the pudgy bespectacled Mister Diebele, a head shorter than his wife, manages to return by noon of this granitic day in late autumn to his residence, lunch, scan The Philadelphia Evening Bulletin, thence repairing to his backyard, long and narrow, extending to his garage fronting on Ruscomb Street where he proceeds to putter: he mows the backyard lawn, he shears the hedges, he replaces a wooden step leading to the pantry, he remortars a section of brick on the garage, he paints the fence a new coat of black steadily and expressionlessly in his gray and white lumberjacket, pausing every now and then to restoke his pipe and quietly clean grime and dust from the lenses of his spectacles; he whitewashes the interior of the garage, he gardenhoses his Studebaker and then steadfastly polishes the body of the car; he makes certain that the gutter on either side of the pavement running the length of the backyard is sufficiently deep to carry off rainwater efficiently without flooding the pavement should there be a deluge, and he digs with a small spade at any location where the gutter is too shallow; he measures a plank and he saws, pudgily huffing until Mrs Diebele reminds him that he should take a rest in order not to endanger his health which is erased altogether by a neat and effectually penetrative heartattack removing him from the face of the earth as it is known on the Roosevelt Boulevard between A and B Streets; he relights his pipe, he tests the supports of the radio aerial, he does not hesitate to sweep away with his wife's broom any threat of refuse, be it autumn leaf or errant twig or the casual crumple of a torn newspaper page which can mar the exemplary cleanliness of the Diebele backyard, in the face of which, all the other backyards on this 200 block are pigstys, maculated as they are with children's toys, dilapidated swings, forgotten summer chairs, discarded paint cans and the like which Mister Diebele forbids and condemns in his own backyard as justifiable rubbish; when Mrs Diebele appears on the back porch to announce supper, her husband renounces whatever task he is discharging at the moment to courteously respond to his wife's call and vanishes through the pantry. Lee passes the silent empty house of his Aunt Sadie Schwartz, thereupon pausing at the corner of A Street and the Roosevelt Boulevard, where an autorepair shop is located on the southwest side. Noting the approach, and reacting with a sickening lurch of the belly, of the idiot armtwister Ernie Chalk from the ramshackle house on Ruscomb Street, Lee barely acknowledges Ernies fishoutofwater leering greeting, the spittle forming on the corners of the idiot's mouth as he shambles toward the Boulevard in his thinly contorted gait, at every moment giving the imminence that his many protruding bones will shake loose and their momentum carry them through the shabby mottled integument without a drop of blood being shed, the clammy scales of his skin surely fed, Lee hypothesizes, by a kind of underwater moonlight, sufficient only to maintain a single layer, Cmere Lee I wanna talk taya, Lee hears the hoarse hollow voice, a voice characterized by a kind of constant passionate rattling in the throat shaken by a dim subterranean love to come out hardly articulate on the wet gray rubbery toadstools of his mouth, Cmere I wanna tellya somethin, the one sharp spit of a shoulder higher than the other, Ernie beckons to the boy, his right arm perpetually hugged to his ribs and bent at the elbow, so that forearm and upperarm made a steepsided v, while the hand extending from the limp wrist, thumb touching the idiot's chest, makes a pathetic winglike member, presenting a picture totally different from that of Lee's cousin Gus Nathanson. But Lee hurries on, apologizing in a dumb show that he may be late for his classes at Olney High School, Cmere I wanna showya somethin, I got somethin forya, Lee making a ninetydegree angle to cross the Boulevard, the light changing from green to red, so that he comes to the northeast corner of the Boulevard and Rising Sun Avenue which cuts diagonally at this point across A Street and faces the Boulevard Realty Company on the opposite side of Rising Sun, a building of which the second floor is occupied by the office and apartment of Dr and Mrs Milton Kastrow. Doctor Kastrow is a dentist whose popularity in the neighbourhood is not firmly established

I guess Im not too popular at the Wharf, I wont be staying much longer, Laura

Oh Im not that popular myself. But you got what you wanted out of the theatre, didnt you, Lee?

The harbor, silverjowl in the moonlight, spells some watery sense on Laura's jowls, the girl thicker across the jaw than across her forehead, than across her freckled eyes, the harbor retrieves a silver shadow from her face and returns it, the plump arms from the peasant blouse impressing their fingers about the knee of her crossed legs, the girl deferring upwards to the young man on the stoneseat beneath which spume spatters gray spiderwork, the manylegged egg steadfastly deciphering itself with some concentricity and a relaxed victim or two, Victor Nathanson at once lawgiver and victim, Bruno Canova at once victim and lawgiver, the fly must christen the ointment, the glistening brown sticky paper at Cuchiarra's Barbershop on American Street occasionally alive with a feebly struggling insect asserting a leg, insisting an antenna, tiredly tipping a head in the brown light where Levi sometimes waits with Lee on the heartwired backs of the chairs, Levi perusing the Jewish Forward and Lee leafing through True Confessions and lingering at a photo of a feebly struggling female thigh in the masterful grip of an Arrowshirted male, Cuchiarra doing obeisance with his shears, leering contentedly as he strops the razor, the poster of See Naples And Die on the brown mirror, the brown blue harbor of Naples and the brown faces of railroad men, bricklayers, carpenters bent at the overalls patient to accept the haircut and shave, the smell of oliveoil brownly curling from the Cuchiarra kitchen behind the curled hair on the floor and commingling with wildroot and lathered soap and brown flypaper, the barberchair throne providing a deepening blue view of the freightcars grunting by, traffic stalled behind the obliquely crossed delicate wood narrow triangles, two lowered staves striped diagonally black and white while the gateman stands with his ruby lantern outside his stationary halfcaboose, a gateman of a white mustache, smiling sternly at the petrified traffic, minutes must go by, the motorists turn off the ignition, read The Bulletin by the lowering light, the boxcars and the oilcars making their precise stumbles wheel by wheel into the foreordained tiny chasms between one length of track and another, stumble and grunt, click and recoup, wooden iron cattle bump-wheeled and couplegrind, a brakeman leaning from the iron ladder of one of the boxcars and gracioso cum lento lentissimo gravely and with dignity semiarcing the priestful ruby lantern through the blackening blueness past the warehouses building steadily into dark, vast trailers of brick and concrete glooming over the twostorey slums, the storageplaces abandoned for the evening, the five blueblack silos of the Levi Coal Company grecianly columnar for Lee in the barbershop and stolid Golems for Levi some light somewhere disobedient to brown flypaper and fading off like watercolor, Edith Parker clubbing her white jaw in Stanley's Cafeteria between 49th St and 50th on Broadway asking of Lee that she be given it straight, Tess Rubens outside the Pennsylvania Railroad 34th Street Station waving goodbye to Lee from her convertible, christ youre the first lover Ive had that has biceps, the Philadelphia-New York Express approaching SCHLICHTERS JUTE CORDAGE Ive got to have Rena back, Ive got to have Rena back, Ive got to have Jennifer back shes going to confess in the Arch Street Station or in the White Tower over coffee, let the traffic go through, how long must the watchman stand with his everlasting lantern, when will the barber get to my father, Take him with you, Levi, let him watch you get shaved Rachel pleads with her husband, take the boy with you, he likes to go, All right already, Tell whoever the officer is part of the truth, not all the truth, just tell him what you tell me, theres nothing to rehearse, tell him youre tired, you dont want to go anywhere anymore, just keep repeating that Lee, you understand Harry Ring handhips before him, Rena grinning worriedly under the tiny stolen Klee from the Museum of Modern Art hanging in Harry's apartment, it isnt a fly who struggles off the sticky paper, this requires human attributes, will, determination across the space between father and son each in their barbershop rocks, the bulk of communication between the two political discussion, governmental systems, religious persuasions, abstractions connoting whatever love flows between the two, abstractions for the most part compromising feelings of comfort the two have in each other's presence, God and Roosevelt and Socialism, the mayoralty election and Sholem Alechem which Levi can no longer read, the abstractions of his youth, the terminated culture, the act of indulgence with his lastborn as the lastborn does an act of indulgence, condescension cradled in pathos, with Laura

The girl is a peasantdress and a printdress. The girl is a swirlskirt and a leanto blouse, frecklenosed and frecklebreasted on the nightsand with the darkblondburnt Jane Pickens serving the theatrepeople hotdogs and marshmallows around the beach bonfire, the apprentices gazing in shocked longing at the star, how unpretentious she is, how she makes no distinctions between the cast on the one hand and the flatpainters and the students on the other, sliding down the sanddunes of Race Point into frostchickled Atlantic, twisttided and bloodcrackling in the midst of stuportime Gee I want so badly to be an actress, Lee, I want it more than anything else in the world

are the phrases disguises in the interminable inch of repetition

and here the man staged to let the girl in with the identical common decency

in the grip of the expected twinge

the anticipated urge toward rebelliousness that we shall not be commonly decent

that we shall be ugly

harsh

crude

but the wound is as hackneyed as the decorum

the cruelty handmedown as the benevolence

the silence brutal as a wordspate

turn away and be done

kiss her and be done

splurge yourself upon the Atlantic

withdraw to dry land

grotesquely become laura ingersoll

remain lee emanuel

the sensation of the actlessness of choice the dimension of the impossible

impossible to be impossible

the sole uniqueness the lust for the impossible but for each impossibility got we have the emergence of the possible courteously reminding us of the impossible

what then such a lust

of what is it the disguise

but the disguise itself is only the action of the urgency so that instead of tearing off the disguise we construct additional disguises

realizing that to tear off is only to construct

realizing that to pare down is only to fatten

realizing that both fattening and paring down is simply the act of frantically adjusting to the unchanging urgency to the impossible

the impossible is simply the notion of omniscience; the dumb need for omnipotent control so as to make all men a myth, the girl the instant spring of the beautiful

and instantly we ask vengeance, vengeance: in that the beautiful cannot be done; vengeance—to tumble in and contribute to the already destroyed

I want to be an actress more than anything else in the world Stay with me tonight, Lee the triumphal rafters of the prayinghand roof supporting teapot and confetti in the seaweed saturated dark Lee and Laura in a fingertoil on the wallnext bed. Because its your last night the fake fishnets as puncholed flypaper looped from the rafters after the party, were the only apprentices left How many people are ahead of my father he doesnt have such a heavy beard anyhow it doesnt show as much because hes blond Its impossible Jennifer should be with anyone else she promised dammit she promised with a snicker on her teeth

Sy knows nothing of politics

Sy can only dance

Sys only successful with women

Sy can talk to girls endlessly

Sy isnt aware of anything important

He goes caddying in New Hampshire

Sys still a virgin too

with all his talk

tales of women

tumbling in the hay with this one and that one STILL not yet STILL he hasnt had one not really

not really

all he can do is ride horseback

golf

dance

I got to get Rena back

Ill call her from new york

Ill say shes got to sign papers

here

thats right

and when she comes in to put down her signature Ill RAPE HER TAKE HER SHELL KNOW WHOS SHE IS GODDAMN IT THATS WHAT ILL DO I CANT SLEEP ILL GET UP FIVE IN THE MORNING ILL PHONE PHILADELPHIA

I cant stay Laura, Ive got to pack

No you dont its early

Its not that early

But look on my watch it says

Its wrong its slow

its flypaper

when will the freightrains stop

Lee.

Yes?

Please stay. Please.

I got greasy thighs, everythings infected, Im infected, shell be infected, shell scream, shell vomit, shell throw me out I COULDNT STAND THAT I WONT STAND THAT and I want her like knuckles in my throat clenched knuckles in my adamsapple I got a scholarship in my pocket I dont want to come to america I want to stay where I am not on 4th and baindridge I wont cry nobodyll see me cry Ill pass it on,

somebody will inherit by grimacedback sobs

my sperm will clench its fists

my sperm that will make boys will not weep

theyll hold back

GODDAM YOU LEVI WHAT ARE YOU DOING I cant help it I dont want you go away be in N'muxt stay in Lithuania what am I doing in Province-town with Laura Ingersoll

I have something to tell you, Lee.

Yes?

shutup, Sy, come in, Newhampshire let her be your responsibility I want none, Im not constituted for responsibility, I hate it, my fathers responsible, youre my friend arent you

yes

then be my father take care of laura anybody take care of her Im not supposed to be here

Lee, Im illegitimate. Lying on the bed, drawing away from him in the fishnetted confettied teapotted dark, saltsodden, the wave grows underneath the foundations washing at the wood, coming against the stone, slurping like a dead drunk under the shack on the pier, waterslosh and stuporous beat, she weeps in a kind of felt, in an insulatedness, soundproofed weeping

I knew it had to end, Lee,

no, no, let the gate up, watchman with the snowy lantern, bored with the true confessions because all my fathers waiting for is a shave, the thighs are flaccid in my dozing lap

but youre what I dreamed of, the offtheshoulder casual gulp in the voice, tall and

and;

and;

and;

Very brave now is Laura. Stoic expressionlessness the freighttrain gates crossing and crisscrossing the dim teartracked face under the fishnets, a spider spinning a silken blessing over Laura and Lee from the ceiling as the stalled traffic reads The Daily News, the boxcar waters slipping into their steady slots and a rubyglowing nightlamp sways from the rafters. Lee passes a hand over his face: he needs a shave. Crosslegged, Laura prim plump unprotectedness armored in a dullvoice

My mother was a private secretary to a Minneapolis tycoon I wont mention any names

I actually for the moment want a shave, Lee thinks. Why should I care if youre illegitimate, he smears the sweat from his face. Frogs croak in the swamps behind Commercial Street. Opposite Town Hall at two in the morning swamped with beer he and Sy and Sam cavalierly zip down their flies moved by a simple urge right where the street crooks closer to the harbor a bent vagina and shower the pavement with three streams which if examined closely gives the illusion by way of the moonlight playing upon the streams of the sound impulses converted into visual waves upon the oscillograph.

Well its a sad story Laura says, dont you like sad stories? I want to be sad. Let me be sad. I was never introduced to my father. How would you feel if you were never

Well like feet, Lee says. Like lots of feet. Ive got to get back to pack.

No you dont its early.

Its an hour ago and you say its early, Laura.

If you let me come with you Ill help you pack and then you can come back here.

Thats impossible theres an awful lot Ive got to pack itll take me a long time just to know where to start

You just dont want to stay with me.

I do want to, Laura. Feet

Why are you talking about feet, why

I dont know. You mention illegitimacy

It hurts

All right a little like feet maybe it hurts

I dont understand you, Lee, her little face screwing up like a small whirlpool going round and round and sinking into the fishnetted dark go throw a line if you can Lee go throw

Feet on Commercial Street, Laura.

What?

I see them, thousands. The very fact you construct an illegitimacy, well, I see Laura's legs, thighs, hips, I mean, I dont care if its true or not.

Youve got to care, its the one thing I want you to care about.

Not about love, then, but illegitimacy, the latters more important, I must be struck by it, I must carry Laura's wound, I should own your sore, not mention it to anybody else, but youd know youd told it to me and be proud I knew and loved me for it. Loved me that I was proud of your illegitimacy, then partake of my pride and walk approved by my side, the wonder of it that nobody should know and the notknowing shining on your face, I share your illegitimacy, you have a father

Oh dont be ridiculous, Lee, I dont see you as a parent, now stop.

Excuse me. Its coming.

What is.

I meant to say youd have me as a brother, Laura.

Youre making me hate you.

I dont want you to do that.

The hell you dont you bastard. You better stay here. Its so warm, Lee, why dont you undress, I might even have some pajama tops, you could choose one, why dont you undress, I dont want you as a brother, its our last night, Lee, our last

No it isnt Ill see you again

No no no, its impossible, theres no again. Why are you afraid, Lee?

Im not.

yes you are oh yes you

Laura.

Yes

Is it true

What

That youre illegitimate

Im not sure, Lee.

Certainly you know one way or the other

Why do you have to press me

Dont you want me to press you

Yes, Lee. Press me, press me, force the truth out of me, please, do, yes.

Well

All right, Im very ordinary, theres no illegitimacy, but why should you want me to be ordinary? Couldnt I be illegitimate just for you? Let me be that way. Cant you be fair to me and believe in my fantasy?

You adopt it as a mark of attractiveness, as a sexual comeon.

Isnt that fair

If it works, Laura.

Why dont you let it work?

But if I pity you, Laura, Ill pity myself for the pitying.

Isnt that what you want to do, Lee

Yes and no.

Laura gurglegiggles. Darling, she says.

Huh

Youre sweating through and through. Here, let me take a button, its very simple, first the top one, then the one next to the top and then

I cant.

Youre tall and dark, Lee. It was when I straightened up from painting the flat I saw you this is the one I said to myself this summer this is the one Ive got to Ive got to.

Got to what?

I havent wanted to do it with any other man, Lee, I mean Ive wanted to but I never could make the decision to give myself, it was all legitimate, too legitimate, but with you, you see, Ive no father, I could want to make you pity me, I could invent any kind of fantasy just to persuade you any whichway because I want you to have me Ive decided, I decided that day right out on the wharf, I want to with you, Lee, I want to, awfully, awfully, to let myself go with you, why wont you let me, why, why

Im leaving in the morning, Laura. Its nearly light now. Ive got to make that bus. Ive no more money

Ive got money, dont worry about

My people are expecting me

Who?

My people.

Who

My father and mother, Lee says.

Laura laughs, doubling up on the couch. Oh your mother and father. Oh, oh. Are they married? Are you legitimate, Lee? Are you for real?

You sound a little hysterical.

No. No Im not, Im fine, oh Im so hurt, you just dont know, Im such a big illegitimate, I made up everything for you, I wont ever be an actress, Ive failed, gee oh gee, oh gee boy but Ive failed

Laura, Laura

Dont. You go to your shack and you pack. Go on now, go ahead, youll be late

Laura

You just get out of here, you get out real quick, oh Ill see you off in the morning at the bus, dont you worry, youre all forgiven, Ill survive somewhere else in my illegitimacy, itll work somewhere

somewhere.

past the mind like a black tar road sinuous through the white Provincetown dunes

Well you can have some coffee with me, Jennifer.

The girl with the knotty lowlying calves scratches at her wristwatch with the bitten fingernails and then flings back her pageboy, her face offhand stern looking up at Lee on the southeast corner of Broad and Vine Streets, the Scottish Rite Temple of the Masonic Order on the opposite corner across Broad its grim gray granite facings and window slits noon of the day in the late summer matching the grim rosegray granite facings of Jennifer with her narrow bluegray eyeslits, redrimmed and caked with white deposits. Brown's Delicatessen on the northeast corner displays its ornate arabian neon sign, a long narrow establishment its booths perpendicular to Vine Street so that one can see the businessmen on their lunch hour masticating pastrami sandwiches, lox and cream cheese and whitefish with rye bread and washing these solid fragrances down with light clear amber beer from coneshaped glasses. Two pigeons, on their way to City Hall, sniff and peck in a few moments of tarrying at a burst bag of popcorn near the White Tower at which Jennifer and Lee are standing. Two pigeons, purple and blue and slategray, waddle arthritically round and round the yellowwhite popcorn, their little smooth skulls rocking back and forth and dipping to the kernels, dipping and rocking in a plump reconnoiter, their glittering eyepellets shooting at the kernels and bouncing back, their hips heavy and rocking, their rumps tapered and uptipping, their tailfeathers applauding before they continue their last leg to City Hall located at the intersection of Broad and Market Streets, a blackened massive stone structure relieved by the slashes and spatters of yellowgreenwhite pigeonturd, a ragbag of the Greek, the Roman and the Byzantine served with huge helpings of castellated Gothic and Georgian dessert topped by the statue of William Penn brimhatted and lacewristed, housing the offices of the Mayor of Philadelphia, the City Council, the Water Bureau, the Tax Bureau, the Bureau of Vital Statistics, the Police, the Bureau of Real Estate Assessment, the Philadelphia Art Jury, the Courts of the Common Pleas all served by wirecage elevators and commodious stone stairways at whose bottoms and tops and loitering as well outside ammoniacorsaged mensrooms stubbystatured snapbrimhatted plumpvested men may be encountered authoritatively idling away the time, discoursing with equal facility on precinct politics or the sixth at Havre de Grace, tipster sheets and The Daily News wadded under their armpits

All right, Jennifer says, low thuds in her voice. One cup.

Sure, Lee says.

People pass. Cars, north and south on Broad, east on Vine dedicated to oneway traffic. Its not fair I dont know all the people, Lee feels. I dont want to discriminate against any of them, white or black or occasional yellow.

theme song:

> somewhere Ill be illegitimate
> somewhere a parental absentee
> somewhere somebody will truly care
> that Im not what I am
> but what Im supposed to be

today is Lauraday in New York's Washington Square, a moment like a child rushing into the simple nozzle of the spouting fountain, while on the rim of the surrounding stone circle sophisticated balladeers sing

> somewhere Ill be illegitimate

to naive inverts in pageboys and bluejeans, to maidens who blush sallowly

anything could be interrupted for Laura, Lee says to Flikker who chins himself on the monkeycage with the other children while Lee describes enormous arcs in the swing he preempts from a little boy

is she back in Minneapolis Flikker grunts

or here with Lee in the swing Lee whees at the top of the arc

She holds an anomalous position, Flikker asserts. Shes neither alive nor dead.

Till I die, Lee says, Laura can go on and on in a billowing peasant skirt trying to keep the skirt down with one hand and waving to me departing in a bus with the other. What do you make of it, Lord Flikker?

Flattery. Sheer flattery, Flikker hugs his sides, his lowflying forehead wallowing in wrinkles. She says goodbye to you, smiling and weeping simultaneously. What could be a larger flattery than the mixture of laughter and tears? Lost, illegitimate, lusting, frustrated, you pack a bag instead of a vagina, she looks on you as fool and boy and departing wish of a man, her summer all mocked and yet in the larger mockery evanescing, going, seated in a bus, a man of no dreams vanishing with a dream, the wondrous impossibility of it, not, mind you, that she seeks to keep her skirt down over her legs so that others might see them, oh no, Lee. Rather, that you might see them. Why should she let you? She will keep herself as you keep her, prim, maidenly, modest, she insists upon your own lie and waves it away at the same time, its a triumph for her that tears her apart, in that you will forever keep her with you, the final image the most vivid, she has her revenge

and a strange revenge it is, too, Flikker. At night, whenever Im depressed before falling asleep, what image comes to mind to make me smile, to dissipate the terror? Always, always I think on Laura in billowing peasant skirt, trying to keep it down in spite of gusts of wind while she waves goodbye to me at the station in Provincetown, and I fall asleep with my heart something like that skirt, feeling a ridiculous delight, if you will, a droll nostalgia, night after night she comforts me

Still? Flikker swings his legs over the stone rim, peering at the headdress of the fountain

somewhere Ill be illegitimate

Less and less, Lee admits.

She may die, Flikker warns.

Not till Ive done with sorrow.

You may someday be done with sorrow before going to sleep at night—and then, wheres Laura?

When Ive sorrow only in the day and not before sleep at night—why, no Laura.

You may kill her, then.

Yes.

Without even being aware of it, you may kill her. Joy before sleep will kill her, and youd not even know, because youdve forgotten to be sad.

Yes.

Lord Lee, how can you? She gives you the best moment of her life, the moment that can dispel your melancholy if ever you experience it before sleep—and you may kill her? For God's sake, man, the least you can repay her with is your melancholy. Flikker flings his arms wide and bows in utter servility. The girl is too young to die!

Im thirtyfour years of age, Flikker. I cant go to sleep with a toy for ever.

You would do away with men's charms, Lee? You would murder all their teddybears? This is akin to the murder of the innocents.

But this is the horror of us, Flikker, that we seek to retain the innocents within ourselves, and so we abhor with the profoundest hate the sight of children in our conscious hours. I will tell you, that if we murder our charms, it is the one crime for which we shall not be held accountable, and we may love children then.

Flikker most airily responds: I shall never love children. And, now and then, Laura will return to you before you sleep. So, youve no more than part murder, a botched killing, by halves, by quarters at best, fragments of all our time sticking out of our skins, drawing blood or tickling us, one or the other, crimes both laughing and brooding, never thoroughly settled, no one thing totally alive or totally dead, you understand, Lee? We are things of segment, sometimes twitching, sometimes somnolent, sometimes inert, sometimes adazzle at the top of the fountain. Dont be afraid to think of Laura before you sleep.

Stiffly, Lee stands. Im not afraid to do so.

The hell youre not. You tell me now only no more that youre afraid of being abject in the dark. You dont deserve Laura at all. You despise gifts, dont you? Youre afraid youve got to give something back. Thats her revenge: she gives you a final image, knowing that you must experience distress in order that that final image be evoked. So, she serves you with years of distress. Marvelous, marvelous—women are fantastic. Bravo, Laura! Flikker does a caper on the stone rim
                     somewhere Ill be illegitimate
whitetowering, the philadelphia day, over the half eggshell for the bandconcerts in Reyburn Plaza its rows of woodenslatted benches where six bums sit silverbeardedly dozing in the sun their backs to City Hall
        the pigeons disconsolately hopping and waddling at the bums' feet
        the trolleycars lumbering east and west on Arch Street
        UNITED GAS IMPROVEMENT COMPANY UGI
        HORN AND HARDARTS
        (looking north, that is)
        MASONIC TEMPLE, a black commingling of Romanesque and Gothic
(looking east)
        (looking west)
        BENJAMIN FRANKLIN PARKWAY
        FRIENDS SELECT SCHOOL
        (looking southwest, now)
        PENNSYLVANIA RAILROAD SUBURBAN STATION (south)
        THE CHINESE WALL TOTING THE TRACKS OF THE PENNSYLVANIA
RAILROAD PAST THE BROAD STREET STATION ORIGIN OF LOCAL TRAINS

PROCEEDING TO NEW YORK CITY AND IF YOU PROCEED EAST ON MARKET STREET YOU MUST ENCOUNTER THE READING RAILROAD STATION SCHEDULES TO REACH ALLENTOWN AND READING AND THE RICH ANTHRACITE LANDS OF PENNSYLVANIA

(west again)

THE RODIN MUSEUM A REPLICA OF THE THINKER BROODING BEFORE YOU AS YOU ENTER (northeast from reyburn plaza)

THE GLEAMING FACADE OF THE PHILADELPHIA EVENING BULLETIN THE NEWS OF THE HOUR ON THE ELECTRICLIGHT CONVEYORBELT SIGN BULBS FLASHING TO COMPOSE LETTERS WORDS SENTENCES MEANINGS MEANINGS BY GOD MEANINGS TO SIX SILVERBEARDED BUMS DOZING IN THE PLAZA FLOCKS OF PIGEONS PRECARIOUSLY WADDLING AT THEIR FEET SOMEBODYS GOT TO FEED ME WADDYA MEAN I TRANSMIT PNEUMOCOCCI ILL NOT BE OUSTED FROM MY NATIVE CITY IF NOT FOR ME WOULDNT CITY HALL LOOK ALTOGETHER LIKE A DUNGEON DONT I PARTIALLY SANDBLAST THE STONE WITH MY YELLOWGREENWHITE SHIT THE CITY COUNCIL SHOULD TENDER ME A VOTE OF THANKS THERE SHOULD BE A MUNICIPAL TROUGH IN SHEER GRATITUDE I WHITEN THE ACADEMY OF MUSIC AS WELL ALSO THE MASONIC TEMPLE ALSO THE BROAD STREET STATION AS A MATTER OF FACT THE WHOLE OF CENTRAL PHILADELPHIA INCLUDING WANAMAKERS BENEFITS FROM MY BLANCHING PROCESS WHY IM SUPERIOR TO THE VICE SQUAD I RAID RITTENHOUSE SQUARE WITH FAR GREATER EFFICIENCY WHO CAN MAKE THE HOMOSEXUALS VACATE THE SQUARE WITH AS MUCH RAPIDITY HELL IF THEYD LIGHT UP THE PLACE AT NIGHT AND STATION PIGEONS IN EVERY TREE ID MAKE THE SQUARE COMPLETELY SAFE FOR HETEROSEXUALS NOT ONLY THAT BUT ID BESPATTER THE WINDOWS OF EVERY BOOKSHOP SELLING OBSCENE BOOKS SO PEOPLE WOULD KNOW NOT TO FREQUENT THEM ID DESIGN SOMETHING IN WHITE IN THE SHAPE OF A JEWISH STAR LIKE THE NAZIS DO PNEUMOCOCCI MY ASS WHO THE HELL DOES THE CITY COUNCIL THINK THEYRE KIDDING IF THEY WANNA STIFLE GERMCARRIERS WHY DONT THEY CLEAN UP THE CESSPOOLS IN KENSINGTON SOME OF THOSE OPENAIR URINALS IN THE STINKING COURTYARDS BETWEEN FRANKFORD AVENUE AND TORRESDALE AVENUE WHAT KINDA CRUMB THEY THINK THEYRE THROWING THE PEOPLE BY A HANDFUL OF MASSHOUSING UNITS IN THE SLUMS THATS ABOUT WHAT THE PHILADELPHIA CITY COUNCIL IS FAMOUS FOR ITS VAUDEVILLE I KNOW ONE COUNCILMAN WHO DATES HIS FAMILY BACK TO THE PAY-

FLOWER EACH TIME I DECORATE HIS HAT HE CANT IMAGINE WHAT HES
BENG PUNISHED FOR BECAUSE HES JUST FIXED UP A TRAFFIC TICKET AT
THE MAGISTRATE'S COURT AND GETS A SERVICEMAN AND HIS GIRL MAR-
RIED WITHOUT THE USUAL THREEDAY WAIT THATS ONE HELLUVA BUSY
DAY LET ME TELL YOU RIDING AROUND IN HIS LIMOUSINE THROUGH THE
FETID ALLEYS OF FISHTOWN HIS PARTICULAR BAILIWICK NO SIREE YOU
VOTE REPUBLICAN YOU AINT GONNA STARVE

Jennifer.

Uh. She nibbles at the faint traces of a maze.

Want a

No. Thanks. All her stiffenings in the process of breaking off, startled
at random I havent much time the knottycalved girl is furtive. The White
Tower plateglass window is bent double and billows quietly convulsive
transparencies into reflection onto Broad Street. They stoop, Lee and
Jennifer, at a redtop table, whitelegged. Incessant stillnesses lean behind
them on a redtop counter

Why dont you look at me

might feel like changing. Its hard not to do what you want when I
look at you somebody left a maze on the table reflections bite their fingernails too a razed Rena bite their reflections on up to people they say dead
people's nails continue to grow the least mourners could do is to bite their
dead beloveds' fingernails

Like that Sunday at my parents house. You did what I wanted

I couldnt, Lee, I was frightened if Id given in I wouldntve been able
to bite my fingernails Lee bites Rena's between her thighs nobodyll know
youre nervous down there

Youre still frightened.

Maybe

Of me

Yes.

You wrote me only once at Provincetown

I was busy. You know, Lee. Jennifer smiles shakily, shoulders cocked
up into a crawl, a taped squirm in the seat, apologetic. Square white glis-
tenblanch teeth the maze loses itself in Jennifer, searching. The maze of
somewhere a m

the wiliest of bewilders; she has brushed herself buff clean but smells
Jennifer stinks if youre too close, the martyr Jennifer she contends,

plucking all stenches from you, anyone close, to take them upon herself she grins, not as if shes been running, finally, in her search for the maze on the tables of things, white reflections on scarlet, but because you have just stopped running and the sweat avalanches on to her, so that she, too, must run if she must own up to the stink at all, her eyes running, her tongue, veins, the incessant stillnesses in her become tomboy, hooting, she must not be caught hunting for herself, what a childish prank for the square nordic face, the pageboy in noonday theater cut. Broadshouldered, thinwaisted, fingers long and squaretipped, the lateyellowgray eyes

resemble my father, Jennifer.

I try very hard, she says, dry, glancing at him feebly. Then, in spite of herself, held. Stop it

What

Looking at me that

What does it do?

want to stay here, in this stupid White Tower hamburger joint

With me.

With

Why didnt you write me more often at Provincetown

I didnt want to.

Why not.

I wanted to break it, Lee.

Why.

I had to

Why

Its at an end

Is it.

Looking at me that way.

What does it do

It makes me want to stay here, in this stupid White Tower hamburger joint.

With me.

With you.

Why didn't you write me more often at Provincetown

Why didn't you write me more often at Provincetown

I didnt want to.

Why not

I wanted to break it, Lee.
Why?
I had to.
Why
Its at an end
Is it
I think so.
Now, Jennifer?
I cant say it is right now, not with you looking at me
Then how do you know
Because I want to know
Youve been with other men.
Yes.
Did they make love to you
Yes.
All of them
Yes
Did you want them to?
Yes
Did they touch your breasts?
Yes.
I think so.
Now, Jennifer?
I cant say its right now, not with you looking at me.
Then how do you know?
I cant find the maze, she says quietly.
Add enough men and theres a maze
Yes. Yes
And they made love to you
Yes.
Did you want them to?
Well, you know, she grins sourly, you run into them in the maze, sacrifices get to be enacted onstage, the audience becomes more and more important
They touched your breasts.
Yes
Did you sleep with them?

Ive got an appointment, Lee. Let me go.

Drink your coffee.

Its cold.

Drink it.

Its the way you look at me.

How do I look at you, Jennifer?

Like theres something inside of me you know how to meet.

What is it that I meet?

I dont know, I dont know. But I dont want it to happen.

You love me?

No— yes— how the hell shoud I know? The girl sweats. Lee can smell her across the table, through the onions, the mustard, the garlic, the goatish stench of her that he likes, the acrid stink, the essence of armpit, he enjoys the granulated eyelids the same time they make him nauseous, the face a feminine replica of his father's, the jowls not so heavy of course. Youre the only person I know who can make me feel diminished, Lee, far smaller than you, Goddam it, the only person I feel inexorably committed to being serious with. I dont want to be serious, or act serious, I dont want it, I wont have it.

You finished?

Yes.

You love me?

Its impossible, Lee. You oppress me, I cant absorb you or throw you off you know like a glancing blow or a reflection and yet Ive seen things with you that Ive never seen before, Ive been content simply to walk with you, talk with you, sit with you in Rittenhouse Square, listen to music with you, watch light on the Schuylkill River with you, all the simple common things that I used to despise, laugh off, be flip about. You know all the mornings and afternoons and nights weve walked miles around Philadelphia but I cant go on, its got to stop, it is stopped, its done

Danny wrote me youd been seeing Guy Schonfeld.

Dannys a gossip, maybe you dont know that about him

He wouldnt write me what isnt true

Maybe not, but does he have to write it? Hes rather jealous about you

He admires you.

Perhaps, but that doesnt compel him to like me. But I dont care if he does or not

Hes a brilliant guy

What do you have to defend him for

Were off the main track, Jennifer. I want you.

The girl swings her head down over the table. She crawls her fingers along the red tabletop, the nails bitten and dirty, she hasnt taken a bath in two weeks, he can envisage the dirt line on her neck, she must be crawling with sweat, what the hell does he want her for, the nordic, the whitecaked eyelids, the filthy body, the goatsmell, the baritone voice, the snigger, the dancer, the runner, see how she dances away, football with the kids along Park Avenue behind Temple University, catchball with the boys, soccer, composing the school musical in collaboration with its outstanding fag Harley Semple.

Forgive us our egos, Jennifer. Better present the icy petrifaction as we become more intimate with you than the wilt.

Bravo, Lee. May I go?

You marrying Guy

Maybe

You love him

Yes

Youre a liar

Ah. Ah. Youre such a delight. Stop looking at me for Christ's sake. I dont think I can stand it.

You still havent told me why.

Theres a sort of a twist that happens, between you and me. A twist, dammit. Dammit

Such twist as occuring between Jennifer and Lee taking in some measure from the nature of the shared abscess that refuses to burst, in which both probe with a kind of silken hook, a cowardice at spilling the contents of themselves. The twist a sort of skirting that each does along the frayed parts of themselves. The twist of the nature that each dares the other to obliterate all sense of mutual communication, a daring that each can circle without end about each other, without renewal of any sort, without the riddance of feces, without the ingestion of food, without sleep and without motion. The twist that in a surpassing folly of imagination posits the extirpation of the whole of the rest of the species, that Jennifer can give this, that Lee can give this; that, to shake it off will invite the loss of their specialness to each other. The twist that is of the animals who stop just short of devouring each other, but who do not wish to surrender that unique keenness of sensation which precedes the devouring and who wish to keep it in suspension. The twist that is enamored of suspension itself, that may insure some brand of immortality, though both Lee and Jennifer may hate that they happen to be at this point of time the two components. The twist of infamous servitude, in which both are servile to each other, in which neither is master, in which neither can imagine any mastery whatsoever, in which a rasping degradation collars them both, in which they both taste the raw meat of each other without chewing it. The twist of a running hunger insisting on denial of satisfaction, and the laughter at each other for such fatuousness, Jennifer and Lee yoked to the same ridicule, the twist that they have no knowledge of each other, not the least iota, and would challenge each other to remain together and preserve inviolate that enormous dumbness

Guys got a big nose.

So?

A very big nose

What of it

Practically bigger than the rest of his face. Isnt that all you feel when you kiss him? See and smell and touch? The nose? Youre engaged to a nose that teaches sociology, that ferrets you out. Youll be pregnant with a nose.

Like I was pregnant with your eyes

At least you dont have to blow eyes.

You bastard. Jennifer smiles feverishly, theres no Broad Street, no Scottish Rite Temple, no Brown's Delicatessen, no pigeons waddling. Simply: Lee's long hands, ruddy, burnt. Lee is complimented by the term bastard. He swells but at the same time he doesnt know what to do with his brains. He knows hes got brains, he knows theres some sort of pulpy mass vironed by bone and impulsed to eyes, nose, tongue, ears. But he doesnt want to think. In this instant he wants idiocy. In this instant he wants to set the pulpy mass loose from its moorings, pounding

But the pounding is only converted. To alcohol, to drugs, to thievery, to sex.

Of course. The pounding against the wall does no more than either break the wall or the skull. Whereas, theres a certain additional variety to the conversions, which are means of survival.

Predicated on the wish to survive.

Of course. Either you die right away or survive for awhile and die later. What else is there? Its all very simple.

Theres the desire for a third choice to come into being. The choice involving the sense of transformation. There is that that can make one want to pound the skull against the wall and set the pulpy mass loose.

Because Jennifer is obdurate? Because its impossible to sense any transformation in her, you want to sense it in yourself.

But none of us are closed systems.

You would go mad were you to experience the reality of quanta.

I wonder if the schizophrene is exactly that.

No, he is not. He is the ultimate horror involved in the enclosure of multiple closed systems. He is the common madness of proliferating closed systems. What you ask for is the uncommon horror of knowing the open system, which is no knowing at all, so that you defeat any and all purpose altogether.

But in terms of quanta none of us are closed systems.

Only partially are we human in terms of quanta.

But that invokes a paradox: how do we manage to create the illusion of the closed system while in reality at all times we undergo transformation in terms of quanta?

That is the defense of the quantum against itself.

How do we manage it?

By death, of course. We keep the illusion by dying, by gross transformation at the point where we are in danger of beginning to sense the minute transformation.

But how did we originally manage to avoid the sense of the minute transformation?

By the act of reproduction, in which we are content to observe the variation of our own kind, as a sop for our inability to perceive transformation.

That does not meet the essential question, which is, again, how in an open system have we managed to fashion the illusion of the closed?

Obviously, by an ingenious combination of the animate with the inanimate. You must not for a moment suppose that the human body is every inch alive. We are not constantly registering, therefore, on what we understand to be live tissue, but on intervals of live tissue. It is the sense of the interval which is the provenance of the closed system illusion. I will tell you, Lee, that you are the kind of individual who does not wish to accept the necessity for one sort of sacrifice or another. In order to perceive at all, we must inhabit a prison. You want to avoid that sacrifice, but successfully doing so would entail total blindness. You would be blind now in the presence of Jennifer

Jennifer.

Yes? Why do you smile so sleepily?

Did you ever experience the sensation of shaking your brains loose from their moorings so that they become a sort of fish swimming around in your skull and once in a while look through your eyes. The fish looks at you now

Quit it

Oh no. The cold scaly fish sees a girl sitting at a table. Her nose is redtipped. Its dark inside the aquarium skull, Jennifer, and the fish swims around and around, the gills brushing against the ears—I hear a fragment of you—a word—quit it—quit—then it makes for the back of the skull, the tail pointing at the eyesockets—do you see its tail? Is there love in the tail? You can see, I cant, because the tail

He chuckles, deep in the throat. The fish executes a loop, stares at lips being bitten, fingernails bitten, patches of white and red on a face

The fish doesnt understand, Jennifer

Go to hell

Weak

cold in the skull. got to change the water, wholl change the water, where do I let it out, wheres the drain? But then—then the fish will flounder

ho

(fish: can you joke? pun upon yourself? The miracle of the punning fish—)

and be

dry.

gasp.

Why you breathing so fast, Lee?

Theyre changing the water. My whole body is lying on its side

for God's sake Lee control your

I dont want your pity

who are you talking to

Rena screw your pity

pity for fish/the fish that peers into the television screen new years eve

fresh water. but equally cold. Jennifer. your names Jennifer. Danny. Yes.

I needed this walk around the fountain, the giant greenscummed maidens tossing their fishbreasts into the nightair Danny Danny I hate her I hate I hate her. Youll forgive me, of course. She went and married an Armenian, Ive nothing against Armenians, youre one youre

Yes yes, really, Lee

I finally got the nerve to talk to her, during the intermission, Id seen her five successive times at the Philadelphia Orchestra concerts. Alone. Tall, a little stoopshouldered. Why I havent been seeing you, she said she attends Swarthmore, sister of a famous female tennisplayer, older than she, brilliant in school, summa cum laude, but not her, she had to plod, fearful of examinations, her father a professor, her grandfather an emeritus at Harvard. All right. I even comforted her when she got a B in one of her courses, she knew nothing, took her to the Tenderloin once, she couldnt believe her eyes, the seedy drunks, the—yes. Well. And the automat. Couldnt understand people served themselves, thatd never happened to her, then she went back to her home down south, married an Armenian, I—

Rage, Lee, rage

Yes. She sent me an invitation to her wedding. The Armenian a professor of neurology I hate her I hate her I hate her I want to rip off her stoopshoulders and and and stuff them up her cunt, let her have

a

stoopshouldered

cunt

Jennifer.

Well?

Youre inanimate. Thats how I adjust. Besides, Im a woman, Im marrying a professor of neurology, Im jealous of my sister, Im as nordic as you are, why do you seem to gravitate toward Jews, Jennifer? Can you cheat them more easily

I dont think of you as a Jew

What of Guy

Yes, of him. He is a Jew

So you wont be my mistress because you cant think of me as a Jew

Partly. Does your mother want you to marry a Christian

Lee they dont really like you to believe me take the Diebeles for instance she smiles at me I smile at her were friendly were neighbors even next door the Forstens even though we tell each other's business and Id do worlds for her and she worlds for me theres a difference in their heart of hearts I know they dont like me inside theyre antisemite sure they wont tell you theyd deny it theyre good people who has anything against them but I can feel it Lee Im telling you your mother knows Ive been through life and you havent take my word for it dont ever think of marrying a Christian you think youd get along but believe me the first argument shed call you a kike and youd call her names dont you ever dare bring in a Christian girl in here I wouldnt talk to her and if youd ever marry one youd break my heart

oh mother

im telling you my heart would break, Id never get over it, I just cant think of it, to have that kind of daughterinlaw, listen Lee theres plenty nice Jewish girls they got money theyd be only too glad to get somebody like you why cant you find a nice Jewish girl the congregation has plenty you should take them out

You dont feel my mother in me, Jennifer.

I might marry you if I did

To get back at her

The girl smiles pinchedly. With Lee you analyse and analyse and analyse, which she wants to shatter once and for all. He slices little pieces of abstractions, which you must stamp on. Because the little pieces of abstractions tend to crowd out the sense of life in you, tend to bombard the sense of light within yourself, the sense of no relationships, while Lees constantly making relationships, tying you in, not even that youre so much opposed to that but that you feel Lee is only making a fiction of relationships, relating the sense of one of his feelings to another of his feelings and embracing you with that and never relating the whole of himself to the whole of yourself, which you must resist too because you do not wish to admit the totality of yourself and Lee at the least makes a presumption of that, how dare he, how dare he as a matter of fact attempt to define you, how dare any man seek to do that, its not fair, because in a man defining you you would loan out yourself to him by way of being familiar: since he knows you, you can let him have you, youre sort of interchangeable, he can take care of you without your lifting a finger because he bears you around in himself, all of which is fine, really, yes, quite convenient, you can walk around the streets of this earth just taking care of your inmost secret and letting the man that has you take over all the other things, like providing for your belly and your vagina and the clothes on your back while you, your deepest secret of self, can be sort of free, leaning against a wall in the sun, laughing to itself, the deepest secret which is your sense of aliveness, of simply being on the earth which nobody else knows because theyre so busy getting things to eat and places to live in that they forget what their deepest secret is, that sense of sly aliveness, of simply leaning back against the wall in the sun without a belly or vagina or clothes, but if you let a man do that, which is all right for awhile, suppose the sense of aliveness, that deepest secret, suppose it doesnt work out, suppose some day you stop laughing to yourself because you feel too queer doing it, youre apart, separate and youre made fun of, and all of a sudden you want to run away and youve got to get your whole self back to run away and the man wont give you back to yourself because he feels so goddam princely keeping you, youre a subject hes gotten used to being proud of, so to hell with anybody trying to define you, you wont attach to that kind of man at all, but rather to some man who knows his place with you, which isnt Lee at all, not that he wouldnt keep his distance with you but that hed make you enraged and unhappy by dissecting what the very distance itself means, so you want somebody who someday you can simply snap your fingers at and be done, whether you have a child from him or not, not that you wouldnt have a child, certainly you would, youd go through the act, but its quite mechanical as far as youre concerned and youll keep it so because a child tends to define its mother and youd be damned if youd let a child do what you wouldnt let a grownup come near to doing, so youd let your divorced husband have it, let the child define him, he can have it, yes, this whole goddam worlds full of people trying to make you aware of your limits, not that Lee does that, at least not in one sense, because while he tries to define you he tries to extend you at the same time, push back the limits, but thats dangerous too you see, because thats already admitting limits, but she concedes shes attracted to Lee's attempts to push back her limits, she likes that, she may even love that part of him that does that, but that means loving your own possibility of limitations, so that the very love has its consequence in fear of herself and thereby fear of Lee

Shed be the only person I could get back at in you, Lee. Your mother. And thats not enough, not near enough.

So youll marry someone, like Guy, whom you can get back at fully, thoroughly.

If Id say yes to that, Lee, Id only do so to please you for the moment

You want to please me for the moment

Just for the moment.

Then right here just for the moment were in love.

What more could you want than such a concession?

The coffeecups on the redsurfaced table jitter from the rumble and lowboweled roar of the BROAD STREET SUBWAY underneath the White Tower, warming the anuses of Jennifer and Lee. The counterman flips the hamburgers on the aluminum grill, three rows of four apiece he flips them methodically, eyes a shrugdrug against the pink of the meat dirtying into a smoky sizzle at fourthirty in the summerlate afternoon, the traffic proceeding south on Broad Street thinning out, the traffic proceeding north thickening with Chevys, Studebakers, Buicks, Fords, Packards, Nashes, the rumbleboweled roar of the subway increasing in frequency, Jennifer wanting to disadhesive her ass from the vibration, Lee wanting the concentric shakings quoiting her intestines to continue

behind the Emanuel garage in the driveway up against the Diebele garage wall the looted brain of Ernie Chalk trickles spittle from the mouth and intimidates Lee against the brick, Ernie keeping his frozen uppawed right hand against his own sparrowchest and with his left seizing Lee's hand, spreading the palm and compelling it backward unnaturally, bullying the boy so that his knees bend a little. Le me go Ernie, please. Nah I aint gonna letya. Let me go. Nah not yet, ya gotta beg me, Ernie pulls back his lips from his lonely separated teeth, the gums practically bloodless, a graypink, his breath stuttering with decay, his upinwinged right hand shivering slightly, his body like an old chassis with the motor just turned on vibrating, he will cow the boy, he will wail a whimper out of him, he will make the boy the very jelly of himself of Ernie Chalk. In the jutting corner house directly across Ruscomb Street, sitting in the rocker on the open porch, is a sixtytwo year old man by the name of Shatzky. He is paralysed, from a recent brain hemorrhage; his stillness of white hair and swarthy flesh is the sole presence overlooking Ernie and Lee. The rest of the street is deserted. Shatzky stares. Paralytic, idiot, boy.

I want you to be my wife, Lee says

For one thing, youve no money, Jennifer says. You may have, eventually, but Ive no idea when, and neither have you. The hamburgers flip and sizzle on Jennifer's heart. A paralytic stares impassively from across the street. Ernie pushes Lee's hand backward, the wristbones thrust, you call ya mother an youll really feel it Lee. The afternoon shadows slate across Ruscomb Street, Broad Street is blueserge, why doesnt my mother call me, why doesnt she come through the garage, isnt she back yet from seeing Uncle Victor, shes been gone an awfully long time, let me go, what do you want to hurt me for, I havent done anything to you Ernie/yeh thats what you think/well what did I do you Ernie/plenty plenty/whatever it was Im sorry Ill never do it again Ernie I promise I swear cut it out huh that hurts that hurts that/that hurt Lee/yeh/that hurt Lee/sure it does Ernie/does it hurt more now maybe/yeh it hurts me please stop I met Guy's father Jennifer hes a druggist isnt he

Yes.

A little man isnt he

Yes.

With a big nose and a high voice an awfully high voice when he opens his mouth youre awfully surprised arent you Jennifer

Yes.

Because you dont expect it to sound like a womans do you

No.

It sounds just like a woman's doesnt it

Yes.

Thats Guys father

Yes.

With a soprano voice

Yes.

I know his sister too, she had a job done on her nose, I felt her up in a closet once at a party shes marrying a dentist with an excellent income I can feel my neck like a wrist being bent backward into the coffeegrounds

What do you want from me Lee what does any paralytic want sitting in a rocker

He wants to rock

But he doesnt rock

The rocker is still

His eyes thump and jitter at the spectacle against the Diebele garage wall, the paralytic Shatzky belongs to Ernie and Lee, hes theirs, possessed by them in his own stillness watching the idiot bend the boys hand backward that enough Lee yes sure yes I gotta do it a little bit more please dont youre hurting me a little bit more I cant stand it sure you can Lee no I cant Ernie let me alone beg Im begging that aint enough

Lee Ive really got an appointment Jennifer cant twist her head around to look through the plateglass window at the granitic niches of the Scottish Rite Temple across Broad Street all the niches are monopolized by Lee

I didnt think youd make it a matter of money Jennifer why are streets deserted in the traffic sometimes

down ruscomb street a grocery store a candystore a butchershop nobodys out playing softball lets choose up the hands of the two leaders climbing past one another on the bat towards the top the last full grip obtains the first choice of the available players Lees the last always the last to be chosen hes too fat to run fast hes too unsure of himself to hit the ball with any consistency he gets too frightened to make a throw with any habitual accuracy

Let her go Lee shes no good for you I dont want my sons marrying Christian girls I dont care if Sue is Dave's wife now I wouldnt have her in the house why didnt he work it out with Betty Bettys a good woman for him look at all she stood for from him he could still do it if he wanted to Lee's hands and Jennifer's dipping into the red surface of the table

surrendering is the most difficult possession

Ernie let me go my motherll wonder what happening to me I wont tell her I wont tell anybody just let me go Ernie wants to see the boy down on the ground

Rena Im down on the carpet

Youre not seriously suggesting I wait for you Lee are you? What do you expect me to do after I graduate from the university? Can you in all honesty suggest I wait for you

the paralytic has been a Democratic committeeman all through the

Republican years Harding and Coolidge and Hoover he suffers the hemorrhage of the brain upon the election of Franklin Delano Roosevelt he has done favors for everyone on the block in the ward all through the Republican years each of the days before Election he has personally come through the kitchens of every family in the ward and asked the husbands and wives to come round to the polls tomorrow and vote come out and vote this year I should be able to get the traffic light at D and the Roosevelt Boulevard so the children can cross safely I know theres been three accidents there with children during the past year if you vote the straight Democratic ticket I think we can get a traffic light FDR do you remember Shatzky the Paralytic well let me tell you his wife is selling cheap dresses from the house now to support the two of them and does seamstressing for extra dollars while the paralytic sits overlooking Ruscomb street peering with blazing petrified fury at the idiot hurting the boy

Jennifer's hamburger heart is a rich redolent chocolate, garliced and onioned and relished, and she thinks of spreading mustard over it and munching on it but she is a paralytic in the face of Lee why doesnt his mother save him everybody saves him anyhow Harry Ring wants to save him from Rena

Id no idea your values included money, Lee says.

They do now, Jennifer says

On your knees

Saul thats the first and last time Im on my knees

What are you searching for

Its not what Im searching for but that I must be on the ground some rare object that thousands of people must bend down to and look for

Ill give you a sedative. Rena Ill give him a

Give him something for God's sake I cant take much more of

My wrist hurts my neck hurts my waist hurts being arched back Rena Ernie Chalk Jennifer Ernie Chalk Levi Ernie Chalk

The trouble with you Lee is that you look on the world as if its some drooling idiot and you the child the idiot seeks to force to its knees

Doesnt everybody so look at it

Were not supposed to admit it

We must seek constantly to convert that knowledge and search around the feet of the idiot

at Provincetown the commercial street feet Laura

the idiot is a virgin too

and look for money. There is an alternation of idiots in the relation-ship of two people. You and I Jennifer, for example. Im the idiot whos forced you to her knees and you search around my toes for money

I dont see any.

Youre mindless now as you search. There is the idiot with power and the powerless idiot.

the earth is all we have, Lee. It is you who does not want the earth. It is you who are in the extrapolative habit, the infinite springing away because Jennifer is a jot you cannot have. So you intend to gain what you cannot define because you are unable to hold what can be defined

Isnt that in itself a gain because some of us cannot obtain the jots? Arent some of us denied certain possessions so that we can seek to gain others which belong to nobody

Thats an excuse/a rationalization

Doesnt rationalization play its part for the individual so that he does not need to hold on to his regret

Then what the hell are you holding on to her for

For as long as I can in order to understand her and myself in our connection

So theres fear of a disconnection

Is there any knowledge that does not have its matrix in fear? And there is nobody to stop us. Shatzky the paralytic cannot move, cannot interrupt Ernie Chalk who has the boy down on his knees up with his head against the Diebele garage brick wall. The humanitarian cannot intervene.

The termination of a particular sector of knowledge is the only humanitarian. You understand that, dont you, Jennifer.

Yes.

It isnt Lee Emanuel you want to have money so that you can share it. Would you be my wife if I had money

Somebodys waiting for me

Theres always somebody waiting for somebody else. Dont forestall me with the commonplace

The unique never forestalls anybody. We can always deal with the unusual

Then deal with me forestalling you from keeping your appointment.

Thats a commonplace

How long must this be continued, Lee

Till we know each other.

But Im no longer here, Lee. Im simply your image. Ive long since departed. Im married, Ive a child, Im divorced, Im remarried, Ive a mansion in Jenkintown.

Isnt it incredible how we avoid the present, Jennifer?

Lee grins magnanimously. His face lengthens in the late afternoon. Jennifer feels like the macadamized granite blocks of Broad Street, the traffic wheeling over them at the end of the hot day, the macadam a slick-stickiness, the sound that of adhesive tape insistently unreeled from the stone by the turning wheels, Jennifer's own flesh the adhesivetape stick-slickily unwound by Lee while underneath she knows her granite blocks will never be moved. As Lee strips her, she only reveals her stolid underpinnings. Pitiable man who must so pinion her against a White Tower Restaurant. So awkward of him. Lees never graceful. She merely suffers him and is amused. The poor man is indulging in a kind of necrophilia. The girl is no longer germane but he persists in keeping her in his grip. Cant he feel the statuary? She has become perfect form, but he insists on treating her as a piece of chaos, as if he cannot endure relinquishing his tools. He has already fashioned her, but he goes on measuring, reassessing, as if in the hope she will once again assume life and so relieve him of the necessity to strip her, so that he can once again work with her foundations

No I would not be your wife if you had money, Lee. The girl's voice is curled around a whisper

Your thighs are dry, he says studiedly. So: theres no marriage, no child, no divorce, no remarriage, no mansion in Jenkintown

we slip back and forth between perfect form and life itself

What?

Dry, I say. He stares with the end of his nose, splayed and slightly bulbous, like his mother's. His dark brown eyes are closely set. He misses verging on cockeyedness. Rubbing his left leg against her groin in the livingroom of 236 East Roosevelt Boulevard with the single fake french door shutting out the inclosed porch he says I can feel the granulated eyelids of your thighs on the sofa. Your thighs are red and whitecaked, he tells her in the gusts of goatishness from her. Let me up, Ernie.

No.

Your knees hurting me, your motherll be here soon.

No she wont, Lee.

When he puts his hand on her bare thigh he draws it back in sudden disgust.

Look at it, he tells her in the White Tower.

I wont.

Look at it.

Her jaw plummets, her eyes are lustreless, there is no sense on her face whatever as she regards Lee's hand now covered with a sugary deposit of white crystals, a little sticky. No wonder theres dried semen on your eyelids, he laughs at her. You try to get it up into your eyes: its perfectly all right to have a male's discharge up there, isnt it? It distracts us from the male member between your thighs, doesnt it?

Thats a curious jest, she says thickly. Ive no penis.

Havent you?

No.

Feel for yourself, he says.

Its you who want it there she says dully, two red points in the middle of her corneas, her blonde pageboy in a brown lustreless finish under the waning light.

Put your hand down there, Jennifer.

The very act of my doing so opens me up to total ridicule.

Are you more fearful of ridicule than your genitals?

We all are.

No, Jennifer. He shakes his head gravely. Were afraid of finding genitals all over us, didnt you know that? Sprouting in the unlikeliest places—as, for instance, from our buttocks. Can you imagine breaking wind through a penis? Why, we could waft our fertility beyond the farthest borders. Put down your hand, Jennifer.

I didnt want you to be able to laugh, Lee

I know

I mean its all right for me to laugh and you not to

I know.

I dont like both of us laughing.

I know.

It really puts you on my level and, because youre a man, above it

I know

And if I dont laugh at all, I may never be the same

I know

I want to be the same. Always. As I was. I dont want to change. I want to laugh now.

Put down your hand—maybe thatll tickle you.

Suppose I actually find a male member between my thighs. What then?

I should think that would greatly satisfy all the latent homosexuals you intend to marry.

Its a trick. You masturbated yourself under the table and came and let it dry for awhile and now youre showing it to me.

Its simple enough for you to find out, Jennifer.

The girl rises, carefully, her lower lip bitten by her top front teeth, her shoulders bent, her brow furrowed. She moves her legs with the greatest care, inch by inch, as if afraid something may jiggle. Her expression is that of someone who has just encountered an extremely severe stink. She slides her shoulders against the chromiumframed glass door, leaning her weight against it, so that she slides herself out onto Race Street and then step by step she drags her feet to the subway entrance and there grips the manyfingered brasscolored rail so that she can let herself down the steps, one by one

You shoulda helped the old lady down the steps, the counterman accuses Lee

he clenches both his hands suddenly into a double fist and brings it hard up against Ernie Chalk's groin

the idiot screams

and limps painfully away from the Diebele garage hoarsely scream-ing turning his head back blubberscreaming You shouldnt oughta hit a girl in the crotch

as, with a gentle swash, the gas lamplight at the corner of A Street and Ruscomb

NEXT STOP NORTH PHILADELPHIA STATION NEXT STOP NORTH

if youre going to survive you may have to do so as an ancient as an old woman or as a castration

PHILADELPHIA STATION NEXT STOP NORTH

Lee scans the slowly spreading city through the trainwindow. Not dusk yet. But autumn, and Philadelphia, like Shatzky the paralytic, immobile on a rockingchair on the open front porch; but Shatzky dozes; the lion of a man has eaten his fill dumbly of a little boy who with clasped two fists has driven an idiot adolescent's maleness so far back into a bleeding bladder that the idiot in that stroke maintains with empty urgency that all along he is shrinking Ernestine Chalk. Shatzky cannot bray with satiation; he must sleep. Vote Democratic. He can return to no electioneering at the polls. Mrs Emanuel we need your vote for the next President of the United States as her eyes water from the onions she peels in the kitchen. The soup simmers, the coffee percolates, the brown roast halflids the consciousness, she shells the peas, she takes out the aluminum pot, she scours it with Bonami, she steelwools the dirty pan from the morning's eggs sunnyside, she turns down the gas on the stove from high to low, she peels the potatoes, she mashes them, she pours milk into them, she sticks a toothpick into the roast, she sprinkles a smidgin of thyme, she cuts some parsley, she chops up the apples, she stirs the gravy, the breakfasts and the lunches and the suppers, she places the knives on the table, the forks, the spoons, she puts the rye bread on the tray, she heaps the green-white lettuce, she slices the scarlet tomatoes, she fills a pitcher with water, she fills a small schnapps glass with scotch for Levi, she switches the light on in the breakfast room, she forgets to put on the light in the kitchen

Mom why dont you use some light in here, Lee says.

Ah I can see without so much light, she waves him away.

Its not good for your eyes.

I can see, I can see, go way, Im busy.

Hows gramma feeling?

So why dont you go up and ask her?

Lee mounts the stairway and peeks into grandmother Hilda Nathanson's room.

So gramma how are you feeling?

Whos that whos that its so hard for me to see? The lady under the coverlet smiles tremulously and squints through her bifocals. Oh its you Lee, its so nice you should come in to see me. Gramma nods in sharp little jerks, a few gray hairs wisping from her chin.

I think youre gaining a little weight, Lee grins at her tenderly.

Oh, oh, youre making fun, youre making fun, she shrills up at him in squeakshrills, speaking loudly enough to hear herself. You look in my pocketbook, Lee, you should take out half a dollar.

Lee makes no move. Go on, go on, I want you should have it.

With cupidity and unwillingness Lee takes the half dollar from the pocketbook. Thanks, gramma.

I wish it could be more, Lee. My youre such a tall boy now, youre so tall I never would recognize you.

You didnt tell me how you were feeling, he shouts at the half deaf lady.

All right, all right, she waves the question away, it is of little moment when the grandson is here as she peers up at him through the tiny bifocals, the small locketshaped face seamed and bony on the mere stem of a neck on the clippedin nips of shoulders. She hardly makes a stir under the coverlet. There is hardly a body there at all. There is more gray hair than anything else, piled atop the spare dab of a skull, the steelrimmed bifocals occupying most of the face, the lips a suggestion of a cleft, the whole body of Gramma Nathanson a squint to see who her grandson is standing at the foot of the bed in the spare room, the official spare room of the house where odds and ends of blankets are stuffed into the closet, odds and ends of old hats, discarded clothes that Rachel cannot find in her heart either to sell or give away or burn up, odds and ends of underclothes all thoroughly laundered, nothing dirty, Dave's old highschool baseball uniform with the letter G on the front left standing for Germantown High School, a fourletter man, baseball football backetball and soccer. One thing Dave omits: swimming; the one sport Lee enjoys and is moderately competent at. One large window looks out on the blank buff wall of the Forstens' house, two feet away across the alley. Who her daughters youngest son is here in the spare room of the odds and ends, to which Rachel takes Hilda Nathanson against her will from the perfectly cheerful oneroom apartment she maintains in West Philadelphia near her son Victor, where she has her samovar and makes tea three times a day and reads the Jewish paper and dozes away the afternoon, the only reason she permits Rachel to take her away is the indisputable fact that she can no longer climb the stairs. Also she finds shes constipated. She can sit on the toilet and nothing will emerge. She has pains in the lower abdomen. She is very weak. She must lie abed. She prefers her daughter to take care of her rather than Victor. Theres nothing like a daughter to understand a sick mamma. And in the fading light of the spare room with its odds and ends she discovers that things are new again because she cannot remember very much. And thats good, she thinks, for her old age. If she cannot remember Odessa, there is the spare room instead, and Lee inquiring about her health. If she cannot remember what she was, then the six months or so that are left her are no threat. Because Hilda Nathanson cannot remember that there is a tomorrow. So she glows with all the perkiness of the wonder of her grandson, so sudden before her, so completely sudden, such a miracle in God's name—He seems the only one she has not really forgotten—that the death of her husband Joshua has no meaning whatever. She has not forgotten God; so, she supposes God has not forgotten her. Neither, it seems, has her grandson. God and her grandson it is possible could be one and the same person. In this odds and ends of a spare room world, it is hard to say that that is not so. You dont have to stay here, Lee, she nods at him, Go. Go already, you must have lots of things to do, Im only an old lady a little tired in bed, what do you want with me here, she motions him away, Gramma Nathanson does. Im fine, Im fine, she wrinkles her nose at him. Tell Rachel Im not so hungry tonight. Maybe a little tea and thats all. Tell Rachel. Youll tell her?

Yes, he says.

But he is loath to go. Somehow he doesnt want to leave her. For one thing, he can hardly see her under the coverlet. Shes only a faint mound, a little heap the colored girl might sweep under the carpet. You could make a mistake here. You might not recognize this is my grandmother lying here. But she is, the same one whose photograph in the ornate gold frame sits on top of the glass cabinet in the dining room, a photograph of her in a stiff brocaded dress, old even then to Lee's eyes, possessed of the dignity of age, while in the photograph in the same gold frame next to her smiles Grampop Joshua Nathanson with the bartender mustaches and the hair curving down and up over the forehead. Heres my grandmother. Something is true about that fact, and something is not true. Lee would like to understand where his grandmother is going

As he understands he is going to 3892 Frankford Avenue to talk over a possible reconciliation with Rena

he leans against the kitchendoor jamb watching his mother gather up the sodden yellow carrot peelings in her hands and then place them carefully in the bulging garbage bag. See, she says, you have to shop for yourself, its no good phoning the order in, I never saw such rotten carrots. Wait till I talk to Rosen. Hell hear from me. See, Lee? Ah, fahchap! she slops the carrotpeelings into the bag, irritated. Thats what happens when a grocerystore has no competition. Youd think hed be grateful, Rosen ought to thank his lucky stars for fifteen years everybody in the neighborhood buys their groceries from him, he made a fortune. Now he doesnt care. To hell with the customers! Its because of us, the customers—who else?—he could send his two boys to college—and you, you Lee, whats the matter you dont want to go to college, heres a family can afford and you dont want to go, I just dont understand, maybe you can explain, Ill understand, I was one of the brightest girls in my class—oh that lousy Rosen, may he rot! Im telling you it dont pay to be nice to nobody, they only stab you in the back. You think Dad would phone, hah? if hed be late? I'll throw the supper out, thats what Ill do, what good is it? Its burnt to a crisp, what could it taste like? Youll see hell phone, the drivers are late, hes got to go to the barbershop, Ill slam down the receiver, how many nights Lee supper is burnt to a crisp, here I go to all this trouble preparing it and what thanks do I get. Youd think I could be proud of my sons yet. Dave? I dont even want to talk about him. In Texas somewhere mittendrinnen. Does he write even? His mother's heart could break, but not a line. Not from my son, oh no, hes with his gentile women, does he think of his father and mother even? You, you he doesnt even write a line. Not a postcard even to his brother. Some brother you got, let me tell you. Such a ballplayer. A fine profession for a Jewish boy. What did it get him? Im asking you. What? Heartaches for his mother, headaches for his father. His father treated him too good, that was the trouble. Both of you we treated too good. Parents should throw their children out on the street, thats when the children respect the father and mother, they come on their hands and knees to them, thats right, am I wrong? Tell me where Im wrong. At least you, Lee, you should know better. Brains you got, not like Dave, not that he aint got brains you understand, he just doesnt use them—its in a ball! His brains are with his women, with the likker, all he knows is to have a good time. Are you any better? Do you study like youre supposed to up in your room? Shut up, dont lie to me, you think your mother dont know whats going on. I can hear you up there making speeches for actors, crazy speeches. How could I give birth to two such sons? What did I do? What sin did I commit? Why is God punishing me?

Rachel Emanuel begins to weep, sniffling, lifting her apron to daub her eyes as she inspects the readiness of the roast in the oven. Lee controls himself. Hed like to slap her across the mouth, but he sits

Gramma told me to tell you she isnt so hungry tonight, all she wants is a little tea.

Oh she dont know what she wants, Rachel grumbles, she in her second childhood, I get so mad at her I could kill her

SKF BALL BEARINGS, Jennifer Hazlitt's husband, the train responds to the steady braking, the clickclickings slip into the ear at a slower pace. The shadows on the eringreen lawn fronting SKF unlimber, splay and multiply till babyspots recessed into the earth are somewhere switched on and the green in calcined, the SKF sign is bright black white and bold armstilted callingcarded to Lee eyebackwarding from the train window, his concentrate on Rena lulled, he idly supposes she is waiting volubly with her footdoctor Nate Goldstein and his wife Hannah at this residence on 1829 Clearfield Street where Nate houses his office as well complete with xray apparatus and a son Chuck and a daughter Linda; his little satanic majesty, Chuck, beginning to stutter like his father. A woman called Tess Rubens will be consulted in downtown Philadelphia recessed babyspots, leaning his elbow on the sill, Tess's nipples are recessed till you, not so Edith Parker's on Avenue B from which vantage the United Nations lulled by the existence of feminine members besides Rena, to whom Lee remains officially married, is Rick Russo's status precisely determined? Curious Harry Ring being in South Philadelphia living with that squarebodied sculptress supporting a child, herself and Harry by colortinting photographs

the train again like the couch on the open porch on Roosevelt Boulevard as Lee stares at the traffic with his left ankle in a plaster cast

after the performance in the rear of the President Theatre the playwriting instructor shakes Lee's hand, Thats what a play should be like, the New York part of Rena standing proudly by, the Philadelphia part momentarily obscured, the massive copper disc with the Japanese symbol theron meaning Wisdom hanging over her rustcolored sweater and between the junoesque breasts, the brassburnished shoulderlength hair furnishing in itself copper and rust

its hard to lie beside you Rena and not do anything

Im asking you not to, Lee, but its just a question of time

lined up for chow in the North Carolina woods on maneuvers before the North Africa invasion the platoon sergeant thumbs Lee and Ivan in the thickening dusk I want twelve volunteers who are accomplished swimmers for a rivercrossing full field pack

twelve volunteers

you and Ivan are two of the twelve, got it?

Yeh.

Youll be a waked at 0300

dwarfsize in height but barrelfat in leg, belly, shoulder, neck and head, Bruno Canova saunters into Victor Nathanson's office at the Nathanson Moving & Storage Company in South Philadelphia

Lee glimpses brassstriped hair swirled through the revolving door of Horn and Hardarts

suddenly awakening Rena feels the whole weight of Harry atop her her bra flung aside and the man trying sweating to slip it in

I cant believe that, Lee says quietly

Oh I dont want you to blame him, Rena says, he was really only doing it for you

murder

murder

plunging on the monorail through the dark Lee clutches his mother

look Lee dont worry that I cant come the usual way please dont worry you go right ahead, Edith tenderly urges him in the winter night, and if you feel like it later on and it doesnt disgust you Ill be able to come if you use your mouth is it good darli

ver

even though I cant come this way you feel awfully good youve got such a nice big long one oh God its marvelous maybe someday Ill be able to come the regular thats right hard

you dont mind

no. no. hard as you can that, yes, Jesus

NEXT STOP NORTH PHILADELPHIA the blacksuited goldchain across the vest conductor nods through the car

SCHLICHTERS JUTE CORDAGE

Of the motion of the self. Lee pauses before the window of the Boulevard Realty Company at five minutes to nine in the morning, on the corner of Rising Sun Avenue and the Roosevelt Boulevard. Fear. Someone will see, notice, record, report Lee Emanuel. Another little candy store around the corner on the Avenue, The Inquirer and The Daily News on the rusted orange racks outside. The boy straightens himself

stand up straight, his mother advises

you want to grow up stoopshouldered?

youre tall you should be proud of it

lots of men would like to be tall

the mother is a body of doctrine:

dont tell somebody else your business

your father and mother you can tell anything

the only people you can trust is your mother and father

nobody has to know

keep things to yourself

tell pop about it, he likes to be consulted, after all hes been through life, he understands a lot, he can give you good advice

study hard, get good marks, after all your father isnt a millionaire, get a scholarship, look at Sadie's children, Donald and Clara and Ethel all got scholarships to the University of Pennsylvania and look at your cousin Russell everybody looks up to him hes so smart so clever and with such a personality hes got a silver tongue

dont stay up so late at night always remember you have to get up early in the morning and your mind should be clear

dont be afraid of people you should mingle with them as much as you can

youre as good as the next one

and you should think of yourself better than the next one

dont be so frank in public people dont especially like to hear the truth

the truth hurts

but with your parents you can be honest

your parents will never hurt you

always remember you can come back to your mother and father

your parents are the ones who really love you

you dont do always what we would like you to do but that dont mean we dont love you

were the only parents you have

you got to learn to be independent we wont be here forever

someday your mother and father will be gone and youll wish youd never hurt them even in the littlest way wear your rubbers in wet weather so you wont get a cold

your health is the most important thing

keep the muffler around your throat thats the easiest place to get a cold

dont let the coat flop around it doesnt protect you that way

afterall if you get sick who has to take care of you but your mother and Im not so young as I once was its not so easy for me to run up and down the stairs

dont smoke so much you want to get cancer?

that Eli Berman that nut he was the one introduced you to smoking thats all that nut is good for to get people into bad habits look how fat hes got look look there he goes hes peeking peeking he wants to see if youre in quick lets go in the livingroom he shouldnt see us I cant stand the way he talks Oh Mrs Emanuel you look so young look look hes peeking the nut, what a nut, does he still paint, how can he hes got a wife to support and a child that wife of his she looks like a nut too shes cockeyed oh poor girl look she walks like a truckdriver some pair they are and Eli is so fat I hear hes a salesman for a notions firm thats what you get for trying to be an artist

Should he risk the exams in Latin and Geometry and Chemistry or take the A Bus to the Logan Square Library? The candy store and high-school examinations. The stupefied man behind the counter in a woolen buttoneddown sweater selling cigarettes, sodapop, papers, candybars OH HENRY MILKY WAY TOOTSIE ROLLS LICORICE STICKS BUBBLEGUM, the rack of tattered rental books, 2 cents a day, the browntopped circular revolving stools running the length of the counter, school stationery, lined and unlined paper, notebooks, varicolored pencils, the calendar with the pinup girl, a baby yawling in the rooms behind the store

Above the boy in the sky the clouds thin, pull apart, sunlight slits through and fizzes on the minutiae of quartz in the pavement beneath the boy's feet

FOR SALE PROPERTY LOCATED AT 5409 BOUDINOT STREET, TWOSTO-REY HOUSE, $5890

FOR RENTAL STORE, 1862 WYOMING AVENUE, INQUIRE WITHIN

Lee walks rapidly west on the Boulevard, past a brief row of semi-detached sham Englishstyle homes and crosses Masher Street, casually glancing down Masher as if to promote the impression that he may be seeing it for the first time rather disinterestedly, three blocks north looming the neoGothic facades of Olney High School, Mister Emil Finsen the Principal. His breath in a vise, Lee hopes he will not run into a teacher arriving late. He looks behind him. At B and the Boulevard a green doubledecker bus is momentarily motionless. The boy steps up his pace. Surely he will be caught, reprimanded, suspended, his mother will scream at him, his father gently remonstrate—goddam his gentle remonstrances—his mother will have to accompany him to school, the sixteen-year-old by the side of his mother, an infamy, a shame, a ludicrousness. At school he will be quietly lectured, his mother standing silently by, shaking her head. My boy is a good boy, my boy dont really mean to

The bus ought to be here. Lee stands stiff, looking neither right nor left. He knows no one. Hes in a study, hes absentminded. If anybody recognizes him, he will ignore the person and later plead he was concentrating on something else. The redgoldyellowpurple maple leaves speculate at his feet, the wind flicks his hair, the maple trees keep regular order east and west on the Boulevard, four lanes of highway separated by wide strips of turf now a lifeless green, a green now only habitual, but the present-arms of the sun sass any remaining patches of gray on the morning, tumbling them, routing them, sending them flying as the doubledecker bus lumbers to a halt at Lindley Avenue and Lee boards it, extends the fare, a token worth 12½ cents sedulously avoids looking either left or right, perhaps one of his mother's friends is sitting there, the boy is dry with terror, nearly losing his balance down the aisle as the bus buffets itself once again into motion, Lee apologetically at a woman passenger whose foot he nearly squashes My goodness cant you look where youre going Sorry lady I hope I didnt hurt your foot Oh you boys are so clumsy, till he reaches the cursory narrow spiral stairway up which only one passenger can ascend or descend at a time at the rear of the bus where he grasps the handrail worn to a semblance of silver and pulls himself up, his body lurching, swaying, but hes letting the fear go now, he feels he has outsmarted the day, the public school system, his parents, necessity, duty, routine, examinations, marks, inferior and superior, grades, past and future, restriction, constriction, he has routed time itself so that as he finally seats himself in the deserted upper section of the doubledecker, gladdeningly leaning and bracing and grasping and bouncing and smiling on the curved woodslatted seat as the bus crosses Wyoming Avenue at the point it makes a diametric across the Boulevard, an isolated section of cartrack no longer used embedded and gleaming in the macadam, Lee is expansive, smug, indolent, that swinging trapeze melody of the last movement of Beethoven's Sixth Symphony just after the musical thunderstorm has subsided blaring out in the boy's mind and echoing throughout his torso because hes riding and riding and riding and looking at the world from the top of a doubledecker, a second token in his pocket for the ride home and an extra twentyfive cents jingling for two hotdogs hell eat at 17th Street and Vine, a block away from the Library, and a hot cup of coffee to wash down the lunch

FRANKFORD JUNCTION the train glides by and the snatch of length of cobblestone and cartrack Frankford Avenue with a puny skyline south in the distance Central Philadelphia City Hall the Philadelphia Saving Fund Society whose abbreviation has given rise to PISS SHIT FUCK AND CORRUPTION the LincolnLiberty Building which houses Wanamakers Mens Store the Philadelphia Suburban Station. But the rest is flat. Two and threestorey houses PHILADELPHIA CITY OF HOMES. The textile mills of Kensington. Shibe Park where the southpaw Grove winds up for a fast one the batter cant see on a cloudy day, Jimmy Foxx signaling behind the plate, the tall cadaverous Connie Mack holding up his scorecard in the dugout STEEE-RIKE THREE. In the National League the Phillies are still in the cellar. The shipyards lining the South Philadelphia waterfront and the oil refineries stinking up South Philly generally. PUBLICER DISTILLERIES, WHITMAN SAMPLER their cubistic trademark man lighting up in multicolored jerks on the electricsign carrying the box of candy, sweet-smelling chocolate passing under the huge steel giders of the Delaware River Bridge anchored in their massive concrete blocks dwarfing to the east the newer tollbridge TaconyPalmyra darkening in the rapidlyfilling lanes of dusk

sombre. The cells close to the ground of macadam and cobblestone, mile upon square mile, huddled down side street and Germantown Avenue sourcing in the sedate flowings of the Wissahickon to make its way through the burgeoning negro slums after catty cornering Lehigh Avenue. Block after block of row houses in dull redbrick, squat fat woodporch columns and facings in the section known as Strawberry Mansion sharply delimited on the west by 33rd Street, the eastern limits of the monstrous acreage of Fairmount Park and the Reservoir the city seems not dead but holding secret counsel under the miles of cartrack and cobblestone and overhead copper trolleywire and rowhouse

AMERICAN CYANIMIDE

HIGRADE FRANKFURTERS

Lee can hear it as he sees. Beneath the steel humpings of the train-glide. Beneath the callous drops of the wheels into the slottings of track

ALL OFF FOR NORTH PHILADELPHIA ALL OFF FOR NORTH BETHLEHEM STEEL

the vast cylindrical structures of the United Gas Improvement Company reservoiring and supplying cookinggas to the million homes of Philadelphia and along broad thoroughfares and stubby streets the illuminating gas to the

streetlamps, gwashHOOL and the long all through the night sharp suspiration thereafter

so that, pulling into the North Philly station, the city at last with GWASHhool and the sharp breathy sassing of the steady yellowgreen gas comes to some light, a curious old light sassing over Hunting Park Avenue

Chestnut Street

Spruce

Erie

Old School Lane

Twentysecond Street

Delaware Avenue

South Street

Buttonwood

Bodine and Federal, Broad Street and Market, Cobbs Creek Parkway, Locust and Clearfield, Juniper and Race, Schuylkill River Drive, Brandywine Brandywine Brandywine

and Lee is born, a midwife in attendance, at 7th and Berks. The gaslights make little hoops of illumination in the city between the two rivers. The gaslights gently push aside modest areas of dark among the maple and elm and oak thrusting up from the pavements along Moyamensing Street and Wingohocking and the classical porticos of the Stephen Girard School for Orphaned Boys and the quiet blocks around the walls of the Eastern State Penitentiary, the gaslamps flaring yellowgreen at the foot of the crude crimson electricsign rearing over Strawberry Mansion as 33rd Street empties into Girard Avenue ICE NEVER FAILS

gently hissing through the night greenyellowgreen in their glass enclosures coiffed by a metal peak whose sides are ornamented in scallops, something like a faceless figure of the Middle Ages supported by an iron pole, sometimes obscured by the foliage of trees so that the light is burdened further and falls in leafy patterns on pavement and street, thousands of gaslamps in an ancient radiance in the distance give the city a parchmentyellow twinkle so that Lee is loath to surrender his seat in the train as it gently stammers to a halt, preferring to be bemused through the window at the city

JOHNNY WALKER bright and jaunty on the sign on the east side of Broad Street

the hissing parchmentyellow twinkle under the El, down Old York Road, Wellens Avenue, Rockland Street and

Ruscomb

the boy places the stiff straightbacked wooden chair at the bedroom window, sits and stares through the summer screen at the new hanging ball of an electric arclight which can be seen over the street behind the Emanuel garage.

Even the summer screen suffers from the same odd parallax. The spaces between the wire mesh are as minuscule as ever, but the whole screen seems distant, yet terribly close. As near as he puts his nose, the mesh nevertheless recedes and at the same time expands. Lee is silent. He doesnt want to confide in his parents sleeping in the front room of house at the opposite end of the hallway. Each object in his room is strained through the same distortion. The chest of drawers is enormous, apparently appallingly ponderous and overbearing, yet possessed of a puffy quality as though it may float away at any moment, and seen withal as through the wrong end of a telescope. The walls, the foot of the bed, the very covers respond to the perceptual delusion. Lee's own body feels precisely as his eye registers: overblown, weighty. He puts his thumb before his eyes: it is gigantic yet distant; he can hardly lift it yet he feels it may be blown away. Closing his eyes does not change the situation: the field of blackness behind his lids expands prodigiously and is as heavy as a great boulder; but while it threatens to roll down upon him, crush him, engulf him, it sustains itself featherily and seems as remote as the farthest heavenly constellation. But the boy will not tell his parents. He believes he can solve it. And solve it he does, each night, but only temporarily, for it insistently returns, as insistently as the recurrent dream he has of his maternal grandfather, Joshua Nathanson.

The Nathanson farmhouse in Lansdale, a Philadelphia suburb less rolling in its countryside than the typical unfurling Pennsylvania valley and Appalachian, locates on comparatively flat land. The farmhouse is a rambling somewhat reminiscently Georgian structure of slanted roofs and eaves, overstuffed but fragrantly cool and delicately spoiled by the whiffs of the advancing age of two of its occupants, Hilda and Victor Nathanson. Five more live within: Victor, their son, sallow, thinlipped, harried and stooped; his wife Helen, opulent, widehipped, creamtoothed, scarlettongued, owning a buxom laughter interlineated with a wasp-ish temper; and their three children: Gus, the oldest, his brain fixed at approximately eight years of age owing to a cranial injury in infancy—with wavy light brown hair and an easygoing expression; the next old-est, Charlotte, of faded blue eye, buttercolored hair and onionwhite skin tentatively washed with pink; the youngest is Stephen: he most strongly resembles the lean elfin quality of his father's face but lacks the tense downdriven mouthcorners and mottled flesh and has taken the merrier moods of his mother. The rear of the farmhouse commands an old dirt pike, rutted and ravaged but altogether shaded over by elm and sycamore. Across the pike from the upstairs bedrooms can be seen an expanse of meadow, overgrown with weed and chunks of purple from masses of vio-let, and yellow swatches of buttercup, daisy and dandelion. Before one can enter the farmhouse proper, the rotting timber of a gate must be swung in, which Levi must always leave his car to do, irritatedly, Lee chuckling in the rear seat, so that he can then drive the Buick in and around to the front of the house, which is inordinately wide and boasts a sunporch with stainedglass windows running the entire span.

It is only nominally a farm. Joshua speculates in realestate and is building a string of bungalows on the southern line of his property. But the principal Nathanson business is in moving and storage and the offices are in South Philadelphia. In Lansdale they reside more comfortably than they would in the city and with considerably more space. There is a cow in the barn providing milk. There are chickens for sumptuous meals in poultry. And, some hundred yards down the twisting path, a good dis-tance behind the barn, is a pond, greenscummed and dragonflied, water-bugged and frogcroaked, stocked with perch and trout. Fishing tackle leans against the sagging split boards of an afterthought outhouse on the sucking mud banks; the outhouse door is half off its hinges, and undulant spiderwebs, coruscant in the sunrays slanting through, relieve the ochre interior.

Even on this comatosely hot and humid day little Hilda Nathanson in a heavy shiny black dress with a frilly white collar serves steaming tea Russian style in water tumblers placed on white saucers, because Joshua exacts this particular tribute in all seasons, a squareheaded man in high-colored faceflesh and curtly cut bristling white hair, still practically stomachless, his legs crossed by the side of the table its oilcloth in red and white squares, his white mustaches creamy and springing, and tan spats arrogantly concealing the laces of his fawn shoes. For the moment his starched high collar is doffed but a collarbutton continues to secure the neck of his white silk shirt striped vertically in scarlet; elastics on either arm prevent his sleeves from edging too far down his wrists. For all his seventythree odd years, Joshua Nathanson is a man of some fashion and undulled appetite; Hilda seems no more than an appendage; smiling absently and occasionally shrill, she is a little hard of hearing; but she scurries about with the teakettle and the saucers, the glasses and the napkins in silver rings. In spite of the heat and the steaming tea, Victor sits with his arms crossed as if to hug himself close to the massively ornate castiron stove while Helen giggles at one of Levi's sallies.

Why is it each time we come, Rachel says solicitously and accusingly to her brother, you look like you caught your death of cold. In the middle of summer youre shivering.

Hes a frail man your brother is, Helen the milkmaid howls at her sisterinlaw. What dont he have? Hes a little jaundiced, he catches cold it doesnt matter what the season is

Victor maybe youre working too hard, Rachel scolds.

Im not working too hard, Im not working too hard, Victor mutters rapidly, his face pinching itself.

Lee maybe youd like some tea, Joshua beckons to his grandson. Youll see how good it is even in hot weather, itll make you sweat and cool you off, come take a sip.

The amber liquid rests on the same level as the boy's eyes as he approaches. Grampop's dark brown eyes flash challengingly through the beetcolored flesh, the mustaches crossed white sabres on the red wall, Lee twirling his mustached attitudes toward Gia Antonelli and Rena and Edith and Tess and

Try it with a sugar domino between your teeth, thats how a good Russian drinks it, Joshua counsels his grandson.

It tastes very sweet, Lee says gravely to his grandfather, and Joshua removes a shiny silver quarter from his pocket, handing it to the boy. Lee swallows, overcome.

So tell grampop thank you, Rachel incisively reminds him.

Thank you, grampop, the boy unswervingly directs his gaze at the old man

(the doctrine of Rachel Emanuel includes the injunction, Always look a person in the eye

dont look away from a person hell think youre afraid of him

also if you look straight in his eye hell know youre listening to him and meaning it

also hell think youre honest

not that any son of mine isnt honest

I pride myself my sons are honest

never so much as a cent did they ever steal

Id crack them across the hands if they even thought of it

of course David never really stole its just hes a little soft in the head)

So hows Stephen, Rachel says to Helen.

Fine, fine, Helen chuckles heartily, he suckles at me like he wants to eat a steak already, hes asleep in his crib

Helen Helen, Rachel says, knitting her brow and signifying the unauthorized and immoral interest of her son and Charlotte in Helen's bawdy reference.

Rachel whats the matter with you they got to learn sometime, somewhere, its better than the street, Helen says with raised arms, her breasts billowing under the coarse cotton blouse.

I know I know, Rachel says, but theres a

(time and place for everything

before you say anything you have to know who youre talking to

theres no reason you should make an outsider feel angry at you

never confide in an outsider

a stranger is always a stranger I dont care how close he is to you he isnt your own flesh and blood

theres no substitute for flesh and blood

you should never tire yourself out thats how you get sick right away

its not good you should be so much by yourself Lee

mingle

mingle

mingle

why should Dad have to bring a stranger into the Business

theres nothing like your own flesh and blood

dont be so quick to show affection to a stranger he can stick a knife in your back

see what Hitler did to the Jews

the German Jews trusted the Germans

the Kasters next door theyre German Jews you think they like the Russian Jews the Kasters are snobs

mom what are you lowering your voice for

whats the matter with you Lee, the voice goes right through the walls even the walls have ears like they say if I had Hitler here I would cut him up in little pieces,

her voice is loud and furious

mom youre raising your voice

thats all right I dont care who hears what I have to say about that dog Hitler I would stick his pieces into the oven and I would roast them thats what I would do to him that dog that)

Lee you want to play catch, Charlotte pleads sweetly.

Sure.

Take Gus with you, Helen rasps at her daughter.

Gus is crooning to a doll in his lap on the other side of the stove but Charlotte takes his hand and pulls him up, Come on were going to play catch, Gus. Gus smiles gratefully at Charlotte and Lee and the three race through the screen door down the yielding wood steps and over to the newmown vast green lawn its single craggy walnut tree in one corner and the white chased dogwood in the other. Charlotte's dirtsmudged smocked white organdie puffing over her knees, Gus startled and still under the walnut as his eye blinks the butterflies stumbling crazily in the air round the treetrunk, the girl scoops her whole body from a crouch and catapults her arm and softball toward the whiteblue sun at two in the afternoon, the arm in spite of herself stubbornly refusing to be unsocketed but punching up the shoulder and lifting the leg and laughing up the mouth and rolling back her eye and head to tickle her throat as she points to the ball whitening and smalling and pinpointing toward the high sizzle in the sky, Lee his arms tentatively crooked and his fingers partially sphered maneuvers in abrupt arc, rectilineal curt dash, bitter backtrack, triumphal sidle, his nightblue rayon shirt blackening with sweat, his blackbrown eyes flushing the sky under the downchuting ball, breath sprinting back and forth in the throat, stacatto rushes through the parted lips, there must be a catch of the plummeting roundness from the bigger stationary roundness quartzlit and bluewhite blinding, from which the boy must snatch the momentary weight of impact, the point of stinging completion isolated from the girl though partly pulled into the being of isolation itself by the potential murmur of her satisfaction at Lee capable of catching it stronger than the disappointment satisfaction if he could not, the former gratifying her the more because she is more loath to feel it, and he while aware of her bank and shore and his connexion thereto nevertheless the lonely champion of the betweenness, the lord of will he or wont he, the aristocrat of the perhaps decisionmaking, praise involved in suspense itself, the boy squints at the expanding circle, Charlotte chipping at her teeth as she swings her clasped hands back and forth between her spread legs in a chopping stroke. But his shoe slips on the grass, he falls to one knee and the ball grazes a nail of his extended fingers, hurting it, and caroms off to the dogwood. Charlotte pouts, mocksympathizing. Lee lopes to the tree and retrieves the ball but Charlotte switches her pleasure, runs to the boy, flips up her legs and bounces down to the grass on her buttocks, looking up in dubious astonishment as he tentatively rocks the ball back and forth between his hands, spuriously examining it, its ascent and descent continuing to cling to it, Lee's expression makes as if to impose upon the ball infinite alternatives, substituting assumptions of not having been thrown nor attempts made to catch, playing down the takenplace action by the falseserious consideration of what can be learned from the mistake, thus lightening the possible seriousness of the mistake itself, we are so aware of ourselves that the error may not have been important at all. But Charlotte is already beyond success or error, except that his failure gives her some sense of wanting to play with him other than so. Besides, shes too far away from him in a game of catch;

further, too much of the game is dependent on Lee because she doesnt care one way or the other if she can catch the ball or not, so the fun is too much his, or the shame of not doing it well is dominantly his, Its too hot for catch, she says, propping herself back on her elbows. Lee crouches down in front of her, casually rolling the ball on the grass against his open palm. Uhhuh, he says, avoiding her eye. Gus is content to be smilingly remote sitting crosslegged in his knickers under the chestnut and clapping his hands intermittently at a butterfly stumbling by not so much as if he wishes to catch one but more as if to cause the creature to stagger more pronouncedly, more intricately, Gus's jaw dropping like a toy trap when a butterfly dares brush his chin. Charlotte swerves a glance round to him every now and then, to make sure he has not strayed, and then with a finger describes swift circles around her own ear, gesturing with her head at her brother, Cuckoo, she chirps to her cousin, cuckoo. Lee studiously keeps his attention on the ball under his palm as Charlotte draws up her legs and clasps her arms around them, leaning her chin on the knees, her buttercolored hair in ringlet and dogwood shadow, her eyes bluer in the shade, a faint down of sweat on her forehead. Lee wants to look at her panties but refuses. A slight breeze stirs a pale chill over his chest and spine through his drenched shirt. Momentarily he squeezes the ball against the grass. Oh dont do that, Charlotte says, you might squeeze the air out of it and it wont be any good after that. Okay, he says, relenting his palm. Guess what I saw yesterday afternoon, Charlotte proposes

I dont like to guess

Oh go on guess.

I dont feel like it. If you dont feel like telling me without guessing, dont. Thats all, he says.

Charlotte bends backward again, repropping herself on the elbows and scissoring her legs back and forth to make a breeze. That makes me feel a lot cooler, Lee

Sure it does

Guess exactly where it makes me feel a lot cooler.

Where does it

I said guess

I told you I dont like to, Charlotte.

Oh come on take a chance

I dont feel like it

But I like you, she insists, troubled, frowning, I like you an awful lot, I love you.

The boy reddens. No you dont, Charlotte.

Yes I do, too

Well whats that got to do with me guessing where you feel cooler

I dont know, but its got lots to do with it

For instance.

Oh youre too picky. Charlotte nudges her torso to one side, leans down on her upper arm, her chin nudging blades of grass, one knee up in the air and the other leg flat against the earth, her dress fluffing up and around her belly. I know what, she says, snickering

What

Youre afraid to guess where I feel lots more cool

No Im not.

Yes you are, oh yes you

Bouncing, the ball flounces past her nose, missing it by a fraction. With soft appeal, she pouts her eyelids, big balloons of pout drawn back from her eyes, Gee you mad, Lee?

He squirms down on his belly and licks a blade of grass. No, he says

Charlotte sits up. Because I dont want to make you mad

Okay.

Anyhow yesterday afternoon I was supposed to be taking my nap, but I didnt.

Lee raises his eyes. To the white onionskin calf and thigh. He keeps running his tongue along the blade of grass till it begins to wilt from the spittle

Tangled in the rear seat of Perry Marx's car, Lee and Charlotte exchange spittle. Perry and another girl are altogether out of sight on the front seat, the whole car parked at a tilt in a culdesac path off the main road in Fairmount Park ICE NEVER FAILS glowing scarlet far above in the distance. Gus Nathanson mouths an offkey gibberish rocking back and forth on the porch facing Fairmount Park at the point where the museum piece trolley with its wooden seats and openair sides emerges from its slow meander through and across the Park beginning at 33rd and Lehigh and ending at 35th on the other side, Lehigh no longer in existence

Its sort of like a little knob Lee can you feel it

Well

Thats right, right there. Lee

Cant you spread y

Im trying, its pretty hard in a car, all right, I dont know if I can stand it, Im

There

Yes. Maybe youd better

Whats the matter.

Well if you do it anymore I dont know if I can control myself, more, faster, faster, cant you do it fas. Uh, uh, uh youd

Look Im going to

No. What do you think. Maybe

Well

Because I dont know how long I can

Well maybe wed, I dont know. Cousins

What I thought. We could go too far and were

Cous

Gee Im sorry Lee Im

Its all right. We were getting too serious

Dammit, Lee.

Sure

I mean we couldnt

A pale yellow stain on the girl's panties. Lee jerks up the blade of grass Well what were you doing instead.

Listening.

Where

At the keyhole of the toilet on the second floor Rena has crabs in Harry Ring's apartment I mustve got them sitting on his toilet hes got all kinds of girls coming here Lee you know its nothing Ill get some of that purple stuff that potassium permanganate I was sitting down looking at my crotch and I almost screamed I saw something jump

What are you so nervous about?

I dont know, Lee, Ive begun to bleed again he chews on the blade of grass, the dried sweat sticky under his armpits, a yellow glow starting to suffuse the western sky, he wishes his mother and father ready to go home, an ant starts to crawl across the yellow stain, her thighs embowered with leaves of shadow. Suppose the ant will take flight? Suppose it makes a hole and takes flight? He would like to tickle Charlotte with the wilted blade of grass

Did you hear anything?

No, so then I looked. Butterflies

What?

Yellow butterflies beating at her crotch, my Uncle Aaron has antennae, the vacant wings of Gus, Hullo Lee

Ah hah ahhahah Helen Nathanson pokeshrieks at the air in the West Philadelphia house, the toonerville trolley an insect across the street, see he recognizes you ah hahha hah aah, Lee, the senseless wings of things grouping at beginnings at 7th and Berks, Lee, its Lee aint it Uncle Aaron peers closely at the adolescent, I havent seen you such a long time why dont you come down to the business say HULLO to your Uncle Aaron dont you think Im good enough for you hah her strong even milkwhite creamcoated teeth projecting nipples Lee wants to grab his aunt's tits and hang onto them and swing from them

Come on Lee if were going to make that movie, Charlotte stands at the door, embarrassed

Ahhahaaahhahha youve got plenty time, Helen as if drunk on milk, the black eyes merrymeddlesome, the twin hunks of beef booming from her chest Gus aint no lazybones are you Gus Helen claps her son's shoulder, he goes to the store for me, he scrubs the floor, he earns his keep let me tell you, the countrywoman yells, she strides constantly at the top of her voice

so does my mother at home, not in company LEE ITS SEVENTHIRTY GET UP GET UP YOULL BE LATE FOR SCHOOL HOW MANY TIMES DO I HAVE TO TELL YOU NOT TO COME HOME LATE OH THE SONS I GOT DID ANY OF THEM GIVE ME PLEASURE NOT ONE GIVES ME ANY PLEASURE MOMSARUM BOTH THEY EAT THEIR PARENTS' HEART OUT

the mother's doctrine: come home by one oclock in the morning, theres nothing you cant do by that time

butterflies and the leaden weight in Lee's legs waiting for Charlotte's report

Lee hullo Lee hee hee hee Lee Gus strums his own tongue, quartertone slides up and down the scale, an eastern witless music the audience chanting, drugged, Aaron, Ernstine Chalk, the millions of Asiatics, numb from the spawn of countless spawn, Perry Marx has mongoloid features, Im contemptuous of him, his father little than he scurrying round his jewelry shop in downtown Philadelphia FELS NAPTHA SOAP

CUNEO PRINTING

GIMBELS

the brass nozzles projecting from a stubby pipe from the department stores near the pavement water in case of fire water in case of

ICE NEVER FAILS

Lee oh oh oh, he may distantly remember a name, thats all, he cant remember me, its not permitted, idiots arent allowed to reach back for me, why am I frightened of them. Because they remind you of animals unclassified. A separate species sitting under a walnut tree who gives me butterflies in the belly, brings back the infancy of ants on the ground, evokes the unregistered, HULLO LEE, baring his spit, letting it roll down the sides of his mouth, strumming on all the hollow instruments of Lee himself, conjuring all the unidentifiable spaces in the boy and the adolescent and man, dont touch me, DONT TOUCH ME he hurls the blade of grass away but its soddenness prevents it from traveling more than a few feet, thats as far as we can go, a few feet away from the void snatching at yellowgreen butterflies, no wonder I dont want to fill Charlotte up with sperm I wont insist sitting on the runningboard afterwards in the summernight Gee I got hot Lee I almost let you I wanted you to for a minute there I thought I couldnt control myself I got awful hot

You were wet allright it was squirting out

Dont talk about it youre making me, look touch it again, touch, they dont know up there in front theyre busy, allright, nah, its starting to hurt

Her mother's teeth belong on the yellow stain, Dear Rena

Nobody mentions Uncle Victor father, father, you know theres a father in this house, FATHER, he carries in the wash ahhahaaahhahha Gus is a good boy he knows how to go to the bathroom

DONT YOU

he dont even play with himself hahahaaaaha

DO YOU

What did you see, Charlotte

Now the two crouch forehead to forehead, buttercolored hair against blackbrown, onionskin flesh against the sunburnt ruddiness, white organdie against sweated blackblue in the purpleblue shade under the dogwood white on the yellowgreen grass, brothercousin Gus waving under the chestnut to the saffron butterflies, panties cut in the shape of wings, Jenniferodored, ammoniacal, the moment Lee is discharged from the Army of the United States is

odorless

sightless

soundless

tasteless as though no induction no training no thirty mile hikes no maneuvers no dust no rage the moment of discharge

(two children conspiring put conspiratorial adults in the sun. two children conspiring are completely serious, hidden, authentically clandestine, absolutely surreptitious. the adults on the other hand seem to be playacting, pretending they are children. it is impossible to conspire with any selfbelief when one is an adult; it becomes a game; with children it is no game. not that the children keep the secret; never; the wonder of the conspiracy is to spill the secret, get rid of it, pass it on—what good is a secret if it is merely kept between the two conspirators? on the other hand, the adults take on the impossible: they attempt to maintain the secret which is always discovered and which children immediately know: after a moment, they share. not so the adolescent and adult: they risk death to keep the secret: they are after all not so vitally interested in fleshsurvival as the child is: the adult wants the secret to survive down a conspiratorial line, as if a secret is immortal, as if by secrecy the conspirator confers a magic upon himself. children know magic is momentary and must constantly be reinvented in a variety of forms. the adult believes magic singular

)I musnt tell you, Lee I am concerned, seriously, it was a terribly overwhelming sight, should I tell you, him, she frowns matronly, she is her mother's mother, her grandfather's grandfather in the uncanny mimicry of unknown knowledge that is the matrix of knowledge, she is carefully laying the bed, tucking in the covers, preparing herself, testing the springs with the utmost seriousness

I musnt tell you

Come on now. Darling Rena

Okay. Grampop was sitting on the toilet seat cover with his thing up in the air you like grampop dont you

Yes

and my mother was sitting on his knees and playing with his thing. They were naked. Grampop looked funny because his skin is like the silverfoil you wrap chewinggum in only his isnt silver its lemony and wrinkled just like when you roll the silverfoil in a ball and then stretch it out again it has sixteen trillion wrinkles maybe a trillion trillion and then my mother sort of stood up you know not all the way but something like a monkey with something between its legs and moved over to where his thing was sticking up and sat down on it it went right up where she has a lot of hair I dont have much myself, I guess I dont have any would you like to see?

No

Come on Ill show you

No

Dont be mad.

Im not mad.

You sound mad.

Im not

You like grampop dont you?

Yes, uhhuh.

And my mother she was just smiling all over her face all over. And grampop he took one of her boobies and put it in his mouth and she smiled even more then but what was even funnier was she went up and down on his thing and instead of smiling all over her face she just smiled on her mouth and didnt move her mouth she just kept it open a little and made a sound like a little sheep does way up in her nose I think and grampop began to hang on to her boobie by the nipple my mother has a great big nipple well gee it isnt as big as a cow's Lee but I bet its half as big as grampop's thing anyways and she jerks it around like she wants to get rid of it like she wants him to bite it off and grampop he just looks at it all cockeyed and shes jerking his head first this way and that way and making that sheep sound way up in her nose and bumping up and down on his thing and hes getting awful red in his face and his thing is real shiny and then all of a sudden she says hahaah hahaah and jerks her boobie as hard as she can I think and quick stands up and the next thing you know theres something

glump glump glump Lee rubs the scar on his right little finger from the glass washboard, rubs it against his teeth, stands, the blood making a lake around his face

white and oily from his thing it shoots right up and hits her under the boobie and she gets down on her knees and puts his thing in her mouth and like Stevie my brother sucks her boobies she does the same thing to grampop yes she does I just couldnt believe it Lee and grampop is looking I couldnt tell where but just as cockeyed and I had to run away because I was going to start laughing any second you know why?

Lee shakes his head

because my mother she twisted her boobie so hard it pulled out grampop's false teeth and the false teeth they were swinging from her nipple right when she was on her knees sucking the white oil from his thing Lee where you going you like grampop dont you

False teeth, Lee says, halting, looking down on fluffed organdie, the scar on his little finger throbbing.

You cuckoo or something?

Youre a liar, Charlotte.

No Im not.

Yes you are.

No Im not.

You didnt tell the truth.

Yes I did.

No you didnt.

What do you want to bet? She stands, indignant, hands on hips, Gus making now a circle with his arms, a sort of hoop he tries to make the butterflies stagger through, an angry bliss on his face, he himself staggering round and round the walnut tree, the farmhouse its stainedglass fourbyfour windowpanes red and green and blue Whitman Sampler jaggedbrilliant in the sun, the multicolored checkerboard flashing in the scalding saffron light, mechanical, a sign going on and off, the Whitman Samplerman carrying the box of candy under his arm along the whole front of the house, staggering mechanically in the background, Lee can smell the heavy odor of concentrated chocolate, Lee's blood going on and off in brilliant checkerboard all over his body, a little man inside him jerking up his knees and walking, marching, toy soldierlike, fake candy under his arm, his grampop going to present Lee with a box of chocolates, but all wrong, too much an advertisement on the top of a building overlooking Delaware River Bridge gently arcing over the Delaware, the samplerman jerkily crossing the bridge, a tugboat hooting, hooting, somebodys hooting at grampop and Lee, the boy doesnt want to come back from Atlantic City and return to grammarschool, he wants the summer never to end, his father is the one making it end, its his father's fault, he spoils everything, he makes things end, not like his grandfather carrying a glass of amber tea, its his father whos spilling the white cream into the tea, Lee doesnt like tea with cream, he likes it plain yellow against the panties, Charlotte pees tea hot and scalding, thats not the person it should come from

How will you prove it, Charlotte? He sticks his little finger in his mouth

Ahhahaha she mocks him, youre still a baby, you suck your finger ahahaha she dances away from him backward toward Gus, toward the hoop for butterflies, you suck your finger, youre still a baby Lee

Just dont you follow me he yells at her

still a baby still a

running down the path behind the barn

baby sucking his ahhahah youre

running through briar shining poison ivy swathes through buttercup and dandelion and violet moooooooooooooooooooooooooooooooooooooooooo moos the cow mooooooooo moooo moooo

a ba

his own teeth are false and he abruptly jerks his finger away from his mouth sneezing

he starts sneezing kneedeep in goldenrod sneezing kachoo moooooooooo kachoo

mooooooooooo

kachoo his head snapping back and forth cant get rid of the false teeth his head snapping

KERCHOO

tears streaming down his KERCHOO little boy fights through gossamer web treehanging his head snapping teeth chattering he spits

spits

spits

KERCHOO

the cow the teeth the boobie pursuing till he slogs through the mud on the pondbank oozing he snaps his head jerks he shakes his head things stick

stick

slime

webs

pulls at the outhouse door

crowds himself in

sneezing frantically brushing away the spiderwebs clear

clear

he fights his breathing. make it come slower. breathe through the mouth

not like the mother doctrine: dont breathe through your mouth Lee but through your nose because thats where the germs are caught otherwise the cold air goes right down your throat and you catch a cold

He sits on the toilet seat. No. He moves over to a corner, away from the hole in the seat. Quiet.

Swimming in sweat. Sweats prodigiously like his mother.

drink plenty of water his mother says

sweating is good for you keeps you cool

but mamma says she shouldnt sweat now as much as she used to, it makes her weak

mamma dont die

daddy dont die

Quiet. Darling Rena he writes in the barracks quiet

The air is still in the outhouse. Lee doesnt want to go anywhere Just tell them that Harry advises, always tell the truth its more convincing not the whole truth, understand? Part. Keep repeating you dont want to go anywhere, over and over and over, Harry grins, hes got false teeth too, Lee loves and distrusts him, Grampop Harry Ring, Rena looking worriedly down at Lee I dont know whether I can go through with it she says You dont have to do anything but tell the authorities this is how you found him, understand? Children, children, children, Harry throws up his hands, but Lees got to be protected, well fox them, Harry chuckles, because Lees extraordinary and he shouldnt have to be bothered with the Army he doesnt want to go anywhere he dont have to not till his mother calls Rena youre not my mother youre not my its nice and quiet here he begins to observe the outhouse. A square of a glassless window cut out near the top. Cut out the boxtop from thirtyfive billion POST TOASTIES and we will send you free of charge a genuine Tox Mix sixshooter

Lee grunts, for the moment tickled

A blade of sunlight balances itself perfectly like a tipped seesaw through the window, Russell Zion unseen on the high end

why dont you be like your cousin Russell Rachel Emanuel enjoins him you never heard him criticize his parents

each time he comes into the house Russell kisses his mother

not that you have to do that with me every time, Rachel blushes

watch out who you kiss generally

believe me you can get germs from kissing also

I hope youre careful the girls you go out with Lee

its easy to get into trouble

you dont know like I do how much a girl wants a man, believe me shell hook him any way she can

you come from a nice family, Lee, a girl would be glad to get you believe me

dont you think I was glad to get Dad

of course I had lots of beaux but Dad was the one I fell in love with

one of the men in love with me is a wealthy man today I couldve had lots of money but I knew Dad would always support me you think things were easy with us Dad started out with a grocerystore

money dont grow on trees

you should save your money get into the habit

dont squander your money

i know you Lee just like your brother David hes got money in his pocket it burns a hole

dont smoke so many cigarettes its the same thing burning up your money

money is very important

you cant do anything without money

keep your health and your money because a girl you can always get there are millions of girls and theyre all looking out for a man

you can be choosy

dont be hasty

any girl you like you bring her here provided shes Jewish of course Ill tell you what shes like believe me your mother knows I can tell right away and dont tell me a girls Jewish if she isnt because I can recognize a Jew right away

dont ask me how I can tell, I can tell

something tells me
a little bird tells me, who else?
i can tell a shicksa right away
you should think of other things besides love when you think of marrying
because love flies out the window when theres no money like they say
you cant live on love like they say
you can learn to love like they say
and falls athwart Lee to shimmer a spiderweb in the corner on the
flooring.

It is very quiet. Lee looks through the doorway. The dragonflies that
sew up children's mouths shuttle back and forth over the filmed pond
surfaces. Waterbugs scuttle, frogs sound as if theyre choking to death.
Tree and underbrush enclose the pond. Reeds and weeds conceal the
shape of the banks. It is thick with quietude. A vague amber is diffused
through the treebranches. Lee vows he will forever resist anyone trying
to fit his mouth for false teeth. But he chuckles as he swears. Charlottes
lying. But he doesnt want to see her. Not ever again. He doesnt love her
though she avers she does him. She doesnt really love anybody. The boy
shakes his head, clotted. His nose is full of mucus, from the sneezing,
but hardening. He wants to feel the comedy of the false teeth clamped
on the nipple but his diaphragm wont budge the iron laughter vising to
it that the chuckle the boy had sent down after it is trying to dislodge.
A lie has an effect. You may not believe the lie but it poses the alternative, in this case the girl that is Charlotte implying herself by her vision,
whether true or no, in opposition to the boy's grandfather. Actually in
opposition to Lee through Joshua Nathanson; and, really, opposing her
mother as well. There is no end to what she as a little girl wants to destroy,
seeing everything around her through the vacancy of her older brother,
Gus, having to take care of this vacancy, cherish it, protect it, be cautious
with it. Her father, Victor, is a wisp, a frailty. It is her grandfather who is
the ordering authoritative voice in the farmhouse. But she can have no
effect, certainly, on him, nor on Hilda; her father will not listen to her;
her mother would slap her face. She cannot operate on Gus. She chooses
a relative stranger, someone of the family who visits now and again, who
entertains some affection toward the grandfather, to sink the false teeth
of her fantasy in, someone she can really reach, who belongs to the child-

hood category, because he, Lee, must be condemned for developing affection toward her grandfather: Lee has no right to love that man in any way. How dare Lee feel love for a man who is her father in the actual emotional fact? Lee isnt Joshua Nathanson's son, not while she must be treated so cavalierly as to be Gus's keeper. But she feels warmly towards Lee. Therefore she must hurt him for two reasons, to disentangle him from Joshua so that she be the only child who can love her grandfather while at the same time venomously besmirching him in her imagination in order to degrade him to her chronological level in which Joshua will be aware, at least in her desire, of her; and to make the boy focus on her, even in venom if necessary, as long as he will generate some kind of feeling toward her; so that this rosetinted onionfleshed buttercolorhaired little girl may entertain two males within herself, one very near and the other distant, an ideal situation; and certainly she must keep them separated in reality as she has them revolve within herself intimately—in a vacuum, senselessly, perhaps the only sense being the terribly remote one that she really wants her grandfather and her cousin for brothers, to replace Gus. The younger brother, Stephen, is beyond her ability to cope with altogether; she avoids him as much as she can, acts distantly to him, expressionlessly, as if he is a part of the farmhouse's decor, no more. Her main drive is the incessant force in her to disgorge Gus; he has disorientated her, all but shattered her; she must minister to this idiot whom everyone avers is her brother. Thats manifestly impossible yet she knows its so. Therefore, whatever relationship she has or wants with her mother, grandfather, grandmother and father, she must make them all behave in some aura of idiocy—to produce the believability of Gus; and she makes Lee run away from her. He is an opposition she can have effect upon and she brings it into being. If she can do that to him, now, she will manage it on others later; she will cut herself altogether off from Gus, from her mother; she will refuse to visit her father in prison; she will finally have no family except those making up the one of the man she will eventually marry. The believability of the idiocy of Gus must be extirpated ruthlessly and she will erase him from memory. She intends to remember only one member of her immediate family: her grandfather as her father

Do you remember that tale you told me about grampop being with your mother, Lee asks her, ICE NEVER FAILS, on the runningboard of Perry Marx's car.

Mutely, Charlotte shakes her head no, the warm night disembodying her face.

With your mother in the bathroom of the Lansdale farm, he insists.

No. What would they be doing there together?

All right, then, Lee tells himself, its possible the tale is true. On the ground that Charlotte is not the emotionally complex girl he premises. Perhaps he wants to premise her complexity in order to absolve his grandfather. He concludes she indulged in fantasy so that he can whitewash Joshua and this is an error. But the feeling he can whitewash Joshua takes place only in his later years, that is, that the feeling he can absolve Joshua is a true feeling only subsequently developed. The necessity to absolve is a rich one. He would like to pick his nose now. In the outhouse he begins to pick his nose of the clotted snot and flip the snotballs at the shimmering spiderweb, making it sway and disconcerting the somnolent spider. As a boy, making the judgment that Charlotte's tale is a fantasy but unable to unincorporate the fantasy from himself, he wants his grandfather to die. Because the fantasy corresponds to a real event

Lee walks down the hallway, past the bay window looking into the bedroom of the one of the Kaster brothers next door, past the head of the stairway. Its five in the afternoon. Hes in his stocking feet and he walks warily, not making a sound. He knows his mothers in the bathroom. He can hear her pissing into the toilet. He knows she thinks hes taking a nap. It is the moment he has been waiting for: for years he has wanted to see his mother on the toilet. A simple enough curiosity. Hes believed she has a fascinating body, if only he can see her naked. The bathroom door is ajar. But the hallway flooring creaks.

Lee his mother calls out.

Uhhuh.

You want to come into the bathroom

Uhhuh.

Ill be out in a minute.

Lee walks into his study, next to the bathroom. Then he stops. He stretches from the doorway. Its only about six inches around to see into the bathroom. He senses his mother never looks up while shes on the toilet. He feels that when shes in the bathroom shes inspecting herself in one way or another. Hes right. Shes looking down. He can see her now, craning his neck. Shes in her winter underwear which comes down to her ankles, thick and woolen winter underwear. There is a flap on the underwear so that she can defecate. Shes through defecating. She wiping herself. The front of the underwear gapes. He sees her breasts. They are long and flat and hang to her navel. He sees the region of her groin: it is black, thick with black hair. She is completely unprepossessing. This is nothing. He feels nothing erotic. He only feels terribly disappointed. Is this all there is a patch of thick black, breasts hanging to the bellybutton and a hand wiping the ass with toiletpaper. This is his mother

This is all his Aunt Helen must be, therefore, no matter what she appears to be when dressed. Why, then, must his grandfather have the sensualism that Lee cannot experience. The boy feels his grandfather when seeing a mother like Helen naked should react in precisely the same manner that Lee does visavis his own mother, Rachel. It is disgusting that he cannot, that is to say that if Lee can permit Charlotte's fantasy to remain within him, if he cannot brush it aside, then he must suppose his grandfather capable of reacting sensually to a motherfigure such as Helen, and this is insupportable. It is disgusting, offensive. Somewhere inside the boy Lee is the fear that somebody can find a motherfigure erotically arousing. He wants to eliminate that fear, that possibility. So: it doesnt matter whether Charlotte's tale is true or no. The tale stimulates the fear that mothers are sexually provocative. He hates his grandfather, he wants him to die. Joshua does die, in fact. And the boy develops guilt over the death, a large, strong, blatant, powerful guilt which Lee must attempt to exorcize. The tremendous power of the guilt demands equal power of exorcism which, if successful, will cast out many other irrational fears which gravitate to the big grandfather guilt. If the big guilt does not exist, there is scant chance for the manifold fears of a child to be eventually uprooted because they havent been crystallized, collected, congregated. The tale about his grandfather and aunt can serve a purpose. Certainly he can never really know whether Charlotte herself is complex or not, the disembodied sweet face of her looking at him innocently in the Fairmount Park dark. But you must premise the complexity of every human being. You cannot predicate simplicity. You cannot arrive at simplicity. You may have the desire to do so which in itself is anfractuous. Suppose the story is true. All right. Most of us proceed on the basis that children blurt out everything they see or hear or sense any whichway. However, while children are given to blurting, they are equally given to secrecy. But lets narrow it down to the blurt, what we believe is the simple desire to tell an experience, a daytoday sensing. Charlotte doesnt narrate the story, supposing its true, to her father, or grandmother. Only to Lee. She makes a choice for the exposure. Suppose she doesnt resent her mother or father; suppose she has no particular feeling about her grandfather; suppose shes quite happy about taking care of Gus. Why, then, would she want to relate a picture of coition to Lee? We say, readily, to erotically arouse her cousin—if nothing else. She would perhaps like Lee to do to her what she saw took place between her grandparent and her mother. Where? On the grass before the farmhouse? Obviously not. Perhaps she wanted to suggest a clandestine meeting. Shes two years younger than Lee. Still nothing unusual: children dote on clandestine arrangements. But, if this so, shes not afraid of Lee's genitals. Why should she be? Shes seen animals around the farmhouse. Shes seen the cow give birth, seen it mate with a bull. Does she actually think Lee will be either like a bull or like her grandfather? Perhaps. It begins to become more curious, a bit more strange, then. But lets presume she makes in her young mind the necessary corrections. Lee will have a smaller penis, she a smaller vagina. She knows she has a small vagina why shouldnt Lee be subject to the same laws? Good. But now: will Lee hang onto the nipple of her breast? What breast? Her chest is as flat as Lee's. And she doesnt believe Lee has false teeth, so she wouldnt be able to dislodge the nonexistent. Then the girl seems to be an explorer. She wants to know what this coition is like without teats, without false teeth. Will it be like the bull charging the cow? What mimicry will transpire? She says she is about to laugh when she sees the false teeth clamped onto her mother's teat. She may now be disposed to laugh, if Lee tries to fornicate with her, at the nonexistence of false teeth, which in itself predicates a sense of paradox in the little girl Charlotte. She might want, then, the paradox to come to fruition: she might want to laugh, want to very much. We must remember that she didnt reach the laughter: she fled as the laughter began to come upon her watching the two principals through the keyhole; and then her laughter sank as she fled. Charlotte is frustrated—not sexually but with respect to her sense of humor. What it comes down to, then, is that Charlotte tells the tale to Lee in the hope it will sexually arouse him so that he may attempt intercourse with her so that she can laugh. Not enjoy sexual congress, mind you, but enjoy laughter. Our sense of simplicity is outraged. In the outhouse behind the barn at the pond Lee chuckles. He feels, later, an iron laughter clamped to his diaphragm, refusing to come up. It does not come up because he is outraged if only on the level of simplicity: he feels, somewhere within him, that Charlotte has wanted to use him in order to laugh. She isnt a little girl. She doesnt correspond to what he knows of little girls. He doesnt know what she is at all except somebody who has told him something vile and extraordinary, and that could be anybody. This in itself is a vast matter. She exceeds little girlhood. She ceases to be dirty white organdie. She is not a child. He doesnt know what a child is now at all. All he knows is that human beings are foreign matter and he gouges his left index finger into his nostrils, scraping off the snot, kneading it between thumb and forefinger, at the very least deriving pleasure from that tactile sensation, the rubbery cohesiveness of the snot, the green yellow black purple tones of it, squeezing it, feeling it yield deliciously as it hardens little by little so that he can shoot it at the spiderweb and cause the waddling spider to shift cumbrously, perhaps to ingest the snot, the viscid stuff, as viscid as the white oil Charlotte describes emitted by the grandfather, so that perhaps the spider will die as Lee wants his grandfather to choke on his own discharge, not caring now if Charlotte wanted to use the story for her own purposes of laughter but only caring that this august gentleman, this kind man who gives him tea and shiny quarters, who is so benevolently patriarchal, who is so much like what a father should be, so unlike his own father, so much like what he wants his own father to be, iron in kindness, not softness in kindness as Levi is, but arrogantly benevolent, whitehaired, fawnspatted, silkshirted, that this handsome old man should even figure in a lie as something comic, losing his false teeth over a nipple, losing his discharge in a woman's mouth, be painted as cockeyed, even as Lee has a tendency towards being, the man who has patted him on the head, smiling at him, who has never criticized Lee in any way—could so disgustingly stick in his mind is too much for Lee. He accuses the old man of being capable of sticking in his mind as a sorry degraded figure. Lee feels there must be some truth to the story if it can so affect him, and he despises the old man. The boy doesnt want to be discovered. He wants everyone to forget him. The spider scurries away through a crack. The shimmering web, multicolored in the beam of sunlight, is dotted with snotballs. Lees finger is spotted with blood from scraping the membrane in his nose. He can hear the frogs croaking inside his brain. He can feel the dragonflies skimming behind his eyes. The green scum of the pond veils his face. He sits very still. Perhaps a web will be spun around him, thats what everybody deserves—to find him encased in a web, paralysed, the sun shining on him, ready to be eaten. And he experiences a twinge in his belly. It must be four oclock. The spiderweb has lost its gleam. Only the snot balls festoon it, weighing it down. Another bellytwinge. The pond darkens. Its impossible that he could be hungry. He isnt allowed, not ever again, but the pit in his belly deepens. He starts

LEE

its his mother's voice, distant

LEE

he starts to cry, his nose filling

LEE

he wipes his nose with the back of his hand, smearing, and stumbles from the outhouse

LEE ITS TIME TO GO HOME

all right mamma he stammers to himself, stumbling up from the bank, the tall weeds slashing his face

LEE

yes yes yes. Its his mother calling, he could kiss her. But he wont. He wants to kiss her. But he wont. But its enough for the moment that shes calling him, calling him, his name

his name

his name

thanks mamma

thank you thank you thank you

Levi

uh

get up, the phone its

what?

get up I said the phone its ring

what did you say what did

somethings the matter the phone dont ring three oclock in the morning

all right Ill go downst

Lee starts in the backroom, the voices muffled through the long hall-

way
    I know somethings wrong I just
    what could be wrong
    Levi a phone dont
    all right, Rachel, all
    the boy swings his legs over the side of the bed. exhilarated. an excitement, a cool shaft of air shining down through his mouth all the way down to tingle his feet
    a hulking tousled figure the boy sees shamble from the front bedroom, the nightgown gaping at the neck, his father, sleep stunning the sweetness of his eyes, the boy peeking through his bedroom door
    Lee
    what do you want pop
    go back to bed
    whats the matter
    nothings the matter Lee, go back to
    okay
    Levi put on a bathrobe Rachel says
    leave me alone I dont need a bathrobe
    the phones still ringing I cant imagine yes I can I got a feeling its
    shut up already Im going down
    so hurry
    Im hurrying
    tensely Lee sits up in bed, the covers over his legs, another spring time, but the cool of early morning chilling the room, the arclight through the back window curving silverblue through the dark, something marvelous is happening, he wont have to go to school, the world in a whorl, he wont be required to act, hell be swept along, hes not really affected except by the excitement of the thing
    the phone stops ringing
    the boy stands again at his bedroom door
    his mother worrystreaked stands at the head of the stairs Lee go back to bed this is none of your business
    I cant sleep mom
    try LEVI
    SHUT UP RACHEL IM ON THE PHONE
    LEVI

WAIT A MINUTEFORGODSAKE
he asks me to wait a minute when Im on pins and needles
slowly ponderously Levi mounts the stairs
so what is it
Joshua
whats the matter with him
hes sick it was Victor on the phone he
whats the matter with
he wouldnt say Rachel he just says to
hes not just sick hes
Rachel thats not what he
something tells me inside something
Rachel stop imagining
Im not imagining I got a feel
he just said come right away
sure right away right
Rachel control yourself

Im controlling Im controlling what do you want me to do Levi what
WHAT she wrings her fingers, wrings the bone out of them standing at
the rail overlooking the stairway

Lee stares wideeyed, tiny stickinesses of sleep in the corners of his
eyes

Lee you better get dressed
all right mamma
get dressed quick as you can
all right mamma
Levi I dont know what to do first Im telling you I know pops dead
Rachel Lees awake
all right all right but dont tell me
all Victor said is hes very sick
yeh yeh very sick that weakling brother of mine and that big cow of
his wife why didnt they do something
CONTROL YOURSELF RACHEL
how can I control, its my father, Levi, my, hes
no he aint
what do you know, how can you tell, Im telling you something inside
me, they wouldnt call three oclock in the morning just if hes sick I dont

know the first thing to do my mind isnt what it should be, the diamond rings on the fingers begining to be arthritic scraping against the mahogany rail

just get dressed Rachel

jouncing in the rear seat as the car bumps over the pike the boy luxuriates in the jounce and the springtime and the aquamarine morning rising on the fanning rose horizon, his mother and father quiet, a snivel every now and then escaping Rachel, Lee secretly exulting in the grim face of his father and elated by the tears of his mother, no school today, no school, no school because somethings wrong, not with him but with somebody else and theres nothing better in the world than to have something wrong with somebody else, it makes the boy glad and blithe and gives him a feeling of power, hes not afraid of Charlotte now, she can say anything she wants

they are told to play quietly on the grass. Gus hums solemnly to himself, his cheeks between two fists, his elbows on his upraised knees as he sits on one side of the new playswing. Charlotte grasps the two metal chains suspending the wooden seat and lifts herself onto it, peering quizzically at Lee on the other side.

Give me a push, Lee.

Big or little?

Just a little one.

He looks pensively down at the grass twinkling with buttercups. He looks up to see Charlotte's eyes twinkling with buttercups. The arc has lost its momentum and the girl is disinclined to spend more energy on it.

Isnt it a pretty morning, Lee?

Itll be awfully hot later.

I guess so. Her thighs plump out of the dark brown frock.

Her calves and ankles are slim and curved. Her hair is braided and the two braids fall over her cheeks. Her pale blue eyes look up from the grass and, as the buttercups drop away, there is the expression in them of something having been struck, so that the pale blue comes in waves, like Harry Ring's paleness of eye gives the sense of something having been struck, so that cornea and pupil seem to recede. Did you see grampop?

Uhhuh.

In his bed?

Yes.

With his eyes closed?

Yes.

Hes dead.

I know.

Gus hums, up and down the scale, softly, a distant siren. Shut up Gus, she snaps at him.

I aint doin nothin, Gus says.

Yes you are. You quit that humming. Its awful.

It is not.

Yes it is. I have charge of you and youre supposed to do what I say, so you shut up.

Ill hit you, Gus says.

Just you dare.

His gentle brown eyes subside. He looks at her warily around the side of his face. Whatll I do?

Pick a daisy.

Whatll I do now?

Pick off the petals one by one, and when youre done that pick another one and you do that till I tell you to stop and each time you pick off a petal you say to yourself real quiet she loves me and then with the next petal you say she loves me not and with the next she loves me, thats the way, Gus.

Whos she?

Mamma.

He pouts. She loves me she loves me she loves me she

Oh all right, Gus. Its only a game. Dont you even understand a game?

But she loves me.

Its only a game.

She loves me not? he wrinkles his brow at his sister as he tears off a petal.

Thats right.

But she loves me dont she dont she, his mouth opens as if hes about to cry.

Dont you dare cry, dont you dare, Gus Nathanson!

Mamma loves me, he shakes his head yes.

Charlotte describes a circle around her ear, looking at Lee, Hes cuckoo.

You stop sayin that about me, Gus pouts at her.

Its only a game when I say youre cuckoo, Charlotte laughs.

Cuckoo, he giggles. A game?

Thats right.

Okay. She cuckoo, shes cuckoo not. Is that all right if I say that about mamma?

Yes.

Happily, plucking the petals, Gus intones, Shes cuckoo, shes cuckoo not, shes

Lee.

Uhhuh.

Whats dead? Charlotte asks very seriously.

Shes cuckoo, she cuckoo not, shes

You mean grampop?

Uhhuh.

The boy runs his open palm up and down the links of the chain suspending the wooden seat of the swing. The girl sways gently from side to side. Everybody knows what dead is, he says condescendingly.

Well tell me

Well

Shes cuckoo not, shes cuckoo, shes

Huh?

I didn't start yet, Charlotte.

Oh. You sorry hes dead?

Arent you?

Maybe

Dont you know for sure?

Im just a child, Lee, Im not supposed to know for sure.

Yes you are. You better. He shakes the chain and she nearly slips off the seat

I almost fell off Lee. You keep it up and Ill tell your mother

Please dont tell her, Charlotte.

Ill see

Promise

No I wont promise. Ill think about it. Ill tell you what.

What?

You tell me what dead is and I wont tattle on you

Shes cuckoo not, shes cuckoo, shes

Well whats a dead worm?

Well gee Lee a dead worm isnt anything, I mean its dead and thats all, but grampop dead, well, thats not like a worm

Sure it is

Shes cuckoo, shes

Charlottes exasperated. Hes is NOT like a dead worm, Lee, thats all.

How do you know?

Well a dead worm is awful small

The boy would like to escape but hes bound to this girl swaying in a swing and to Gus

shes cuckoo not shes cuckoo shes cuckoo not

bound. To answer her question. The pale buttercolored girl is a thrust, a swing, an axe in a dark brown dress against the carmine slashes down the morning springsky. He must make his grandfather dead to her. He must give her the death of the grandfather, as if he must give her his own death, youll see, yes, little girl, little poutmouth. Hell kill his grandfather for her. Grampop is still alive for her. An unparalleled opportunity for Lee. Strike Joshua down in Charlotte. Lee wants him dead in the eyes of all. Not a spark left. Why should Charlotte retain Joshua? Unspeakable. Dirty

Shes cuckoo not, shes cuckoo, shes cuckoo not

Did grampop move in the bed, Charlotte?

No. But that could mean hes asleep

Sure it could. But did he breathe?

I couldnt tell

Why not

I didnt get that close, Lee.

Why didnt you?

I didnt like the way he smelled. He stinks.

Did he stink that way other times?

Yes he did, Lee, yes he did, Charlotte crows, throwing her head back and tipping the swing. He stank that way when he was sitting on the toilet and my mother was going up and down on his thing

Maybe he was already dead then, Lee hurls at her in scorn, derision.

But you said hes not supposed to move and he was moving when my mother went

Cuckoo, shes cuckoo not, shes cuckoo

You mean you could smell him through the keyhole?

Thats right.

How come hes smelling like that now in the bedroom upstairs when your mother isnt going up and down on his thing how come how

Maybe just before he went to his bed she went up and down on his thing again.

Thats just a maybe. Did you see them?

No. But thats the way he smells, Lee, you go up there and smell real close I dare you I deedoubledare you, I triple deedoubledare you

Why are all the people here? Whys my mother crying and your father

My mother isnt.

She looks sad though.

She looked sad right after she got through going up and down on him right before she knew the false teeth was hanging from her boobies

Why is my mother and your daddy crying over him? You didnt answer that.

Because he wont wake up from his sleeping.

Did that ever happen before?

No. Youre mean, Lee, youre awful mean

Shes cuckoo not, shes cuckoo, shes cuckoo not, shes cuck

You think hell ever wake up?

That dont mean hes dead.

Then youre a liar all the time, you know what dead means, otherwise you wouldnt say it that way.

Yes I would too because I hear people saying it that way just like you do too and Ill bet you dont know what dead means youre just copycatting grownups

Hes going to be buried

Whats bur

Theyre going to throw dirt on top of him, theyll cover him up with dirt but first theyll put him in a coffin, thats a wooden box and then theyll dig a hole and put the box in it and cover it up and you wont see him anymore thats what dead is.

Charlotte tightens her grip around the chains, around her mouth, hunches her shoulders and shakes her head violently no no no, I wont let him be put in a box. Shrill, her thin neck pitted with pulsing shadows.

Then, a spout of triumph pops her head up. You lose you lose, yes you do, Lee. I got you now. If hes dead like you say how come I can see him if I want to when I think of it? How come I can hear him talk and move and everything if I think of it?

Can you make him get outside of you?

Charlotte stops her abrupt swings. She slides off the seat.

Shes cuckoo, shes cuckoo not, shes cuckoo, shes cuckoo n

Her throat twitches. She walks over to the walnut tree and leans against it. Then, slowly, she rubs her back up and down on it, never for a moment taking her eyes off Lee, the pupils and corneas receding. Then she beckons to him with a curling finger. Come real close, she says. Warily he stands only a few inches away from her. I can make grampop get outside of me, she says, if youll help me. Then she sneers. You dont even have to help me. Just watch. Watch me at the pond. Will you? Gravely, leaving Gus, they march down to the pond and into the outhouse. Charlotte takes off her panties and inserts her finger, staring scornfully at Lee. In and out, in and out, faster and faster

Shes cuckoo, shes cuckoo not, sh

Is he coming out?

No.

Now?

No.

Do it faster. Can you still think of grampop?

Yes.

Faster.

Shes cuckoo not, shes cuck

No, he

The girl beats on the toilet seat in a fury, Ill make him Ill make him Ill

Yes. Grampop, grampop. She runs from the outhouse, through the weeds slashing her face, cutting it, faint scythes of blood fanning down her cheek, barnacles inland, a hundred miles from the sea, the canoell capsize

She throws herself on the ground behind the barn, the cow staring at the girl, moo, moooo, moooo

Cuckoo not, shes cuckoo, sh

Mooooooooooooooooo

Again she jabs in her finger, in and out, in and out, and throws herself from side to side on the ground, capsized, the streaks of blood smearing her cheeks, Lee make him come out make him come out he isnt dead he isnt. She slams her buttocks against the grass, bouncing them as she jabs her finger, hiccuping now, wildly glaring at Lee watching her with his mouth gulping great chunks of the morning air

You see him, Lee?

No, no

She springs to her feet and springs up and down on the grass like a jackinthebox

Shes cuckoo, shes cuckoo not, shes cuckoo, shes cuckoo not, shes cuckoo, shes cuckoo not

Grampop grampop grampop she yells like a cheerleader

Yay team team team Lee howls at her

Grampop grampop, dancing, Come out, come out, please

And she races up the path, Lee pursuing gleefully, back to the swing, heaving herself onto the seat, propelling herself into larger and larger arcs, Live live live she yells at the top of her voice, GRAMPOP you get out of me you hear me you hear me

He cant

Gus stands gaping at his sister, his daisies dropped but his mouth slowly forming the syllables Shes cuckoo not, shes cuckoo, shes cuckoo not

At the bottom of an arc she slides off the seat and smashes into Lee, both of them rolling down onto the ground, Lee seizing her and pinioning her foamflecked bloodsmeared face and shoulders against the green grass as he straddles her

Could you get grampop out, heh?

She twists her head from side to side. No. No.

Thats dead, Charlotte, when you cant make a person get outside of you. Is grampop dead, Charlotte?

She whispers.

I cant hear you.

Yes, hes

Shes cuckoo, shes cuckoo not, shes

made of walnut, the grain undulant and gleaming from the burnishing and the convexity of the lid. The coffin rests in an empty room, empty except for the bed in which Lee sleeps. Then the boy awakens and tosses aside the covers. The lid section, however, supposed to fit over the head of the coffin, is nowhere to be seen. But Joshua Nathanson's head, propped on the satin pillowcases of the coffin, is quite clearly present. His expression is quite amiable. Theres no reason for the boy to feel misgivings on that account. What gives Lee pause, of course, is the fact of the expression itself; where there should be eyelids kneeling over the sockets, are open eyes, of a disturbing bluish brown; further, the lips are parted and apparently in the act of breathing. The boy nevertheless is absolutely sure that his grandfather is dead in the coffin: the mirrors in the Nathanson farmhouse have their faces to the wall; the windows of Joshua's bedroom are covered with his clothes. Despite these certificates, a high natural tint cheers Joshua's cheekbones; his yellow brush mustache does not seem in the least faded. For the moment grandfather directs his gaze toward the ceiling. Lee feels his own heart cease to beat, as if, indeed, he has transferred systole and diastole to the man in the coffin; but before any words are exchanged between the two Lee notices the final peculiar touch: the satin pillowcase, on which his grandfather's head lies, pours like seashore surf—of which the boy is instantly reminded, much like the surf experienced during his summers at Atlantic City—over the rim of the coffin to momentarily engulf a line of ants dancing along that rim; but one of the ants, the leader, the only one playing a fife, of all things, by which Lee is marvellously tickled—the fifeplaying ant takes the instrument from his mouth and swings it over his head and down upon the surf—like an axe, absolutely like an axe, Lee thinks, so it must be very important—so that the satiny surf is cut off and the line of ants reappear as if by magic along the coffinrim and dance once again to their fifeplaying leader—until, once more, the satin surf spills over, and the entire action is repeated. Its too bad, the boy thinks, that his grandfather is here to spoil his delight in the endless victory of the fifeplaying ant: the fife of the dancing ant axes off the surf, the fife of the dance. But though the boy wishes above all to concentrate on this phenomenon, he is distracted by the sight of Joshua raising himself to a sitting position in the coffin and turning his most benign gaze upon him, beckoning at the same time with his beautifully manicured right hand and saying in the kindest of tones, Come, Lee.

What about the ants, the boy hears himself saying.

The fife of the dancing ant axes off the surf, Joshua says sweetly, explanitorily, his eyes now the color of the tea in the glass he gives to the boy.

I know that already, Lee says impatiently.

No you dont, grampop quietly says. Thats why I want you to come with me.

With his fists the boy pushes himself back against the iron staves which form the head of his bed. He shakes his head no. Grampop keeps on beckoning, the satinsurf swallows the dancing ants, the leader ant brings his fife down like an axe upon the surf and cuts it off, the dancing ants reappear, grampop beckons from the coffin, Come with me, Lee, dont be afraid, the boy shakes his head no, the satinsurf

I wont hurt you, Joshua Nathanson says. Dont be afraid. Come with me, he says, curling his little finger, The fife of the dancing ant axes off the surf

Mommy, Lee pronounces it accusingly. But no mother comes. Instead, as the boy pronounces the word, the leader ant increases enormously in size and raises the fife above Lee's head as though it is about to be brought down. And down it comes, and down, and down, the boy crouching and shriveling and contracting as the fife comes down, and down, and down, Joshua himself in the coffin growing larger and larger and his voice booming You come with me, dont be afraid, I wont hurt you till the blade of the axe is about to touch Lee's neck

Mommy. But his voice is only a whisper in the room as he finds himself curled against the head of his bed, the cold iron staves raising goosepimples on the exposed section of his flesh between the parted pajamas. He dares open his eyes. No grandfather, no satin surf, no ants, no fife. Only the sensation of the vastness of the chest of drawers, the window, his finger. Their great weight and yet their puffiness and remoteness. Their weighing him down and at the same time the sensation that they are anchorless and might float off any moment. Lee springs out of bed and sits at the room's rear window, huddling, breathing the fresh air as deeply as he can and staring out into the sky and the stars as far as he can. The sky and the stars are the sole objects which refuse to be subjected to the parallax. The great distance is constant. Night after night the boy starts out of bed and sinks his stare into the nightsky above the Ruscomb Street twostorey houses, moon or no moon, when the rain runs along the gutters of the garage roof to enter the rainspout and rattle tinny

152

drums, tinny coughs and sardonic metallic snickers on its way down, when the rain sweeps along the thick halfscreen put in the window for just such weather, longvented for the entry of air, but spray seeps in just the same, icy and lonely, as if it must force its way into Lee's room for warmth and companionship as the boy draws back from it in the chair, sneezing a little in the dark, fearfully glancing at the door from time to time, hoping his mother or father will never discover him at the window and ask him questions he does not want asked—he does not want them concerned with him at all. As for his brother David, he wouldnt be interested; he doesnt live in the house anymore anyhow; hes in another house at the corner of Lindley Avenue and Warnock Street in Logan with his wife Bettie and their first child, Fay; Dave is twelve years older than Lee, which is the greatest distance of all. But there is only the distance to shut out the closeness, the sound of the rain in the spout, the clatter of the bouncing water against the tin, the sight of the ricocheting speckles on the garage roof in the light of the overarching arclamp on Ruscomb Street against which the rain wavers and rubs like innumerable cats disintegrating into spiderwebs pearlfurred and fizzing as the boy's bladder fills, but he doesnt want to piss till the objects in the room resume their normal dimensions, and then not for awhile, because if he returns to bed too soon after the usual dimensions are reasserted then the enormities will rematerialize and hell have to go back to the window anyway for another half hour, another hour perhaps, alone again with the distances, the small dark boy looking through the windwrinkled window, staring relentlessly and worriedly, the brow fraught with the necessity to disgorge and exorcize the huge heaviness, the gauzy behemoths, the leviathanic remotenesses, the crushing balloonesses issuing from his eye that he seeks to blow out of his retina onto the night, onto the winds from the northeast that bully and chivvy the ballroom clouds amongst the silver clatter of bits of moon

a silvertwig vibrating on a telephone wire there

what of the species of the telephone poles, the doublebarred crosses:

I see two Christs crucified, Lee tells Danny Naroyan in the parked car before the Roosevelt Boulevard house at threefourteen of the long summer night. The emeraldcornead Naroyan, sitting at the wheel, looks through the windshield at the uptilting triple highway, all the way up to the Catholic church at C St, blond hairy stubby fingers grasping the wheel, imitating the squarerigger THE MISS GRACELY head of the Olney High School Music Department conducting the school symphony orchestra, auburn ropes in ornate boxes piled atop her largecubed skull atop a cablecorded square neck founded atop a great storagebox of a torso to which is nailed on the ventral side two smaller boxes nominally known as the mammilaries, and to the dorsal proceeding floorward again two smaller boxes accorded the buttocks, NOW

IN A PERSIAN GARDEN IF YOU PLEASE LETTER D, she sights the tame young bull of the concertmeister, imperiously confers her baton for the moment upon the invisible upper plane, her brows contracting, her squarerigged features all meeting in the center of her face in wizardly concentration, her left hand pinning back the page of the score on the podium, the students poised upon the MISS GRACELY VALKYRIE, cymbalist his two platters aerial, the kettledrummer his pompons addressed to gravity, the racehorses of the string section their bowbottoms a fraction above the catguts, the flutist his knuckles in pure beggary above the little holes and his mouthfrowns discoursing to MISS GRACELY she DECAPITATES

the whole Catholic Church is corrupt, Danny snorts, when my brother used to work for the State Liquor Store hed bring over orders of brandy and bourbon and the best scotch to the parish house. Of course theres no reason they shouldnt live well but the hierarchy might be going a little too far by showing itself at the Baths and letting somebody go down on them. I find it extraordinarily difficult, Lee, to reconcile the beauties of nature with some of the behavior of Man who is a sadistic animal, Danny shakes his round balding skull

accidents survive

Schweitzer the perfect example of the pure humanitarian.

I dont think thats quite true, Lee quietly says, for all of his ironic jest of showing the visitor the trees along the road with bullets embedded in them and saying They couldnt run away, and his apologetics anent the microbe that he kills it only to insure the health of a man. Crud, absolute crud. The man is a terrorstricken sentimentalist. Ill concede his musicianship on Bach, if you say so, I know nothing about it except that Ive heard his organ renditions and think them altogether dull. But his humanism is a harrowing lie because of its final limitation; he too at last makes a value judgment and decides there are classes of living organisms which must be extirpated in favor of the human species, and narrowly practices his value in the depths of the Congo. He has a right to practice it, of course, but let him spare the world his cant of justifications and muzzle his eminent disciples of whom Einstein is not the least absurd when he calls the good doctor a great man because of his selflessness. Surely nobody with any logic can demonstrate why man should aggrogate unto himself the rights of survival over microbes simply because he is capable of a Bach. Does Schweitzer anesthetise the microscopic organisms with measures from the Art of the Fugue before he stains them for the study in death? Wuchereria bancrofti doubtless evinces gratitude before it goes under and expresses regrets that it never experienced the fortunes of the twelve-year-old Mendelssohn when he first laid astonishment upon the forgotten cantatas; or perhaps the parasitic worm may whisper, I regret I have but one evolution to give to my Schweitzer. Anyhow, I see two Christs crucified

His analyses of Bach are very profound, Danny certifies.

They may very well be, except for his and any exegesis upon the Master which attempts to prove his abiding religiosity. I will accept Bach's devoutness, you understand, if we list Religion as one of the branches of Art, a Position itself benignly touched by the Gulfstream of Sex which laps at God and Music with something less than gentleness on more than one ceremonial occasion. The conception of Divinity, singular or multiple, is one of the more masterful strokes of the Esthetic; indeed, in its singular formulation it has prodded the science of an Einstein to express it in unified formulae. Parenthetically its amusing to observe the antics of Science lustily howling how its discoveries generate impacts upon men, complacently asserting that the impacts are measurable in many respects; conveniently choosing to ignore, of course, for the very reason that they are immeasurable, the impalpable edifices of a tune constructing impact responses, the consequences of a Picasso Guernica, and the hours upon hours of incalculable subtleties of joy and expurgation from a Quixote and a Hamlet. Anyhow, I see two Christs crucified

On the Roosevelt Boulevard, part of US Highway Number One between New York and Philadelphia, the traffic thins. The firegutted house adjacent to the splinterfaction synagogue at B Street is still boarded up though Mr Sherman has long since moved away. Levi Emanuel snores, while Rachel presses an electric heatingpad to a pain in her side

Why two, Danny lilts at Lee, challenging chuckles in his voice.

Oh I dont know. When I was younger late at night Id sometimes stare at the telephone poles receding into the distance, and Id imagine a crucifixion. But I just couldnt see Jesus as one individual up there on the Telephone Pole as God's Linesman splicing the broken wire all by himself, Lee laughs into the dark. I figured Christ had a brother. I figured, if you will, that God had acted rather like Aristophanes's divinity and had split his Son in two so that the brothers could seek each other and finally, in a dramatic rendezvous, meet each other after a life's separation upon the Cross to prove their Father's immortal point, namely, that one could not really suffer alone but that one had to suffer with someone else, with one's brother; that single suffering was a delusion as was single joy. Of course, Lee shrugs, shooting a long leg out the open window of the car, the exact opposite may be held, perhaps an even more dynamic idea, that Christ was crucified all by his lonesome to show the sheer illusion of trying to exist by oneself. So God forsook Christ because the boy had dared to announce openly who he was, the Son of the Almighty; having done that, there was no recourse but elimination. It wasnt the Jew or the Roman who killed Christ, but Jesus's Father, the Angry Vengeful Terrible God of the Old Testament. Lee grins at Danny

it was simply a matter of the Old God having caught up with the new-fangled New Testament. For awhile it seemed that Jehovah had got left behind—there was his son preaching Mercy, and Turn the Other Cheek, and Render Unto Caesar and all sorts of gentlenesses. Adonai had got oldfashioned, was a thing of the past. Well, sir, hed be damned if hed let Christ get away with it. Yahweh had no intention of letting himself be supplanted, so he murdered his Son. Naturally it was His worst error. He made a martyr of the boy

Snickering, Danny couldnt contain the query. Why do you persist in referring to Jesus Christ as a boy?

Lee shrugs, spreading his hands fan wise. Well, for Godssake Danny, he certainly wasnt a Man, was he?

We dont know what his disciples covered up, Lee.

True, true—Lee sometimes generously concedes a point. But nobody has ever come forward to assert that hes the illegitimate son of Jesus Christ. I guess if someone did hed be jibed off the planet. Still, you know, Danny, if hed had any illegitimate issue, his father would never have killed him: hedve given him credit for showing some terrestrial sense. But, par example, Jesus was a Boy Not Of This World and he had to go. The damaging thing was the admission. If only Christ wouldve kept his mouth shut, his Father wouldve let him go on being a living boy. But Jesus bragged. That was unforgiveable, in very bad taste and inhuman. God certainly wanted no inhuman emissary upon the earth. He wanted his Son to be one of the boys, to do a little proselytizing here and there, unobtrusively you might say. In that way Jehovah would still be undisputed. With Christ the Lords disputed. Of course, the disciples got clever about the whole thing: they didnt want that rather obvious Rivalry bruited about because the propaganda mightve unduly suffered and the converts might not have got so numerous. So, the idea of the Trinity occurred to them. Brilliant. Solved the whole thing, burying the old Jehovah pretty quietly in the ThreeInOne, as pretty a piece of metaphysical trickery as has ever been devised. Christ got really palatable then, having absorbed his Father. Which was in accord, if you think about it, with the growing independence of the Son in the family, or at least with its initiation, eh? Even more importantly, perhaps, a new law of civilization became quite cogent, namely, that Fathers couldnt go around anymore murdering their Sons with impunity. No sir, they couldnt, or theyd be incorporated into the Body of Christ. Take a look around you, Danny, and observe the waning influence of Fathers and the ascendancy of the Marys, the Mothers of Christ. It all fits, huh? It wouldnt surprise me a bit if the next revolution in religion would involve some woman coming forward and crowing that shes the daughter of Jesus Christ.

And instead of the Trinity? Danny innocently says.

Very simple, Lee says. The HoleInOne

The battered Ford creaks with Danny's whoops. Lee raises a tickled eyebrow and detaches himself from the car. I think Id better say good night.

Listen, Danny momentarily detains him. Theres a woman down at the National Youth Administration I want you to meet, Ive told her all about you and she wants me to introduce you. I know youll like her, dont be bothered by the way she looks.

How does she look?

Well its her hair, I think it frightens some people off. Its carrot red and wild.

Whats her name?

Terry Shannon. Im having an NYA Orchestra rehearsal tomorrow afternoon at three, Ill take you down to her office. Shes no kid, Lee. Shes about forty. Okay?

Sure. Good night, Danny. It was a good night. The tall boy clenches his hand on the carwindows metal rim and grins at Danny, grins wide, showing his two upper front teeth with the generous space between them, and the crazily crooked lowers like a jumbled group of little tombstones for dogs, for animals of every kind, Danny thinks, with a bottomless affection for his friend, this ungainly lad three heads taller than he with the tousled black hair, one lock inevitably falling over the right side of his forehead, Sy had caught him well, Danny agrees, in that swift watercolor he had done of Lee last Sunday on the Emanuel porch: in ten minutes he had captured the large closelyset darkbrown eyes with a hint of protuberance, the small ears sticking out a little from the heavy curling hair, the long line of the jaw narrowly avoiding the lantern type; only the pout of the lips was more Sy's than Lee's. Danny's broad round beaming blond peasant countenance watches Lee turn to the house, smiles as he sees Lee suddenly remember to correct the stoop to his shoulders and straighten up. Danny waits, waits almost as a mother, to make sure the lad has his key, turns it in the lock and opens the front door, at which he looks over his shoulder and flicks a tentative forefinger at Danny protruding through the carwindow. Good night Lee, Danny calls with a soft stridence and shifts the Ford into gear to pull away, compressing his mouth, his eyes misting a little as he makes the swift left at B Street and another left to go west on the Boulevard toward Wyoming, thence to Lindley Avenue and at last to Old York Road, his home, feeling the shattering gusts of departure even on this summer night, feeling as the trafficlights change red to green and he makes a right onto Wyoming along the treelined avenue and the Ford grinds its way through foliaceous shadow past the squat rows of the silent twostorey residences bulgingly dark in the moonless, windless, warmcool summernight, past Fifth Street with its sudden clatter of trolleycar tracks and commercial shops on the vision but silent this late upon the ear—there should be sound, there should be sound Danny insists—past the church whose distinctive claim to the neighborhood was its scarlet cross atop its spire, endlessly revolving and visible for miles around, reminding Danny of the scarlet sign in Strawberry

Mansion ICE NEVER FAILS, and that perhaps this church should flaunt that CHRIST NEVER FAILS—feeling now as always that tomorrow should signal his leavetaking from his mother and father and brothers and the rug business in order to pursue his musical craft but just as immediately providing himself with reasons why he shouldnt go, that his father is an unlettered peasant who is lost three blocks from his home, that his mother would have no one to scream at or to talk intelligently to if Danny is not there, that the oldest brother is ashamed of his Armenian background and that his older brother is an oaf primarily fascinated by women and cars. Impossible to leave the Naroyan Rug Company now. Next summer perhaps. Besides, he refuses to accept an assistant conductorship; he will be a full conductor, and be paid accordingly, or nothing. Besides, Curtis Institute is the recipient of many requests and when he graduates he will surely have an offer. Besides he is still learning. Where else could he be so exhaustively instructed in composition? His teacher, Rosario Scalero, has no peer, for all of this old man's crotchets and senile envies. Then, envies pour upon Danny: he envies Lee's physical height, his handsomeness, his relative freedom from responsibility and physical labor. Before Danny assumes his duties as head of the parttime NYA Music Project in Phila- delphia he delivers freshly-cleaned rugs on the Naroyan truck; he collects rugs to be cleaned; he helps clean them in the Naroyan plant, scrubbing them down, dragging them out on the grounds to dry; he plans advertise- ment by handbills and attends to invoices; only then he sits at the piano to solve a problem in counterpoint for Scalero. There will be no strength left over to go away, finally. Danny feels himself a kind of muscular little Christ. He disagrees with the conventional portrait of the Saviour, a kind of tall dyingswan man. Danny sees him a bustling little dynamo, trotting from parable to parable. The gingerbread mansion the Naroyans rent at Old York Road and Lindley Avenue rises stoopshouldered from the emi- nence on which it was built and Danny guns the Ford up the incline and parks it in front of the garage which is used for the rug cleaning. A bitter- barking coloraturathroated pomeranian flurries out from the kitchen in a gossip of flitting feet to greet Danny who laughs delightedly and drops to the lawn and rolls around with the dog squealing PINKY PINKY PINKY PINKY PINKY PINKY

KLOONG KLOONG KLOONG KLOONG the Gilbert clock chimes as Lee warily mounts the stairway in stocking feet

Lee?

Uhhuh. Go to sleep mom.

I cant sleep. I was just dropping off and you had to come in late, its so late, what were you doing out so

Goodnight, mom

You know how Im such a light sleeper

Uhhuh

Dont ever come in so late again

Ill try not to. Patient.

You hungry?

I ate a little in the kitchen.

You should have more consideration for your father, you know hes got to get up fivethirty to get down to the Yard for the drivers

I know.

So?

Im going to bed now, mom.

Its about time.

Go to sleep already.

Im all awake now, Lee. Ill never get to sleep again. Ill be up all night now.

Theyll kill me. One way or another. Lee doesnt want to get off the Number 50 trolley. Running half the length of the front section of the trolley are two long curvedtofitthebuttocks benches facing each other across a wide aisle. Painted red but dimmed by usage. You can sit in this section and not pay your token or its equivalent of 8 cents (two tokens purchasable for 15 cents) till youre ready to leave the trolley, at which point its mandatory to pass by the conductor who stands and sometimes sits on a little circular seat, which he can swing out of his way if he chooses to stand, located in a hiphigh booth jutting into the aisle and narrowing it. Opposite the booth and perpendicular to the side of the trolley is a more or less hiphigh black iron guardrail separating the long bench on the right side (from the point of view of entering the trolley) from its continuation about four feet into the rear half of the trolley where the paidup passengers sit (the bench on the left terminates at the conductor's booth). The righthand bench makes an inverted L with the bars of rows of benches, upon which only two people can sit at a time, separated by a narrower aisle, extending to the curious semicircular bench which conforms to the curved rump of the trolley's rear. The motorman stands at the front of the trolley, also served by a small circular seat upon which he can sit or swing to his rear out of the way, where he manipulates a knob attached to a horizontal lever capable of making a half circle: the shifting lever, announced by periodic clicks, controls the halting of the trolley, a single rear speed and three forward speeds from low to high. The motorman, as does the conductor, wears a black uniform and a cap remarkably like those of trainconductors or French officers; his vision is served by three large windows precisely like those at the rear of the trolley except that they are not cut short by a seat placed in an arc. The conductor, however, seems a far more important functionary: both his jacket and vest seem slit by a multitude of pockets from which protrude varicolored packets of passes and transfers, some of which are free and enable a passenger to transfer from one trolley to another at a stipulated junction to continue a ride without additional cost, but for others, depending on direction and length of route, he must pay another 3 cents; dependent from a chain attached to his vest is a metal puncher which the conductor utilizes to punch a hole in a transfer precisely indicating the time of expiration; bulging from the conductor's belly and strapped round his waist is a shiny metal object made of stubby vertical metal tubes, varying in size to accord with quarters, nickels, dimes and pennies which he inserts through slits at the top and disgorges, when he is making change, by little plungers on the side. Sitting in one of the twopassenger seats, side by side with an elderly gentleman who has a disposition to doze, let his head fall on Lee's shoulder and jerk to wakefulness each time the trolley stops to unload and pick up passengers, Lee would prefer to change his seat, but its Saturday and the trolley is crowded with shoppers on their way to the central section of the city, to Market Street. The sallow conductor grins at Lee's discomfiture; the other passengers smile at each other slyly; one woman frowns disapprovingly at the elderly gentleman altogether. The passengers swaying and hanging on to the celluloid nooses—the straphangers—which are secured to iron bars running overhead—crane their necks contemptuously at the dozing man. If only to liberate himself from the embarrassing position, Lee wants to get off, but that feeling is insufficient to counteract the stronger one, the sensation that he will be murdered. One way or another. If not murdered, then struck, wounded, knocked unconscious. Not long after he begins his walk east on Montgomery Avenue. Of course, its ridiculous. But the fine mist falling is indistinguishable from his sweat. Perhaps the mist will have kept them in, in their bedrooms, or their livingrooms, or their poolrooms. Them. The menaces, the murderers, the thieves, the idiots, the povertystricken Guses of the neighborhood, the unshaven ones, runted and stunted, the inhabitants of the caves. Lee prays that the Guses and the Aarons have been driven in by the spring drizzle. They are not here this morning. They have vanished, they must have. They should not be allowed to live, much less to stand on streetcorners. They should themselves be murdered. They threaten the boy. Any moment theyll leap at his throat. Lee's shoulder-blades gnash, huddle, gnash. His father shouldnt demand he come down to the Yard once a week on Saturday mornings. To learn the Business. Make himself useful. Five dollars for the day. The overpowering brown bulk of the Stetson Company on either side of the street, connected over-head by galleries. Through the open windows the men in undershirts sweating over the machines shaping the felt. His father has no right to bring him down here because Lee wants to love the murderers, the thieves, the menaces, the poor; he wants to espouse their cause, right the wrongs of the exploited, but not in their midst, not threatened by them; this is manifestly unfair; he wishes to do it in his own way, safely removed from the masses, not jostled by them, not taking the chance of being jeered, spat on. He doesnt trust the murderers, the thieves, the idiots, for they understand nothing. He is quite sure they resent him. He is certain they want to leap on him and tear him limb from limb. Because hes Levi Emanuels son. The boss's son. The favored, the pampered, the inheritor. He wants to shout at them he has no intention of inheriting his father's business; he wants to plead with them that he likes neither leading nor being led

RADBILL OIL COMPANY. A singlestorey white structure, against which railroad sidings abut

its impossible that anyone will be out on this kind of day. But there they are, as Bodine Street comes into view, across the littered empty lot, where his father has a LaSalle parked this year. A block from the saloon

one block. He shoves his fists into the raincoat pockets. The bills against the saloon's brick walls

TOMMY LOUGHRAN VS

to one side of the two rutted marble steps leading into the office of the at the open gates for the coal and charcoal trucks. Uncle Aaron in his floppy shoes smiles unseeingly

The knot. The group. The huddle. Kids. In their middle and late teens. Standing. Kneeling. Rubbing hands. A fade on the crapgame. But the Yard isnt his. He will publicly disavow it to them. He wont run them. He wont tell them what to do. But theyre waiting for him

TOMMY LOUGHRAN VS

HOME GAMES SHIBE PARK ATHLETICS WITH WASHINGTON ST LOUIS BOSTON NEW YORK

Its not my fault. I didnt want to come down. Id rather be home. Please dont do anything to me. I havent hurt you

From the dice the murderers the pimps the thieves with concealed knives concealed guns concealed brassknuckles

look up. One by one. At the boy, who smiles, tentatively. He might have to run. He might have to scream. For help. For his father. Theyre afraid of his father all right, afraid of his brother. His father's biceps will squash them if they dare lift a finger against him. Im not my father, Im only a kid. But theyre no older than he is. Theres a confusion, then. Lee thinks himself younger than the spawn over the dice, at the entrance to the Yard, swinging their cigarettes as from a lariat of snot, spitting, gesturing with little knowing nods at the boy warily approaching.

Theyll kill him. He knows they want to kill him. He knows they hate him. Look at the venom in their cigarettes, biting around their eyes, their eyebrows as if caps pulled low, deadly, sickly, thin, charged with muscle, rip and claw, with no clothes, no money, with only their verminous caves to go to while Lee lives on the Roosevelt Boulevard with its treeshaded highways, sedate houses, bonamild interiors. Hes got more than they have. Why should he? By what right? Because hes Levi's son, son, son. But I like you, Lee thinks. I really want you to have as much as I do. I dont believe you should be poor, I want you to have as much to eat as I do, theres no reason you shouldnt and Im going to argue for it so please dont kill me I beg you

They spit. Growl. Mumble. What are they saying? Theyre talking about Lee, of course. Theyll gang up on him. Nobody inside the officell know. Before he can shout a word, itll all be over. The idiots, the thieves, sallow, thin, with weapons of all kinds

Hes got to get through. Grin a greeting. No word. Just grin, like youre one of the boys, like you belong, its only an accident youre the boss's son, thats all, you know that. Dont touch me, dont touch me, dont TOUCH

Jaw clenched, a quiet grin, fists in the raincoat pockets drenched, Lee walks across Bodine Street, twelve feet, no more, the drizzle matting his face

The crapshooters indifferently move aside so he can go up the two rutted marble steps

One of them momentarily tilts his skull back in a snivelsneer, says, Levi's son.

Another answers. Yeh. Getting big, aint he. Guess hell take over when the old man kicks off. Dave dont want the Yard.

Lee forces out a chuckle, opens the office door

MYGOD LEE CANT YOU GET THE ADDRESS DOWN CORRECTLY

Waddya yellin at him for Hymie Krause gnarls his fingers around the wire caging separating the corridor from the office proper, you been years in the business Levi you expect him to pick it up all in one day

Whos talking one day, but the least he can do is get the address down right. You know what it costs to send a truck to the wrong address

Lee sits at the desk, silent, chickles of sweat sticking to his ass

Christine Novak turns to him, Dont mind the old man, his bark is worse than his

Lee for God's sake the next time make sure you realize we lose money when

I cant hear right, Lee mumbles

Waddya talkin you cant hear right, cant you hear on the phone

Henry Feinstein, globefaced and bespectacled, at the desk near the weighingscales, Levi's office manager, clumps a fist around the phone's mouthpiece, Levi

Hurry up Henry what

I got the Reading freight manager on the phone

So what are you asking me Hymies screaming in my ear hes got to get home hes got to get home his sons getting barmitzvahd

All right Levi all right so I got Big Bernie waiting on the scales hes yelling hes got to get out on the street

Well.

So theres a delay on the two cars of stove coal but theyre tracing them down now, they oughta be on the siding early next week

Tell that sonofabitch what does he want me to do with my orders, am I supposed to cancel, its bad enough as it is, the competition with oil-burners is getting worse all the time, tell him I want those cars in tomorrow, I can do business with Lehigh Valley, whats he think Readings got a corner

You tell him

Youre on the phone Henry you got a mouth Lee your phones ringing you gonna wait a year to answer Henry get on the scales all right Hymie Krause so how many bags

Christine slams the ledger shut, Levi youll just have to get another girl in here

Lissen I got plenty overhead as it is

Im tellin you you gotta get another girl this Social Securitys drivin me nuts

Eddie Jackson lumbers into the office from the back door, the huge hulk of a negro, exsparring partner, Levi what the fuck am I gonna do about the stove coal

What are you asking me for what am I supposed to do the God Almighty Reading Coal Company, get back into the Yard and leave me alone, I got a million worries, Dave wants me to switch a coupla cars to his Yard

Hes running short already? Hymie is incredulous. What the hell does he do with the stuff

How should I know, am I supposed to be a police officer over my own son

Cal Lacefield with the white scars in his cinnamon mouth silkily leans over Levi's desk, Levi that cable out there sure is runnin mighty thin, I wouldnt be too sure about the bucket

Ill be out in a minute

Chief Aaron wobbles his skull on a poke through the front door, You hear about Shorty Maples?

Hymie says, Chief you oughta get back in the Yard they shouldnt shortweight the bags

Aaron's eyes wobble in his face, fifteen sizes too large for his eyes, the jowlfat dripping on the floor, Whats the matter with you Hymie aint you got a heart

Yeh I gotta heart, I should treat it special?

Youre supposed to be superintending outside, Levi tells his brother with unaccustomed sweetness

Whats the matter with you Levi?

Christine snags a drink. Henry busies himself at the scales, clicking on the lead counterweights

Shorty Maples, little Shorty Maples, waddya know, Aaron intones, clucking, I never woulda believed it. Did you hear, Lee? Where you been such a long time

I was here last week, Uncle.

Yeh, yeh, thats right. Shorty Maples dead and buried, I cant believe, last week with my own eyes I saw him leave for the mines, did you know that, Levi?

I knew it

Sure why shouldnt you know it, he was driving one of our trucks

We all expected it, Aaron.

Not me. I didnt expect it, Aaron innocently says.

What did you expect from a man

What, man? He was twentyeight. Christine, thats all he was, wasnt he?

The girl sniggers. Thats all. He drank too much.

Oh you know that, Christine, Levi says heavily.

All right, Levi.

The drivers tell me he never got back to Philadelphia, thats the truth, Levi?

Thats right, Aaron, so go

On the road he died.

On the road.

Aaron grins. So tell me. Aaron is very secret. How much did he drink. Aaron is a little boy, the candy is all over his face, the candy of death, white and sticky, his neck gulping

Ah Jesus Christ Aaron, Christine shoves a deskdrawer in with a bang, stands, hands on her hips, you really wanna know he hadda habit drinkin a fifth before he started out to the minefields, another fifth on the way and one more before he went to bed and he never lost a truck, did he Levi?

Grudging admiration, No, never. Never got into an accident, you could never tell he was drunk. Once every three months Shorty Maples

Really hung one on, Henry chimes in gleefully, remember Levi? Really got dead drunk. Couldnt walk, couldnt talk, used to hole up in a gutter

Waddya know, Shorty Maples, some drinker that boy, hah? Aaron pouts

On a gray drizzlefine day Lee and his father are fishing from a rowboat on the open sea. A dead calm. Except Lee isnt fishing. Only his father. Lee doesnt say a word. He knows the man at the opposite end of the rowboat is his father, is quite certain, except that Levi's body has another face, the face of Harry Ring, the man at whose apartment he lives before hes taken to Governors Island after his furlough. Anyhow, Levi Harry Ring Emanuel is fishing on a gray drizzlefine day in the open sea. The fishingline makes a little hole in the water. Then the father begins to row. The ocean is exceptionally calm. As he rows, Lee observes a great ocean liner in a distance, slowly crossing the horizon

the fife of the dancing ant axes off the surf

Nevertheless, the ocean liner is not so distant that Lee fails to observe a matronly woman standing on the upper deck at the rail. She, too, oddly enough, is about to fish. As yet she hasnt cast. She resembles both Rachel Emanuel and Lee's wife Rena. At this point, his father with Harry Ring's features slowly commences to turn the rowboat in a circle. As he comes about, Rachel Rena casts her line and the hook flies out to embed itself in Levi Harry's eye. Levi Harry suddenly rears in the rowboat and clutches at his eye with the hook in it, blood gushing from the socket. And, soundlessly, the father falls out of the rowboat, still clutching at his eye, and into the ocean where he sinks. Lee leans over the side of the rowboat at the same time that the ocean liner disappears beyond the horizon. He peers down at his father's body plummeting down through the water. The water is so clear and calm that Lee can see him sinking all the way down and down and down, continuing to clutch at his eye from which the blood continues to pour. He watches him plunge till he can discern him no longer

KEEP IN STEP GODDAMN IT forward MARCH

My Darling Rena M1 Garand look. I cant put it off any longer, I wont, Ive got to see you, I dont care what happens to me All Right Emanuel this is your barracks I thought Id be stuck in the stockade No the stockades overcrowded besides all were doin is holdin you here till we hear from your outfit the bars on the windows oughta be enough Im going AWOL, I wont use that many days for a construction of desertion to be put on it. Sheer cowardice, perhaps, I admit it. Of course I realize its wartime but Im not in combat Im simply with a combat outfit and were still in the States, so dont worry I couldnt possibly get a long jail sentence or even be dishonorably discharged and certainly not shot Rearing up from his desk the Captain EMANUEL screaming EMANUEL WHAT THE HELL DO YOU MEAN BY DESERTING YOU REALIZE THIS IS WARTIME YOU REALIZE YOU COULD BE SHOT FOR SUCH AN OFFENSE NOW EXPLAIN YOURSELF in an office the color of wet sand Im sorry sir WHAT THE HELL DO YOU MEAN YOURE SORRY YOU REALIZE THIS COUNTRYS AT WAR yessir the captains face is the color of wet sand tinged with pink The quiet boy in the bunk next to Lee at Fort Dix with the sad face Ahm charged with homicide, whats yo name. Lee. Lee Emanuel. Mines Chester Rowland. Slim, the color of dry sand. Now ah want you to know it wasnt premeditated murder or anythin like that, naw, it was a lotta people call one of those crimes of passion, ah jus caught mah wife with another man an ah carved them both up, thassall, now ah think that justifiable homicide now dont you

In the South Philadelphia office of the Nathanson Moving & Storage Company, the color of damp sand, the globular dwarf that is Bruno Canova twirls himself like a child in the swivelchair to one side of Victor's desk. Victor runs a skinny finger down a yellow sheet itemizing and tabulating the household effects of a family he has just moved, In a minute Mr Canova I

Sure sure take your time

Victor Nathanson is a finger with a head whose hair shoots up to one side, grayblond, yellowskinned, wetting his fingertips, his bluegray eyes smiling to one side of the sockets. Distracted, The chair, Mr Canova

Mi botherin you? Hey I dont want to upset, you understand, throwing his arms out, balloons of embrace

No no, its these itemizations

Sure, Victor. Dont mind me calling you Victor, eh? I had dealings with your father Joshua, he never mentioned me, hey? Victor blows a touch of dust from the yellow sheet, carefully lays it on the desk, face down. Wary. No, he

Well I just came in. You know. I hear he died.

Yes.

I was sorry to hear it, real sorry, Victor. Victor okay?

I think so, Mr Canova

Bruno.

Yes. Bruno.

Pumping himself up from the swivelchair Canova straightarms himself onto the edge of Victor's desk. Very sorry for the old man.

Thank you.

Prancing his bulgehead around the office, Pretty quiet, huh? The Depressions no help to nobody. Lissen I was pretty intimate with the old man. He pumps himself off the desk and begins to walk around the office in the circle of his body.

Is that so?

Mostly realestate. I got a lotta property in South Philly. Hell it aint worth much these days but I figure if I can hold on to it, know what I mean? Sure you know what I mean, youre a sharpie like your old man.

Victor abruptly purses his mouth and rips away a finger, the rasping sliver of a fingernail in his mouth. He spits it out. Tests his fingernails against his thumb. The bitten nails are jagged, rasping. Before he can stop himself, hes a sliver of rattling tongue thinking of Helen, Stevies growin up, Charlottes in her teens and what did your father He gives a sliver of a laugh He looked out for me, Mr Canova

And the color of damp sand, not only yellow, sand swirling around the office set in motion by Canova's swivel

Bruno, Vic.

Yes, he looked out for me, with his realestate. Bites a nail. And his idiot son, Gus. Cranial injury. He doesnt believe it. Lots of children cranial injuries when theyre babies. Had to sell most of it for taxes, you know how it is

Sure Vic.

Would you believe it Mr Canova my father

Bruno

Well Bruno he left me without a cent. Nothing. Realestate, to pay taxes, he creaks up from the chair, rectinlinears around the office, Bruno retreating to the window OC EGAROTS & GNIVOM NOSNAHTAN to momentarily lean his swelling puffs against the wooden pole to which a curtain waisthigh is attached, blue, sanded over

Business is slow, heh?

Well, the whole country. Biting off the nail of the filing cabinet, Victor clicks a drawer open and shut, open and shut, open and shut, open and Rachels a good sister. Levis a good brotherinlaw. A two thousand dollar loan. Generous of Levi, he can hardly spare it himself, he can himself hardly rattle his newspaper over the sound of Gus's lowsiren moans in the livingroom, his wife duckwaddling her breasts through the room, he bites his fingernails, bluegray, sand flowing from his fingernails, damp and rasping, one livingroom set, item one mohair sofa, item one mirror mahogany frame, item one lamp brocaded shade, Helen tossing her duckwaddle tits at him, turn this way and a tit, turn that way and a tit, turn the other way and a wallop of a hip, her sex crowding in his bluishdamp fingernails, his bluishsanded eyes, this is what youre here for, item one tit, item one crotch BROCADED AND FRINGED, what the hell more do you want Victor Nathanson and a slim blond daughter Charlotte Daddy, Daddy, Daddy, Gus go upstairs to bed fuchrissake Dont yell at him Vic he didnt do nothin Helen turns on her husband, turns, swivels, no wonder he cant keep calm as Canova swivels open and shut, open and shut, what is a man, what is a man How you figure you can hold on to your realestate Bruno?

The barrel of a dwarf hitches up his pants. Gotta develop somethin on the sides the only answer Vic.

Youre lucky youve got another business.

Im lucky. You believe in luck, Vic?

Victor slides himself into the deskchair. Its all luck

luck something to brood on, luck in small letters on the window, kcul, crawling kcul, or in gigantic letters like ICE NEVER FAILS over Strawberry Mansion, the luck of the Irish but not the luck of the Jew, lucky sweepstakes winners, lucky millionaires inheriting but he couldnt even keep the Lansdale farm, maybe its lucky he had to give it up, lucky Joshua died, lucky hes got an idiot son, lucky he cant have sexual relations with Helen, lucky hes nearly bankrupt, lucky he cant get any more loans, lucky hes got a sick mother but thats all right though, Rachel can take care of her but wholl take care of Victor Nathanson, maybe hes lucky nobodyll take care of him, maybe hes lucky his youngest son doesnt know him very well yet, lucky his oldest son Gus is an idiot and cant know him very well, lucky Charlotte is a girl and wont be part of the business anyway, lucky shes attractive and blond and slim and somebodyll marry her quick, quick, but shes not old enough yet and he cant push it, he cant push the years, he cant find her a wealthy husband, but maybe thats lucky too because it means everything depends on Victor Nathanson and hes got to find out what luck means, its got to mean something to him, luck that can be spelled in dollars or loans or pity, he must be the lucky type somebody can have pity on because hes shivering, hes cold, its his damn circulation, it never was any good, maybe thats lucky too, maybe the circulation will withdraw, sink back, concentrate on and hole up in the heart, his bloods got to find someplace to go because the rest of his body is thin, his toes are pinched, his face is squeezed, his hair is frizzed and skinny, his nose is bony, his eyes are pale, his eyebrows are hardly there, his chin is pointed, all this means Victor Nathanson is lucky, only he feels a little faint, a little bit like his sister Rachel she gets faint too, shes got low blood pressure, its not such a strong heart, but hes a man, his hearts got to be stronger, its advertised that way, wives say so, children demand it, hes the man of the house, the hour, the time, he, here, man, heart, luck, Victor Nathanson, luck must come through

You gotta slam that desk drawer so hard Vic?

I was? Im sorry. I got things on my mind, things

Look, theres a Depression, it aint your fault.

No, it isnt. Lots of men

Plenty

What kind of business you in besides realestate, Bruno?

Howd your family take the old man's passing, Vic?

Vic makes his lips disappear, as if sucking. Not hard. Maybe my mother, but shes a little confused in the head. You know. Im glad you came in Bruno, things are slow, theyre bad. Since the old man died I havent had a chance to get things off my chest, you know how it is, I didnt want to worry my sister, her husbands got enough—ah, what am I talking. Good to know an old friend of my father's, but youre not so stylish as he was, jesus he was stylish

With the cane

And the spats and the gold teeth in his mouth. My was he proud of the gold teeth, smiled whenever he could, unnatural sometimes, you remember, Bruno?

Who could forget?

I can joke a little.

Sure.

He couldve left me a couple gold teeth.

Bruno folds his sausage arms, his pudgy fingers. I know what you mean.

All that style but he left us nothing.

The old man used to tell me he could con your wife's mother into a coupla loans every now and then.

Lena? The old Mrs Cherny?

Thats who, thats who, I remember her name. Shes still alive, aint she?

As tough as they come. My wife takes after her.

Bruno plumps himself down on the swivelchair and gives himself a couple turns. Victor smiles at him slackly. He feels slack, for the first time in days. Tough as they come, heh? Bruno puffs out chuckles, puh puh puh.

Thats her. His heart slows down a little. He joins Bruno's chuckle. Youre not worried, heh Bruno, about the times, the Depression?

Whats to worry?

You remind me a little bit of Joshua. He was never worried. Me, Im a born worrier, like my sister. At least she worries a lot about me, if Ill catch cold, my liver, my blood. Worries more about me than my wife or daughter. You—you paisans, you never worry. Me, I got a business to lose. If I last three more months itll be a miracle.

Believe me, youll last, Vic. You got my word.

I understand, youre trying to make me feel good.

I believe in that, Vic. I believe in making people feel good, I go around alla time doin that, everybody likes me. In a way, Bruno Canova would like to fatten Victor Nathanson up. But he knows this is impossible. Impossible, anyhow, from the outside. From the inside, maybe possible. To coat the thin man's nerves with fat, more fat. To spread tallow over Vic's brains. He doesnt approve of jittery men, uneasy men. Bruno Canova wants everybody relaxed, as relaxed as he is, soft and plastic as he is. He doesnt believe in hard things in this world, he believes in the roll, the cushion, the slow bounce, that everything hard and angular should be absorbed. He enjoys absorbing, drugging, making people sleepy. He believes nobody should be on their guard, that you die when you die like a slowly bouncing ball into the soft turfy grave. He wants to put everyone in this world off his guard, its a favor hes doing them, each man should be like a quiet village, rich or poor, it doesnt make any difference. If a man wants to be rich, hell help him, somehow; if poor, hell assist in that, too. And, certainly, all nervous men want to be calm, as Vic must lust for tranquillity instead of sex, as if there are some men who want the peace without the necessary antecedent orgasm, thats Vic, whos had his orgasms and found them wanting or found himself lacking, so that there must be some way to avoid that intermediate step, Know what I mean, Vic?

Looking at the dwarfed fat man, Vic feels his heart approaching a kind of float or as if hes being massaged. You must be a religious man, Bruno.

Yeh, Bruno is caught by surprise. Yeh, I never thought of it that way before. I guess I am religious. Dont get me wrong, I dont go to church no more, I aint been to confession in years, but I think I know a little what it means to be a priest. I feel a little like a priest, Vic. Thanks.

So thats part of it, Lee explains to Danny in the red white yellow black Naroyan kitchen. Uncle Aarons an example on my father's side of the family, and my Uncle Vic on my mother's side. Nothing like corned beef, eh? the spit smuggles the spices into the whole body and the next thing you know you feel as if youre consuming contraband. Same thing with Nova Scotia lox, rolled beef, hot pastrami, sour tomatoes, Lee hunches over the table, jawing the great slabs of spiced meat between shaggy slices of pumpernickel. I frankly dont know whatll happen to me under pressure

My sweetest darling Rena Hell I havent even learned how to field-strip the M1 Garand rifle. I dont intend to learn. As far as Im concerned Im going to let the whole goddamn barrel and firingpin and trigger and muzzle rust. Because Im not going to use it. Maybe I shouldve told the examining psychiatrist at the Armory about Uncle Aaron and Uncle Vic, but I couldnt. I couldnt put myself in the same category with Link Cornwall, not at that time, anyhow. No, I dont resent Link. All right, maybe I do, in a sneak sort of way. But I like him too. Remember that party of his we went to at his Spruce Street apartment? Sure he was aleady drunk when we got there, but the only thing he did to me was to gently pat my balls and then my ass, a kind of fore and aft greeting. You didnt mind. Nobody couldve. From a homosexual that kind of greeting was positively respectful. He was certainly drunk enough later on to take a girl into his bathroom

Dear Lee I doubt very much if Im ever coming back from Europe. You and Rena were the only ones I hated to leave, because you were the only ones who ever treated me with any kind of respect. I didnt want to leave you. In that Marley Road doorway I cried probably for the last time in my life and I cant remember the time I cried before that. Its really no use trying to get me to do anything, to be creative in any way. I cant. I just cant sit down for that length of time or stand in one spot or simply think in a sustained manner. Of course itd be wonderful if you and Rena could get over to Paris. I guess I could show you just about everything and introduce you to just about every kind of person you could possibly imagine. I think Ive met the range. Its been five years, hasnt it? Ill end up here. Away from my brother. Hes been here and gone. He wont return to Europe. It was France and then England and now back to the States. Hes gotten along very well, successful. Hell, a lord and his wife kept him for three years in a Scottish castle. I hear hes designing sets for a new Broadway opening. He has that facility, yknow. Thats all hes got, hes a mediocre prick and the bane of my existence. I suppose you can call it sibling rivalry if you like but I cant quite explain it that way. I hate that bitch called my mother and that bastard called my father. Now why should I form a fix on either of my parents, both of whom I detest? My brothers an invert too. Theres nobody in my immediate family I have any affection for at all. Im afraid you wouldnt recognize me, Lee, Ive grown terribly fat, extremely gross about the hips. I used to pride myself on a certain charm of figure I possessed but that was boyhood more than anything else and Ive let myself go to excess. The other night I slept with Jean Marais whos slept with Cocteau who slept with Andre Gide. I havent written you for awhile because I was in the hospital with some goddam cocci of the mouth which Id got from a onenight stand with a beautiful little Arab boy. It was a messy sort of thing and rather painful but they finally got round to treating me with the new antibiotics and so far as I know I havent a trace of the infection now. Im leaving for Switzerland in the morning with an ancient Marquis. Skiing. Im so tired. Im so very tired, Lee. I guess Ive crossed and crisscrossed Europe now at least three dozen times, lived in one chateau after another and one hovel after another. I never have enough money, never never never. I hear that nasty little Dell Sergeant is having a Broadway opening. I detest that facile little prick. Do you remember that afternoon on the Naroyan lawn—after Danny had moved to Ridge Avenue—when we were all sitting in a little circle and Dell with his fantastic pretentiousness remarked that all he wanted to do was to get just one play on Broadway so he could be picked up by Hollywood and there, eventually, persuade some producer to consider doing a screenplay on Proust's A la recherche—only a section or two of course which Dell would naturally adapt. I hate that pretentious little fag. But I suppose he knew all the time exactly what he was about. He sucked around Letitia Rollins long enough and wrote his play with her in mind for the lead—and she was sufficiently superannuated enough of an actress to be sucked. Hell forget adapting Proust, of course. The whole idea is a pretentious faggy idea to begin with. What shall I do, Lee? Tell me what to do. Im so tired I want to die. But Im incapable of committing suicide. I pity myself every conscious hour, pity myself and hate my brother—I suppose ever since he was such a goddam honor man at high school and my mother adored him, adored him, adored him and abhorred me. My father never knew what to do with me. He tried, on several occasions. Tried to understand. He never disputed my intelligence. Ill never forget how flabbergasted he was when I reeled off the property values of a hundred midtown Philadelphia houses and the types of their architecture. Its really all over now. You know it was mainly at his instigation that I left for Europe in the first place; the family wanted to get rid of me, they couldnt stand the notoriety I constantly created. But I couldnt resist it. Ill never forget that afternoon concert at the Academy of Music which I attended attired mainly in a cape, and when I described that old whore of a WCAU announcer, that Forrest Guest, I simply couldnt resist standing in my box and howling down at him Bonne matinée Father Guest, hows your corrugated cock? I recall quite vividly that in uncontrollable response he turned round and turned all colors—frankly I hadnt thought him capable. My father sent me a hundred a month for a couple years and then he wrote me his business couldnt absorb my cost any longer and that Id have to return. But I couldnt, then. So he cut off the allowance, I havent had it since. Pity me, pity me, pity me, Lee, I beg you. Now Im crying. I said I hadnt cried since I left you and Rena on the Marley Road steps that night. I could hardly stand up for a moment. I knew I wouldnt ever see you again, that the gross probability was against it. You and Rena. Rena was the only woman I ever liked, too. Oh, I hated her at first, I suppose because she was your wife. But later, later I terribly enjoyed being with both of you. Now Im crying. Im sorry if Im smudging the words, you do see the stain of my tears, dont you? Oh Im such a flabby impossible person, I dont know what you see in me at all, I never could understand. But you respected my wit and perception; I dont think Ive any of either left. Frankly, I dont know whats left. Im part of that new—or old—race of the homosexual gypsy. I guess Ive done about everything, Lee. Im sure you must have only the greatest of contempt for me. And you should have. Im worthless. Thats something you dont like to admit, do you? that anyone could be worthless. I am. Totally. Im nonsalvable. You must permit yourself to recognize that about me and forget me. Theres no point, really, in my writing you ever again. Ill only whimper and whine more and more. Im so cold now. Tomorrow itll be better, with the Marquis. Ill be warm and Ill eat again. I havent eaten for three days. Oh, Ive been through this sort of thing before, too. I really dont think youd want to know me in Europe. Lee, Lee, Lee—Ive stolen, Ive raped, Ive forged checks—Ive committed just about every possible kind of crime and gotten away with them all. Ive even smuggled dope across the border. You remember that bust of Beethoven I hit a sailor with when I had my Locust Street apartment? You remember how he staggered down the stairs and left a trail of blood, all the way into the street? Because the sonofabitch wanted money from me for sucking me off. I got enraged, I was furious, I couldve killed him. I meant to kill him when I struck him with Beethoven. Well Ive used busts again and chairs and anything that was handy to hit people with. The one crime I havent committed is murder. I might, where and when I dont know. And I dont care. I never cared who I hurt. I felt no twinges, no qualms, no remorse. But I never wanted to hurt you, and, later, never Rena, either. You had complete aplomb when on meeting you for the first time at Winston Murchison's I made you a butt, and you replied in kind, but then later told me itd be ridiculous to continue in that kind of relationship when you so much liked me. You told me straight out that you liked me. No nonsense. And that you didnt want to be made love to by men. I knew exactly where we stood. Perhaps that was why I liked you so much, that I felt asexually tender toward you: you made it clear that you wanted to know my mind because you enjoyed my mind. Nobodyd ever said that to me; if they had, they never meant it. I felt you meant it. How is dear fatuous Winston? And that hairdresser lover of his from Cologne who claims that, really, really, some of his best friends are Jews. That poor bastard and his nightmares, always the same, dreaming of himself as a little boy pursued by an old man—you know I used to run into him now and then in the men's room of that allnight movie—whats the name of it? right on the corner of Market and Juniper, on the northeast side—ah, yes, the Family Theatre—cruising desperately for a pickup, desperately, a mania. Thank God I never found it quite so difficult. Switzerland. And then Ive been invited to spend the summer at a Normandy chateau. How will I end up, dya think? My body dumped in the Seine? I know I wont live long. Please be sorry for me. Always love, Link

Cornwall, Link, on the bluegreen bright winterwhittled day presents himself, with raincoat reaching to his ankles, a derby hat on his head and an empty pictureframe under one arm, to the army officer at the reception desk, a kind of enclosed reviewingstand, of the Armory in West Philadelphia, observing dryly, I dont know why Im here in the first place: I voted for Wendell Willkie. Note, I am a Republican. I cannot suspect a single reason, therefore, why I should be given a physical examination for the army of Franklin Delano Roosevelt. In his other hand, Cornwall, Link, carries an open umbrella. He is, perhaps, five feet four inches in height, but is disproportionately commanding. He rests the tip of an umbrellarib on the officer's desk. My name, he says, is Mister Link Cornwall, of the Germantown Cornwalls. At your behest I have expended a single token minted by the Philadelphia Rapid Transit Company for you to be graced by my presence. I will expect to be reimbursed for that and for an additional eight and onehalf cents return fare. I hope I have made myself clear. I voted, I say, for Wendell Willkie. Now, will you inform me where I am to undress?

anyhow, Rena, that was the way he began. He did undress in a barn of a lockerroom where another thousand or so young men were doing exactly the same. The Armory had a high flat ceiling squared off by row upon row of skylight, and the bright winter light flooded the thousand naked male bodies in various postures of kneeling, sitting, standing, jumping (for the cardiologist) and bending. Link Cornwall insisted on retaining his empty picture frame in one hand, the umbrella in the other and the derby on his head. Otherwise the boy was nude. When by some act of magic he managed to remove his derby to wipe off the sweat, his auburn ringlets in their dampened condition clustered more thickly on his skull. He had made sure to forget his spectacles and squinted his green eyes malevolently over the multitude. He made a point of not recognizing me. I had an unmistakable desire to mimic everything that he did, but found myself incapable of doing so. His angelic freckled face atop the softly curved body, which tended to protrude more pronouncedly at the hips, was ashamed of nothing. It cavorted. Link cavorted. At first he went around from naked ass to naked ass, paternally patting them down the line as each waited its turn for eye ear nose and throat, urine, heart, chest and the remaining structures which offer the human form. When a patted ass got its first view of derby, empty picture frame and umbrella, astonishment uprooted irritation and the men began to laugh. Turn the cheek a little more this way, he said to one, so that I may appreciate it the more. Link was carrying the empty pictureframe on one naked shoulder now. A couple officers gently admonished him: he was, after all, still a civilian. They gently pleaded with him to conduct himself with more propriety. They remarked to him that he was becoming too much of an entertainment and was upsetting the orderly examination procedure. Link listened stiffly, picture frame, umbrella and derby; he was a model of unruffled naked dignity as the watching eversomale men sniggered and whooped, their testicles jiggling, fatty teats quivering and lean teats stretching thinly over rib. He bowed ceremoniously and conferred the honor of assent upon the concerned officers. When they wandered off into the dense immensity of the naked bodies, their uniforms incongruously out of place, Link began hopping, first on one foot, then on another. This was followed by a scratching role. He scratched under his armpits, on the back of his neck, in his navel, in his crotch, at his ass and behind his kneecaps. I itch terribly, terribly, terribly, he explained arrogantly to anyone who turned an ear. And resumed his hopping, one foot, then the other, umbrella askew, pictureframe jumping, derby sliding

derby sliding, picture frame jumping, umbrella askew, hopping down the line first on one foot, then the other, Cornwall, Link, presents himself to the proctologist, scratching himself furiously in the crotch, the anus, the armpit, the navel and the back of the neck

Bend down, says the proctologist.

Link divests himself of the pictureframe and the umbrella but keeps his derby on. He complies with the proctologist's request and the derby slides off and strikes the wooden floor. It rolls a moment, settles on its crown, rocks momentarily, and is still, proctologist and Link watching the derby expressionlessly. You do apologize? Link asks the proctologist from his bent position. The men roar. The proctologist restrains himself from reply. Instead he says quietly, Bend down further.

Angel Cornwall does so.

Now spread your cheeks, the proctologist demands.

Link spreads his buttocks. A smidgin. He arches his neck to stare at his forlorn derby on the floor with something like nostalgia. The proctologist bends down to look at the anus. But insufficiently bared.

Spread your cheeks more, he says impatiently.

Link widens the breach, in which the proctologist pokes his eye. What he is looking for, or what he will hope not to discover, is evidently still not evident. Spread em some more he bawls.

Cornwall, Link, auburn cherub and ringleted angel, slowly straightens himself, saunters to his derby, retrieves it, dons it, reinvests himself with pictureframe and umbrella, turns and stalks to the proctologist. My dear fellow, says Link, if you want my cheeks, as you so Christianly refer to them, displayed in greater aperture, spread them yourself.

With this, he hops off, first one foot, then the other, scratching, forever scratching

and it was this way that Link Cornwall finally reached the examining psychiatrist, continuing to carry pictureframe, open umbrella and derby. Even as he sat down before the skullskinner, he managed to twitch various members of his body, including his penis, and scratch at them

your name, please

Link Cornwall

your parents, please

Letitia and Roger Cornwall. Rachel and Levi Emanuel

two sets of parents?

republicans are known to have two sets of parents, doctor. I voted for Wendell Willkie. Im here under false pretenses

do you have any objections to be inducted into the Army of the United States

did you?

I would appreciate it very much if you attempted to answer our questions to the best of your ability

Yes, doctor

do you have any objections to

none at all. I want to be inducted. very much. when may I be inducted. will there be very much of a wait? I dont think I could tolerate the waiting. I rarely could. impatient as I am

is that why youre scratching yourself

I scratch because I itch

for how long has this been going on

why, ever since I entered the armory, of course. the itching began. I cant get rid of it. I tell it to go away. I say to it, you may prevent me from being inducted. But its no use, doctor. it stays. its an itchy itch. I mean by that that the itch has an itch. I dont know which to get at first. Lee, I say to myself

Lee?

Lee Emanuel, my name. Ive two sets of parents. I told you. Lee, I told myself, when you were nine years of age you were sucked off by a boy of ten, a very fat stupid boy, in the alley between the Forstens and the Emanuels. I enjoyed every moment. I had no shame. But I refused to copulate with any male since. as Lee Emanuel, that is. not as Link Cornwall. But I did itch directly thereafter. My father Roger has an itch, he says it comes from the blood

my blood is too rich, it tries to thin itself out by itching look at his hands. scaly, like Jennifer's eyelids, the flesh keeps peeling off, I was going to be inducted into the Czar's army

this is not the Russian army. The Russians are our allies

not for Link Cornwall, nosir. I voted for Wendell Willkie, Im republican, to hell with the Russians

we crawled and crawled and crawled, Lee, till we were over the border

thats why youre itching then, from the crawl, from having scratched yourself over the Russian earth, you still bear it with you, you said nothing to me about wanting to escape service with the Czar, thats whats itching you, you really didnt want to be a scholar at all, Levi, you had guts only for crawling, escaping, eluding

that takes a certain amount of courage

yes, a certain amount, but Im not impressed

are you calling me a fairy, son?

how do i know what you are

with the other boys and girls when wed go to another Lithuanian town for a dance, wed tumble in the hay, I knew what girls were

bravo, bravo, you knew what girls were

well now, look, doctor, isnt that proof Im fit for the Army of Franklin Delano Roosevelt

this is not the place where we come to certain conclusions

well youve got to declare me sane, you understand? what will my friends think if you dont. how can i carry the onus of insanity around with me

I didnt want to do that, Rena. but now I know what i want to do. im through, they can have the fucking army, Ivan take care of my rifle will you Im going into town

fuchrissake we got a thirtymile march coming up at three in the morning

I dont give a fuck, I gotta get into town

whats Columbus got

its got bars, its got hard liquor

Lee I cant stand another of your letters, theyre driving me insane, stop it, its enough I have to get up on the stand and sing with my mother calling me all kinds of names, my brothers calling me all kinds of names, stop it with your letters, yes I love you, yes, I love you, what more do you want me to say, no I dont know anybody who could get you shifted to a non-combat unit, stop torturing me, I know youre unhappy, I cant bear it, stop threatening me youll do this that and the other thing, do it, I dont want to hear about it anymore, I dont mean that, Lee, because I love you, truly I do, theres nobody else in the world but for God's sake have some pity on me I couldnt stand working in the Frankford Arsenal over that drawingboard so I took a singing job with another girl in Atlantic City, you wont like me, Ive gained so much weight, please try to take it, Lee, it cant last forever, only stop torturing me

do you approve of the war

certainly I approve it. war is to approve, isnt it? periodically weve got to kill, slit throats, bash in the groin, roll in muck and mire, masturbate to our heart's content, fuck men, consent with the whores of all nations, run away from wives, mistresses, girlfriends, mothers, fathers, brothers, the cities we were born in, the jobs we got stultified in, certainly I approve of war, any war, American and British and Chinese and German, what the hell difference is it what side you fight on so long as you fight, wound, terrify, rape

Im Link Cornwall, I wont die, Rena, Im a nance, I prance, I fag, I like boys, the only women Ive enjoyed are those forty years of age or older, look doctor, get it over with

Id like to go in that Armory, Rena, and shiek and pansy around and hit the psychiatrist

go on, I dont care what you do so long as you keep out

I cant, I owe an allegiance, Im a jew, theres Hitler, there are six million Jews, I cant let my friends go and keep out myself

what about Danny, Sy, Al Gordon. Danny made the excuse hes running a business for his otherwise incompetent family. Sys the only support of his heartdiseased mother, Als got a trick knee, your cousins got a trick knee, what do you have

I dont want to go, I dont want to go, I might die

are you afraid of death

yes

thats normal

whats normal about being fearful of the inevitable

Lee has no grace

the hell he hasnt. He got inducted, didnt he? it was all he could do to admit he suffered from chronic allergy and had ringworm since he was twelve years of age

I got in, but somehow Im getting out, like Aaron got out, like Uncle Vic got out

now look here men General Patton in his high voice addresses the 2nd Armored Division the German and Italians your enemy, you got to go over there and grab him by the family jewels

the family jewels

jewels are Jews

Jews are jewels

preserve the jewels

survive the jewels

discharge more spawn

are you interested in having a family Mister Cornwall

no

you want no children

funniest goddamn thing at a party I got sucked off for kicks by a dike who was pregnant at the time, shell make a fine mother, no Im not the father, you know what I tried to do for her, Ill tell you, reverend doctor, I tried to suck off the pregnant woman's fetus, now there a trick by God, I was experimenting: can a fetus if a male experience an erection and what the hell does it look like in the womb and, furthermore, will the mother then feel as if shes being screwed by the embryo, and if by the embryo does the catholic church approve, is this incest, if so, what variety and can we thereby excommunicate the fetus. point, how is the fetus to be excommunicated? will he be refused entrance into the confessional. when was the last time you confessed an embryo, father? what sin had it committed with Lee Cornwall

do you like boys

I love boys, I cant wait to get into the army of Franklin Delano Roosevelt, come on, doctor, lets get this over with and maybe you can see your way clear to coming up to my apartment tonight

Levi this is Link

Mr Emanuel I do so much adore those silos in your coalyard, I can conceive of no greater thrill than to have them stuck up my ass

are you afraid of going mad

oh JesusChrist doctor, didnt you know that all madmen are homosexual, all womeninsane are dikes, you think a male paranoiac wants a woman? you think a female hysteric really wants a man? never, never—they want their own sex or even better they prefer to screw themselves

I think I have sufficient information Mister Cornwall

let me tell you more

it is sufficient

nothing is sufficient, doctor, thats why I cant stop itching, theres no end, nothings exhausted, no terminus, no death: THATS WHY IM AFRAID, because I wont die, not completely, NOT SUFFICIENTLY YOU UNDERSTAND, parts of Lee Cornwall will go on twitching, scratching at the earth hell be buried in, let me out

let me in

let me out

let me in

Levi cant sleep nights from the itching. he takes a bath, thats a temporary relief, counting the years spent at the coal business. counting the next payment on the bill. counting next week's income, number of trucks, number of coal bags, number of clothes, number of times hes talked with Dave, with Lee, with Rachel, with Vic, with his weigher of scales, number of days in the year, month, week, number of his own years, counting numbers, on the pages of The Freiheit, The Jewish Exponent, The Philadelphia Evening Bulletin, the number of miles on his Buick, number of friday evening services, counting, counting the scales on the palm of his hand, blades of grass on the lawn, taxes, number of days left for sister Bella Zion to live, thats why you should learn to be good at mathematics, Lee, he grins crookedly, everything involves mathematics, counting the number of hours till the light comes out of the east, is he the only counter? counting how many days to Pesach, Rosh Hashonoh, Christmas, Purim, counting how many years he has to live with two heart attacks now, how many hearts does he have

I read about the mechanical heart

sure all the organsll be replaced with mechanical or electronic substitutes and nobodyll die except by suicide

I insist you give me my eight and one half cents what do you mean Im rejected

the armorys in an uproar, Cornwall slapping as many asses as he can lay his palms on

PLEASE go Mister Cornwall, heres your token

you realize youve wasted my time

yes, we realize

you realize that Ive literally been on a wild goose chase

yes we realize

you realize I havent made a single man here Im frustrated

your token, Mister Cornwall

WHY DIDNT YOU LISTEN TO ME IN THE FIRST PLACE I TOLD YOU I VOTED REPUBLICAN

will you go now

Link Cornwall departs, raincoat down to his ankles, auburn ringlets confined by his derby, green eyes asquint as he smirks at the sun, angelic snubnosed countenance sweating with innocence, empty pictureframe under one arm, unfurled umbrella held by the other.

Ive been invited to spend the summer in Normandy

the summer heat in Georgia, Rena, is a foul and squatting thing. The prisoners from the Fort Dix detention barracks in New Jersey wear

fatigues with large white Ps painted on the backs. Shambling prisoners in the hot summer evening rain, floppy puddlehats on their heads,
the guards with their carbines, awri awri get yr ass outa the sling Lee
only half believes it, halfbelieving a halfinvolvement sure I can stop off
at Philly on the way back to Georgia and see Rena and fuck her AWOL,
have her body in the halfing, but half having her, not quite believing it,
because it would be impossible to have anyone else here in New Jersey
where theres a ride with a psychopath, believe

believe

believe hes a psychopath thats what Barry Handler says and Dr Lobov
the Goldsteins' alternate family physician

or in Georgia or anywhere else in the USA. Only Rena a foul and
squatting thing, not her, impossible to visualize, the incredulity of over-
riding ego

TRENTON

ATLANTA

FORT BENNING after reveille the rows of cots and the rows of huddling
men. Humps. The dark has many lumps in its throat, these men. A bugle
falls. Bereaving reveille, somebody inserts a trainwhistle in the pinesome
slot after the bugle the men shambling hulking drooping sliding sloping
into the Fort Dix messhall

P

the orderlies slam down the mashed potatoes the hamburger the
tomatoes the bread and the

HANDS THE HUMPING LUMPING KNUCKLING SLIDING SLOPING SHAM-
BLING CRABBING FINGERS UNDER THE WHITE PRISONER LIGHT SCOOP
SNATCH SNAG SNAP JAW JERK HUG HAGGLE THE FOOD INTO JIGGER AND
JOWL AND HAWK AND HUMP AND COSSACKS OF THE TEETH THE SLEDGE
OF THE TONGUE THE BADGERING OF THE SPIT THE CONGA OF THE LIP

eat it

wheah the fuck ya think ya gone with the spuds

PICK up the meat

eat it

eat it

make a prisoner of the food DOWN BUCKLING ADAMSAPPLE DOWN
THE CHUTE OF THE EYE DOWN THE PLUNGE OF THE NECK

ya dont grab it ya go hungry

ya dont fight for it ya wont get it
ya dont stuff it down yr belly ya can fuget it

I dont know what youre talking about when you talk about a man. I dont know what youre talking about when you talk about an animal. I dont know what youre talking about when you talk about a living thing or a dead thing or anything in between. I only know what youre talking about if you tell me about certain forms in army fatigues with white Ps on their backs who bend over pine tables chunking down spuds and hamburger and tomatoes and things they call greens and iodine-flavored scalding coffee. Sometimes with forks, sometimes with spoons, sometimes with knives. But most of all with curved palms, with fingers. I only know what youre talking about if you tell me the meat and the spuds shoot up and plaster white and yellow and brown teeth and clog the inside of the mouth and get sledgehammered into a belly. I dont know whose belly. It doesnt matter whose. You cant name the belly, you cant name the crouching form, you cant name the fingers and there is no speech, neither English nor French nor German nor any any other known language. There is only the belch and the fart and the hiccup under the white prisoner light in the army mess barracks at Fort Dix in the army of Franklin Delano Roosevelt. The crouching forms are hungry and build up an enormous heap in their bellies so they can slide down off of hunger into a luxurious valley of waiting shit. I dont know what youre talking about when you call them Americans or Italians or Chinese or Nazis or Fascists or free men or slaves. I dont know what I am, Rena, slogging in the thirtymile training march on the hot clay Georgia road. I know Im whimpering. I know Im cringing. I know Im full of hate. I know Im sweating and lusting for the green tall pines on the side of the road. I know I hate the sweating sergeant and sweating little Ivan by my side. I know I would like to slam down the Garand and the full field pack and the bayonet. I know I want to kill the captain and the sergeant and the general whoever the fuck he is and Secretary Stimson and President Roosevelt and my mother and my father and any sonofabitch who managed to stay out of the draft. I know I want pity. I know I want special attention. I know I want to be excused, let off, discharged, be called incompetent, neurotic, psychotic. But I march. Its nearly fifteen fucking miles weve been marching but I go on. I want to stop. I want to sink on the Goddamn hot clay Georgia road. I cant feel sick for the poor nigger slobs we pass with their blackandwhite prisoner stripes and the chains on their feet, the libertarianlyscreamedabout Georgia chaingang repairing the road. I pass them. I look at them. Dragging their chains, the chalksweating niggers. I dont feel sick. I feel maybe a tenth more hate. Kill the guards. Why should they be alive? Its a simple question. I feel like this: with authority I would condemn the guards to death and the warden and the whole Goddamn fucking population of Georgia that permits the chain gang. No mercy. No trial by jury. No commonlaw protection. Did the niggers get commonlaw protection? Did they get uncommonlaw protection? They got sentences, five years, ten years, twenty years, thirty to fifty years. Very simple: kill the Georgia judge and the Georgia jury and the Georgia prosecuting attorney and the Georgia governor and all the polite softspoken liberal men and women of Georgia who yap the southern white man knows how to treat the nigger as a special problem. I dont see why they should be alive when these dragchain niggers pulverize stones in the onehundredten degree Georgia heat. I only pity myself. Im sorry for myself and I dont give a shit who knows it. Im a Goddamn crybaby inside, Rena, Im slopped up with tears and self commiseration. The snots running down my throat. The snots running down from the eyes into my mouth. The sweat is one long crawling biting scratching chigger under the fatigues. The Goddamn captain of the company is red in the face. He breathes fast, then slow, then fast. The poor Marylandborn sonofabitch has had it with his DROWLING YAYEKCENT. You put one Goddamn rubber knee in front of another. The orange clay road winds, ups, downs and has chevrons of heat ascending from its surface. Theres a ten minute break awri fall out you guys fall out you pricks you miserable laughable training sonsofbitches, take a rest, take a breather, take ten, take five, find some shade, take a salt tablet, dont gulp down the water from your canteen, be smart and take a sip and roll it around in your parched mouth, anybody who cant make the hike fall out, drag behind, let the medics take care of you, youll go back to camp in a halftrack you poor weakling, cant take the gaff eh, you dont belong in the armored infantry, you dont belong in the colossal Second Armored Division, you dont belong to your country oh no no no no we wont think any the less of you, youre just a little overage or you got a hernia or youre a fag or youre psychoneurotic but brother you better have a good excuse if you fall out, I dont want one man of Company C to fall out the redfaced farmerboy maryland captain

YAYEKCENTS, hell answer to me, we dont want any slackers in this heah company, unnastan naoaw? I want to ram my bayonet up his ass, I want to make that cold steel freeze his sweat and make his balls go POOF like a couple of wrinkled little balloons in his fatigues, red balloons no doubt for the red white and blue. You think of the pines. You think of the barracks with running water, water running. Of a shower. Of a beer. Of a whisky sour. You think of dying. On the spot. No trouble. No regrets. To hell with Rena, with fuck, with food, with mother and father, with friends OUTSIDE THE ARMY MAY THEIR SKULLS BE STUFFED WITH THE ARMY'S POWDERED MILK, kill Sy Tarassoff, kill Al Gordon, kill Danny Naroyan, kill your stuttering brother Nate and your cocacola drinking brother Herb, the footdoctor spared for the civilian population and delicatessenstore brother spared for his little daughter his little lousy baby girl he masturbates against with his own ringworm infection of the groin. You want to die. To hell with going on, with getting back or going forward or ascending or descending or any imagined motion whatever. No motion. Screw motion. Die

    die

    die

    die

    so therell be no more sweat, no ten thousand pound fullfield pack, no forced march, no training maneuvers, no war, no white prisoner heat, no hate or anger or selfpity. Nothing.

    Can you imagine wanting nothing? Im not the only one. The othersll joke about it later. Not now. Nobody says a word, got that, Rena? Nobody smiles, nobody grins. Got that, everybody? No defense. They make comedies out of it, later. They make tragedies out of it, later. But now its not tragic, not comic, its just plain disemboweled sweat, reduction, a piece of itching flesh with five hundred other bodies of itching flesh walking down the Georgia road. Itll get worse in combat. Im not going to fight. Ill be goddamned if I will. You want to murder just to change the itching and the heat and the exhaustion, just to get on the back of a variable. Just to feel hot blood thats icy in relation to the Georgia heat or the Italian heat or the Normandy heat or the North African heat. Theyll make faggy little dramas out of it, later. Theyll make cute conflicts and counteractions and the grandstand play of tactics out of it, later. Theyll make men out of us or bestial animals or howling maniacs. I dont know what theyre talking about. Theyre a horde of defensive liars. Theres nothing complicated. Were simply columns of exhaustion and hate in what we call human form. Not regular columns. Uneven. Straggling. Halting. Halfseeing. Half believing. But altogether exhausted and altogether hating and altogether selfpitying. But I wont die. Ill survive. They wont even put me in a position to be slaughtered. Im going to get out, one way or another. Because were decimated, Rena, decimated. You dont know. Ivan says so. He writes me from the 41st Armored Infantry Regiment, writes me when Im in East St Louis undergoing the first stage of flight training. He writes me Im a lucky sonofabitch. In the North Africa invasion Company C loses fifty men. Up the Italian boot they lose fifty more. The regiment is decimated. The division is splintered. On the side of the road. Through the trees. In the ditches, Lee theres nobody left youd remember or know, only me, you dont know how lucky you are and I dont blame you. Oh shit shit shit BLAME ME if you want. Call me a fucking coward. Sure I am. Even the courage I show is for the purpose of cowardice, survival, call it what you want, call it even the white P on my back. I must survive. Ill get out of it any way I can. Special Service is no good. Good christ Rena theyre calling everybody from the airfields, all over the midwest for the Battle of the Bulge, every day theyre taking more from the Garden City Army Airfield. Ive got to write a letter. They need me here. Im in a special Airforce outfit, they call it Ground Safety, I make reports of accidents involving aircraft and personnel and air force machines on the ground, in the shops and hangars, Im a Goddamn sergeant, I write the head of Ground Safety at Randolph Field, no, wait, thatd be stupid, I write my friend the sergeant, the attache of the major in charge of ground safety and I make no bones of the matter. I write him theyre taking us all to throw in the garbage heap of the Battle of the Bulge, I write him fchrisake do something I got a wife Rena, cant he transfer me fuhchrissake, quick

    quick

    quick

    maybe tomorrow theyll take me

    Im hysterical

    Im in a panic in our little farmhouse apartment in Garden City TRANSFER ME FOR GODSSAKE IM HONEST I DONT WANT TO BE SHIFTED INTO COMBAT

Im scared
I
dont
want
to
lose
my
life
   you dont know what youre talking about if you think im lying. All
Im lying on is a chill macadam road. Its midnight. Weve slogged twenty
miles. We eat. I dont know what Im eating, Chassid. Maybe its the State.
The State supplies my food. His honeycolored beard is still in the evening stillness. No air, no wind. Something rubbery and greasy and hot
and cold and solid and gelatinous and slimy and charcoaled and liquid
on my plate and I drag the stuff into my slackmouth sitting on the side
of the road, the pines above me, the tips of glow in the dark, all voices
basso, faint rumbles, I dont need to take a shit, its all hard in my bowel
or caked at the entrance of the asshole, its all sweat I cant tell the difference, Chassid, Ive no idea where Israel is, no idea of six million Jews in
the crematoriums, I dont care, put six million more in, Kill them all, kill
them and the Nazis and the Fascists and the Americans and the French
and the British kill the whole human race I dont care. I wonder if you
understand that. Harry Ring does. But I want to kill him too. He doesnt
register for the draft and gets away with it, or he lies, or maybe he says
hes got diabetes, hes too sick underneath to serve the Army of the United
States so kill him too, wretched, wretched, wretched under the Georgia
pines, itching in the groin, they try a salicylate on my fungus of the groin,
it works sometimes, the heat of the day cools off sometimes, I dont chew,
the food goes down in lumps, with a shrug, my body is a shrug
   maybe the macadam roadll be cooler
   its prisoner white in the moonlight
   its better than the earth
   its straighter
   it straightens out my wrinkled lumpy body
   my throat open at the neck
   my body
   in a sweet

small
arch
over the moonlight of the macadam road, sweet pines, no trainwhistle, no regrets, no army, no glowing cigarettes, I just dont
have
to
do
any
thing
nobody tells me
no sound
no order
no kiss
sleep

sleep is the condition of the State on the long low Mediterranean
swell of the Georgia macadam road, Chassid. The condition of the State is
the attrition of the abnormal, the slow wearing down of the position that
there may be the notknow, from which we think we may never recover
the conscious, but that is a peril of the individual that the State would
seek to annihilate, there must be no precious danger of the individual if
the mass is subjected to danger; relieved of a specific uncertainty, we are
permitted the public uncertainty; as you proceed to your State of Israel,
so do I proceed to a unit of men in which the State would have me believe
as a minuscule state, the smaller fully representative of the larger, that I in
this responsibility to the smaller absolve any responsibility of the Larger
to the microscopic; whatever the makebelieve of this condition, the gas-
masks are slung by one's side, and are finally forsaken by the side of the
road in that the actual human faces are finally similar, and at last undif-
ferentiable, as Victor Nathanson's from Bruno Canova's, though the one
is thin and the other fat, each is drained through the other, as I perhaps
drain one State through another, unable in hate and in fear to tell any
apart and in the prospect of death gaining an omnipresent irresolution
for I do not in truth or in fantasy know vaguely or precisely what to say
to the decimations, to the men of the 41st Armored Infantry Regiment
who fall in North Africa, in the Italian boot, in the Battle of the Bulge, to
my own nephew Stephen, nineteen years of age, a whiff of smoke on the
deck of the destroyer struck by the kamikaze, Stephen Nathanson, son of

Helen and Victor,

whether theirs is a terror which cannot at last be named, the terror of the threat of dispossession by the State, the terror that they may not be mimics, the terror that they may not at last resemble each other in the common gesture toward the grave, that thus does my friend, thus my cousin, thus another American or German or Italian or Englishman, that we are not so various as to fail to be capable of agglutinating, this the final mortal chance before chance itself is removed, before the describable can no longer be called upon; describe me, sire, and I am a fool, or an ingrate, or a savage, or a buffoon, or a poltroon—or a supporter of a family, which in itself may be reckoned with, but if one is unmarried, if one has no sick mother or mad sister, one is the State's, under the premise that if the State fails to be defended collectively it will have to be fought for individual by individual, and that therefore the individual has a greater chance of survival if he subjects himself to an ordered mass, in consequence defense obtained by appeal to individual cowardice which may be engineered into collective heroism; therefore, if I do not fear my own death, I will rebel against the State; if I do not fear the death of many, I will rebel against the State; if I say, let every man, woman and child fight for himself, I am a rebel against the State; if I say that fewer men would murder each other if faced with the prospect of individual combatancy, I am an enemy of the State, I am a collective coward because I do not want the State to fight but rather each of its members, but wherein may this be related to Victor Nathanson and Bruno Canova who circle each other in the office of the Nathanson Moving & Storage Company, circling in the quiet savagery at pediatrician. Incredible! You may possess me. You may burn times of the men of the armies who have strange relics in their skulls of known intimacies far from where they are, not that the intimacies are either loved or hated but that they are intimacies, proofs, demonstrations of derivation and involvement with other men and women, to which one has some fealty, some debt, that one must pay oneself off somehow, that one must continue to be to them those intimate relics, otherwise there has been no birth, no naming, which is insupportable, one cannot live in an air of incredulity, one cannot doubt oneself constantly because this may attract other men and women constantly who would want to dispel that doubt and involve one even more deeply with others, so that, after all, the identification that one must return to is nothing more than the safety of but semiinvolvement, semirelationship, so that one at any given point could go ahead and make other relationships and alter former ones, which one cannot do if one believes one has no importance, no value, no identity, because certainly in such a condition someone would all the more fiercely and frantically claim you and you would be locked forever in one type of intimacy, in the profoundest kind of spirallingdown knowledge; and this, the State realizing full well, makes capital of, exalting the familial relationships, that they are conformations to return to because they are breakable, changeable; to utterly doubt oneself is to open oneself up to an unalterable link which Bruno Canova and Victor Nathanson must perforce deny, must, to commit what must be committed, but that I, Lee Emanuel, in my own world of proliferating doubt upon doubt, was not necessarily subject to. I do not love; I feel some sexual tenderness. I do not really hate—I feel an extravagant selfpity and fear; I do not really become angry but feel magnificently murderous—and will not kill; I feel the spirallingdown and up of astonishment that I am where I am, do what I do. Astonishment: that is something which is the foundation for the deepest involvement. I am the man who must laugh at the fact that I am with anyone at all; I am the man who must scream within myself that I live either by myself or with anyone at all; I am the man whose mind gapes at the fact that I am here, with my mother and father, with Rena, with Sy, with Harry Ring, with Saul Reed the me with your lust to prove you are connected to me, I will shrivel in agony. Either it is the astonishment or the absolute indifference, that defense against astonishment, the ultimate defense, the complete absence of feeling except that which informs you you operate in a body. But at any time the astonishment may burst open, and I am not Lee Emanuel, I tell you I have no name, I tell you I have not been born, I tell you I know nothing about death—I can tell you only that I fornicate, eat, shit, feel terror—but that that could be anyone walking down the street, ascending a stairway, interviewing a prospective employee, compassionating a beggar—I ask you: who does not feel all these things? Is this a distinctive personality? a precisely differentiated human being? who can possess at times the faculty of total recall and in other hours remember only a jumble. I submit myself to you, as Victor Nathanson submits himself to Bruno Canova.

RACHEL EMANUEL ANNOUNCES: MY CORNS AND BUNIONS ARE HURTING ME: THERELL BE A CHANGE IN THE WEATHER attesting hereinunder to a type of love Rena Emanuel bears Lee Emanuel because hereinunder on the 24th day of December the first day of their arrival in Fort Worth Texas they are invited to Dallas by old Philadelphia friends of the Goldstein family for a Christmas Party at a select house on a sinuous outskirt of Dallas drive hereinunder at said house Lee Emanuel in acute discomfort from previous removals from Garden City Kansas to Altus Oklahoma and at last to Fort Worth Texas as a sergeant in the army of the United States, hereinunder buck sergeant, three stripes, Sergeant Emanuel as he is known, further drained of essential energy by the quality of the company in the outskirts of Dallas abode, old Philadelphia friends of the Goldsteins' as aforementioned, become firmly affluent by reason of having transfered the commonplace practices of cutrate Philadelphia drugstore houses to the conservative trading abided by in Texas, taking the Texans as it is said unawares and hereinunder establishing a temporary monopoly Im tellin ya they dont know nothin theyre naive were cleanin up as long as itll last by that time well make a fortune, hereinunder try a bourbon Lee, sample a vodka, now hereinunder you take three jiggers of rye, the rooms of said abode hereinunder as it is common practice in Texas to utilize the vast resources of natural gas heated unit by unit by small gasheaters flush with the wall hereinunder, including the oblong with the toilet facilities toward which Sergeant Emanuel makes his dreary way, said abode resounding with the shouts and giggles of Jews in their preChristmas celebration of cutrate prices and the expeditious movement of accumulated stock, all old Philadelphians hereinunder, Rena herself in scarlet attire flushed with ambulatory spirit and prancing hips, the tall lean buck sergeant a little stooped and in something of a maze from the glaring gasheaters in each room and down the corridor and the rye and the gin and the vodka and the bourbon liquids of Christ about to be reborn upon the earth, hereinunder bestoops himself into the lavatory and therein proceeds to unbutton his olive drab trousers

at altus oklahoma army airfield sergeant emanuel assigned to the message center is directed to keep posted and uptodate the volume of army directives issuing in countless and endless number from the Pentagon, alterations, deletions, additions, alternatives, cancellations in the room next to the mail room where an Oklahoma girl perhaps sixteen years of age and a bonafide native constantly distracts the seageant's alterations cancellations deletions alternatives additions by alternately snagning snot from her nostrils and doubtless due to the Oklahoma heat frankly scratching at her crotch with an entirely ingenuous expression upon her olive complexion and jetblack hair as she sorts the mail

which drops in uneven quoits about his ankles as he squats upon the toiletseat a completed horseshoe hereinunder and therefore a false one and perhaps more akin to an english saddle but nevertheless cool to the ass not that the buck sergeant must defecate hereinunder but simply to enjoy the quietude of the Nathanson outhouse where he may permit a urinary trickle every now and then simply to hear the gurgle of the perch and the trout hereinunder but not wishing any longer for his mother to call him back to the farmhouse nor wishing to play with the drunken Charlotte nor to listen to the quartertone moaning of idiot Gus Nathanson without observing that the sun has gone down and the flaring lights are out and that there is simply hereinunder the gentle sassing of the winds through the thick undergrowth and the branches of the trees and the susurration under his eyelids why in preChrist's name there should be that pounding of the surf in the distance and the cry of the ants hacking off the surf from the sweet cool polished wood of his dozing he cannot understand, the nickel sheen of the faucets in dulling lustre hereinunder and under and under all he wants is for somebody to light his cigarette dangling between forefinger and third which he shouldve lit himself but the enamel washbowl darkens in the distance and a grin topples off from his lower lip and hangs from his chin but the pounding goes on and on and on

LEE

all right

LEE ARE YOU IN THERE LEE

sure im here fuh preChrissake

LEE CAN YOU HEAR ME ITS RENA RENA RENA

listen to my wife the cheerleader

LEE YOUVE BEEN IN THERE AN AWFUL LONG TIME

awri awri preJesus im pulling up my pants now

there it is. Up with pants. Roll on the socks. Button the shirt. Comb the hair. Comb the breastbone, clean out the navel, look yourself in the eye, in the mouth, under the armpit hereinunder, arrange yourself, he could see the population of the world all at once

PUTTING ITS BEST CLUBFOOT FORWARD

SMEARING VASELINE ON ITS COLLECTIVE HARELIP

IS THERE CAKED BROWN ON MY UNDERPANTS AH WEAR IT THE SEC-
OND DAY WEAR IT THE THIRD DAY WHOSE GONNA LOOK IN THE CREASE

is Buddha gonna look in the crease?

Moses gonna look?

the President of the United States gonna inspect

hereinunder sergeant emanuel unlocks the door and a semihysterical Rena blurts in The gas is out Lee the gas is out couldnt you see the gas is out.

Stupidly he peers at the gasheater, grins with a onesided gape, peers at the cigarette still dangling from his hand

Thank god you didnt light the cigarette, Lee, she half laughs, gurgles, whimpers, her head crawling over his shoulder

Yeh

I missed you, she says softly. You were gone an awfully long time. You always do take such an awful long time in the bathroom but this time you took even longer and I got scared you couldve

Yeh

You couldve

Yeh

But you

Yeh

Are you all right, Rena says, her black lashes so black as to seem like paint perfecting hazel eyes and the swart flesh and the brasscolored hair, the hair the color of rotten oranges, as preJesus preJesus the fullness of the girl, the sloping bosoms of the girl, the five feet eight and a half inches of her, the eleven years of the girl and the woman a channel through his bone and a flak through his synapses till flesh go fuzz on the firmament and the bowel be a beetle on the turds at the TajMahal IN THE WEATHER CHANGES

At once, under the louring cloud

The point is, sure, Bruno, my oldest son is an idiot

But hes not handsome, Harry Ring turns to Rena, Lee greeting the two at the Fort Worth depot. He looks like a man. Hes not pretty at all. A mensch. You dont have to worry about a thing, he assures Lee, well plan the whole thing out. You spent four years in the army, right? Thats enough for any man. Its time they should let you go. To hell with them sending you to Guam. Aint the war over? No Germany, no Japan. So to hell with the Army. You got a perfect right to get out. Harry Ring will figure a way. Thats why I took this Goddamn trip all the way from New York. This is Texas, heh? They can shove it. Jesus what a crosscountry trip. Hot all the way, phew, a curse, an inhuman world, look at my white ducks I started out with, black, the soot, couldnt keep the fuckin trainwindows closed, who wanted to? Thinshouldered, nohipped, cragfaced Harry Ring. Look at his eyes, he whips at Rena. Lee's eyes. You think he isnt seeing a thing. He dont think hes seeing a thing. But the eyes are taking in everything. Hes got eyes all over his body, heh Lee? Eyes back of the eyes yet. Everything is put down, the hint of a nuance, my dirty white ducks, We were three seats apart most of the way, he tells Lee with a canny quirk on his mouth, it was that crowded. Harry laughs abruptly, uproariously, everybody in the depot turns to look. Look, everybody, he yells, Im a civilian in dirty white ducks and sneakers, theres no more war. Youd think there used to be a war, he tacks on, in a hoarse whisper, to Lee. War is for people, I dont qualify. Monkeylike he legs his walk through the depot. First thing I gotta wash up. Renall tell you, in my east Thirteenth Street apartment I got a shower rigged up, the toilets the cleanest room in the house, I take a shower once a day, I got to be clean. Dont worry where Ill sleep, Ill flop on the couch—you gotta couch, heh? I wont disturb you, you dont like to be disturbed, heh? he sneaks it across to Lee, Lee to crack, not now, not after her mother Esther in Atlantic Rena focused on Lee, she worried and smiling, she doesnt want Lee to crack, not now, not after her mother Esther in Atlantic City with the first heartattack, Rena wheeling her every day from the room her brother Nate engages at his expense, wheeling her to the boardwalk and having to keep her mother down in the wheelchair, she wants to get up and walk the following day, Im all right, I cant stand being in a wheelchair, I have to be active even if I die her highpitched giggling speech under the faint hairiness on the upper lip, the black hair mounted in tootsierolls on her head, the magnificent black hair with the ruddy glints and the red sashes of her lips under the ticklesome black eyes, I dont want to be wheeled around, N-n-n-now m-m-m-mom, Nate says, you g-g-got to d-d-do what the d-d-doctor says

  Its the last hill, the platoon sergeant says, cherrycheeked and little black popeyes and neatly nurtured mustache and bluetinted freshlyshaven

skin, to the fifteen men as the dawn bluetinted and freshlyshaven lami-
nates and builds up under the dark in South Carolina. The last hill, then
its all downgrade to Rocky River. Take five and then were going over. The
Blues are on the other side. The mssion is to cross the river swimming
with full fieldpack and rifle without enemy detection. Its a shallow river
most of the way, but theres a good ten yards deep channel and a fast current. Good luck.

good luck Lee, Tess Rubens

gee from the first moment I laid eyes on him when he walked into the
Walnut Street art gallery I never got such a charge there I was sitting at
the desk and Lee walks in and I thought it couldnt be true and then when
he opened his mouth I thought it was impossible

good luck Lee, Tess stretches her arm forth from the blue convertible
in the 34th Street Station, Pennsylvania Railroad, trains west, trains east,
I never had a lover with such biceps, theyve all had thin biceps, even Bill
Sachs with the black turtleneck sweaters, nonobjective biceps she plummets her cheeks into dimples, and he was such a serious young man playing Vivaldi by the hour

good luck Lee, Tess honeysuckles the dimples into the dusk, into her
valentine face with the titian striations through the deeper red.

Was it what Rena told you

Oh I guess, partly anyway, Lee, gee I cried and cried and cried that
night after she told me I didn't want to have anything more to do with
you, but it wasnt Rena altogether, the dimples straying to her eye comers,
the ponderous columns of the GraecoRoman depot grimming in the dor-
mant dusk, the ironrumped dimgreen subwaysurface trolleys on Market
Street to the west of the depot grinding out of the Schuylkill River tunnel, the blob of jellyfish light cycloping their convex muzzles, I guess its
mainly the guy supporting me and my boy, he IS responsible for all my
furniture you know, though I guess I can admit I wasnt going to see him
anymore at one point, Lee, because of what happened at a party we both
went to, the psychoanalyst we both went to was there too and can you
imagine what he said to the analyst right there in front of me Lee, Tess
titianstriated in all her available innocence in the convertible, the valentine dimples overarching her eyebrows, sweetening the long green eyes

No

Well right in front of the analyst he says to the analyst you tell her doctor you tell her Im all right enough for her to marry me, Tess littlegirls her mouth in the dumbing dusk, the parked cars the dusklight tripping over their gleaming surfaces, the GraecoRoman 34th Street postoffice on the opposite side of Market Street write me write me not write me write me not write me shes cuckoo shes cuckoo not shes cuckoo shes the subwaysurface trolley urging the rod through which it receives its motivating current from the dull copper overhead wire against the wire its roller sizzling against the wire the pale copper sparks flitting through the air to the cobblestones, Tess copperhair, the valentine received through the dusk, will you be my, will you not be my cuckootine right in front of me he says that Tess Rubens squeals at Lee holding his briefcase with the toothbrush the shavingcream the manuscript the dialog, the calftones as well in Tess hair, the green eyes circling her head horizontally and vertically, the corneas marining all over her head in the dusk fishbowl Jennifer I told you the copperfish would finally emerge from the skull and swim all around it whilst dropping their white granulations from their anuses, pasting Tess's flesh, white as sugar, the fishes lapping at the sugar, Tess sucklemouth bubbling all over her face and I told Edith Parker in Stanleys Cafeteria after Id picked her up from her cashier's job at the 45th St and Broadway moviehouse PRESIDENT TRUMAN JERKING AROUND THE NY TIMES SIGN RECALLS MACARTHUR DUGOUT DOUG THE BASTARD WITH ALL THE PHILIPPINE PLANTATIONS I met somebody in Philadelphia I fell violently in love with in love with

in love with

the burgeoning hips

the teats very interesting teats the kind with the recessed nipples Tess gravely informs me when manipulated they can be lazarused from their retractions and sure enough up they came

up

up

the nipples from under the water of Rocky River oh dont look so close Lee Id rather you wouldnt see my varicose veins Tess says, you musnt, sssh, now just you wait, you must be so impatient, just let me put out the light, I dont want to take a chance of my son suddenly coming in after all hes only five and a half

LUCK

in love with

well right then and there I very nearly left him what RIGHT did he have to say that to our analyst of course he was drunk

and I was tight

and the analyst was loaded

and I didnt think the analyst was being very ETHICAL do you? because the analyst said oh very gravely yes I would say hes ready to marry you Tess

can you iMAGine?

I remember what your son said in the restaurant, Lee shifts his brief-case.

Those biceps, I never had a lover who good LUCK

As you sipped the dry martini you said mummy I love you

in love with

I love you very much mummy but you DRINK too much

gushing rose over her sugarwhite skin, Tess says, Children, why you never, but I just cant leave him Lee, you understand dont you? I just cant and I might as well tell you he gave me an ultimatum and I guess he was in the right I dont know it just seemed so, you know? because he paid for the furniture and he pays half the rent on the apartment and its HIS convertible and he heard about you Lee and he just told me it had to be either or and youre just too much like Bill Sachs oh I know your biceps are ever so much more bigger but youre like Bill in so many ways and youve been having trouble lately and its just been the third week of the affair and ONLY on weekends you can hardly get any words out of me at all but I just thought at least this you ought to know, the worried valen-tine recessedly copper floats in the convertibles front seat, the hand on the gearshift, and wed just repeat what you and Rena and besides, Lee, oh Lee, besides, besides, I just cant let him go, he just couldnt do without me, you just dont know what kind of past hes had, its just too awful to talk about, I just cant tell you who he is, hes awfully talented hes an inte-rior decorator, oh not just THAT, hes a CONSULTANT, Lee, yes, who do you think DESIGNED my apartment, Tess turns the ignition on, hes just too pathetic for words, you dont know, his mother, Lee, its his mother, youve no idea what KIND of mother he has why when he was fourteen years old just FOURTEEN Lee, thats all he was, she used to, Tess swallows, blushing her valentine, undulating the titian striations, the dusk deep in the green airfoils whirring around her face, the creamy dimpled waters, his mother

would masturbate him
    whisper
    yes
    whisper
    masturbate him and then THEN when hed
    whisper
    yes
    whisper
    when hed . . . .
. . . come, shed SLAP his face in
    RAGE CAN YOU IMAGINE?
    good luck Lee
    Laura Ingersoll waves holding the bollowing blue convertible down over her knees as the briefcase departs to the GraecoRoman temple you go back now, you wait for the New York express, you hear the announcement in the boomlooming spaces, you take the escalator down to the trainlevel, you go back now, the sea waving to the departing swimmer, the undulating foam of light receding into the dusk, many things are over, how many times may things be over. Ah, but the biceps. The big biceps. Tess runs her motion over the biceps. Comments on them. Praises them, the first lover with. The biceps fill his brain, bulge in the sea, he goes back with lauded muscle, the advertisement to himself, sold unto himself by three weekends with Tess Rubens, the reward the swelling in his upper arms, the contracted disease of himself, the transient virus of the ego infecting him, scratched into him by a red fingernail, five bulging barnacles on his upper arm drawing the blood of pride to the surface and disguising the toothbrush in his briefcase, the shavingcream, the manuscript, so that he must roll his shirtsleeves up further on his arm practically to the shoulder, his biceps falling shoulderlength like a girl's pageboy haircut, he shakes his head, the biceptresses trolling his entire body, he flings back his flesh to reveal the disease as he brings back his weary swimmer father to the shore titled:
    THE RESCUE OF THE BICEP
pumping bicepbreath into the lungs of the Tesschoice drowned on the other side of Market Street at the postoffice, theres nothing you can do for her
    father

nothing at all

shes quite dead. Yes. Oh, certainly, theres a masturbated gentleman in the picture whos trying to masturbate some life into her, but its no use. That will never resuscitate her. He simply has no biceps in his onanism. No power. Thats one corpse hell never decorate the interior of. Because a fiveandahalfyearold boys its only resident, and hes slapping his mother's insides in a rage each time she raises a bicep. Slaps her down dead, mummy I love you but you masturbate too much. Take that

and that

and that

sperm streaming in tears down his innocent face

arent you ashamed to be alive. Take that

and that

and that

no use

shes quite dead. Her analyst and her paramour keep vigil, thinking that perhaps the child may be delivered by a psychoanalytic caesarian. But theyre barking up the wrong fallopian: the tubes are tied up in an alcoholic afterlife rage. The analyst puts the coffin on his couch: just indulge in free dissociation he tells Tess but the boy slaps her vagina each time it opens its mouth. The boy cups his hands in the tube and yells out at the analyst, I dont wanna come out, I just dont wanna. The analyst places some sugared trauma at the mouth as a bait but the kid wont bite. I prefer my masturbated serenity he calls out haughtily. The paramour persuades his mother to enter the tube, telling her, At least this much you owe me. Perhaps you can entice the child to come forth. But his mother is caught midway in the tube and now cannot move in either direction. She dies too. The sacrifice is in vain as the little boy holds his hand over the mouth of the paramour's mother:

MURDER IN THE UTERUS

the newspapers blare. Mother's supreme sacrifice the subhead reads. Could a mother do more for her son than to expire in the vagina of her son's mistress? Lee boards the New York vaginal express, good

luck

cuckoo shes cuckoo not

Violet snow softens the steaming black iron railroad tracks along Federal Street. The raised lettering of Nathanson Moving And Storage

Company wears violettufted shoulders. That failure among the locomotive hierarchy, the freight engine, the tugboat on wheels, hudgehudgehudges along the steaming violet iron tracks past the amputated sidings, dwarfing the little woodenposted houses with their green and white boxes at the windows of denuded plants on which a violet petal pauses, melting at its catch, the violet moisture trickling down stem and branch. The gray cheeks of the Federal Street cobblestones through which the brown bare earth where in a later spring grass conducts an isolated wag can be seen, tilt violet scales that run down the gray of Victor Nathanson's face inside the office and touch up his temple gray, as if the pinched man wears an ancient cosmetic and will have a boy at all costs before he makes his way to the symposium in the same office with the globular dwarf Bruno Canova

Might say Im a kinda agent, Bruno plucks at his chin hairs. All I get outa this is ten percent. Now that aint askin much of a man.

Lena Cherny, Vic peppers his features with scales of smile, his flesh overloaded with cosmetic: violet gives way to green, green is undermined by yellow, yellow taken by burnt umber on the narrow gardenspade of a face, the lean gardenspade of a body, the childspades of fingers scratching at the inventories on his desk, the long crackle of a nose sniffing at his son Gus quartertoning on the stool near the safe

But I wish youda left the kid home, Vic. I can make myself comfortable in all kindsa situations, but I wish youda

Hes my ten percent, Vic says. But he dont know anything. Hes fourteen but he knows less than he did when he was six. He gets worse and worse, he apologizes softly. He dont know what youre saying, do you, Gus?

not, shes cuckoo, shes. There are violet pockmarks at either corner of the mouth.

Large pools of pocks concave Vic's flesh. When he shows his teeth they are pale yellow narrow gardenspades digging up the pale pink gums, completely disgusting to Bruno, bored in the violet light of the snow, his stillness churning in the plump boredom, this must be his last effort, for he is bored with the series of resistances to his panacea. True, the resistances are overcome; true, he is gratified by the sudden affluences of the men and women he has helped though they show him no sign of gratitude: the event itself must for him be their act of gratitude. But the act for him is a touch insufficient: they do not bless him. This begins to rankle somewhat. He can understand that for purposes of security in the face of the police authorities they would tend to sever contact with him once he receives his percentage. But certainly among themselves they could very well form some sort of organization of the assisted. Naturally, it would on the face of it have to be nameless. But they must know that he would nevertheless be aware. But they do nothing. As if they are dismayed by the one act of daring they are able to summon up from themselves by reason of his intervention. As if that single stroke of daring burns the rest of their lives away. How can they be so ungrateful as not to bless him for destroying their previous histories of doubt and vacillation and hopelessness and helplessness? For he shows them that the victim need not forever be a victim. He shows them that if the social fabric is insufficiently tough to reduce their misery at privation and want and anonymity and anxiety they can then therefore tear it at their will—not by long years of collective effort toward a Fascist or Nazi or Communist goal but by a piece of individual ruthlessness which takes advantage of the very advantage which eats away at them: it is the American way of working within the democratic system itself, Im a good American Bruno contends, Im loyal, Im a good naturalized citizen, Im somebody for the history books, because if a guy pays forty, fortyfive bucks every three months on his insurance his whole life why shouldnt he get the whole ten thousand or twenty thousand or thirty or whatever the hell hes got on his own Goddamn life, heh? Why should somebody else get a hold of it especially maybe when he needs the whole ten thousand or twenty or thirty or whatever the hell it is to make his life comfortable so it aint a spittoon for somebody else, so he dont hafta worry for the maybe ten or twenty years comin too quick outa his bowels. Whatsa matter with you Vic? Sure, a guy cant make hisself a stiff. He cant even pay on his own insurance these times, so it lapses, dont it? All ya get is what ya paid into it, some lousy piece a change, heh? So ya twist it a little. Every solutions gotta twist to it, every big deals gotta twist, the only way ya can get ahead is with a little twist, am I right? Who kept up Lena Cherny's insurance? Who makes ya go broke keepin it up? Your wife, huh? The wife thats the beneficiary. Lena Cherny dies your wife gonna keep all the money? Heh, Vic? Shes gonna split it with ya, because didnt you pay inta it? Shes got a conscience, believe me, Vic. So outa her conscience you pay me the percentage. Ten percent is after all a very modest return for infusing a man with the courage to commit a marvelously daring act. But what is it that has none of them bless him? It must have something to do with a loss of memory. As if in the commission of murder everything which precedes the act is obliterated. It is impossible for them even to see the humor of the chemical agent which is invariably utilized and which proves so invariably effective, the humor of course involved in the fact that each of Bruno Canova's disciples accepts the suggestion of arsenic. An arsenic ring, an arsenic brotherhood: Bruno Canova, though he would be the first to deny it, implants a mysterious collective effort in a segment of the bankrupt middle class in South Philadelphia. But the obliteration of the memory of all that has gone before in the life of each murderer and murderess—this he does not bargain for. That they remember murder and murder only begins to annoy him. They cannot remember they have been in want. They cannot remember their financial misery. They cannot remember they have lost their jobs, that they stood in breadlines, that they saw their savings wiped out: all their memory consists of is an act of murder, as if that act of absolute removal removed not only the life in question but their own past lives, as if in the murdering of another individual they committed suicide. Disgusting. Victor Nathanson is his last case. It isnt that Canova needs the ten percent. He needed it in none of the cases but he does require it as a signature. For if those he has helped do not love him, they will hate him, and in the engendering of either emotion is a possession. He is at the least, at the very least, ten percent of the commission of murder. But none of them love him, and he is as much bored with the lack of gratitude as he is with its monotony—which he did not count on. A certain amount of hate, yes; but there should be some love. Not one case responds with love. As he barrows his stubby portliness past the rows upon rows of twostorey red brick houses in South Philadelphia, the men and the women on the concaved marble steps and the wooden porches begin to whisper fearfully about Bruno Canova. And Bruno Canova is above a whisper. Bruno Canova is a man who likes to be out in the open. The enormous act of his compassion requires the clandestine but he would like everyone to know and to reveal it in a shout. If people must whisper about him, then he must prefer to remain unknown, he must quit, for it is right that man either be shouted about or utterly unknown; it is womanly that a man be whispered about, referred to as some little horror of a bogey, used to threaten erring children with—he is not born a man so as to frighten children. Therefore, either he must confess to his ten percent murderousness or cease to be the helping angel. But, he considers, if he confesses to his tenpercent involvement then that must inevitably be misinterpreted; he knows he will be named a monstrous kind of coward, a man who seduced others to murder but who himself never once committed murder directly. They will not admit that the seduction is the prime murder itself. They will name him an accomplice. They will not award him total credit— they will give him only ten percent. And Bruno Canova does not believe he can tolerate such ignominy. It is profoundly unjust and he believes wholly in justice: Is there not justice in the fact that Lena Cherny is an ailing human being? Not once does Canova choose a person in the best of health; he has rejected pleas for planning the murder of perfectly healthy individuals. It is only those whom he adjudges already want death he lawfully takes under advisement. Helen Nathanson's mother is admissible to the charmed circle touched by Bruno Canova the bachelor. Admissible for other reasons as well. The choice is dictated by certain stipulations, not only that the victim be incurably ill according to Canova but that he be either the mother or the father of a man or woman in a married relationship; also, the married couple must have one or more children. The ten percent that he exacts as his signature he remits to his own revered mother and father in Milan, not to help them financially, which they do not need since they themselves are quite comfortably fixed, but as a dutiful son's transferal of the signature which, once he enjoys in possession for a brief interval, he feels they should permanently have as a token of his connection to them while insisting they remain exactly where they are— in Milan: the ten percent he sends them is enough for them to have of Bruno Canova, quite enough of their son, for them to know that he is altogether independent of them while nevertheless paying them his tenpercent recognition that they are his origin which he recognizes is their due the moment his first victim commits a murder, so that in his own mind he feels that while the ten percent he sends his parents is a long overdue announcement that he is alive and well in America, it is at the same time a partial destruction through those murdered of himself in his parents' eyes, a destruction in the making out in himself of a debt to his parents to whom he has never felt indebted, a matter which is intolerable; but the debt must not be clean: it must be stained, and stained without his parents realizing it, a supreme satisfaction, the more so in its utter silence, for which his parents would be the first to congratulate him had they the mental dimensions to appreciate it, which he knew they did not, so that murder once removed is one method for punishing them for their limitations, their simple belief that life is best furthered by more life, by the nine brothers and sisters, in fact, of Bruno Canova the bachelor, Youre gonna be the twentieth in the ring, he at last announces with open brutality to Victor Nathanson. My twentieth, he says, an Im done.

Im not so sure, Vic says, abstracted in the coarse crinkly brown hair growing low over Gus's forehead shes cuckoo shes cuckoo not shes

my mother talked to you more than to anyone Ive ever brought around Tess complains in wonder, She likes you

Thats an interesting layout shes got on Delancey Street

Colonial. She likes Colonial

the leaves of blue shadow low over the forehead of the lamplights radiance on the thicklythwarting snow

My feet are getting all wet Tess squeals

Youll live Lee says. Colonial. A spinningwheel, British chinaware, 18th Century hurricane lamps

My father divorced her a few years ago Tess says flatly my feet are getting all wet do something do something do something shes cuckoo shes cuckoo not in Philadelphia you can hear the freighttrains hudge hudge hudging the gaslight low over Gus's violet eyes. Daddy you ought to kill her. Theres Stevie on the deck near the depth charges and Gus is a kamikaze pilot in a clear violet world, the hudge hudge hudge of the engines behind him. Bruno Canova is a bulging propeller in front of him, the little globulars whirling and whirling shes cuckoo shes cuckoo not. Im going toward my head, you never knew that, did you, Daddy? Violet snow descends in parasols over the field behind the Lansdale Pike because the head is the place to hit at the same time you strike out with it because Charlotte bounces a violet balloon in front of me and thats something I can hold on to and fall with as I fly, Im flying toward Stevie, hes my brother, hes a little boy and hes starting to shoot at me but if only hed shoot with the depthcharges but he wont there he goes

there he goes

to the machineguns

hes going to try to murder his own brother

if I close my eyes, daddy, I can see violet streaks. Flak under my eye-lids, Im a United States of America Destroyer PLUNGING through the briny seas, escalatoring up and down the waters

hold me tight mommy

on the monorail of the mind

down

something whites coming up as we go down theres only one thing to do with old Mrs Lena Cherny daddy and thats to kill her just like Bruno violet Canova says. Ill tell you why. Because she looks like cuckoo mommy, Helen Nathanson it says on some violet letters. Gee I dont care its not so much she LOOKS like her but that Mrs Cherny is OLDER, now you cant let that be. Mommys not supposed to get older because IM not supposed to get older. You said so. Charlotte said so. Stevie said so. Mommy said so. So you gotta kill MY mother's mother. Gramma, oh yes you do, youd bet-ter, because I want to sing about it up and down the scale how the big old lady takes her tea and she drinks it and she falls down dead because SHE wants my purple balloon. Charlotte promised it to ME. I want it. Look at Stevie, hes another reason, because hes shooting machinegun bullets at my purple balloon but Bruno Canova the fat little propeller HE wont stop HES on MY side so he keeps turning around and around straight toward my brother. Look, daddy. Hudgehudgehudge, thats how I feel late at night when the heart is a purple balloon, just like yours, daddy, and theres no use hanging on to that, is there? because it floats down to all those gray cobblestones from the stool by the safe in daddy's Nathanson Moving And Storage Company. Moving and storage. Oh my, daddy. You know you dont believe in moving and storage, thats whats discouraging you so much, and Charlotte because shes so blond and she doesnt look Jewish because shes so white and tall in the moving and storage hudgehudge-hudge Im a freighttrain moving along gray tracks and the snow is melting low over my eyes and my breath is just like when the lamplighter lights the streetlamps gwasHOOL my breath goes on and there I am hissing and hissing and hissing wissing everyboydy and girl go, im sure sorry for you because you know I gotta have the purple balloon of the heart

because once I didnt get it Charlotte took it away when I moved to it and youve got to give it to me now

youve got to be a daddy. Youve got to stained up and if theres anything thats storage youve got to stirage it in the gluz tay grampop uzed to sigh with prizzon. Im your risen for mereder. Youve got to crawl along the floor on your hinds and nose and sirch for signyor bellyoon. Im your dumbson, DROP it. Charlotte held out a purple balloon. Hold out your goaway for me, mothers cuckoo, Charlotte shall unsister me, Stevie nonbrother dumbgus. Dumbgus waves his arms, go, go, go, I wish thee not, thourt allstranged, mama makes me scour the floor, mamma errands me hire and thyer, im but a bucketthing, balloonflatted as I sing, go murder, go kill, alls seperable, severalable, make descissions, daddy, do. Hudge hudge hudge I am a hudgeback if any must know along my graytrack and I am melting violet snow on cobblestone hearts. Thourt faint, thourt no sock o the walk, thourt graynosetipped, I felt thee not in Helen, sire, no never, thou wert a daub upon her, and therein was I disenchanted, conceived by crook no hook

I am a crything, daddy. Charlottes out. Stevies done. Helens an escalator on grampop's thing. He left you naught because he wished not, he had not known who in the pale conceived thee. Not him, surely. His wife, yes, but what hed to do there with a shiftless fuck? Then kamikaze the crinkled dame, for thoult be guiltless, no money yours for the purple balloon will float above the prison walls beyond Aunt Rachel one morning, on a vine of vain, abstracted in the crinkly grayblond hair of his father's triangular head

When I was a kid in Milan I liked the guy with the balloons, specially the violet ones, Bruno says.

Eh? Vic is startled. But murder.

It aint murder when ya prick a balloon.

Vic's fingers jaggle, chip away at the desk, the freight engine hudging, the violet snow parasoling, Gus crouching on his lips on the stool near the iron safe. Theres nothing in the safe, Vic says. He snorts. Thats why I protect it with my idiot son

Ah ya shouldnt talk about him that

He dont know nothing. Some safe he is, no valuables in him.

Ya shouldnt talk that way about human life even if hes a dummy.

Suppose shes in pain.

Nah. Little by little ya do it. No pain, Vic.

I mean she dont have to know the pain. But inside her little things know it

I dont know about little things, Vic.

You should, Bruno. The little things get the pain, not the stuff behind the eyes, behind the ears, under the headhair. The pains in the bellybutton, under the armpit, and its a jealous pain because it wont say anything to the brain. What do you do about that, Bruno?

They get all doped up. Nothin inside knows anything. Jesus what a Vic Nathanson, a little Jewmouse. The office windows coated with violet steam, violet hudgehudgehudge. Bruno rolls over on his violet balloons to the window and draws a little fat man in the steam. Like in a turkish bath, he says to Vic. Like a turkish bath? I love em. Jesus I love em. Three times a week I go. Steams everything outa ya. Before ya start with the arsenic, take a turkish bath. Each time you slip it into her drink, take a turkish bath. Its easier that way. Youre all tired out before ya start the killin so you dont feel anything either, all ya feel is clean, Vic, got it? You gotta get real clean before ya kill, okay? Violet beads droplet on Vic's forehead. One droplet is his sister Rachel, nobody else knows him, not his wife, not his daughter, not his son. Only Rachel. Stevies nowhere, a baby. Babygurgle, daddy littlething, no report. Vic has no sensation of growth. Any time. Any year. Not since childhood. As soon as he begins to work with father Joshua Nathanson he has no sense of growth. Well what do you think, he sniggers at Gus, shall I do it to your grandmother Cherny?

You shouldnt oughta ask him. Bruno suddenly turns accusingly at Vic.

Why not ask my own son?

Its a sin to ask a dummy. They could talk back. And what a dummy says is like God.

Gods a dummy?

Sure, He cant talk, he dont know no language. Its a risk to ask somethin from God

Thats only Gus

Only only—you dont know what he is. He could surprise ya, he could strike ya dead

Whats dead? Eh, Bruno? Charlottelee, whats grampop, she wouldnt believe

I dont know. All I know whats dead maybe ya get money from, Vic. Thats dead, see? The loot. Ya pick a corpse's pockets. Whats the Cherny use it for anyhow? Doctorsbills? Shes givin the stuff away as it is. Be a doctor. Im a healer, myself, a tenpercent daddys little helper

Itll be my only act of daring, Vic says.

But that isnt fair to the rest of my life. Thats not what I am, Vic says. Its not true. I got to be fair to myself. Im no criminal, no, Im not, ah, no, there it is, though, right there. Yes. No criminal. If the violet balloon of the heart floats above the prison walls after Im indicted, therell be no trial

You aint gonna be indicted. Who says theyre gonna find out.

Suppose they do?

So my violet balloon couldnt take it. Id have an attack. Id die before judgment.

Nobodys gonna find out

How do you know?

You want somebody to find out?

Maybe.

But what about me, Bruno Canova? They find out about you, they do the same about me.

You afraid to take a chance? Vic crows at him. You dont want to go through with it now?

I didnt say that.

I know about me. I couldnt be judged. You they might judge. You afraid of judgment?

No.

I knew I couldnt be a criminal, Bruno. Ill kill her.

No. Ta hell with it. Let it go.

No, well go through with it.

I changed my mind, Vic

I dont think so. You change your mind and Ill go straight to the police.

With what kinda story?

With Gus's story. With my son's story. Hes here.

He dont know nothin. He didnt understand.

You take a chance, Bruno. Vic goes to the window and draws a thin man in the violet steam. Ill take a turkish bath first, he says. Its all right to murder if you wont be judged. I mean for me, he pats Bruno on the shoulder. I dont talk for anybody else. I got no right. And maybe nobodyll find me out. But if I thought they wouldnt, I wouldnt go through with it, because there should at least be an indictment. At least suspect me. Nobodys ever suspected me of anything. Im clean before a turkish bath, he laughs. He wipes out his drawing on the window. I can see right through myself at any time. Because Im not constructed. You got any idea what it means not to be constructed, Bruno?

No

I never felt I had a framework. No bones, just skin. My sister tried to make feel like I had bones but thats because I looked like a man to her and I was older. She always felt more toward me than to anybody except to her husband Levi. Not to her children at all. Little by little I got to be her child. Shell forgive me because Im her child. She always wanted to make with a big forgiveness toward somebody she loved: such a person ought to commit a crime—for her. If her sons did, she wouldnt forgive them because she doesnt love them. Im it. This is for Rachel. I commit murder for her so she can retire from the world. Thats what she wants to do anyhow. Why should I deprive her of that? Shes a Jew but she wanted to be a Christian so she could be a nun. When she was a kid she used to envy the nuns. I know why. She wanted to hide herself because she looked like such a woman even as a kid, with her big tits and big hips. Shell get her wish now. A Jewish nun. Thats pretty funny. I can laugh. She wont. Shell become my bride, shell think back to her youth that she told me about nunhood and Ill be her shrine at which shell make vows. I know her. Shell be all in black when she visits me, already withdrawn from the world. Her big brother hath decreed it, she will say to herself. Shes all Ill have, shell think. Im deserted by wife, sons, daughter. But not by Rachel. Im her cross, the Jew hath a cross, did you ever think that, Bruno? Did you ever think that what the Jew wants more than anything else in the world is a cross? If only some nonJew would come along and be crucified, the Jews would flock to him and call him their saviour, eh Danny? Look at all the money you could make as the Armenian Christ

Do you hate your uncle?

He wasnt tried. He wasnt declared innocent or guilty. The compromising sonofabitch

Rena,

Yes?

What do you do?

Slaglight drifts through the burlap drape over Harry Ring's eastside apartment, Lee sits sweatless in a low easychair I want to go through with it

Rena says I wont have any trouble

I know you wont but I want to hear it, Harry laughs. Come on. A couple children I got, he slaps his knees. Rena apologizes all over her face, a smile here, a smile there, the slaglight stopping short at her complexion's own lowkey creamlight

Well I make a phonecall to army headquarters in Manhattan and I tell them Im very worried. Theyll ask me what Im worried about and Ill tell them its about my husband hes here on furlough visiting a friend of ours in New York.

Lee giggles.

Giggle, giggle, Harry says. Good for you. Get all the giggles out. But Im not saying if you feel like giggling when theyre here you shouldnt. Every bit of truth helps. Giggle then if you like. It helps with the illusion. You understand, Lee?

Yes

Then what, Rena?

Then theyll ask me whats making me so concerned and Ill tell them he keeps repeating over and over he isnt going anywhere anymore and he keeps sitting in that chair over there just where he is now and he wont move.

And what do you say, Lee?

Only that Im not going anywhere anymore, Im just not going

What do you feel like doing while youre saying that?

I feel I wont want to look at them.

Then dont, dont look at them. And dont say anymore than the simple insistence that you dont want to go anywhere. If they have any questions of any kind, you answer you just dont want to go anywhere. Never get complicated, it can trip you up. A simple phrase will do, you understand?

Yes

Rena, make the call. You frightened?

No.

Lee, you frightened?

Yes.

Good. Keep feeling that way. The truth always helps. Make the call

Gus has violet hair as he climbs the last steep ridge before Rocky River. My name is Gus Nathanson, he keeps repeating to himself, Army

Serial Number 32866709

Do you know your serial number, Sergeant Nathanson? The drifting slaglight piles a soft transparent dune in front of his lowered face. He sees torsos of officers uniforms

32866, 32866

Is that all you can remember?

Thats all I can remember

Do you remember where youre supposed to go after your furlough ends

Im just not going to go anywhere, I dont feel like going anywhere, I just feel too tired and Im not going anywhere, his voice keeping low, patient, reasonable, sane, as if patting a child's head, Im not going anywhere, I just am not going to go anywhere else, Ive moved enough

Its all right, sergeant, the officer looks down on the stretched head-lowered man in the low easychair, the slaglight from the burlapped window in a dune before the man as his face slidesdown facedown on the dune

Im just not going to

You wont have to, Sergeant Emanuel

My name is Sergeant Nathanson and Im not going anywhere I absolutely refuse. You see you can do anything you like to me, you can put me in prison or you can kill me if you like you can do anything you like to me, sir, sir, sir, but Im not going to move anywhere at all in this world anymore because

very quiet, the slaglight filtering down through his voice

Im so very tired

You wont have to go anywhere at all, sergeant, we just want you to come with us

But Im not going to move anywhere

I promise you

the officer without the face has a mellowkind voice, a voice with the slaglight in it, burlapped and filtered as Rena looks worriedly at the little group chewing on her fingernails

Will he be all right Doctor

I wouldnt worry if I were you Mrs Emanuel

My name is Sergeant Gus Nathanson

Yes of course and you wont have to go anywhere if you just come with

us, well take you to a place and you wont have to move after that I promise
you

You really do promise me? Gus's voice is ingenuous, guileless, trust-
ing, he looks up a feather of an instant that as immediately comes floating
down once again upon the slaglight dune

Yes. Whose place is this Mrs Emanuel

A very good friend of ours. Harry Ring

I see

Do you want me to come along with him?

No, that wont be necessary

This is something I must do. I must keep repeating I wont go anywhere. I musnt look up at anyone. Just keep looking down at my feet,
the worst part will be going through the hallway and then outside on the
street I can feel the people looking at me as I go into the ambulance. They
stare curiously at me. Im doing something to the people that I dont like. I
cant name what Im doing. In a sense I think maybe Im frightening them
in an odd way because my head is down, the kids looking up from the
gutters, those are the violet faces that I can really see, theres no escaping
the children, men I can look at halfway but not at kids because the only
way I can avoid children is my shutting my eyes and I just wont be led
blind across the sidewalk into the ambulance the people say nothing and
the kids dont say anything I just hear the faraway noises of Manhattan
the traffic I feel the height of the great buildings

an orangepeel

a red toy whistle

a green celery stalk

shoes

the kids' faces rolling a toy truck. The point is, Will the walls of the
people crumble and will they pile in on me? That Im really terrified of.
Im escaping through the channel made between the people, the avenue through the red sea but I dont feel like a fleeing Jew at all, just a
fleeing human without racial tie, without name and they dont say anything. How will it be when I return here? Will they recognize me? They
probably wont. Theyll forget. So all of my feeling here is insignificant
and this is exactly what they may be silently accusing me of, what right
have I to be insignificant to them. Theyve seen me before, seen me come
and go in a perfectly normal way and now I dont tally with their mem-

ory which was fairly significant. They see me helpless, being led, being propped up, a man in an army uniform, and somehow they understand in their griefless happyless way that what they saw of me is no longer to be seen, their comment is a pause in the business of whatever theyre doing whereas before when they saw me they never paused, I was part of their movement, choiceless, not determining. But now theres a choice and they pause to witness it whether they know my choice or not. But the fact that its a choice is its insignificance because they must know that in choice is the insignificant—and this halts them, to ask of themselves what manner of man is this who makes some kind of decision, how small he is even though he is tall, look how he shambles, see how he sags in the shoulders because he chooses between one thing and another, because he will not go to Guam if the many go, or to the moon if the many go, or yet to the grave if many go, yes, heres a person who would choose life rather than death, an incredibly insignificant man who goes alone. Let me pass through quickly into the ambulance, one of the noncoms says you wanna smoke, yes, Gusll take a smoke, but he cant look up, he musnt, it would shatter him to look in a man's face so that, rocking in his rocker up the last height before Rocky River he sees only the back of the man ahead of him, the violet light of the early morning, petrifyingly hot, knowing his cousin Lee Emanuel is in the van of the platoon, up ahead, probably already making the descent toward the river with the Japanese plane overhead still a distant pinpoint, suicide takes a while to descend while Vic waits for the opportunity to slip the poison into Lena Cherny's tea, the fullfield pack and M1 Garand smarting into Vic's left shoulder, rubbing it raw, the sweetsmelling pinetrees descending the ridge with veils about them, Aunt Rachel shouldnt be visiting me Harry did you make sure my father wont come and visit me wherever Im put yes I made sure I told him to keep away you dont want to see either of your parents Lee no Doctor MacFarland I dont want to see my father or my mother if you bring them here I wont go out to see them I absolutely refuse I just dont want to go anywhere anymore I just dont want to shes cuckoo shes cuckoo not shes no nobody I havent done anything I dont know anything about Lena Cherny being poisoned I just dont want to go anywhere anymore Moyamensing prison a quiet cold place iron bars and steel mesh its a padded cell on Moyamensing Island

I have violet hair and the ridge is all quartertones and eighth tones and sixteenth. I suppose the dawn can be like that. The dawn is the moan of a siren. Lee doesnt hurt me, he takes out my sister. Aunt Rachel has a violet veil, she doesnt want to be recognized. Her sisterhood friends might ask her wheres she going. But, then, nobody knows that. That flat violet icefloes along the Raritan River in New Jersey are in the best of us, and the odor of gasoline in the cold. There is the peculiar sensation of ascending the last ridge in a car, the red warninglights of the autos ahead in my mind, red on violet. Its true Im cold in the heat. Its true Lena Cherny is a miserable creature. What did grampa Nathanson leave me? Nobody mentions any money. Theres a discussion in the Roosevelt Boulevard living room about Uncle Aaron, downright outrageous and unfair Levi thinks, Uncle Aaron left ten thousand dollars insurance and were going to divide it among all his brothers and sisters, but only Ben and me spent money on him, by rights we should each have five thousand apiece and let the rest of the family go hang, we spent a helluva lot more than ten thousand on him. But what about me, Lee accuses in his mind, didnt Grampa Nathanson or gramma leave me any money, wasnt I supposed to get two thousand dollars but Im afraid to ask, it sounds awful to be demanding money of the dead was that all I was interested in having from them and how do I have the right of asking it at all from my father whos been supporting me after graduation from high school and has spent far more than two thousand on me, but nevertheless I feel if she left it to me then its mine but how do I say it with any conviction and I wont accuse Bruno Canova of putting murder in my mind, why should a nonJew have any credit at all when the fullfield pack is so heavy and my heart is so light, light as a violet balloon, Lee dont become oversweated its the worst thing in the world for you you can catch your death of cold Lee look where youre going watch both sides of the street look right and left

right and left

but Rachel is the traffic right and left, violetveiled Rachel running up and down the ridge in the pines, the mother is the exclusive traffic

trudging up the ridge, Lee far down in front, makes Gus feel like an idiot. He could use Uncle Aaron's removal from reality, he could use the ten thousand dollars he left for some independence from his father, he would have to ask Levi for anything

Vic is certainly happy that hes out in the air at last in the morning among the pines of North Carolina, reminding him of the Pennsylvania countryland, Lansdale, running down the cowpath through the pasture to the little outhouse on the pond where he can be by himself, away from his idiot son, his lustful wife, his domineering father, his clinging sister, his gentile-appearing daughter that Charlotte

Well Doctor MacFarland thats pretty horrible isnt it

Just how do you mean that?

Well my niece, thats my brother Dave's daughter, I was babysitting her one bright sunny afternoon and I was at least fifteen at the time and I guess Fay was no more than two and I just couldnt resist it I just couldnt

What was it that you

I was exploring her. I wanted to. I wanted to see how shed react. It gave me a thrill to do it. I put my finger under her diaper at the entrance to the vagina and I massaged it, oh, I assure you it was just for a moment, just for a moment doctor not more I swear it wasnt more and she liked it she liked it a twoyearold cuckoo shes cuckoo not cuckoo shes

This isnt going to hurt, sergeant, and itll give you a long rest, itll just be a sort of pinprick

My whole body is rocking. Up the ridge. Legs up front. Ive got to get to him. The pale violet pine trees smell of Rachel's lavender sachet she keeps in her upstairs chifferobe, everything kept behind the trees that a son unlocks and explores little by little, a vagina here, a vagina there, Rena I may never see you again, my mouth might be locked up in my mother's chiffonier. The kamikazes nearer. I can all but see the pilot. My own cousin, I thought he was up ahead in the platoon. Look, mother, Id like to tell you what Vics going to do, but if I did, why, then he might not die. If I tell you hes poisoning your mother, youll stop him and I dont want you to. Besides Im not supposed to—youve made me an idiot and I wont violate that. Im a reactionary, Im not radical, I do what Im supposed to. Idiots are very orthodox. They join the army like everybody else. They dont rebel, Rena. All of us, were divided into two compartments so that if one is flooded the other one can be made airtight and will keep us afloat. One compartment is the idiot, the other the great intelligence. My grandfather drinks a great deal of tea. Now I know, now I know

Victor Nathanson poisoned Joshua Nathanson. He didnt need Bruno Canova at all. What a joke on Bruno. Yes, thats how Joshua died, heart-failure by way of arsenic, so Vic had to kill Lena Cherny, he had to be susceptible to Bruno, he had to atone for the first murder by committing a second. Certainly he mustve been aware of Helen and Joshua. But to kill his father didnt require courage, no, no. That was a terribly orthodox act, prescribed in all the civilized manuals—son must kill father and kill him doubly, doubly if father hath carnal knowledge of son's wife. Ah, of course. Orthodox. Then, overcome with the orthodoxy of his act, the very mechanicalness of the matter, its inexorability, he must atone for his mechanistics, he must turn tables on his automatism, he must expiate his lack of courage. Yes, courage wasnt in the action at all. The cowardice of his mechanistics is overwhelming. He must show himself he is capable of sheer guts in the violet icy afternoon, the freightengines hudgehudgehudging on the slategray rails, and Bruno Canova names the one he will dispose of. Canova the namer, the baptizer, the christener, nothing more, a mere tool in Vic's hands, the more so since Bruno is totally ignorant of the matter. A tool is always ignorant. Thank you, Bruno, I mightve overlooked myself. The poison for Lena Cherny, indeed. My wife's mother. Perfect. My wife wont visit me in prison. Neither will my gentile daughter. Nor my baby son Stevie. Certainly not my idiot son. Illve cursed the whole family and wont be tried for it but will die out of one compartment, the balloon hearts, the deficiency. While, you see, the guts of me will not have failed. My digestion will remain perfect, my feces will emerge imperturbably, I will die out of my weakness and not out of my courage, die under indictment, never brought to trial. I will show myself I can murder out of sheer radicalism, not out of reactionary behavior patterns. Bravo Victor Nathanson! You are a great soul! And what greater revenge upon one's idiot son than to tell him the whole story but its a long climb, uncle, and I want to stop. I want to lay down. I cant make it. Ill have to drop out. Fifteen miles through thicket and bramble, over a hundred hills, the sweat caked inside my nostrils, Lee a blur up front and a blur in the sky, where the fucks Ivan that Goddamn stubby curtnosed little American, the little russianbackgrounded steelworker from Pittsburg, carrying his heavy little steel ingots in his pants, I didnt take a shit before we started and I shouldve, its an ingot of steel in my bowels, how many loads are there in this fatuous existence, the worst the load in your ass

the worst the load in your ass EE

Jesus

my bunion hurts therell be a change in

EEE

219

Not Lee. They keep Lee in the padded cell one day and one night and then release him into the Governors Island psychoward, windowbarred, true, but unpadded, six white beds on one side, six white beds on the other, each occupied.

But at night a redfaced soldierboy is brought in straightjacketed, unconscious. The psycho prisoners are uneasy. Lees got the bed next to the padded cell where the unconscious man is locked, Doctor MacFarland, gray, lean, crinklehaired, supervising, late of Merrills Marauders, Indonesia, the Burma Road, dysentery and malaria, the rank of a Major in the Medical Corps, psychiatrist and son of a minister, a fashionable civilian practice on Long Island, My father taught me Hebrew as well as Greek, Im partial to the Old Testament he tells Lee, youll be all right as soon as youre released from the Army, youll have to stay with him Mrs Emanuel after hes released he tells Rena privately, Im much more rapt by the vinegar and thunder of the old Hebrew prophets than the milkiness of the New Testament, I think you can go into town any time you like now, simply report here every morning and youre free the rest of the day, Ive made out your discharge papers, itll be a matter of about two months incredible incredible incredible

Doctor MacFarland, is incredible, But theres one thing I must ask of you Lee once youre discharged, it will be better for you if you dont try to reach me later on. I want you to forget this as soon as you can. I want you to forget me. Youve got a wonderful wife, gray, lean, crinklehaired, Major MacFarland, dysentery and malaria, the Burma Road, Indonesia, late of Merrills Marauders, my fathers a minister

supervising EEE. Not Lee three in the morning the redfaced soldierboy vet EEEEEEEEEEEEEE in the padded cell. The psycho prisoners sit up in their beds, Lee next to the padded cell, he might break loose, Im the one nearest to him, hell go for me, hell kill

kill

kill

MacFarland comes. Not running. Quickstepped through the double-barred psycho door, the nuts on either side of the ward sitting forward in their beds, Lee's hands gripping corners, terrified of the insane who do not recognize the sane. Never. Its not their policy. Because: the sane have sold out, have become hypocrites, have made adjustments. We hate the sane: they move here and there, they accept external conflict as a balance to internal conflict. Not so with us. Never. Nothings external. Alls inside, where we can keep it, watch it, guard it, roost over it, lock it up. We possess ourselves to the very limit. Not so the sane: they do makeshift with the world and satisfy themselves with outside possessions. Thats simple, easy. The trick is to make a circle over oneself. The trick is to persuade yourself that you are singled out, that nobody else is around; and, if they are around, they serve only the purpose of singling you out. Man is single. Not alone. The insane is never a lonely man. He is the collective cellular group with the Master in perfect control, the master being the one who is mad, because all the other cells would like to break bread with other cellular collections; theyre weak, insecure—but the Master whiphands them, forces them to be content with His recognition. Ah, you see, then. Madness is the recognition of oneself par excellence, therefore, I, redfaced soldierboy, awaking from the dope theyve shot thru me, I, I am very angry because theyve tried to stop me from recognizing myself. The doctor comes in warily but without fear. I like him, I respect his courage, but I cant let him know this and hell never know how much I love him I love him I love him want to fall all over him and eat him and ingest him and digest him and make him one with me. But. Instead. To the absolute control, the utter selfmastery. Theres the plane, overhead. The German divebomber. What the fucks it doing on Times Square? How dare it? This is America, my native land, my. Nobody else is bothered. Thats the sane for you, never ruffled by strange appearances—thats a German divebomber over your heads. I should get to the foreign newsstand where 7th is confluent with Broadway. The newsstand might understand, theyve got German papers. But I cant move. I musnt move. If I did I might not bring attention to myself so I must choose to stand my ground like any good insane man must. Its diving, the sabres of wings foiling in the sun, down, down, Ive got to stop it, Ive got to scream for attention, the people have got to hear, so: I crouch on the hard sidewalk. I crouch, curve down my head and raise my right arm and make a sign of a V with the two fingers of my right hand

VEEEEEEEEEEEEEEEEEEEEEEEEEEEEEEEEEEEEEEEE

Goddamn.

Lee halts, the scar on his right little finger pumping up his whole hand, MacFarland nowhere to be seen, the sonofabitch is in Burma shuddering with malaria. Lees here, not in combat, this is simply a problem in summer maneuvers, before North Africa, in America, North Carolina, thick with Rachelpines, the ground violet under the early morning light, violet on green, the top of the ridge resilient with pine needles. The psychoward prisoners will be standing on the bank, somewhere a redfaced soldierboy.

VEEEEEEEEEEEEEEEEE

Its a woman's scream. For the second time. Twist a lip. Couldnt be Rachel at the Moyamensing celldoor. Lot of plays to be written, dialog, plot. Shit. The worst the load in your ass, he wishes he couldve gone to the toilet but then Rena would come, shout for him, startle him out of his dying lethargy, his mother call from the farmhouse

EEEEEEEEE

That prick of a captain. Volunteer swimmers. One day of swimming exercises at a lake, men swimming by using their arms only, not enough time to learn the coordination of arms and legs. Fifteen men, volunteers, chosen. You, you, you and you, the captain wants fifteen volunteers, the old Army game. Theres a joke somewhere. Low comedy. Put it in burlesque as the stripper comes out. Audience roars. Yeh, thats the way it was in the Army, yoho and a hardiharhar

Ludicrous. Somebodys got to stop Lee. Somebodys got to make it out that by the time he races to the riverbank all the action will have been finished and that his presence will be entirely superfluous. All the times hes running hes superfluous, the mother superfluous racing by his side. Gus will have accomplished all the necessaries by the time he reaches the bank. Uncle Aaron will stop him. Uncle Victor will recover, Lee wont have to kill Vic and settle that matter once and for all, it doesnt concern you, Lee, youre only fourteen years of age, Rachel says whatever you read in the paper its all lies.

So that running downhill is a lie. No point in it. He doesnt believe it, he doesnt know who else will. Why is he alone? Is it that he is cursed by being the only sane man in the group of fifteen? He, Lee, must single out someone else, because Lee isnt in control. Theres a kamikaze after him and a German divebomber. Theres his father after him, and Rachel telling him her bunion hurts and that there will be a change in the weather. But not the violet hot summer morning. The suns like his mother's orangewhitehot iron over the laundry, gliding through the pines, making stripes, making prisoners and searing somebody in the water, sizzling him sure enough in Rocky River, gliding orangewhite hot over the redface of somebody in the water and making the soldierboy scream like a woman with all the psychos, all fourteen of them, standing on the riverbank, uneasy, while Doctor MacFarland races to the rescue ah, ah, eeee, eeee, that does it, now Lee knows the joke, now hes privy to it as he tears through the brambles and the clutching undergrowth, tearing down through the cowpath to the pond, running from death only to come upon it in the little outhouse, it all fits, dammit, it all fits because the load in his ass bursts asunder, MacFarland the sonofabitch infects him with humanitarian dysentery, its too much, the shit is flowing out of his anus, the world is crazyloose, the loony sticks his V toward the orangewhite motheriron in the heavens coming down to sear the face of the bulgeeyed soldierboy in the water

It isnt fair. This isnt the day of the examination. The test is going to be delayed. Olney High School schedules the examinations for next week, next year, next century for preChrist's sake. Lee can take the bus into the center of Philadelphia. He can hum the morning theme of Beethoven's Sixth Symphony. After the storm, that is. Triumphal. So. Whats with the running? Wheres the excuse? He hasnt planned on it. And yet the opportunitys here. The prick of a Captain wont let Lee take the airforce examinations, hes sitting on the application, Lee is scheduled to go with the rest of the regiment to North Africa, to be decimated, killed, Lee cant get out of the regiment, cant escape into the airforce, hes locked in, his rifles rusty, if and when he gets to North Africa the Goddamn weaponll jam and hell be out of his life before he can fart Tetragrammaton. But this is a helluva of an exchange, a lousy screw of a gamble. He knows what the situation is. Some poor fuck of a volunteer swimmer, one stocky bastard of a redfaced soldierboy is out there in the water, in the racing channel, twentyfive yards wide, struggling for his Goddamn redfaced life in his fullfield pack and army brogans and M1 Garand and bayonet and gasmask on his back and the poor sonofabitch is trying to swim across and he cant and hes screaming because after a fifteen mile hike through the heat of the North Carolina night hes sweated and hes weary to the tip of his colon and the stupid platoon sergeant gives the fifteen a fiveminute break

a lousy five minute break because boys thats all the time youll have in regular combat so start across now

now

now

and the poor redfaced joe in the lead gets to the middle of the channel and develops a cramp and the guy right behind him develops a cramp and the guy behind him in the swirling racing crystalmuddied waters hes got a hard load of shit in his ass that wont burst asunder and together with the fullfield pack and rifle and army boots he sinks right the hell down in the water and drowns its as simple as that, drowns.

Water stuffs his mouth. Water stuffs his throat. Water stuffs his lungs. Water stuffs his belly. Water goes round the hard mound of shit in his ass and stuffs his balls and forces its way into his thighs and his calves and his army boots and drags him down

and down

and down

till hes dead of water

but the guy ahead of him. The redfaced boy with the wife and two kids God bless us it reads like a manual of American family patriotism because yes you guessed it the army awards the soldiers medals to his wife not to Lee

the guy ahead of him slobbers in the water at the sun and man he screams EEEEEEEEEEEEEEE

Its Lees chance. If there are heroics from Lee the captain wont be able to sit on the airforce application, sitting because Lee went AWOL during wartime, the major offense. The captain will be forced to recommend Lee for the exam. That is, if Lees alive to take it. Its a ripe and consummate choice that confronts the young man. Not that a choice is being made. One must hesitate to describe it as thus. The young mans running. No choice. Hes running down the riverbank. After the first pause he runs. Theres no question in his body at all that run he must—and down to the bank. He does that before he thinks of the airforce application, before he thinks of getting out of the armored regiment. On the other hand the choice to run may have been made on a cowpath in Lansdale. Because Gus is rocking in Lee's swinghead. Because Uncle Aaron sees Jehovah in the clouds and its certainly true that something is angry with Lee. Laura Ingersoll is angry with him because hes leaving Provincetown on the morning bus. Jennifer Hazlitts angry with him because she finds out shes a boy in a White Tower hamburger joint. Gia Antonelli is angry with him because he cant get an erection. Tess Rubens is angry with him because shes discovered how hes acted with Rena. Renas angry with him for his hysterical letters to her. His fathers angry with him because he wont learn the Levi Coal Company business. His mothers angry with him because he masturbates and writes plays when hes supposed to be studying his highschool assignments. The highschool debating coach is angry with him because he insulted the judges in a debate with South Philly High. His cousin Russel Zions angry with him because he wont exert discipline and mangled a speech before the Young Mens Hebrew Association. His brother Dave is angry with him because Rachel insists Lee be taken with him when he goes to Wildwood with the semipro ballclub. Nina Tarassoff, Sy's first wife, is angry with him because of a maligning letter he wrote about her to Danny Naroyan. And his commanding officers angry with him because he went AWOL. Not to mention Edith Parker whos angry with him because he says he loves Tess Rubens. Not to mention Esther, Solomon and Nate Goldstein, Rena's mother, father and oldest brother, respectively, who are angry with Lee for not having married Rena and having the intent of marrying her and having the doubt about marrying her and not having the doubt about marrying her. The question is, Lee thinks, who ISNT angry with me? Maybe thats the man or woman Ive got find and maybe the person is down there in the water, drowning; and if somebodys drowning who isnt angry at me, maybe I ought to try and rescue him.

So he runs.

So the cicatrices waxily undulant over Flikker's right shoulder and back under the sun, the Chassid stroking his honeywhite beard, they sit on the concrete coping at the side of the crowded swimmingpool in Riversdale. Flikker's current mistress and her snippynosed son are gamboling hippohipped and snaketesticled in the pool at which the boyfaced Flikker can only sneer. Flikker has it that he received his scartissue in the war when a grenade explodes at close quarters, at which Norma, Lee's second wife, scoffs, They look more to me like burns he got when he was a child. Lees preoccupied with the possibility of recantation

Formulations of power, at once,

changes;

the Chassid on the Mediterranean ship a piece of sculpture in the act of stroking a honeywhite beard, accepted by both Lee and Flikker, If only theyd all drown at once he snarls at the humans squirming, scuffling, scooting, scrabbling and screeching in the pool, diving silvergray from the springboard:

theyd be quiet. We need quiet

(hudge, hudge, hudge)

for these ultimatums to ourselves. Obviously, Flikker says, the small-globed Bruno Canova didnt switch Vic Nathanson one way or the other

Lee, do you play chess?

No.

You ought to learn it. Why dont you

I dont see the point of spending that much time over a game, Lee grins superiorly, unable to manage the truth, which is simply that if he is incapable of mastering a given game or a piece of knowledge at a single sitting he quits further attempt. If he cannot comprehend any piece of phenomena within a short period he dismisses it and tells himself that it is unimportant for his purposes, that he trusts the greatness of his mind to make choices of its own accord as to what should be assimilated and what should not. He cannot stand looking at the possibility that in a large number of phenomenal areas he may be quite obtuse, the word obtuse preferable to the word stupid—which nearly unseats his selfcontrol. He informs himself that his ineptitude at mathematics, categories of science and languages is a subconscious choice; that such might be ascribable to a deficiency in general intelligence is a possibility he cannot abide, just as he cannot possibly admit to himself that he might be other than a genius; if he does not possess genius he cannot see any point to his life at all; should he entertain the supposition of geniuslessness, he might seriously have to deliberate on suicide and that is absolutely out of the question—seriously, that is, for he can permit himself to toy with the idea of suicide when he is not paid all the attention he would like to have or when he is criticized in any way. He can never commit suicide: he is a genius. The matter is settled, once and for all: he thinks of himself as a playwright whose imagination belongs to the Shakespearian level and that one day the world will be astounded to discover, in all probability posthumously, that an American Jew operated dramaturgically and poetically on the Shakespearian plane. Therefore, what he does not understand is trivial. He does not have to understand, as a matter of fact, at all, because, as he puts it, he creates which should alter your idea of Stalin.

Under the coping, which forms a kind of bridge over the pool at one end about ninety feet in length and about two feet wide, the water seesaws and nuzzles a wall. As the late afternoon sun strikes the small crosscurrented waves made by the various thrusting angles of the bathers, shadows of the waves are cast upon the wall in a ceaselessly motile network, much as if a registration might be made on an oscillograph were it capable of testing a number of electrical devices simultaneously. A flickering scartissue. Brightlight guttering through the waves upon the wall. Each of the shadows is bounded by a lambent lariat of light, never coiling, ever uncoiling, bright thinlight spun through the shadows on the wall as if a network of light is being brought in from the water and mounted upon the wall, as if silently protesting children are being slithered in from the water in the late afternoon with brilliant scartissue on their backs. One could stare at the phenomenon endlessly. Lee could, were his belly automatically filled and his feces similarly disposed of. As the headlights of passing cars on the wall inside 236 East Roosevelt Boulevard, on which the conditions of power have negligible bearing, the white scar on the little finger of his right hand a matter of light through the shadow flesh, Flikker's mistress considering marriage to an icthyologist

Anthropologically the king and the shaman were themselves virtual prisoners of their subjects

And God? the Chassid formally interjects.

And Hitler. And Bruno Canova. Lee is dispirited. It is a matter of ineptitude at replacement. If Vic poisoned Joshua Nathanson not so much out of filial rebellion and automatism as he did out of the recognition that Joshua was nothing at all to rebel against, nothing to be rid of, that is to say if Vic felt he were getting rid of an entity that was in fact inoperable and incapable of being rebelled against, then he was doing so out of a sense of having been cheated, of discovering that nobody had ruled him, nobody had dictated to him. Possibly thats the most monstrous shock of all. Nobody, as a matter of fact, even cheating him. Helen dominates everyone. Joshua is autocratic toward everyone. Not toward Vic particularly. Theres nothing personal about their behavior; that Vic is within their orbit is a description of anyone at all in their orbit. With the same logic, then, Vic must murder Joshua. Or is this so? If it is so, Vic must murder any and all objects within his pale—and he doesnt. Vic personalizes, which must be the essence of the thing. He is as determined to personalize as his father and wife are determined toward impersonalization. Then his act of murder is a differentiation, and it can only be done extraordinarily in terms of unique objects. Vic, therefore, ascribes importance to objects and unimportance to himself, whereas the reverse, importance to Joshua and Helen and unimportance to their objects, is true of his father and wife.

Pop.

Well?

Toward the violet dusk of the nearsummer evening the western traffic along the Boulevard. Levi reclines on the violently floral upholstery of one of the orangecolored wickerchairs on the porch, a footstool under his legs, the pale aquamarine beams of passing headlights flaring through the descending violet. The porchwindows are open for the warm Sunday. The pavement outside is deserted in the dinner hour. A first firefly can be seen, blinking pale yellow. Rachel is in the back of the house preparing supper, always on the weekends cans of salmon, slices of scarlet lox, smoked whitefish, strawberries and sourcream, fresh red Jersey tomatoes and heaps of pale green and dark emerald lettuce. Pumpernickel and ryebread are being sliced, the coffee begins to gurgle in the percolator and its sweetlyburnt fragrance dabbles in the air. Outside the maples are cumbrous in their leafage. The brown shades as always are drawn down upon the windows separating the Emanuel porch from the Kasters next door. The geraniums and rubberplants on top of the kneehigh stone wall, in which the front windows are set between their jambs, relieve the stem white enameling upon the stone. The squarefaced ruddyfleshed Levi, his great biceps swelling out of his white linen shortsleeved shirt to support, as it seems to Lee, the thick ruddy neck, peers graciously from his Sunday Jewish Forward, its loathsome brown glossy rotogravure section, captioned both in Yiddish and English, spread on his chest and lap, at his skinny son standing on the stone step between the livingroom and the porch, leaning against the shiny metal weatherstripping calculated to make the livingroom heattight in the winter and thereby save on the fuel bill. No rings adorn Levi's fingers, thick and square as the rest of his hand, on the back of which thick blond hairs grow profusely. His widely-spaced graygreen eyes look on the boy with their usual candor, but sweetly, as sweetly as Lee hears him describe a few hours before the sounds of the New York Philharmonic broadcast from the speakers of their spindlelegged Majestic radio as Toscanini negotiates the slow movement of the Brahms First Symphony, the Sunday broadcasts which Levi himself introduces Lee to, urging him that afternoon to listen, that maybe he will like the music as much as and perhaps more than the saccharinities of Wayne King and the lamenting voice of Russ Columbo and the cacophony of Jimmy Lunceford. There is a difference in the sweetness of Wayne King and that of Brahms, Levi tells him; the former tends to induce slumber, Levi explains, whereas that of the romantic master makes one listen. The sight of the boy to Levi has much of the sweetness of Brahms; and as he is patient with the great classical and romantic music, so he is patient with the boy, a patience tried only when his son works of a Saturday in the coal company office, tried and hurt when his son cannot cope with the exigencies of marketplace trade, not that he feels the boy stupid but that he understands him resisting, shutting his mind, and this cannot do in the world of the marketplace

I wont be here forever, Lee.

I know, the boy all but whispers.

Someday your mother and father wont be here

I know.

So dont you think youve got to learn to take care of yourself?

Yes

You say yes, Lee, but do you know it? Do you know someday we wont be here to take care of you? Nobody likes to talk about, you think I like to?

No

I dont like to talk about it. The world is very sweet. As hard as it is, its very sweet, and nobody likes to leave it. You think I want to go?

Oh, pop, youre not for a long long time, youre so healthy, youre never sick, the worst you get is a headache once a year and you cant stand it. You never stay in bed when you have a cold once in two years

But one day I wont be here. You understand that?

Yes

So how do you expect youll take care of yourself if you cant even answer a phone right for an order?

Ill try again, pop.

You got to keep your mind on what youre doing, Lee.

I understand.

Nobody will take care of you like your mother and father. Nobody. Levi is momentarily vehement.

I understand.

For your sake I hope you do. Nobody has to make you nervous. Nobodys going to eat you.

I know.

I hope to God you do. I wont be able to leave you much. Dont count on it. Not you or David. David cost me a lot. I have to keep working. I cant retire. There isnt enough income. Youll get very little when I die. You remember Wolfson?

Yes

You remember how Wolfson would come to the office in his old suit and old shoes?

Yes

Wolfson died last week. While he lived he never gave his sons and daughter a penny. Not a penny. When they were old enough to work he threw them out of the house and told them to earn their own living. They did and they loved him, they would come to visit him with the greatest respect. He left them a fortune. I dont believe in that, Lee. I dont want you to work yet. I want you to enjoy yourself. But you got to learn too. You think Im wrong—Tell me if you think Im wrong, Im open to reason.

No youre not wrong.

So youll try not to get nervous, Lee?

Ill try.

Im not mean, am I ?

No

it will not do in the marketplace. If he yells at the boy he does so only because he cannot bear to see the child an inferior among the dolts and fools on the other side of the office's iron screen, among the officeworkers and the yardgang. He cannot bear to see the expression of confusion on his son's face. Who in God's name will take care of this confusion when he, Levi, is dead and gone? Why is the boy confused? Theres no reason, hes never even touched the boy, never at any point threatened him with physical violence, nor screamed sadistically at him, nor made veiled promises of punishment, never, never

David Ive given up

Lees exultant, proud

But youre different from David

And the boy is sorry for his brother, laughing at him and sad for him of Brahms. Your son is a genius, Danny Naroyan enthusiastically says to Mr Levi Emanuel

If he is not, and is deceiving himself, it will be almost as bad as if he really is, and who can say

Im an expert in knowing people, Danny blares at Levi, believe me, Mr Emanuel, the stubby blond young man thickly blares, his rimless spectacles stabbed by the light of the livingroom lamps

Youre an expert, Levi cannot restrain himself from a short burst of laughter

I know people. I just know people, Danny shrugs, its a gift, the bald-spot beginning to show through his crewcut. Listen, Mr Emanuel, Im part Jew, Danny giggles

Levi grins

I got to be part Jew to know people and look how I run a business. Who do you think is running the Naroyan Rug Company? I took your suggestion by the way, with the handbills. All over Logan I distributed them. Its increasing the business

Levi nods, satisfied

So dont worry, Danny nods sagely, sagaciously, sapiently, Your sons going to be a great man

Lee

Yes?

You heard of Sholem Alechem?

Lee nods, looking across the dark livingroom at his father under the yelloworange stage of the brocaded readinglamp. To its left is a wrought-iron floorlamp at the intersection of the diningroom with its great mahogany round table so rarely used and its enormous plateglass cir-cular protective covering which Lee and the colored girl, twice a year faithfully, slowly slide from the surface, lift, straining, and set on its edge on the floor so the girl can gently clean it with a soft damp cloth and, as Lee continues to hold its pale green balance, the girl then turns to the table's mahogany surface and dusts it off, after which Lee, grasping the plateglass at the floor, lifts and tilts while the girl steadies the other side and at last manages once again upon the great round clean mahogany table, staggering from the release of the load into the livingroom but not before he brushes by and nearly upsets the wroughtiron floorlamp in its lavalier style, teardrop glass pendants hanging by little wires from tiny holes in the florallyspurting iron curves, the pendants gently clashing tokaycolored from the readinglamp

Ive read Sholem Alechem.

I used to too, Levi admits sadly. Its good literature, but all I can read now is the paper and I fall asleep, its hard to concentrate

I understand

He was a great writer, Levi ponderously and portentously pronounces, a wonderful storyteller, but he died a pauper, Lee. He had to be buried from charity

I want to ask you a question

Brahms, especially the sweetness in the boy's large closeset blackbrown eyes, Rachel's, the first firefly slowly blinking more brightly in the darkening violet air, the lemon headlight beams of the cars when the porch is open and the boy's left ankles in a cast, the child ruminant over the traffic

his right little finger pumps

a suspicious ache in his left ankle

and it is not night

it is morning of the first day as the Bible reports of God

it is not night and yet the scene, the steep bank slipping toward the waters

and the face of God looked upon the waters

the fourteen men standing rigid at the riverbank

all: expands,

contracts,

expands,

contracts. Puffy and vast with lightheaded distance.

Nevertheless gigantically near, close, dominating, overbearing, the fourteen men, the river, the steep bank and Lee himself running down with the sensation of suffocation and at the same time the sense of incredible bouyancy

Go ahead.

Its about God, the boy says very seriously, a steepness racing through his blood, looking at the openthroated massive figure of his father on the

violently floral landscape of the orange wickerchair, the green of the geraniums savagely smelling under their armpits of chlorophyll, the burn-
sweet coffeesmell mixing with the green armpits, Lee's belly sliding like
pancakes on syrup, There goes Mrs Sherman wobbling on her high heels,
mom says she dyes her hair red, its frizzy enough, her diamond rings
glinting in the steepening violet twilight

Well?

Whatll I say to Rabbi Silver the boy condescends

Why should you have to say anything to him? The smile glides softly
around Levi's face, Lee proud of his father's perfectly straight Christian-
appearing nose, and his gentile graygreen eyes, he doesnt look like any
of the other Jewishlooking Jews in the Brith Mikveh congregation, hes
the only one who doesnt look Jewish but hes a Jew just the same and Im
proud he is and proud nobody can tell he is too

Well, Lee hesitates.

So?

Is there a God? Lee says feebly.

Do you believe theres a god, Levi heavily intones.

No I dont think there is anything like that, Lee says, quietly. Is there
one?

Well, Levi pauses, clasping his hands on his belly, smiling down on
his hands, I believe a man ought to think whats true. And whats true is
true. And I guess you can say God is a superstition a lot of people still
have to believe in

Do you believe in it?

No. The reply is direct and clear. Its a superstition. Its a foolish idea a
lot of people still have, and believe me Lee theyll always have it, because
most people are foolish, but you got to get along in the world, Lee, and
theres no sense telling people everything you believe and dont believe

Well why do you belong to the synagogue, pop?

For business reasons. But I dont expect you to tell that to Dr Silver.
You got to get along with people, Lee, thats the most important thing you
should believe in, so when Dr Silver talks about God you should agree
with him, and if the other children talk about God you shouldnt argue
with them. But there isnt any God. No

I shouldnt tell anybody, huh?

Thats right.

Lee grins, broadly, from projecting ear to ear, But Im sure glad you know there's no god, pop. My fathers an awfully intelligent man, Lee happily congratulates himself, Im glad I have a father who doesnt believe in God, and pop and me have a secret together

And you shouldnt discuss this with mother, either, Levi says, because she honestly believes and there are some things its hard to reason with her about

All right, pop. Its a triumph, the two males who secretly know theres no God on the Sunday twilight porch on the Roosevelt Boulevard, the first firefly brilliantly citrine against the black violet night, the ceaselessly traversing traffic white shearings in enameled light against black violet, and the mordant chlorophyll a whorl in the sweet butterburnt coffeesmell but impotent against the sudden vast hunger in Lee for the canned salmon, the scarlet lox, the smoked whitefish, the juice of the tomato already smearing his lips

Levi

Lee

Suppers ready

Boy am I hungry and, the kitchen already in his gullet, Lee races toward

Lee and Charlotte leaning over the bridgerail overlooking the continent of the freightyards near 34th and Woodland inset in the raised-arm amphitheatre of the black violet winter night. The freightyards are pincered by lavaliered banks and tiers and clusters of arclight, bluewhite sizzlewhite fat blisters crooked over the dead graylistening swans of rails in the crosstied greatlake, the blindlight roaring in boxed silence of light down which snowpocks in nightdots' feeblefall, the bodies of Charlotte and Lee in reversal, by which the dotlights of pocksnow tingle at their total disappearance in the violet black behind the rail toward the street, save the faces of the boy and the girl in the accident of surviving ornament decapitated by the arclight and propped on the bridgerail looking down upon the hudge hudge hudging of the freight engines on the backs of the immortally shining gray swans in their pale violet ague entangled in curved parallel and straightedged equidistances down and down in the boxed white depths, this buried continent signaled by an underwhited shuffling whistleshrunkshriek, a lanternman now and then leaning far out over the icelighted glacier, a figure in the corner of the map of the ancients, his whole body scrolled near the ornate embossing of the compass over which Charlottelee pours with a youngwhite face over the cavern of the undiscovered and the unknown with the naive pomp and callow circumstance of youth over the distant roll of boxcar and oiltanker in the tiny blinding commerce beneath, ICE NEVER FAILS, ICE NEVER FAILS a slim scarlet scroll over Strawberry Mansion

as, rolling, Lee's head rolls down the long embankment of Rocky River from the guardrail of a momentary still in his pale green fatigues, his green plastic helmetlining bouncing out of the steel helmet itself rutrested whence he comes, his rifle flung off when he reaches riveredge, his fullfield pack with bayonet snapped into the underbush, his heavy leather army brogans wrenched off with scissoring muscle and acid sweat. Twelve men stand mute and immobile at riveredge. The flat pale orange iron of the sun smooths out the shadowcreases along bank, river and sky, revealing primary blue and green in absolutely lucid candor, in solid conflagration without the one consuming the other. Twelve men their faces in lucid candor of jawjammed terror concentrate their coalesced fear on gangleLee in pale green fatigues, his black hair convict crewcut, his big jaw a ram of bone against his upperteeth, his small red ears tiny poppings from the skullsides, the two farcorners of his forehead gummy with glisten, the frownlines of rampant rage and rearing astonishment and bethicketed throethralls of thought and savoirfaired cynicism and erections of barricading sexual charm and cromlechs of bafflement in three encrusted lowlying deepscrabbling cougars upon the forehead's naked chickenpocked wall, the eyebrows thickly graceful over the faintly bulging black eyes, the black eyelashes hardened in long sabres over the squint toward the water, the straight broadbottomed nose a magnified reproduction of his mother's snorted at the nostril sack openings, all put upon the long nerveneck and the slim but now heavily fathermuscled body.

From the ceaseless SCREEEEEEEEEEEEEEEEEEE sireening from the riverchannel it is possible that the man in the water is cousin Gus.

It is possible that it is Uncle Aaron.

The sound is both mad and idiot.

It is a warning sound.

It is a raiding sound.

It is a noonwhistle sound.

It is a sound in quartertone and in the absence of mind.

It is a fiveoclock factory sound and a nineinthemoming factory sound. A sound summoning men toward it. A sound discharging men from it.

It is a sound which tells men to go underground.

It is a sound which tells men they can come to the surface.

It is a ceaseless, endless, interminable, unending, eternal, sempiternal, everlasting, durable, flawless, amaranthine, undying, unfading, sheer perfection, monumental, epic, heroic, neverending, everliving, unbreakable, irrefrangible sound.

It is a sound that in its unanswerability demands a throat around it.

It is possible that the throat around it is Nephew Stephen, a throat grabbing at the sound from the shambles of the destroyer deck in mid-Pacific struck by a kamikaze. It is possible that the throat around it is Sy Tarassoff's nephew in the English Channel, lost from sight as his B-24 sinks under the waves, shot down by a German fighter. It is also possible that the throat around the sireening scream is that of Lee Emanuel himself, in which case he must certainly contrive to encircle it with his fingers and stop the ceaseless, interminable, sempiternal, monumental, undying, perfect, unbreakable sound, the sound of a man gigantically hackscreaming away with a buzzsaw at his lost marbles of a michelangeloesque david, for

it is also possible that the throat around it is that of David Emanuel in some sunwhacked Texas town when a foul ball strikes him outside the firstbase line between his eyes in the bushleague game and everybody yells Clancy Mann deserved it the lousy fuckin ump, Clancy Mann the handle he goes by in the ball circuits

;and it may also be possible that it is the sound of Rena Emanuel in a stillborn childbirth at the Jewish Hospital in Philadelphia, but this is beyond Lee. And it is the sound which may be beyond him which is possibly the most powerful. It is the sound that is made in the water which is not heard. The catsound. The loweranimal sound. The insect and bacterial sound soundlessly evolving from a man's throat. The whimper of his

toe; of his

auricle; of his

tearduct; of his

earfuzz; of his

parasites in the small intestine; of his

fingernail; of his

wrist; of his

birthmark; of his

coccyx; of his

left lung; of his

inner thigh and his brainlining and his hairfollicles and his bellybutton and his

fungus in his ear, each whimper assembled into the congregational sireening scream. The sound as it is crawling

races; the sound as it is racing

crawls.

It is at last and in the beginning an unidentifiable sound. It must gain identity.

The twelve psychos on the riverbank repudiate the necessity of awarding the scream from the riverchannel any identity. The twelve psychos are whitefrocked in their terror, stand immobile and channel their fear at Lee. The pinkplumpfaced platoon sergeant is working with his fingers at his fingers, the sole gesture of any of the twelve. He makes no sound. The twelve are soundless. They have given up all their sound to that evolving from the channel of Rocky River in North Carolina, a sound surrounded by the oscillographic network of pale sunlight on the crystal muddy-violet rushing careering tumbling turbulent twisting waters. Between the offwrenching of Lee's ponderous army leather brogans and his race, slipping and sliding and stumbling along a meanderrow of flat and pulsing rocks deepening into the river's sideshallows to make a flat dive into the waters, is a decolletage that has no mortal plumb. That vaginaprick which continues the decolletage, that meridian of median minds, trestled on unstressed disaster, sarcophagal casserole and ferruled vindication, though I be the crest of species and the condonement of broken breakfast foods, stumblecrack in the midst of homing humility and vassalaged virtue, whatever the course of human misconduct we are the conduits of alloyed misrepresentation, trolling through bluegreen sunshine and whitefrocked psychod philandering as frozen spites spatulate through the heavebellied air in the pith of scream and the rash of all the man's cells to all the cathedraled orifices of the skin, hush rubbles the air, a roused day nightingale plucks its mandolin, Lee the satellite round the surface of the Rocky River earth itself, shot up into magnetic atmosphere, here a bellow there a bellow in the toiletprivy mind, as to who ranks rescue in the realm of murder, as to what idiot child endures a heartfailure in a prisoncell calling out in quartertones to his sister Rachel over the violetdeepening roiled waters of prisonguard and urinedank prisonair, present here, gift there, sallow samba on his yellowface, what shall I die here and what shall I not as my daughter Charlotte unJewed stands with Lee over the snowwhite arclighted freightyard, the freighttrains of Bruno Canova coupling and uncoupling in the poor waters, I know not my own mind when Ive no mind to it. It is this:

That the mind has another mind. That the mind has a tiny attachment somewhere, a little gadget fixed to it, an extra appliance. And it is this second mind, the gadget extrappliance mind that is constantly trying to get rid of its first mind, disavow it. This is why Victor Nathanson murders and why he dies. This is why Lee Emanuel races along flat and jagged rock. This is why Gus Nathanson sings in quartertones. This is why Levi Emanuel advises Lee to stop racing along the rocks, to halt, reconsider. Its the little secondmind, a squirmy little oddbeasty thing that wants independence of the big firstmind. But as in all independence a cord must be cut. Little secondmind constantly searches for the cord. It cant find it. It looks all over big firstmind. Firstminds clever. It hid the cord. Ah. Lee's secondminds looking for it too, only fast now, while Levi's secondmind tells him to hell with the search, that the cords really very well hidden, in fact its already drowned, but that one cant stop that which is hidden for screaming awhile, out of spite.

Are you racing toward the drowning man out of spite? As a roundabout method of survival? The file of the dancing ant axes off the surf I want him to die and I want him to live. Simultaneously. The freshlylaundered white curtain over the lower half of kitchen window is crinklewhite under the seventyfive watt frostwhite bulb in a burst of orange pearl from the inverted platter of a fixture on the white enameled ceiling. The upper half of the kitchen window is black. The boy sits hunched at the scratched white table jawing a pastrami sandwich. The kitchen door is open to the shed and the low hum of the gas refrigerator. Aluminumware and copperware on the shelves of the shed. An iron. Long narrow rolls of drawer paper. Posttoasties. Against the shed window the occasional soft thump of a great furrybodied moth.

Are all the windows locked?

Are all the doors?

Have you made sure that all the gas flues are turned off in the kitchen range?

Is the oven gas turned off?

Have you tried the front door to make sure it cant slip open?

Have you locked the livingroom door?

The shed door?

The kitchen door?

Rachel Emanuel reminds Levi of the listing from upstairs as she stands in her nightgown at the top of the stairway.

Are the spigots turned off in the kitchen? I know you cant turn off the water completely because theres a worn washer in one of them, and it drips. Call the plumber in the morning, Levi, youve promised for a week.

Is the cellar door locked? The one to the outside and the one to the diningroom? Both?

Rachel dont you think if a thief wants to come in a locked door wont make any difference?

I know, I know, Rachel giggles momentarily, but why make it easy for him? The spigot drips. Theres a rust mark on the enameled white sink near the perforated brass drain, which Rachel has the colored girl keep shining.

Are there any lights left on on the porch? Turn out all the lights, Levi. Lee dont forget to turn out the kitchen light when youre through the sandwich. Dont stay up too late. Dont forget theres school tomorrow. Make sure the kitchen door is locked before you come up. Dont come up too late you might disturb dad. Remember he gets up five oclock in the morning and he needs his sleep. You need your sleep too,

Levi you coming up?

In a minute, in a minute Levi shouts back in the thick voice, I got to get a drink first.

There is a second white straightbacked chair under the window near the gas range looking into the Kasters' kitchen window next door. On the right and behind Lee is the cupboard containing the separate stacks of dishware for the meals of meat and the meals of dairy; beneath the cupboard is a tiled surface making a roof over a waisthigh section of drawers; the tiles bear rows of glasses and in the drawers are the cutlery and utensils for the meals of dairy and the meals of meat; beneath the drawers are more cupboards containing dishtowels for the meals of meat and the meals of dairy;

pots and pans;

rolls of twine;

paper bags.

On top of the highest cupboard, above the dishware, standing on their sides, are the great serving dishes for the meals of dairy and the meals of meat. Above the gas range is a stopped hole in the kitchen wall, once serving as a ventilator for a since replaced oldfashioned range; the defacement is covered by a cheap round clock chased with designs of bluebirds; the clock has not operated for years.

Dont get up Lee, I dont want to sit down, Levi quickly says. I only came for a glass of milk, its the only thing can stop my thirst, Im so dry, it must be the herring I ate for supper, Im telling you theres nothing like milk, the man assures the boy, pulling open the refrigerator door and grabbing the thicknecked milkbottle in his ruddy hands, tilting it over the tumbler, the gigantic whitemisted bubbles gaping from neck to bottlebottom, quallop quallop quallop, so dont get up Ill only be a minute, the matted grayblond hairs tufting from his chest at his opennecked shortsleeve shirt, and its such a hot night, all things combined I guess thats why Im so thirsty.

Cold milk and springwater, theres nothing like nature, Levi says. The things of nature are the sweetest things. Milk from the cow, water from a well. I always wanted to live in the country. But mom cant stand the country. Rachel says Levi couldnt really stand the country either, hed get sick worrying the business couldnt get along without him. A couple days he likes the country, hed be tired of it. I couldnt stand the country a minute, the flies, the mosquitos, and youre all so alone, and everything is so inconvenient, you need a car anywhere you got to go, who would want to live in the country but a meshugenah, a crazy, a fool?

But the air, Levi debates, where can you get such air? Its like wine.

Yes the air is good, it smells so good, Rachel says, as the Buick bumps over the country road, smell, smell. Stop a minute, Levi, so I can enjoy the air.

You see Lee? your mother enjoys the air but she couldnt live out here, Ive been trying to persuade her for years.

Never mind, never mind, Rachel says, Ill get along in the city, Id go crazy with the loneliness, where would anybody be without their friends?

But its such a pleasure, Levi says, when you get up in the morning, the smell of flowers and the grass and the fresh air.

Never mind, never mind, I can do without them. Isnt the Roosevelt Boulevard enough fresh air.

What, with all that traffic?

Whats the matter isnt there enough trees.

You see your mother dont understand, Levi smiles at the boy, how its so peaceful in the country. Your father has the right idea, he tells Rachel.

You think my father dont have some crazy ideas too? she shrills at Levi.

Nature, nature, you dont appreciate nature, Levi shakes his head at her. You can see a sunset like this in the city? You can hear the birds like this in the city? Levi scoffs.

Listen I get homesick for the house even in Atlantic City. Its always so good to get back. Good to get away but even better to get back. You never appreciate your home till youre away from it. You dont get the right food in a hotel, theres always somebody telling you what to do, what not to do, Im telling you theres no place like home. What are you sneezing for Lee?

I dont know.

I hope youre not getting a cold, believe me Im getting older and it isnt so easy for me to go up and down the stairs like I used to, Im not a young-ster anymore, I hope youre not getting a cold, maybe you better go see Dr Newman right away before anything starts, I dont like that sneezing.

Okay Ill phone him.

Theres nothing like springwater to quench the thirst, thats the best thing after milk, Levi says to his son as he wipes his mouth with one of the dishtowels hanging from a rack in the shed, right over the drying washrags, not like that chlorine cocktail they call it from the spigot, Phil-adelphia has such rotten water, you can taste the chemicals, tomorrow night remind me we should go to Fairmount park and fill up the jugs, theres not much springwater left.

ICE NEVER

A young man by the name of Kelly singlesculls flashing white and silver down the Schuylkill ICE NEVER. Paul Scull scores touchdown after touchdown, all American for the University of Pennsylvania in Franklin

Stadium, the pennants chipping at the autumn blue, the cars parked by the hundreds in the adjoining lots, I g-g-got a coupla t-t-tickets for the P-p-penn N-n-navy game Nate Goldstein yells feverishly at his mother, the Broad Street subways packed with fans going down to transfer onto the Walnut Street trolleys out to the stadium, the hundreds milling in at Olney Avenue, Erie, Allegheny, Girard Avenue. Kellys nowhere to be seen in the Schuylkill River by night. There are the falls, near the aquarium, at the foot of Benjamin Franklin Parkway, the vast pile of the Philadelphia Art Museum squatting through the trees, the Cezanne painting of the mountain jeered at by Albert Barnes, he owns the superior version he contends, safe and sound at the Barnes Foundation in Lower Merion, the blueshirted whitehaired handsome retired chemist, the concocter of Argyrol, boasting to an audience how he acquired the Picassos, the Renoirs, the Klees, the Pascins, the Matisses, the Courbets, the Monets and the Manets and the van Goghs for fifteen and thirty and fifty dollars a canvas when the artists were unknown even in France, the international sculpture show with the Maillol, his soft serene nude in the quartz-glinted afternoon, the row of thirsty springwater aficionados lined up along a grotto on the East River Driver holding their empty bottles and the gallon jugs at their feet, Lee you wait in line, Dads feet arent what they used to be, the doctor wont let him stand for so long a time, the dusk greening slipshod down the hill, the Buick parked with the other cars down the highway, the Schuylkill a mild broad orangechattered stream under the enormous fat orange moon, Lee shaking his head at the mosquitos, blinking, swatting blindly as they assail his earlobes and the back of neck and his wrists and his eyelids, doggedly standing in the queue with the gallon jugs and the empty tall winebottles as he nears the cold springwater coursing from a rusty pipe in the rocks under the Fairmount Park hill, the ground wet and muddy near the spring, patiently watching those ahead of him at the waters filling their jugs, bending, squatting in the muddy wet, the mosquitos sizzling through the bluegreening still air, the fireflies dabs of sudden yellow at the softbodying night, the river dull orangeoscillographing through the oaks and the sycamores and the wooden green parkbenches on their cement legs, the voiceexchanges droning as the mosquitos, and the sound of the shlippering water of the spring sperking and clashing against the mouths of the jugs, the man ahead of him puffing insistently on his cigar, the kids running and tagging up and down the line, the couples on the riverbenches skulltangled and shoulderswitched while Lee waits for the springwater and his eyes try to jerk the couples from their benches, jerk their mouths to his, slice off a nipple for a Lee, leave a slippery muddy girl's hole for Lee till hes done performing the springwater duty for his mother and father, ICE NEVER FAILS

ICE NEVER FAILS

the icy water at last freezing the knuckles and wrists of Lee I want my father to die and I want my father to live. Simultaneously. For the most part, on the whole, generally speaking it does not matter to him if his mother lives or dies. Of course, there are exceptions. Moments. In the front doorway at 236 East Roosevelt Boulevard, phone number MICHIGAN 23459, the door ajar at seventen in the evening when he bids his mother good night, hes walking over to Danny Naroyan's at Lindley Avenue and Old York Road, a long walk but a satisfying one in the autumn, Lee anticipating the length of his stride, a machinelike abandon if a machine could so unlimber itself, the stretch of the stride so lofting the whole body in the feeling of completion that he can at moments persuade himself with ease that his feet have left the ground itself and that he glides along the pavements several inches above it and that no end will come to the power of his stride, that no weariness shall overtake it. When he bids her good night. He has wanted to get away from her for hours. But when the time comes, and Rachel in all sincerity hopes he will enjoy himself and asks him what time shall she expect him back. Late. How late? Oh, late. By one oclock in the morning. Well, maybe two oclock. Thats very late, Lee. But it wont be later than two, mom. Make sure it wont be with the milkman, his father says with faint sardonics. No it wont be that late, Lee grins shyly at him. What are you talking about with the milkman, Rachel shrills, two oclock at the very latest, even thats a shandah, a shame, suppose one of the neighbors see him, what will they think of my son. Oh they wont be up to notice me, Ill try to make it before two. What can you do out so late at night, especially if youre with Danny. Well we talk. Is there so much to say? You have so much to talk about it? We discuss lots of things. Of course its true Danny is a nice boy, hes a hard worker, Rachel says. Be careful when youre crossing the Boulevard. Sure I will, mom. She smiles at him. Go already, Levi says to him, you going to stand all night in the door? No, the boy turns with some longing towards his mother, good night mom. Good night, good night, shut the door, youre letting all the insects in, what good are the screens. She comes to the door as he ambles down the cement steps past the snowball bush, its burst of tiny white petals losing lustre. Once on the pavement and unloosing his stride, he pauses, to look back. Of course, she stands in the doorway. Of course, she waves. Why should she wave? He will be gone only a few hours. You got your handkerchief? she calls.

You got your handkerchief.

He shoves his fingers into his back pocket.

He nods at the plump figure in the doorway, her apron without a single stain

why is it your place at the table there are so many stains, so many crumbs. Theres none where I sit. And dad never leaves any. Why always at yours, Lee? Why do you have to make such a mess?

Mumble: I dont know.

Watch how you eat the next time, Lee.

Okay.

It makes dirt for me and dirt makes work, she says.

Okay.

I got my handkerchief, he grins back at her, embarrassed.

His mother nods, and he goes on and does not look back. His eyes are wet. He wants to cry. Something burns in his throat. He doesnt want to leave her. Hes sorry for her. His father at eight oclock goes to a school committee meeting at the Brith Mikveh. His mother will be alone. She will think about Uncle Vic. And surely she will think about the first Lee Emanuel for whom Lee is named. And all the radio programs coming over the spindlelegged Majestic will not stop her from thinking about these two, and about the firstborn, David, no longer in Philadelphia, somewhere in a sunwhacked Texas town umpiring in the Texas League; and these three males in her thinking will make her hurt. Three males in this woman's brain will invade her whole body and there will be no pleasure in her for the evening till she dozes off on the livingroom couch, faintly snoring, her dyed black gray hair pink at the roots, the whitepink scalp showing through the thinning hair. And Lee's nostrils fill with snot, the keptback tears. He wishes she would not hurt. He has wanted her fiercely dead on occasion but he has never never wanted her feeling hurt on the account of the first Lee, and her brother Victor, and her son David. How does a boy go from his mother? How does a boy find it within himself, as Lee does time after time after time, to cut himself away from Rachel, to sever himself from his sensing her loneliness for three males, and to stop himself from staying with her? He does not know. He only knows he must walk down the pavement away from her. He only knows that somehow there is absolutely nothing he can do about it. But he must weep for her. His throat is illusorily raw from compressed weeping. Not that he wants his mother surrounded by thousands of people; he never thinks of that, never wants that; only that she should spend an evening without loneliness—nothing more nor less than that. How can any human being be left standing in a doorway calling out to a person has he got his handkerchief? Wheres the merit in this? What impossible significance is contained in it? That a reminder to him of the necessity of possessing such an object is a function of Rachel he cannot abide. He rejects it. Hes furious with it. But then Lee sees himself sitting in the kitchen, rising, walking into the shed of a cold winter night and looking at the frozen washrags precariously balanced on the rack.

Two washrags, soaking wet a few hours before. Now they are frozen. He can hear everyone in the house asleep quite clearly. The gas refrigerator hums. The windowpanes on the little shed window are misted over though he can dimly make out the heavy eyelashes of the icicles. Theres a chill in the shed. Lee shudders violently, once. He expels his breath with a violent thrust, the boy and the young man fascinated by the simple spectacle of momentary condensation. Again he expels. Again. Again. And hes a little warmer

Breathe deeply ten times and youll be warmer, his mother says. If youre hiccupping, hold your breath and swallow ten times, this will stop the hiccups.

Frozen washrags. He shrugs, he digs at his ear, then he digs out some snot as he stares at the washrags. A big blob, kneads it between forefinger and thumb, but its not enough. With his little finger he scrapes the insides of both nostrils and pulls out more—harder strips which he mingles with the soft blobs, giving the whole more resiliency and toughness, making it more durable to his tactile pleasure as he slides two fingers over the little mass, gently pulling, stretching the drying snot like a rubberband, stopping just before it will ooze apart and repressing the blobs on either finger together, squeezing it then, gently, harder, at last mercilessly crushing with as much power as his fingers can summon till squiggles of the snot bubble out from the pressure. But theres a stubborn strip left in one nostril. He can feel it, hard and adhesive and needlelike, more uncomfortable in its inaccessibility than in its stickiness and proddingness. So he digs once again, hard, mercilessly, urgently, drawing a snatch of blood as he snags it at last and draws it forth. The delicate delivery of the hard strip of snot from the recesses of the nostril is by far the most sensuously exciting of the entire process; for this is involved in the disadhesion of the strip from the membrane to which it is attached, and the moment of the yielding of the membrane as several hairs are torn from their roots to accompany the snot is the most spinally exalted, the sense of quivering relief which immediately follows providing the perfect sensual terminus. And the chill settles over Lee. Hes finished with the snot, its lost its fibrous rubberiness; and, rolling it into a hard tiny ball, he flicks it onto the linoleumed floor, black squares on a white background. The frozen washrags continue to provoke his eye. The washrags are gray and redbordered and woven in cords to make a rough meshwork, and their postures are frozen contortions in bulge and swordpoint. They are wiping things. They are plunged into hot soapy water and then sloshed over garbaged, scummy and putrid surfaces and then squeezed clean again under the hot water faucet and then hung up to dry and to freeze in their precarious balances on the rack. In their gelid state, however, they seem more alive than dead to Lee, and quite pathetic. They are hunks of crag; they are humped, hunched and stabbing; they are a man's insides, the washrag of a lung, of a liver, of a heart. Though he realizes hes playing a sort of game, Lee halfbelieves as he looks covertly about him that he would like to take the washrags inside to the kitchen and thaw them out. He halfbelieves he pities the washrags. He believes he halfbelieves. He smiles. It must be partly true that the washrags in their grotesquerie imply a partially magical quality. Not that they will rise up and fly. Not that they will pulse. But that they embody an atmospheric suggestion. That in their wetness they reacted to the surrounding cold and simultaneously withdrew and protruded pointedly. They are fibre, after all; substance; composed of motile nodes; they cannot be responsible for their washrag outwardness; and— they react. The hunched, humped, contorted, pointing washrag is an overwhelming secret poised in a frozen status on a rack. Touch it and it will fall to the floor. It is brittle. It may break. Lee twitches a muscle in his cheek, he moves his ears in threequarter time, he gently expels a milky breath. His father is thirsty, his father expels a foul breath. Why does his father's breath stink? stink as badly as Jennifer Hazlitt's armpits. The boy may not want to come close to his father on the simple ground that his breath stinks. One must take certain advertisements seriously. Bad breath must be explained to a child before he forms an everlasting hatred toward the person who suffers from it. He is thirsty because hes got bad breath. He drinks milk to annihilate the stench, thirsty to conceal his defect. It is the defect which offends. There may very well be a bad breath to the uterus as the child is born. Vaginal halitosis. What infant can possibly withstand this? Of course this is a major trauma. Not the matter of being born, Christ no, one can endure that, one can welcome it. But to come into the world with one's delicate infant nostrils assailed by the mother's stench at her arch—no wonder the child has to be slapped into taking a breath: the infant has already assumed that all breath stinks and has concluded that he must not offend, so to hell with taking on life, it has a lousy odor. Which is precisely the washrag's secret: warm it and it will stink. Lee bends forward, sniffs at the washrags. Odorless. The cold has killed all odor. Naturally—he wants his father dead. But what of Stefanie, his adopted child, his second wife's daughter? In Los Angeles he and Norma treat the girl for her ninth birthday to an evening performance of the musicalcomedy version of Pagnol's Fanny at the Philharmonic. They sit on the top row of the gallery which looks down on the stage from a great height. When the houselights are dark, one feels an astonishing intimacy with the distant stage and the actions proceeding thereon; not so, however, when the houselights are on; the revelation that an audience is present and that one is sitting far above on its rim gives Lee the distinct sensation that the force of suction is imminent and that he may topple forward into—with, indeed, the concomitant feeling that he is obligated to do so—the very center of the spectator mass. He must touch the guardrail to restrain the forward motion of his sensations. On the steep bank of Rocky River there is of course no guardrail; nor a Norma, nor a nineyearold girl. And the sun is on. There can be no fond intimacy with a distant stage, much as he would prefer the substitution; as Lee descends, he wants a force to check him; somewhere at some point his flight toward the center must be arrested, if only by an accidental fall, if only by his craving that his balance fail him. Surely the men at the riverbank itself will hold him back, discourage him, forbid him by direct order even while he knows at the same time that with blatant cavalierism he must ignore such an order. Nothing restrains him. He is distantly grateful for the guardrail at the Philharmonic auditorium; but, possibly, he can be grateful because he knows that nothing need be saved, gratitude based in large measure on the absence of danger; besides, his wife and daughter are present: two such relationships compel resistance to the imminent suction: they are witnesses. No witnesses obtain at Rocky River, the only witnesses, after all, those individuals who bear love for the person committing an action: such witnesses observe everything about the person they love; nobody observes anything about Lee as he rushes toward the turbulent river except the shallow shell of his action; for, if they should actually witness him as those who love him do, they would either condemn him or embrace him; in either case, a restraining hand would be put forth. So that as he hurtles toward the river there is no love within a thousand miles; Rena sings in Atlantic City; Lee could feel the presence of love ten thousand miles away, but at this moment on the hot summer morning love does not exist at any distance, neither in himself nor in any creature related to him. Certainly there is a mother and a father but he can feel nothing transmitted from either of them; his older brother is out of his mind entirely. Fall he must, then, as if almost from grace; and there is, indeed, a kind of dark coloration to the matter, as if in the midst of the sun there is a young man Lee who is full of hatred and is as a kind of Lucifer suffering an expulsion and heading for a region of the damned, two struggling tortured souls writhing in the icy currents of a foaming stream. At the Philharmonic the height is very nearly no more than innocent reminder of the confines of the Academy of Music in Philadelphia where from a similar gallery, though more lustreless, dim and Victorian, he gazes down on the faintly luminous, faintly violet aureole diffused from the mane of Leopold Stokowski who with portentous regality, his back to the audience, awaits the absolute silence before he will raise his arm to conduct the Philadelphia Orchestra in the stately opening measures of the Bach Passacaglia. But what is considerably more significant, in terms of Lee's relationship to his father and his want that he should both live and die, is that, during the last act of Fanny at the Philharmonic, his ninevearold tires of sitting on the hard bench; Stefanie's ponytail tilting with her nose, she turns to him, the short blond hairs on her arms in a trellised subdued glitter, her low brow furrowed in exaggerated complaint, and hoists herself into his lap without a word of explanation, not of course that there need be, and rests her head lightly and fragrantly against his chest and chin, effectively eliminating a good quarter of the stage beneath. Inevitably the child becomes an increasing weight; inevitably Lee curses the discomfort she causes; Norma is all for relieving Lee by ordering Stefanie to resume her hard seat but Lee shakes his head: true, his thighs are sore, his buttocks are rocks of pain, his neck persistently refuses to reach numbness in its strained twist—but he wants the child to remain in his lap, because, very simply, he is quite proud that Stefanie chooses him for an area in which her body pleasure can be continued, and he deems it an unassailable privilege that he experiences acute distress on his daughter's account; he has a right to be made physiologically miserable so that his daughter can uninterruptedly enjoy the performance below; it is a fierce right but one which he thought never possible of occurrence; and for the first time in his life he realizes that his own mother and father must have endured similar situations on his account and loved him for it as he loves Stefanie. But this understanding arrives far too late to alter the petrified equilibrium of Lee's dilemma— that he wants his father both dead and alive; the understanding is significant only in that it intensifies in equal measure the desire that his father live and the desire that his father die; loving Stefanie makes the petrification of his feelings with respect to his father only the more monumental. If his father dies, Lee will feel the sweetness of his father's love for him that much more powerfully. He wants him to die because the intolerable sweetness will ensue. He wants him to die out of sheer curiosity as well, particularly as to how much money will be left him; Lee will not curse his father for leaving too little, nor commend him if the amount is considerable, but a great gratification will come into being by the very act of the money inherited whatever its size. He wants him to die because no other death can be so immense, nor drench him with equal grief. To a large degree this is what Lee lives for: his father's death. Lee curses its inevitability on that very ground; he wants the inevitable done with, hes weary of anticipating the inevitable, and nowhere is the inevitable so enormous, so omnipresent, so arrogant as in the threat of his father's death. He wants to deal with lesser inevitables—they are not so clearly inevitable, they have not nearly so much weight, they seem more swathed in chance and change; but the oncoming of his father's death cannot be changed; it would only be changed if Lee himself died before his father; Lee does not die in Rocky River; the probability is that he will not die at the top of the Philharmonic gallery; consequently, no such change is envisaged. It is entirely possible that he runs down the Rocky River embankment partly at the behest of a want to die before his father and of the want to scotch such a behest, to challenge it so that the grand inevitability of his father's death cannot finally be altered. But let us give a chance for the chance to occur. Lee will leave no challenge unturned in the contest of the inevitable: he gives his father a chance to outlive him. But at the same time he knows his father will not. At the same time he is sharply aware that he, Lee, will not die, so that as he rushes toward the churning waters he knows he is only toying with chance, that really he isnt giving chance a chance at all, that he will save himself so that he can save himself for his father's ultimate death. It is a curious act of hypocritical sacrifice with as much intent that his father live forever as much as die forever. For, patently, his father cannot die: his father's continued existence is a defense against the reality of the past, against the truth of the past. As long as his father lives, no past can come into being. His father occludes the passageway to the past; as long as he lives he neutralizes history. Lee and his father flee from history as from a Sodom and Gomorrah. Back there, at the twin cities of sin, the Almighty razes history to the ground. As long as Levi Emanuel lives, Lee need not look back. History is disaster, fire, famine, flood, fellatio and cunnilingua; history is the very act of sin which the Almighty demolishes. And yes, at the moment Lee and his father race away, the moment Lee stumbles blindly down the embankment, we know the problem ahead: the question of the continuation of the species. There are no two daughters. There is only one other actor in the drama, the mother, Rachel Emanuel, who flees with her son and husband. The conclusion is inescapable. His father is without seed; not only is: must be. In order for man to perpetuate himself—for these are the sole reliques of man who flees, only these three as each family constitutes the sole remainder of the species—Lee must outwit his father and lie with his mother: only so may history relinquish its hold, only so may it continue to be omitted. So that the conflict presents itself: in order for history to be denied, incest must be done. But that will kill Levi. That will cause Levi to look back upon the raging destruction and disintegration that is

Sodom and Gomorrah and turn to a pillar of salt. So that we are faced with the paradox that in the very effort to deny history we create it. It is in this antinomy that Lee wants his father alive and wants his father dead. And there is already, seriocomically, the faint taste of salt in Lee's mouth. Therefore he knows that as soon as Levi dies he, Lee, will die too. Therefore he must have his father live at all costs: his father is physician, wise man, immortal—but he is not God. Levi and Lee dispense with God; neither credit divinity. Lee therefore is left with his father, as his father is left with Lee. This is a curious double inheritance, working in both directions: the moment Lee is born Levi knows that he has inherited Lee, that Lee has been passed on to him through Rachel. When Lee is aware of his father, he knows he has been left, after the death of birth, with a father. Lee mourns the death of birth: he squalls, he protests, his eyes are ringed with black, he is infinitely sad as each child is infinitely sad after the death of birth. It is a short life that birth has led, and one mourns most bitterly the death of the very young; so bitterly does the child mourn it that he must be taught that he is alive, because he mourns his own passing: he has died at birth; he has left a totally different being behind him, himself; he has been murdered in the very act of coming into life; all of his subsequent life he can feel that early corpse within him, a corpse which has been buried—most horrible of all horrors—within himself; and he carries a dead creature within him for the rest of his own life, says prayers over him periodically, lays flowers on his interior grave, visits the tomb by day and by night, tries terribly hard to decipher the inscription thereon which is always blurred even in the brightest sunshine: he cannot make the dead creature out, he cannot describe the lineaments, he cannot recapture its face sweeter than all the faces he shall ever know; in his worst moments—in his maddest moments—he tries to resuscitate the corpse within him; stealthily, he breathes into himself; a little later he doesnt care whos looking, he fairly bursts his own lungs trying to make the creature live again; and fails; and in his failure once again attempts to exhume the corpse, cast it out—by rage, by blandishment, by crooning importuning, by denunciation, by gross entreaty; and fails; the body is there as long as his own body is there. Shall he exonerate his father for having given him a corpse to carry around the rest of his days? For such an act, Levi deserves death himself. Besides, Lee will be doing his father a great boon: for his father must be carrying a similar corpse of which he would like to be rid: let his father die and his corpse within him will trouble him no more—only by such an act will the exorcism operate. But then, one sees immediately, Lee will have to look about him for someone to wish his death, so that the same exorcism will be accomplished; Lee too must have son or daughter; as he hurtles down the embankment he hurtles toward Stefanie; thus, as much as he wants her, he will have to deny her so long as he wants his father alive. For, if his father dies, then Lee will have to make certain in some way that he himself is Lee, that he is separate and distinct from his father. The problem of acute differentiation may no longer be put off. In life the son connects with father; in death, connection evanesces, disappears altogether. Lee is left with himself. But if no connection any longer obtains, then one of the members of the antipodes no longer possesses the reality in himself of being the other end of the pole. He is depolarized, uncharged and becomes of necessity smitten with himself. If there is no father to love, whom can the son love? All other loves are makeshift, pale surrogates. The son enters a type of motion in which he continuously seeks the intensity of the love he bore for his father. This is ludicrous. As long as his father is alive he need not seek substitutes, but generate totally different types of love. When the father dies, substitutes become confused with the generation of other types of love. Lee wants no confusion; Levi signifies a condition of clarity. And yet clarity is dependent on Levi, which Lee would like to reject. He wants to make his own clarity, consequently have his father dead. The very experience of the desire for independent clarity, though that realm in all probability is never attained, is in itself a justification for the advent of confusion; furthermore, Lee's issue will experience clarity, though for him that day may be forever done. Nevertheless, and once again, with the father dead, Lee must feel that he has derived from nowhere, a feeling to be supplemented by the death of the mother while at the same time he will experience the unique and terrifying sensation that now he, Lee Emanuel, has his back up against history. No one behind him now. Only he covers the hole, like that child with its finger in the dike; as each man in his turn must put his back against the pressure of the eons behind him, and hold—hold till the last moment when the pressure will at last have dissolved him. Lee does not want to feel that pressure. So long as his father lives, Lee need not take his place and can blithely ignore—in the feeling-sense—the force of history; intellectually, he knows it is there; but

when the father dies, the intellectual knowledge is displaced—replaced—
by the feeling knowledge. It is the time—in the father's death—when
one's emotions must be on the identical level with the thinking level: for
it is only feeling in league with intellect that can enable one to stand in
courage with one's back to history. And Lee contends that he is not ready;
he cannot vouch for the ascent of his feelings as he can for his intellect's;
therefore, let his father live. On the other hand, he cannot really know if
he will be able so to vouch unless the death occurs. The death itself may
bring up to the highest possible level the condition of the emotions; and
if one feels a paucity of emotional height, then one may wish one's father's
death, in order to see if the requisite richness may not ensue. Have done
with it. Let his father die. Let Lee see. Death of the father may be a prereq-
uisite for the evolution of the senses. This, then, is a kind of murder. The
wish can indeed be the murder. There can be no evasion in the recognition of such. Evasion, after all, is only the putting off of the death; the lack
of recognition the pausing before the murder. The murder weapon is the
most obvious one possible: the son himself. But it is not a premeditated
murder: it is a preconditioned one. The only way the son may escape his
crime is by self-destruction. And it may be inquired if the very act of suicide itself, if it takes place in the son after the father has died, may not
very well be the punishment which the son inflicts upon himself for the
crime. Not the loss of money, nor the loss of status, nor loss of love, nor
ennui, nor the questionable valuation of the worthlessness of life: but,
plainly and simply, the loss of father. Because one is with oneself in an
absolute utterness. But therein is contained the very ecstasy of absolute
miserliness. The death of the father can mean an ecstasy of self. The self
doing some sort of dance about the stone head of the father, Levi's head
in the fairest smilingest stone, without trunk and without limb, set upon
an unidentifiable sand in an empty landscape, the face sandcolored,
though the blue eyes are somehow evident, the ruddy flesh persisting, the
kind squareness of the skull which the dance cannot shake off nor turn,
for the eyes peer in one direction only, intensely dead in their very aliveness, as though they filter through whatever it is that Lee tries to hold, as
though the whole being of his father filters through whatever Lee sees in
his day and night, as though Levi must forever touch but go through him
with the sweet blue eyes, as though Levi must tell his son some irretriev-
able secret that only the father knows, that the father has wished he could

impart to his son when he was alive and now can never do so. Lee has the stone head of his father and must inexorably think: why did Lee not try to make the stone head some special flesh when the flesh was still there? Why did he not make some indescribably intimate use of his father's face when it was still on trunk and limb? He cannot touch it now, although the sense of the touching of his father's face is more feverish now dead than when alive. He can see the spires of the Greek Orthodox church his father rode bareback toward in the tiny Lithuanian town of N'Muxt. His fathers spires are his now. The flashing windows in the setting sun are Lee's now. The horse under Levi is the horse under Lee

and the water that he plunges into are the icy hatchets flowing from the underground stream in Fairmount Park and hacking away at his wrist

ICE NEVER FAILS

Let him alone.

Who?

The young man in the river.

Why?

Hes some other mother's son.

Can you see him?

Yes.

Then hes yours.

The specific is a misleading generality

The waters too large for you, a size sixteen current flopping about the body, so that you lack the medium; as the dimensions are too great for the figure, the figures' extensions in their strain weight the figure down; unreferrable, a man sinks. The drying sweat forms anchors on the flesh, dissolving only at the bottom; the knots of sweat in the pores tie the figure down; having flung knots of snot at your own net

Let him alone.

Whats alone?

I felt my brother's heart and there was no bumping in my palm. I put an eye next to his, and though I saw myself puffed on the top, no breath blew it out. So cold he was that when I put my skin next to his I thought I had a fever; so yellow his color, my son, that I thought primitive physicians had rolled him like a cheese from the womb; I thought I was his sister, but the community had failed. I said his name: Victor. Victor, I said. My mouth made some memorial sense, but no more, and that was not sense enough. I had been kneeling, so I stood; I felt no fever. I looked down on Victor and I was alone. You look down on the young man in the river.

I dont see him dead.

Are you telling his fortune?

He fights

He fights without an adversary. Let him alone.

Then he needs the adversary.

You mean to give him life by having him fight you. He will try to kill you

I know

You may die with him

I know

There is some death in knowledge, then; as if in the knowing, a matter couples to history. Only in the unknowing is there life. You will give him death. He cannot use you.

I will reach him.

The decision hasnt been made.

I will reach him

The decision hasnt

No, it has not.

You may turn back.

I may.

Let him alone

A man is screaming.

Naturally. Do you know him?

Ive greeted him on occasion and Ive said good night.

Will you tell me if he is a broad or narrowwitted man? will you tell me does he love in a tangent exercise, or browse along catalogued passions, or plays a ticktacktoe in the night? Is he some colloquial mind that trusts no accent save his own? Does he scheme in the sun, run foaming impulses under the moon? Is he loyal to lechery, lecherous of delicacy, meticulous maggot

I know none of these things about him.

Does he know these things of you?

No.

What would you aid?

A man who screams. One need know more of a man than that he screams.

Rena is singing

You mention her only because my own lifes endangered; not hers, not yours

She might scream if you died

I cant respond to a speculative sound. I cant posit my own death so that a girl may scream so that thus I may avoid the proof of the supposition. This is cowardice

But you know that you wont grunt the last possible gust of effort to save a man's life. You know that if you see that that last gust can go down with the man you gust it to, you will rack back that breath. You know this and yet you go to him. This is the rawest picture of cowardice that in the depths knows it can be concealed.

I do not know. He may wrench that gust from me. I may lose the final touch of power to resist.

You gamble on your resistance

Yes

You gamble on the strength of your cowardice.

The act of risk partly negates the cowardice

You are less a coward altogether if you go back, in that everyone will judge you one. For that will not be a show. In the showing of utter cowardice is less of it than in the act of masking oneself with some courage, which is the worst of courage and therefore the foulest of cowardice

No one will smell me

Indeed they will not; to do so would be to capture their own stink and betray their own cowardice. The men will hold their noses for their sake, not yours. You had better go back.

Theres considerable seduction in the imagination of consequences in a group of men who watch you. No mother would be worth her motherhood if she did not picture such to her son

I picture your life.

You would fix it.

Do you want to try to save the man so as to unfix me?

You may be fixed in him

That is repugnant

He is repugnant.

He disgusts you?

Yes

Why?

Because hes drowning, a loathsome behavior which insults me, angers me, nauseates and ridicules me. I may want to kill him. I may want to make certain that he will die. I may wish to administer the coup, struggle with him, be in at his finish, use up the last gust of his go, tense him, show him heres a man next to him who might take him to shore, taunt him by my very presence, snag the last piece of desperation in him, make him reach forth and in that very act of reaching exhaust him altogether, and therein inflict mercy on him, mitigate his terror, have him die in the relief that here is an arm he can hold to. Such can be cowardice's mercy, the nuances of compassion discovered only in the severest strain of tantalization.

Then in this moment you are not sane.

Was my Uncle Victor sane? Was my Uncle Aaron sane? Is my brother David sane? Was my father sane when he avoided service in the army of the czar? What does his son do in the army of the United States? that he keels his muscles through the winter waters

The muscle is heavy with unconscious child.

Pregnant muscle. I go through labor

What will you deliver?

Tons of running down a riverbank. I will make motion lie prostrate beneath me. There are already corpses floating on the surfaces of my impulses. I entreat you not to have me give birth, it will be stillborn

But I am monstrous swimming through the waters, I am dripping with muscle.

I hear no screams

Nor do I. Theres no more screaming. In the dumb residue no excuses exist in either direction

Wheres Rena

In Atlantic City, in bed, she says a man forces her at the point of a prick

Lee.

Yes?

Your father isnt here

Wait for him.

But hes waiting for me. We cant have both father and son waiting, wed cancel each other out

Do you know the time

No.

I will buy you a wristwatch, automatic, selfwinding. Be sure and be on hand to receive it. You should be wearing it now: it would have kept you from the stream.

Do you think time an amulet about the wrist

Time is a kind of execution done on the man, an electrode on wrist, ankle and skull which will carry the switch's throw for the rent done on the woman. It is for this that a man does not dive his life away, for he must take all that time straps him to; otherwise, he essays in abandon, he pollutes a watercourse by cavorting into it without gradation. Had you some time on your wrist, you might have sensed the pause's foil, the pain of tightening punishment; to fling a matter off often has the flinger look back on what's been flung, rub a temple smoother to see what reflection beneath might thereby be revealed; that which is unflung, undiscarded, undismissed, propels a man with that much greater thoughtlessness. Youd nothing to give away: therefore, you gave way; youd no time: therein the essential immorality. Who prides himself on timelessness loses the modesty of the moment, credits accident's intervention to the full—as if he leaps fullborn from a distorting mirror, expecting by his very leap that the mirror, smashing, will be corrected by disintegration, and that he will have its fairest form which he will pick up piece by piece in the very act of his crippled search. What piece will you pick up at the river bottom?

I wont go down that far.

Indeed, you will wait till youre in the very throat of heroism and then permit it to cough you up as though Lee's virtue had become Lee's phlegm. When youll be saturated with timelessness, that instant will you think it proper to dry yourself with time.

Illve made the effort.

There is no effort when one stops short of possible further effort. All preliminaries must be discounted. Look at yourself harshly; there will be soft years enough.

Im tired, cold, I seethe with exhaustion.

Aware of such before you flung yourself into the water, aware that muscle would melt, breath merely stare from the diaphragm's pit at the far circle of swallowlight above; measuring in potential your body's turbulence against the water's, and knowing in advance what hooded wave would be the last you could cowl your skull through—how can you study vanity with such blindness as to put a dying man in your experiment?

When we grasp time we may stay still. The twelve men on the riverbank toll time; their heartbells ring vast strokes by dry tongueclappers; within their landscapes they kneel in tawdry churches, listen to the little sermons of themselves and pray for the man who went to the waters. They will not leave their churches till I come back or die; they will not stop their talk with God till the man theyve delegated for collective task vanishes or makes his drenched return. I go to the dying man who screams not in perfection nor in utter nakedness; I go as a man, that is to say as one of my old friend's watercolors, whose paints may be badly smeared in the river; I may lose a sense; from the very shock of terror I may myself go reeling from my retina and slump down in bluegreen caves; I may go numb or claw in cramping spasms at myself till I snag forth my guts and wave them in futile semaphore at dumb fishes. I go in the hope that Ill return, be lauded and let go from a group I abominate. I go that I may save some semblance of a life. In short, I go briefly as a man, telling myself that I cannot die, that the screaming man cannot die, that all will be faintly well, that I will insure myself as I can in the task, that I will fight to save myself as well as perhaps fight more bravely for myself than for the thrashing, screaming man. I go disjointed, by fragment and by snatch, by horror and by honor. I go by all of myself and at moments only by the pulling scream and nothing of myself. I go because I know I am the only man to go: I know some strokes in the water, I have taken care of myself in the water before, I have lived in the water; which none of the other men on the bank have done; it is not that I am so excellent but that I am the least incompetent; it is not that I am so full of courage but that I am the least afraid; it is not that I do not myself scream at death but that I can still hear sounds of myself beneath, whereas the men on the riverbank cannot hear themselves at all. This being the case, I have plunged in.

B-b-balls

Keep your teeth in

Hes not w-w-worth defending, Rena. He g-g-goes in the w-w-water because hes a f-f-fag, he f-f-feels for a man, thats what hes f-f-feeling for, there, around in the w-w-water. If he had any real f-f-feeling for you, hed stay the hell out, hed act l-l-l-like a m-m-man. But he isnt. Somewhere in the sonofabitch's m-m-mind hes in love with a m-m-man, m-m-maybe not anybody in particular, m-m-maybe the guy out in the water isnt the one. But Lees s-s-sorry for the g-g-guy, awfully sorry, t-t-too sorry. I always told you he was a homos-s-sexual, he had it in him, you ever w-w-watch him? N-n-n-notice how he moves his wrists, d-d-did you? In those l-l-little arcs, like a g-g-girl, and then it goes l-l-limp. And the w-w-way his voice sort of drawls, drags—Ill b-b-bet he dressed in drag t-t-too sometimes. He's n-n-not the g-g-guy for you, Rena. A m-m-man that goes out of his w-w-way to risk drowning. A grandstand faggy play, thats what hes d-d-doing

Sadistic.

To attempt to rescue any man from death is a piece of sadism. A piece of extreme cruelty done upon himself, the whip to the lung, the thrash upon the limbs, the rack from head to toe. But the worst of the torture is done the dying man, who sees a live one waved in front of his eyes and realizes that the live one even though he reaches him will not be able to save him. The most abominable kind of insult to a dying man, wretched, loathsome. He ought to try to drag Lee down with him, its what he deserves, and perhaps thats exactly what Lee counts on, the torture to be done on himself by a dying man. What greater punishment could there possibly be? The dying man will taunt Lee, he will give him an iron hold to try and break, he will imply that this is what Lee has come out to him for, to kill him, to kill the dying man, and to suffer thereafter

I go to commit no crime

All behavioral extremes are crimes. What is an alternative explanation of your action? What, possibly? Look at the thing coldly

I cannot

Coldly, coldly. The man in the water has been out there for some minutes. He has gone down and come up. He has gone down and come up again. He has done it four times, as a matter of fact. Hes in the middle of torrent. Hes being swiftly carried downstream. Hes burdened by a fullfield pack, by bayonet, by shoes. You, Lee Emanuel, are exhausted by a fifteen mile hike. You are not a superb swimmer. Youre sweating, your breath comes in gasps even before you jump in the water. Youve never saved a man before. Youve never had a course in lifesaving techniques. You dont know the first thing about swimming up to a man, diving and coming up behind him to grasp him under the chin. You dont know how to break a man's hold upon you when hes panicstricken. The man out there obviously is. Not even your first sergeant understands the simple problem: he will ask you why you didnt knock the man out in the water. That is exactly what you will try—to knock him out. But you cant. You dont save a man by knocking him out. Thats a myth—or dont you remember the difficulties of motion in water? And yet youre going out there. You must know that you will fail. Why dont you suggest that the men on the bank form a human chain? You dont think of that, do you? Or, if you do, you quickly suppress the idea. That wouldnt single you out, would it? It would comprise a collective effort

I havent been tested before in a life and death action. Ive always dreamed of such a test.

But wheres the test when failure is so sure?

Even when failures a certainty, one has to make the test if one has long dreamed of doing so.

You go out there to act out a fantasy. Infantile behavior at its worst.

The infantile sometimes extends beyond the mature possible. It is the reach to a more highly developed infancy. It is an infancy which you may not even recognize, an infancy more complex that the maturity to which youre accustomed. But it looks like the old infancy to you. But a quality may be brought out in me which Ive never before experienced in action. Would you deny this to me? Besides, a man must know what it is to be at the point of death.

Why then dont you accompany the regiment in its North African invasion?

There are too many points of death there that might be encountered. Is it so wrong of me to limit myself to one?

Then you will not know the limit of limits. You will not experience what it is to be at the point of death not once but many times. Will you deny that this will be an extreme to which you wont be privy?

Yes

Will you deny that you encounter this very point of death so that in the saving of yourself the necessity to undergo many points of death will be obviated?

If I do not so obviate then I will have missed the experience of preventing myself from undergoing the many points of death. From that point of view, then, I put no crime upon myself, because I stop short of the violence of the many. Is that not so?

God was too much in the louring cloud. You go to seek Him under the water

Once, Lee, in the middle of a Philadelphia Orchestra concert in the Academy of Music as I sat way at the top of the gallery

I havent very long, Naroyan

L-l-l-ee and N-n-naroyan, what d-d-did I tell you, Rena, the two of them, the l-l-long and the short

It wasnt until he wrote me about it in a letter, long after the war, in New York, I never suspected

My brother had you watched. He wrote your commanding officer that back in Philadelphia you were suspected of homosexuality

Are you trying to make trouble between me and your brother? Ill face it with him if you want

No, dont, dont, hes weak. Youre not, youre going to save a man

I saw a wisp of smoke curling from the wings.

Why do you tell me this?

There is a relation between it and the man in the water. Otherwise Id never admit it, I havent told anyone else. I thought nobody else had noticed the smoke. The Academy was packed. I thought of only one thing: getting out. I, a superior intelligence. I, whod prided myself on deliberation, reflection, reason—I thought of only one thing: that my life and my life alone mattered. I could imagine panic taking hold of the entire concert hall. I could imagine men and women trampled underfoot. But Daniel Naroyan had to live. There was absolutely no doubt in my mind about that. I didnt give two shits for anyone around me, anyone anywhere in the Academy. As far as I was concerned, that wisp of smoke was curling from the corners of my own heart. I was in the middle of the row. Perhaps I could creep past the others in the row unobtrusively for a natural enough excuse—anyone can be seized with the urge to urinate or defecate even during the sublimities of Brahms. I started to rise, my face white, the cords of my neck twisting like entwined phalluses

(on the Medusahead, of course. Not snakes; rather, writhing phalluses like the motion of my long muscles through the waters. Perseus, who cut off her head and gave the phallic scalp to the Goddess of Wisdom. Later—later, seizing the hair of the drowning man in the water, I wanted only the head, I would salvage the head and the hair—and present it to whom? To the man's wife? Had I a sentimental attachment to a woman whom I had never known? What kind of arcane insult could envisioning this have been? To present the skull and say, The fife of the dancing ant axes off the surf. Perseus seized the writhing phalli and thus held Medusa's head as they struggled and squirmed against his fingers)

(there is the possibility I wish to present the skull to Rena. But I am not that brave, really, to do so. I cannot tear his head loose from his body. But the idea is there. Cast the skull at her. Let me see how her eyes shine then as they do in the presence of Roko, the Negro pianist, at three in the morning in the Chinese restaurant)

(I, too, am capable of extreme actions. I, too, want to loot, pillage, burn, kill. I, too, am capable of enormous violence
am proud of the capability

i dont wanna be called fatty, Lippy
fatty, yella

The plump little Lee walking home from Feltonville Grammar School, turning the corner around Rising Sun Avenue to walk east on the Roosevelt Boulevard, near the end of the school term, in June. Sweating, prodigiously as his mother, squirming in sweat. The scrawny Lippy, who lives six houses away from Lee on the street to the rear of the Emanuel house, Ruscomb Street, on the corner of which the arclight hangs from a tall pole in the rain, in the moon, the bluewhite clouds in a seething glide so that moon seems to race as it hangs perfectly still, expanding, contracting, expanding, taunting his plumpliness, fatso Lee

Im warninya, you been callin me that too many times

fatso fatso fatso in the bared scrawn, the monkeyface with the long lashing lips

im tellinya cut it out CUT IT OUT

fatty Lee fatty Lee fatty Lee

stop his mouth, stop the scrawn Lippy. Lee hurls himself at the boy, grabbing for his skull, eyes half shut, the nostrils half up his face, his mouth a block of gulp. Lippy strikes at him, twists, but Lee doesnt let go, his fingers gouging at the scrawnface, Lippy shaking him as he would a hangdog, the two of them crumpling suddenly to the hard pavement and Lee has the scrawnboy by the throat and it is as if night had abruptly fallen, theres no sun, no heat, no light, the world is utterly dark except for the face beneath Lee that is gasping, turning from side to side as Lee tightens his fingers around the throat, Lippy kicking, his knees hitting at Lee's penis, testicles, but Lee feels nothing but the joy of having the throat inescapable in his circling fingers, and Lippy's kicking is more and more ineffectual in the black black world, lemme go lemme go his mouth tries to whisper but Lee says Im gonna killya, Im gonna killya, I toldya not to call me fatty, I toldya, I toldya so Im gonna killya, I didnt wanna fight

I didnt wanna fight he sobs

I didnt wanna fight

I dont like ta fight he sobs

but now Im gonna killya killya killya because when I do fight I kill I

I give up lippy tries to whisper I give up I give

Im gonna killya

till Lee is bodily lifted by rough big male hands, a man standing over him, Let him go, boy, you win, you win—let him go, the kid cant breathe

and stumbling away, tears churning from his eyes, Lee staggers down the Boulevard, the sweat matted on his flesh, Ida killed him, Ida killed him, he mutters victoriously to himself, I didnt care, I woulda killed him, I still want to the kids on the block looking at him with new respect, the older guys with knowing respect Hey I hear you almost killed the poor kid we didnt know you could fight, Lee, Lippy fearfully keeping his distance blocks away)

when the man next to me whod also seen the smoke and Id been absolutely certain that absolutely nobody in the whole audience had seen the smoke but Daniel Naroyan the man next to me clapped me on the shoulder and stunned me back down into my seat sternly remarking STERNLY mind you, as would a father, You want to create a panic? Ive never been so ashamed, Lee, in my entire life. I heard no music. I blushed. Of course the small fire backstage was put out rapidly while the orchestra continued uninterruptedly to play. I couldve started a panic. I couldve been responsible for the death of hundreds. I myself couldve been trampled. What are you giving your life for? It is an imperialist act of heroism. No Marxist would approve

Youre a kid on the block being called a name. Thats why youre swimming out to the drowning man

The lone Athenian flings himself into the water while from the heights above the Syracusan horde catapult their great boulders

Reserve yourself the right to be the surviving Athenian

Write the history, Thucydides. Record the Merovingian maculations, Michelet. Ride the unicycle, Vico. Put down the Decline and Fall of the Roman Empire, Gibbon. Yang out the Yin, Toynbee

I can see giving your life if theres a Marxist point to it. I see none here. I see only—panic. The panic which petrifies the twelve men on the riverbank. And the panic which impels you into motion, the latter panic you deride. In the uncanny composition of things the single figure separates himself from the stilled group to provide for the group a running object, the requisite intermediary to make transition from themselves to the screaming man in the scream to whom their collective eye cannot directly attach. Fishingline Lee unreels from the groupcast as an acceptible sacrifice to the unacceptible sacrifice. You, uncivilized, do the civilized's work; devised by the group to divine what may come up in the water's oracle, to read by your fingers her foaming lips as to what the group may expect from Rocky River, what life and what death, what shallow and what depth, you the reasonable representative of the group's panic, possessed of their forward motion when they came to a halt. A Marxist would check that law of physics and redirect the energy to the group, return it to the group where it rightly belongs. You subvert, in short, the function of the group. Dispossessing it, you extend it. The function of the group is to examine itself; instead, you bend to its panic and relieve it of selfexamination. You permit the group its luxury and yours. You indulge yourself and therefore the group—and for this you may be traitorous and invite your execution for which the group would have no whit of guilt because it will have been punished by your death and will content itself with the proof of its superstition, to which the oracle will have opened its mouth and swallowed you. What do you gain by striving to rescue him? More loss, Lee, than gain, for if you stand with the group then one more living man will be in evidence to condemn the regimental commander for his orders. The next day his adjutant goes around from man to man of this group. Naturally there will be an inquiry. Naturally there will be depositions. You will be asked by the adjutant to swear that a question was put by the company commander to his company Are there fifteen competent swimmers in the company who will volunteer on a regimental mission? The adjutant will speak in low tones to you, Of course you verbally volunteered, Private Emanuel, you understand that that is exactly what you did. The company commander is to be absolved of any culpability in the matter. The colonel, the regimental commander, issued a written order asking for volunteers—issued it after the volunteers were already picked, the fifteen of them, issued it to cover himself. And what will you reply, Private Emanuel?

I volunteered for the mission, sir

The adjutant, smiling sadly, sadly satisfied, turns away in the pines, down the hill, toward the next surviving volunteer

Lives lost, a certain percentage, is a commonplace in a training maneuver during wartime. A percentage is anticipated. A percentage is counted upon. A percentage is wanted

wanted

wanted.

Otherwise, no mission could possibly be successful. Lives must be lost to certify the competency of the action. Lives must be lost in order to insure the probability that in actual combat the majority of the men involved will survive. If in the training maneuver all the participants survive, then it is likely that decimation will ensue in actual combat because what will have been shown is complacency

Are you intent on preserving the complacency, Emanuel?

I volunteered for the mission, sir.

Yes. For a moment you toy with the possibility of rebellion. For a moment you think of telling the adjutant that you will testify that the swimmers for the mission were each chosen, that there were no volunteers, that that was a covering fiction. For a moment you see yourself on the witness stand revealing that a crime has taken place, that in actuality what has transpired has been criminal negligence and that the commanding officer should be instantly relieved of his command. For a moment you think of telling the adjutant that what happened was a piece of unadulterated rottenness. For a moment. But you quite well know that if you do, your chance to take an examination for cadet pilot training in the United States Army Air Force will be totally nullified. You would then remain in the armored infantry regiment

I volunteered for the mission, sir. Lives lost, a certain percentage, is a commonplace in a training maneuver during wartime. A percentage is anticipated

Will you throw your chances of survival away on a point of truth? No, of course not. There you behave as would a good Marxist. But it is too late to undo your imperialist action of trying to save a man

One must first be an imperialist before essaying Marxism.

Is this your excuse for continuing toward the drowning man?

Let Lee go. The morning sun cracks the shadows, and the young man, running, widens them. Flat blue shadows along the boulders trip and slip the sunlight, retrack the crystal sidewaters. Such innocences that are calf deep swagger hip length later till the whole heads immersed and all goes green before our eyes. Death has many colors; only humans give it black; putrefaction for one exhibits a very laurel of gravid lustres shimmering to invite the glittering hungers of insect and beast

Along Maryland's eastern shore Rena and Lee warily approach a wounded gull

What do you suppose is wrong with it. She wears a simple onepiece skintight black swimsuit, her long copperchrome limbs emptying into the estuary of the hip. The hip in an underground source reaches the waist, that spring bowing under the weight of the breasts. After the breasts she leans back and the neck turns into the childchin, the barest churn of the fullest lip under the hooked nose and the vast blackbrown estate of the eyes

Seafoam comes in on wriggling white chassidbeards

Scraggleclouds crook at raceways of blue. A western sun gingergolds the silverlapped waves. A bare boardwalk dinnerhours. Sand seeps into small windpockets

What do you suppose, she casts a small flare on Lee.

Lets look

Lets not. Lets stay away

Lets look.

All right, then

Following, the gull goes, but they are nearer. Seeing, then, that one birdleg is bad.

A legs broken.

Or foot.

Or

Yes.

What do you suppose we could do for it, Lee takes Rena's hand.

I dont know. Anything, do you suppose.

I dont know

They trick some dab of grimace along their mouths and go toward the bird that, seeing them, hops toward the boardwalk.

It cant go much further

The gull stops when Rena and Lee stop. Waits when they wait. It neither defies nor challenges. Simply it holds a certain distance between it and the girl and the boy

Where will it go if it cant go much further do you suppose

Lets run.

No, Id rather not.

Lets run, just a little.

Just a little

They run. The gull runs. They head it off. The bird turns the other way, hopping

Rena chuckles from the hip. It can outdistance us.

I think youre right.

Either way, it will beat us.

I think so

The bird looks at them, waits. Then it starts to hop toward the breakwater. It seeks to increase the distance between it and the girl and the boy.

Where do you suppose its going

Lee shakes his head quite slowly. I cant tell.

Oh come on. You can tell. There is a sad taunt on Rena's face. Lee feels her shoulder gravely

I cant. But Id like to help it. Because its wounded

But you cant catch it.

It wont let itself be caught

Lee scoops at his shadow on the sand.

Why do you suppose it wont let itself

If I could get it to a vet, Lee muses.

Its not its leg or foot at all, Rena cries, still watching the gull. Sometimes youre so oddly unobservant, Lee

I guess

Its his wing, its his wing. The girl swears her brow, low and on the outside.

The gull, far enough away from the girl and the boy, tries to fly. It runs and tries to be airborne. One wing is superb. One wing stretches, fulltipped, rightshaped. The other wing is Ernie Chalk's, high and folded, that the gull lifts, high, but cannot unfold. Again and yet again it tries to stretch the hurt wing

If I could catch it and get it to a vet

Its wild and wont be helped

You dont know thats so.

She arranges that her blackbrown eyes look down. The suns down

We ought to go back and eat.

Yes, I think so. Im a little chilled

Walk close to me.

All right, Lee.

But they dont go. They look toward the gull. The white chassidfoam seraglios swiftly up the shore.

I hate to leave it, he says.

I know.

If I could capture it and get it to a vet. The wing could be mended.

Yes.

The vets know how.

Yes.

But the gulls afraid.

Is it

Maybe not. Maybe it doesnt want to be touched by us. Cats clean themselves after we hold them

Yes.

Id like awfully to help the gull.

So would I.

Would you, Rena

Yes. Very much

Because otherwise its going to die. Damn it. It wont let anybody give it food. Or anything

I guess hundreds die.

I suppose.

Where will I meet you when I come back from the club?

At the diner.

All right.

You'll be hungry, wont you?

I suppose. You know Lonnie Mahans doing a Moliere play at Rehoboth. He invited us to come to see it. Would you like to on a Monday night?

Not particularly. You go

You dont mind

No.

Youre sure

Yes. I dont mind.

He wanted you to see it too, you know.

Thank him for me but Id rather not go. I want to finish a scene. You understand.

Yes

Hundreds

What?

As you say. The gulls. But his wing. Lee hits his palm with a fist. Theres no sense to the mystery of a wounded gull.

Rena is close to him but his eye picks out the bird only. The sand is chill under the feet, like a hard cold stone that vises now around the calves of the girl and the boy. The scraggleclouds are wentwisps, the sky violetblue, Lee's right little finger pumping, pumping. If I could only get to him, he says.

But he outdistances us, Lee. He does, he does

Will we have to go back to Philadelphia when youre through at the club?

I dont know. I think theres a place in Ocean City that might want me. Ill be hearing from my agent.

You mean right here in Ocean City?

Uhhuh.

Thatd be very nice, Rena

I thought youd like it

But youre not sure yet.

No. But dont worry

Itd be another two weeks at the beach.

Yes. Youll like that, wont you

Yes. I love you very much.

Do you love me very much, Lee.

Yes. Yes.

Tell me again.

I love you, I love you

Ill be late.

Will you always love me, Rena

A soft brown down scatters over her eyes. Yes, Lee. She laughs lightly. Dr MacFarland.

Eh?

On Governors Island.

Oh. Yes

He told me Id always have to stay with you

Did he.

Yes.

Damn gull, he mutters. I dont want to leave him.

I know.

Doesnt know whats good for him.

Hundreds.

Sure.

The sand smarts their eyes. The shadows smart their eyes. The tide is high. Late in the season the chill chaps the darkening air. Girls and boys raucous along the bare boardwalk now.

Where will he go

We cant tell

Id like to be able to tell. Hes going to die.

Weve got to get supper, Lee. Im worried Ill be late Im sorry.

Its all right.

Lets go. Im awfully sorry.

Its all right, Lee.

Will I come back?

I cant tell.

Are you worried about me?

Yes.

Suppose Id drown.

Id die.

Would you? Would you?

Yes.

But Ive got to get to him.

Then go

Ive got to make sure Ill stay alive and be with you again.

Then go.

Rena, Rena. You havent written to me for three days.

I had to get organized in Atlantic City. Im singing and my girl partner does the guitar. Im awfully fat.

I dont care.

Im terribly fat, you wouldnt recognize me

I love you, it doesnt matter

But it does. Im gross. Im ugly

No youre not. You couldnt ever be. Will you write me every day

Ill try.

Will you?

Yes, yes, Lee, only dont importune me, dont beg. Please dont beg.

I miss you

And I miss you too. Believe me

I believe you

Dont take unnecessary chances.

Ive got to see you.

Please dont get into any trouble.

Ive got to see you, Rena

Lee, dont go in the water. Youre not that good a swimmer.

Ive got to see you.

There are other ways

No, there arent. Besides, how can I stand there on the riverbank? Stand and not do anything? I cant, I cant. I must try. You understand that

Yes

I mean, theres a bad wing

Its not the same. Hes screaming for help. The gull isnt. The gulls wild, the man is a tame scream and were not in Ocean City.

Its all the same.

No, no it isnt. Thats your trouble, Lee

Its everybodys trouble and we dont admit it. Suppose the gull is Ernie Chalk. Ernie carries his wrist in an imaginary sling. Ernies so small now, deferential gull, an imbecile, to whom, to Ernie Chalk, I was a little animal, a snail, a rabbit, a moth. The secret of imbecility is that anything lesser than the imbecile in size is a craven creature with whom the imbecile can toy, torment, stroke, kill. And if spit drools from the corners of my eyes, what am I? I will put an imbecile in the water. It is the only way I can go toward the drowning man, he is my fool in the water, a crimson pufffaced clown

Lee laughs as he swims toward the man in the water

Purely a reflex.

Purely?

Cold against a heated body. His belly giggles.

When to the giggling belly the scared cells scamper, on to the navel, a corkscrew lifeboat

Do a backstroke: save the navel

The traitors doing a crawl

Laughter itself is liquid. You mustnt stop laughing, Lee, thats why you must go forward

Della, did you laugh? Harry, did she?

Della the sculptress and Abe the bookseller her husband with his dusty bookstore on Eleventh Street between Market and Race

Abe laughed, Lee

In the South Philadelphia bedroom of Della the sculptress and Abe the bookseller

I wish you wouldnt say anything about it, Lee, Im living with Harry now.

Harry Ring?

Yes.

Is your little boy with you?

Yes.

Harry has a son.

Yes he cuffs him and he buffs him and he roughs him and he scuffs him and he treats him like a little man, and its all right, Lee, believe me, because the boys been around women too much, even his own father

Honest Abe hath round spectacles steelyrimmed, a white brow circled by a white round face and a touch of chin, all to the which his bodys looped, littlelooped, five feet four

Dellas five feet four, theres a sculpher, a kind of hebraic blond monalisa, creamyrocked and greenyeyed, hiefernecked and trucksome titted, dont bother with a waist not she, shoots straight from the bosoms to the hips, stolidsquare on thigh and foot, as boomassed as they come but Harry roughs her, scuffs her, toughs her, buffs her, cuffs and muffs her, and hes a mickey of a man he is not like honest Abe the bookseller, its okay and its all right, he wants to beat me up thats his business, not mine and not yours, why all Abe does is

Whats all Abe do

Whats the matter with Honest Abe

Abes a sweet guy and a neat guy and hes three little loops on hurrying feet

What did you leave him for Della

What did you take up with Harry Ring for

But the sculpher is tearyeyed, Della sniffs and sniffles, Dellas a teakettle handtinting photographs to keep Harry and her kid in food and shelter at Fourth and Federal near a little old askew synagogue, and on top of a tailorstore

Its what your swimming through the waters with, Lee

Mighty suspiciously

And thats whats wrong with Honest Abe the bookseller

thats right

I never wouldve believed it

a clattering of coffeecups in the Heel, a stubby lawyer hees, a bald composer haws, an exballet dancer kicks up her eyes, guy schonfeld the associate professor of sociology at Penn State hiccupples

its true

its true

Della runs around after abe in their bedroom

is that so

sure

hes the one cant stop laughing

how come

she keeps running after him

why

why

same reason Lees trying to rescue a drowning man

no

yeh

its the truth

Dellas naked

Abes naked

and he cant stop laughing
hell have to get a divorce
sure
hes already applied for one
I cant stand it
neither could he
Dellas not laughing
no shes dead serious
she wants him
I dont blame her
but what about Abe
I dont blame him either
tough
yeh its a shame
he cant get it down
what
i said he cant get it down
his prick
yeh
hes got a permanent erection
Jesus Christ
nah thats impossible
who
Jesus Christ
I dont believe it
who
Jesus Christ
well what do you think he looked like on the cross
you mean what was bulging from his loincloth
thats right
he couldnt stand it
could you
no
neither could Abe
he cant get his damn prick down an hes laughing he cant stop
Della get him?
sure

she flops him down on the bed
what the hell
what an opportunity for a woman
thats how she figured
as long as it lasted shes going to get hers
believe me
she fucks him and fucks him and fucks him
and it tickles Abe
certainly
he laughs
she comes
again
and again
and again
he gets up
he runs
the prick still wont go down
does he get an orgasm
of course not
hes out of orgasms
but hes got that erection
like stone
like a statue
Dellas a sculptress
naturally she appreciates statues
statues of a prick
right
she keeps going after him
he keeps running
falls
she jumps
wow
she yells it never goes down it never goes down
a woman's dream
but he cant stand it
he runs some more
all the time laughing

its a torment but hes laughing
he trips
shes got him again
and again
and again
he gets on his pants and runs
where to
his BOOKSTORE HIS BOOKSTORE HIS BOOKSTORE
BOOKS ARE A REFUGE
IFYOURETRYINGTOSAVEADROWNINGMANBECAUSEYOUTHINKYOULL
HAVEANORGASMANDKILLYOURERECTIONYOUREWRONG
up and down on Joshua goes Helen Nathanson
its not true
I got to see that
where
at the bottom of Rocky River
the fife of the dancing ant axes off the surf
Name, please.
Lee.
Lee what?
Lee Emanuel. Whats yours.
Lee.
Lee what?
Lee Emanuel.
How old are you?
Twentythree years of age.
How old are you?
Ten years of age.
Brothers
Yes. that in the general discharge of sperm into icy water the residue destroys the brotherhood, that like a fuckedout fish the body is berated upon its belly floating upward and outward; I will give the semen its due, the salmon leaping upriver, up waterfall, so that I, Lee, standing as a child upon the wet stone lip at the bottom of Niagara, understanding quite well at last Miss Henderson the seventh grade English teacher at Clara Barton Junior High B Street and Wyoming Avenue adjacent to the graveyard of the eighteenhundreds itself adjacent to a mill spinning weaving looming

itself opposite the Wyoming Branch of the Philadelphia Free Library a modest brick structure behind which a playground, alongside of which the little red green twostorey houses of B Street Miss Henderson quietly criticizes Lee that he misspells the word; what word; Niagara. But those tons of churn, those craggymaned waters, lividloomingfoamed, in all throats reduced not amplified to thunder, again some pouring comprehension done on his pate, that here is selected a roar, here a viron degraded to absolute thunder as if the iron heavens above, sluiced of all moisture, emptying what utter cloacae could be amalgamated, collected and aggregated to plume enormous in feathery hugeness upon the boy's two small ears shaken sharded shambled by the cannon of the Niagara, misspelled, misspelled Miss Henderson, dumped and exploded in the whorling ragged serrated rapids beneath, six tons of the waters Lee, six years of his age under the bowelthroated spate of flume and flash, so that in the plunging to it he must erect Niagaras toward a man stupefied and stunned and imbeciled by the FALLS, that my body must take cognizance of itself by way of the genital, standardbearer, talisman, magic that must ensure Lee, hell not lunge waterwards without it, wearing it about his neck, his eyes, his skull, his loins, his kicking feet, that if it is not Lee received, then water itself, Niagara itself must be discharged, the FALLS to cannonade from the penis, hell do Niagara upon the man and upon the river, his mother holding his hand at his side, shy in the majesty of, ooohawed in the blasting grandjesty of, that she may drown with me, that under the sign of the testicles man must live, the two balls in metal signature above his commerce, not three, thats only for idiot and imbecile whove counted themselves too much and shall not perpetuate a mere hockshop of the genes, but the twin wrinkled balls hath shop and factory, work and marriage, mood and mordancy, haggle and harelip penis though they intrude, jiggle and jingle along, cowboy Lee on the watery prairie, the coyote weeds snapping and yowling at his kicking heels, he shall bring mercantile semen to the man though it blow up in our faces, though the FALLS of orgasm beat all living tissue down I will credit exhaustion to the rescue, wild weariness to the renovation; no other recourse, watercourse; the scream of the man coeval and coexistent with the shrill whistle Lee does over the emptied recess of the mechanical pencil hes removed the eraser from, absolute joy as the rest of the seventh grade class stare at him, wicked boy, naughty boy, for he sees in the closet the Clara Barton

Yearbook with the announcement that Lee Emanuel is given the Forefathers Award for general excellence of scholarship; its Miss Hendersons doing and hes in her class with the long oblong windows from ceiling to floor, the long green shades threequarters down to rebuff the hot afternoon sun, the long tawny windowpole in the rear corner of the room used to pull down the otherwise inaccessible windowtops, Lee blows all his lung across the pencil top creating a shrill eerie blast as Miss Henderson enters the room to look at Lee, Im ashamed, Lee, arent you ashamed, Lee, please leave the room and stand in the hallway for the remainder of the period, horsy Miss Henderson with whom Lee is impassioned though shes not nearly so succulent as the blueeyed tacktitted music teacher Now you write down your impressions to this recording of Musorgski's Night On A Bald Mountain but Lee cant keep his corneas off her nipples in the hallway the handwriting female teacher inquires why hes standing there because I was asked to by Miss Henderson What did you do I blew across the top of my pencil and make a screeching sound Too bad too bad little Miss Handwriting says, a head shorter than little Lee, arent you ashamed but he isnt because hes winning the Forefathers Award and hell stand up in front of the whole assembly at graduation from Clara Barton Junior High called to the front by the principal with his mother looking on, that is to say that the rubber eraser has been removed from the drowning man's mouth and Lee knows he must blow across it to make the screaming sound not for the foundation of the matter not for glassy glory nor the trail of awe, but the triumph of the semensalmon leaping up Niagara if only there isnt his brother

    ten years of age.

    His brother.

    There is a body, and it is Lee's, in some silent nakedness that glides around and around on the surface of a certain planet, of a color of peanut brittle, polished umber, though Lee may turn upon his back or lie bellywards, the sphere of the peanut brittle color, of the color of certain sunburnt flesh, it is beneath him and yet above him, that while he curves it is curved about him yet never is Lee within the sphere though it surrounds. Lee, all Lee is a hand upon the sphere burned the color of Rena in the sun at Atlantic City, at Ocean City, at Wildwood and at Stone Harbor, at all of these sandy names. A hand that comes in issue of chin, of mouth, of belly and thigh. But hand, all, that servecurves about the umber peanutbrittlecolored sphere, an abstracted flesh in the most saccharine warmth without gouging the nerves, over which Lee's handbody gliderolls sensing the hairs of the sun saturating the sphere, diffsuffused through the flesh, that the eyelidhand wakesleeps upon, warmcool currying without the comb, honeyburnt and browngold in the long adorumbration

shall you bear to unglide

More like dad than I. Eyes, bluegraygreen. Face, square. Body, a block. Hair, blond. More like Uncle Ben's son, Jared, though his bodys more the longer line, like mine. The features, though, closer to Jared's or Russel's. Lets see, Im born precisely a year after your death.

Yes.

Mother names me after you.

Do you like the name.

Lee, clear and melodious. Mother mentions you perhaps twice a year. Summa cum laude, merry and bright. Healthy. Funloving. Good in sports, in the head, in the heart. Much like Dick Merriwell, a series of paperbacks by Burt Standish with titles such as, DICK MERRIWELL FARTS AGAIN, DICK MERRIWELL REVOLTS THE MASSES, DICK MERRIWELL ANALYZES SIGMUND FREUD, DICK MERRIWELL MAKES NEWTON EAT HIS APPLE, DICK MERRIWELL AND THE PRINCIPLE OF UNCERTAINTY, Russell Zion has stacks.

Is there a stone? No hard feelings.

You mean the inscription at the base.

If you will.

None that I know. I havent the pleasure of your epitaph. In all the visits my mother pays me to the cemetery, I see no marker. As if for me no birth and no death of Lee Emanuel.

Curious you never see a stone for Lee Emanuel Number One.

Am I to urinate on your grave?

Very acidulous. Erosion. If you trail mother, you may reach me.

I am in fact a matter of law. Precedence. Dad speaks of my entering the Law. The urbane of civilization. The litigation involved in Lee Emanuel versus Lee Emanuel.

You must settle it.

You refer to a drowning man.

I am the Resurrection and the Glossary. Find the Emanuel Stone. In God knows how many languages.

At the riverbottom?

The scholar may spend the tenure of his Fellowship wherever he chooses.

Resurrect, for the which the unchewed spirits required, is imagination's fatality. However royal the resurrection, it is unmassed. Resurrection's feet lack arches, a podiatric paradise, manifold cottonmouths at the ache. I cannot put the resurrection down to any figure; it all counts Christ who goes crippled to the Mount. Poor sorefoot Christ, Im guilty of the stones, an awkward slipping on the blood to afterlife however cleansed with water is the promise. Whether I bear springwater to mother and father, or muddywater to a human group, no secondsoul sputters after baptismal. Only Gus Nathanson may take me by the coat and moan in quartertones that he is Christ secondcome. Or those dozen souls in the madman's ward claim they are Archimedes water displaced or Moses dividing the waters of the Reddest Sea or bawl themselves the child Moses in the bulrushes—I must concede weeds enough in Rocky River for such import; or Nelson frigated; or straight come from the Ganges dripping with transmigrations, a very Medusacrop of afterlives waving Come Shelter Me from their infraexcitable scalps. I want no cleanlimbed cloud as the resurrection plane. Is this some masshousing Pantheon, some harpandwinged skyscraper for saved souls? They have meanly pictured it, or humanly, transpose as you will, and as you cannot, the presumption goes, in the barbed abode of Hell. Ernest Chalk can tell me he is Mary or the next Parsifal or the next dragon if enough children shrink at his firespittling presence. I think I have not decided that which to resurrect, not adept at scarce crosses, nor adequately perfumable a fart to charm away gigantic stones upon my sepulchre. I may not be so great a man as to emit the necessary dimensions of a gas and blow me up to mythical paraproportions. I suspect the afterlife conceived by a quibbler, reared by a compromiser, matured by indecision and brought to mortality by thespian theologians trained in disservice to the natural disendowments of a man. Will someone not inquire how much water I may indeed replace without my iniquity knuckling under? My plunge thrashes no Niagara upon the shore. I cleave no dry land through the river. I sense no Archimedean envelopment to prove my endurance. I might with some thaumaturgic theory gape my mouth to the water, jaw it down with an endless succession of pistongulps and piss it out at penisend, some soigné sewer to remain intact after the entire river has passed through, at which one might with some crafty cogency inquire at the condition of that hose painted by a Flemish Master which led directly from the louring cloud above, Jehovahpalpitant, to the splayed thighs of Mary on the thistling ground beneath, the work of art entitled in all devotion, THE IMMACULATE CONCEPTION, which Lee pores over (though we cannot report with what literalness) in the main branch of the Philadelphia Public Library, 18th and Vine Streets, in Pepper Hall which houses volumes of art reproductions from the Caves of France to Pablo Picasso, from Pascin to Fra Lippo Lippi, from the Egyptian Feline to Marini's Horses, from Laocoon to Lipschitz, over which presides a twentyeight year old redheaded librarian with African cones squirting through her silk blouse and black high heels sinewing the muscular saturation of her nylonclad calves as she clatters sicklehipped along the marble floor, Lee's soft prick burning, begging, bucking at the seltzering sight of her so that the hose must at the least snap somewhere along the line and God go one way and Mary another, the conduit finally flapping like a hurtwinged gull in the historical breeze, peeling, exfoliating, I AM THE RESURRECTION AND THE FIFE, THE AFTERLIFE. Lee is. The water is. It is an in and an out of, not a through the. Whatever resurrects must come down. A Newtonian apple a day will keep God away, though Principia dedicated to the greater glory of, appropriate enough for the flyleaf, though Pascal bites his fingernail numbers into the parings of the Almighty. You cannot go where you are not wanted, a simple enough inscription at the base of anything

Intruder. Go back. Do you think it a game of a bobbing red apple in the water.

The game of trying to take a bite out of the bobbing red apple of the drowning man's face in the water

If you bite, perhaps you can swallow the whole apple

The faithful dog returns to his God holding the skull of the wounded gull in his slavering jaw

THATS a nice doggie

DROP the nice man's appleface right here at my feet

delicately

easy now

DONT CRUSH it

let the red apple go

youll EAT later

you cant EAT him just because youve SAVED him

of course i KNOW you wouldntve gone out there in the river unless
you THOUGHT you could EAT him after you brought him back

the eatings not for the doggie

the eatings for Goddie

so

let him go

drop him

DROP him Goddamn it

for Goddie's sake?

My second born wouldntve hesitated a moment in trying to help the
drowning man.

But you said I shouldnt.

What are we to do with FirstLee?

You mean quite clearly that youd like SecondLee dead.

I mean I must always consider and reflect, reflecting, on the contin-
gency, half possible as the boy not yet half a man, whom I should wish
to know, but half the man, which I do not, who, crossing the park on his
return from school, not part of the baseball game nor even part of the
baseball game in which my firstborn David is part of, which is the prefer-
ence, you understand, for there would be recognition present, a firstborn
citing danger to the second, or even refusing to cite it which lessens the
chance of the matter in maternal terms, for this I can overpower, this rise
huge in grief to so far as striking down David without whirling about in a
flat plane quite alone from which everything has been excommunicated,
I denied the anathematization, who, as I say, is about to pass a game in
which other boys between boyhood and men take part, which is perhaps
that which you, Lee, now take part in, without balls, that is to say, without
a ball, except that you yourself are the ball struck in trajectory by the bat
toward a sinking object, my other Lee, as he in truth sinks at the impact
of the hard ball, that is to say, without balls, struck by one of a group of
part boys, part men on a flat field called a diamond, the American game
par excellence, as males mostly men not far from boys stand on diamond-
shaped stones at a riverbank while Lee crosses the stream and fords the
park in the instant, not even looking to obtaining the other side but not
attending the game either, his right temple in the path of the hard ball,

without balls, that is to say, the absence harder in that the balls are not there, half temple and half boy, so that connection without connection is made, the young men staring at him in horror as now they continue to stare at you as you may be sinking, twice ten and three, not so much more than Lee concussed,

concussed

concussed, that you must recover his concunsciousness however the ambulances of the birds siren at the noon of day, for he does not come up, my son, and is dead of the trajectory's hemorrhage in the rising sunskull. They do not mean to kill him

as they do not mean to kill you. How can you then strike that drowning man?

I will seek to strike him because in your thinking of the secondborn you think of noncausality. And for your firstborn and lastborn in consequence you want cause, whether life or death is the result, for this is that to which you may point with pride. To your secondborn you can hardly point with anything. I at least can have perished for my native land. You can do nothing for your chosen land though you are born here: you are too young an American to feel native in it; nor does Levi. Your sacrifices actually are to the European lands you leave behind

The secondborn would not have you act in any relation whatsoever to him. He prefers his unique niche, his unadorned shrine. To die at ten years of age is unadorned indeed. I rather you wouldnt disturb me. Keep me simple: it is a clear sunny day; school is out; I am out; Ive schoolbooks under my arm. Im on my way home. Im in the act of crossing a park. Some boys in their early teens are playing baseball. They may see me; they may not. At any rate in the heat of the game they consider jeopardy to nobody. There is a boy at the plate about to swing at a pitched ball. I may see him, I may not; if I do, my distance from the game evacuates any sense of danger. I go on. I look at ants on the pavement. In an hour Ill be at Hebrew School reading the Semitic characters, something like the ants on the pavement. Im a little hungry, I think of a sandwich. I think there are not many more days till the end of the school term. I am liked, I like. Traffic hudgehudgehudges on the street to my left. Its not much of a park to my right, I can tell you, one of those many small squares that William Penn planned to leaven the crowded residences. But the game is at the far end. In a moment, Illve left the park altogether. Keep me simple on the clear sunny day. The boy swings at the pitched ball. I may see him swing, I may not, but the distance is sufficient protection I do not calculate the force of the pitched ball nor the force of the swing that meets it nor my distance from the ball as it approaches me. The boy who swung begins to run. I may see him, I may not. I may see the ball approaching me, I may not. Home is two blocks away, at 4th and Berks Streets, a little stooped twostorey house in the middle of a block of little stooped two-storey houses. In a year you will be born. I know a sandwich is waiting for me in the icebox, mamma always has one waiting. I can feel the sandwich in my mouth, rolled beef between two slices of rye bread. And milk to wash it down. Mamma always talks of washing the food down. She likes me, I like her. I give her no problems. Im prompt, she always knows where I am, I always know where she is. I get excellent grades and I play good ball with Dave. I spend summers in Atlantic City, poppa sees to that, with mamma, on Maryland Avenue. Im not particularly afraid of anything, and nobodys particularly afraid of me. Im no threat. Im almost a paragon. Im very goodhumored. Id like to go into pop's grocerystore business when I grow up. I think we could have lots of stores, not just one. He likes my idea about that. He likes me. I like him. I swim extremely well, Im good at football and baseball and soccer, as good as Dave was at my age, only I dont pity myself like he does or like you do. Keep me simple on the clear sunny day: I may be other than simple, or not, but it doesnt count today, because, really, I look forward to Hebrew School: Im adept there as everywhere.

But not quite adept at sensing the approaching ball. There the paragon falters

YOU SONOFABITCH

Come, come. The dead have absolutely no right to call the living names

YOU SONOFABITCH

All right, but you hear the crack of the bat. Your sense of placement should warn you, but youre too damn smug. Paragon indeed, with vacuities scattered here and there. Smug, smug

Certainly, then, you must feel overjoyed that the ball strikes my temple, that I lose consciousness, that I fall, that I crumple, that Im rushed to the hospital with a concussion

STOP PITYING YOURSELF

IVE GOT TO PITY MYSELF SOMETIME, LEE, AND WHATS THE MORE PERFECT MOMENT THAN TO DO SO AS YOU SWIM IN JEOPARDY TOWARD A DROWNING MAN, BECAUSE THE BALL KEEPS STRIKING YOUR OWN SKULL AND YOURE BOUNCING IT BACK, ARENT YOU

keep out of it

a tenyearold never keeps out of it. Youre overjoyed that in the morning twelve hours after the ball strikes my temple I die of hemorrhage

no, that does not give me joy

why not

fuck you, why should I tell you

Im with you.

I dont need you.

youre out of your mind

yes.

youre proud of that

yes.

you act senselessly

yes. The first Emanuel that acts senselessly.

Or so you would like to believe.

One can believe in senselessness.

Yes, till you strike meaning. The meaning is in the drowning man.

I can prevent him from possessing meaning by being unable to save him.

In short you will let him die in order to obtain meaninglessness, to really believe in that.

I dont know.

Ah, you stop short of that final arrogance. You cannot entertain it.

I entertain it but do not cap it

A very caviler at cowardice, coward at cowardice itself, a belittler of its reality, a tiny coward, a fear of trivial dimensions. Lee Emanuel the Second, small coward, knowing that he will prove incompetent at the grand cowardice. You do not immerse yourself all the way. It is only a fingernail of involvement, a toenail in the water though your body is largely submerged. But we dont speak of body, do we? Youdve walked a block away from the park where they played the game, not five blocks. It displeases you that Im so cavalier, that Im so much ten years of age, without apologizing for it, without racing ahead of it, without falling behind it.

You on the other hand at ten are far away from it both ahead and behind. At ten youre a child of three and a man of twentythree. You cannot know what it is to be simply ten years of age. You never experience it. Youre terribly envious of me. Do you think you can be ten years of age now in the water?

Any of my friends can tell you that I sometimes have difficulty in hearing accurately

I said DO YOU THINK YOU CAN BE TEN YEARS OF AGE NOW IN THE WATER.

I said what makes you think youre at all hesitating at the premised attempt to save the drowning man?

Hesitation is the medium of exchange

is the lenitive sensation calculated to muffle and mollify the sense of motion

One risks oneself only because one considers it comic to do so. Never seriously

Hesitation in any case nothing more than an uncertain figure of speech, the inability to precisely describe a complicating action

Risk means taking oneself seriously and one's action comically

Archexerting a gangling stertorousthroated figure flings itself into the swifting current, comparing himself for the moment to an outrigger canoe, his arms in, an elbowing on either side, pulling in a mightily capsizing motion against the waters

Can you endure the constrained laughter of the men on the riverbank?

at the notion that the event has already been completed, that the drowning man is drowned, that the drowning man is simply reflexive upon the surface

the event done, why Lee, do you proceed?

I may proceed to race against the oncoming consciousness in the minds of the watching men of the fact of a lag. I may wish to recapture the event itself, the actual drowning. I go forth possibly to reenact the condition, to trick the observers into thinking that the occurrence is still in motion, to keep the constraint upon their laughter. They may never laugh if I prestidigitate the man continuing to drown. They suspect the prestidigitation; in the suspicion is laughter's lurk. But they may not have witnessed the end of the trick. The trick is to insert oneself upon the stage before the curtain. It is known as the triumph of the extraneous.

But suppose you prove maladroit.

But in that very act of magic is the highly moral, the religious sense, for Lee may revive the very struggle itself. For the very possibility of such he cannot be censured. And in the maladroit may be his punishment.

His punishment? The punishment may very well be upon the drowning man, for if the man drowning has any revival potential, Lee's maladroitness may extinguish it.

Then it is the drowning man who takes the further risk.

The drowning man need not go through the reflex action which is not necessarily symptomatic of death. It may signify the trace of life, the drowning man's responsibility. He continues to scream, as well. There is the seduction implicit in the act of drowning. His bobbing red face is a lure which cannot be discounted.

Implying that the drowning man exercises a certain amount of sensuality.

Yes

Theres passion on the mans face.

Yes

As if he is about to ravish a woman.

Yes

Theres no woman available. Only Lee

Theres homosexuality at the prospect of mortality

Even if Lee would not be present. Even if nobody is present

Yes.

The drowning man desires to have self-coition

Yes

At the possibility of lastminute propagation. As if the orgasm will spout up through his mouth and Lee or anyone will be there to catch the emission and swallow it

Yes

This should disgust Lee in the alleyway between the Emanuel house and the Forsten's in the middle of the summer afternoon Come on, nobodyll see, Hank Randall says, red puffs on his elevenyearold bloatface rolling around in a bloatbody set on waddlelegs. The light takes down its pants, showing shadows in the alleyway. How old are you now, Lee?

Nine, Lee says, the oscillograph sending down roots in his belly.

Thats old enough, youll like it.

I dont know. Maybe I shouldnt.

Come on, I wont hurt you. The bloatlips in the urgent smile, a harden of proof in them, a fist deep under the cheeks. Just take a look at my lips, Lee, see how big and soft they are. I couldnt hurt you if I tried. Okay?

Maybe somebodyll come.

Nah, nobodyll come, Ill keep a lookout, dont worry, nobody can see us

Lee feels drained, chilled, cramped, soft, soapy, vaselined, his nose throbbing in his forehead. The older boy has blubber around his eyes, concealing a flat green, a clump of fat around the keen. There is a rolling patience all around him, his blubbernipples heavy through his thin summershirt, his belly a big bag over his crotch. The traffic hums smoothly on the Roosevelt Boulevard. Because of the shallow angle in the alleyway the vertex cannot be seen either from the backyard or the pavement paralleling the Boulevard.

Well what am I supposed to do? Lee begins to shake a little

Nothin much. Just unbutton your pants and take it out. You dont even have to look. You can shut your eyes if you like. Im tellin you youll like it, lots.

Just take it out?

Uhhuh. Ill do the rest. You dont have to do anything. All Im goin to do is get down on my knees, but you dont have to look

His fingers fickle, undaring, all nail, all unfleshed, all bone, Lee unbuttons his pants, his forehead now circling his entire skull, his breath clotted. The summer air is cool in the pants hole

Come on, take it out

I am, I am, Lee softly protests. Gimme a minute

Hurry up

Im going as fast as I can, so

Hot wet, sucking, saturates it, and a faintly rough tongue turns plush upon it, Lee's velveting eyelids slurring down over his sight. The insides of the lips lean lightly on the penis, but exact, demand, pull and push, as if Lee's entire abdomen begins to pour out, as if Hank is mellowly masticating the entire length of Lee's intestines by his gums alone, without the use of teeth, so that Lee himself wants to give, to help, to aid by pushing his penis deeper and deeper into Hank's mouth as the little balloons of fat greased in spit encase little Lee's hard little prick, the fatboy all mouth and quicksand cheek into which Lee is sinking like a rigid tremor, a crystallized piss, his belly now like overlapping plates of steel giving propulsive force to the prick wading around up to its neck in undulant vises of steaming moisture, Lee's legs solidly planted on the pavement, his shoulders hunched, his eyes hunched in on themselves, his ribs fists, he wants to push it into Hank's throat, as deep down as it will go as Hank's sucking flares into Lee's throat and Lee's mouth pops open to give Hank more air, more air, more air, the blubberwrinkles of Hank's mouth creasing like chasms till a sharp jagged chunk rends through Lee's prick like a burning stone and his knees suddenly shimmy, Hank's adamsapple working overtime and his eyes wide as his fat can see as Lee's belly topples over, topples end over end and flops, crazily teetering

Shame, yes. Disgust, no

Lee's belly toppling over, end over end, flopping, crazily teetering, in the cold, turbulent stream

Go through what its supposed to look like, then let him drown. Youll get something out of it, wont you? Youre doing a kind of passive murder on the man. Now thats something I got no experience in. But dont get too close.

Ill have to.

It dont do to get intimate with the man youre going to murder.

Theres a kind of crafty chaos in Lee. I suggest he take advantage of it. Its rare one feels a crafty chaos. Indulge it.

Crafty chaos is a lower animal operation, done with the belly close to the surface of the medium one operates in. A kind of frigid masturbation. Break the habit, Lee

No

You dont have to carry your cold calculation to the limit.

Cold calculation carried to the limit may break up at the terminus. I wont turn back.

Theyre calling for you from the riverbank to come back.

I cant hear them. Besides, if they are, theyre liars.

Their element of truth is that in their judgment youve already shown approved intent which is sufficient for forgiveness, If you come back they will forgive you in truth. If you go forward, they will forgive you in a lie, loudly proclaimed, of course, in proportion to the extent of your insult. The more you go ahead toward the drowning man, the more you insult them, humiliate them. Give your humiliation of them some thought. Youve already sufficiently humbled them. Theyre in danger of groveling

I want them to grovel

No. You want profound reverence from them and you wont obtain that from them if you persist

go ahead

go back

go ahead

go back

youre joking

no, Lee

Russ, youre joking, I dont have the weight

nothingll happen to you, were at steeplechase pier to have fun

youre heavier, youre older, I dont want to go on the seesaw

a tattle of wind about the cheek

a smudge of sunlight from the sea

a boardwalk and rollingchairs

go on get on

all right

dont worry Ill control it

okay

see it isnt so bad is it?

a smudge of sunlight from the sea

a tattle of wind about the cheek

see

saw

saw

see

sawsee

seesaw

up and a down and an up and a down and atop the rollingchairs on the boardwalk and Ill snitch a bit of the sun

its fun

i told you itd be

and down toward the buff caps of the sand THERES THE HIGH DIVE OF STEEL PIER AND THE WHITE HORSES DIVING INTO THE TANK AND THE AERIALISTS AND THE GENERAL MOTORS EXHIBIT AND THE FRIGID-

AIRE EXHIBIT AND MIDGET TOWN ON ONE SIDE OF THE PIER AND RUSS
COLUMBO AND HIS ORCHESTRA IN ONE THEATRE THERES DANCING
TONIGHT SAY THE ELECTRICBULB SIGN KIDDIES FIFTEEN CENTS ADULTS
TWENTYFIVE CENTS AND TOM MIX IN THE OTHER MOVIE AND JOHN GIL-
BERT AND GRETA GARBO IN THE THIRD MOVIE AND ITS ALL FREE ONCE
YOU PAY THE GENERAL ADMISSION THE GENERAL MOTORS CHASSIS SHIN-
ING BLACK WITH THE STEERING WHEEL PROUD AND EMPTY AT THE END
OF THE SHAFT

HAVING FUN LEE

YEH

FASTER OKAY

YEH RUSS WHAT ARE DOING GETTING OFF ILL

F

F

ILL

ALL

FA

RUSS THE SEESAW HIT MY ANKLE RUSS RUSS

Im getting Uncle Ben

Uncle Ben the seesaw hit my

I thought he heard me Uncle Ben when I told him I was getting off

Its not your fault Russ its an accident Ill carry you piggyback Lee

my ankle hurts it hurts awful bad

Ill carry you piggyback and get you to a doctor

a smudge of

a tattle of

wind

sun

chokepeopled boardwalk

I want my pop wheres my pop Uncle Ben

shah shah Lee Ill carry you

but I want my pop I want my pop

Dave alias Clancy Mann says its a chance to win your letter

sentimental athletic exertion

HELP

its not true, theres only a scream, there simply isnt the word HELP

I dont have to depend on the word

I beg your pardon, you do, for the scream is very probably the expression of sheer incredulity at the impossibility. Let him go

I know nothing, therefore I must go

enchantment, Al Gordon says, a transient sorcery, in which you are seduced by an expression of incredulity. All men attempt such a seduction. The worst of it is that you attempt it upon yourself, the notbelieving that you are at Rocky River, the notbelieving you are Lee Emanuel, the notbelieving that a man is drowning, the notbelieving that yourself can drown, the notbelieving that you are either alive or dead, the notbelieving that change is possible from one state to another, the notbelieving that you are exhausted. An enormous negation propels you toward the drowning man. All you have to do in order to turn back is to believe in yourself, to believe that you are in the Army of the United States, to

negate

affirm

negate

affirm

there is this state of Israel. An act of indecency to exhibit one's courage before spectators. One should be courageous in private. Theres no duty worth the seesaw. The fife of the dancing ant axes off the surf, come, I wont hurt you, come with me, into the crooked alleyway of the waters, how can a tenyearold do you harm. Your wristwatch, look at your wristwatch, what is the time, tell me the time,

not till I enter the airforce do you present me with the selfwinding automatic wristwatch, mother, so there is

no time

no time

no time

but the boy speaks of selfwinding automatic time and theres nobody here but the body. Rena sings in Atlantic City. My brother Daves in Alaska. My mother and father are in Philadelphia. Daniel Naroyan is beating rugs. Sy Tarassoff is working in the Camden Shipyard. Al Gordon has a trick knee. Link Cornwall is a homosexual. My grandfathers dead. My brother Lee died a year before I was born. The twelve men stand on the riverbank. There is nobody here but Lee Emanuel. Nobody else is moving but Lee. The company commander is in the colonel's tent. The company sergeant is on another phase of the manuever. Jennifer Hazlitts married to Guy Schonfeld. Laura Ingersoll waves goodbye at Province-town. Dr Newman is treating patients in Philadelphia. Eli Berman is judged a mental incompetent and is rejected from the draft. President Franklin Delano Roosevelts in Washington. Harry Ring doesnt bother to reply to his draft board. Dr Saul Reed is being sent through medical-school free by ASTP. Russ Zion is rejected because of weak bronchi. Jared Emanuel has a trick knee. The Chassid is in the Mediterranean. The Jews are in the crematoriums. Victor Nathanson is dead of a heart attack in Moyamensing Prison. Gus Nathanson cannot serve in the army because hes an idiot. Everybody is somewhere else. I am the only one in the world that can move in this particular unique movement. And the caring is from none but myself for this specific movement and I am jealous of that. Theres nobody in the world that can wrest this from me. No, not the water, not the air, not the stones under my feet, nor any part of myself can wrest the whole from me, that whole which is me. Other beings, men and women elsewhere, try to take me from myself, and parts of my body try to evacuate me, but I wont have it. I stay with myself, all hands will be present, for this is the beast in the hot summer sun that divested of his pack and his shoe and his shirt and his pants and his jockstrap and his gun, that, divested of all things but himself, divested of sweat and cold and all his connexions, flings himself flatbellied into the rushing stream, skullfirst, buttocks pulled after, the beast, as I say, hearing another beast in his final strident coo for the air, must put his teeth about the others, the teeth of one beast upon the neck of the other, for this is the beastplunge, the mother and father and brother beastplunge since no other men can be so sufficient unto themselves as to rebeast thmselves, the teeth bar-ing within the shut mouth, the muddy waters choking at the beastneck and splattering the beasteyes as with acid, the beast in his deepest act of egobeastness, in fury, in selfjealousy, in spit and unhallowed be thy name, damning the transgression of life itself, stomping with the whole beastbody upon mancare, preferring the beastcare, the stupendous blast at all things human that not the multitude will fling itself but that only one beast will so fling as to damn the multitude of men, damn the man-life which is worth nothing to the beast, for the beastbody itself does not pause, does not deliberate, and I hug beast to me, not even thinking of men, not thinking of his own manpart which is left with the comicclothes on the drystones, expending the last beastounce of himself toward that sinking beast with its crimson houndface wailing into the sun, I will sink my teeth in it and shove it back onto the dry land, I will harry and nurse it back to the shore with its two tiny shrunken dugs of maledom on its chest, with its flatworm penis flapping in the wet, with its manburden on its back, man's bayonet a beast should not carry, man's gun a beast should not bear, man's gasmask a beast should not wear, man's fears a beast should not skull, what is a beast doing out there called a man?

There must be enough time. A strange matter, that the hot morning sun steams down upon the water, Rocky River, but turns back at the churning liquid surrounding Lee, like slimy rubbery icicles striating around him. He throws his strokes upon the water as if they are iron pipes and that he must heave himself after them like a big snake. He does not feel his limbs at all: they are the thrown weights which he must positively suck himself after as a dumb thing learning speech by ingesting air rather than by extruding it. He cannot see the drowning man. It, the drowning man, is somewhere out there in the deepest of the channel. Lee knows he will come upon him. He does not know when.

As he does not know what makes this what it is. What is lie of this and what is true of this

Summer it is but there is an armistice for a boy in a Feltonville grammarschool room at eleven oclock in the morning on the eleventh of November. There are twelve quiet children around Lee. There are fifteen quiet children around Lee. From the blinding icicle of the winter sun the long green shades are rolled down. The old female teacher who looks like George Washington, white wig and wooden dentures and all, a hunched portrait by Gilbert Stuart, holds up her hand

Green pines overarch the Rocky River bank. On both sides. Two bands of green separated by slate gray sinuously striped by oscillographic serpents of white

Lee is a discusheaver with his arms in the slabs of the water which he must remove and heave aside one by one,

one by one

monolithic structures of water

kicked in the face by stinging hobnails. Green, slate, serpentine streaks of white, green,

slate, white, green

the Niagara dumped upon the boy, turning to a mother, the tons upon tons of water avalancheening down, but she can only take his hand, he wants nothing more than her hand, he will not have her hand upon his neck nor upon his shoulder let the hand stay simply upon his hand and nothing more, no further touch, any further touch is a disaster, invites repulsion, touch me not, I will throw it off, I tell I will throw

His strokes are shotputs in the water. There is a head. There is a bob-bing apple. Closer

closer

a bobbing red face among the white oscillographings upon the slate churn

a bobbing puffed

bloated

blue eye

not two blue eyes.

Not two. One. A cyclops in the water, crimsonfaced and with a single blue

hudgehudgehudge the freighttrain its amber jelly in the dead center of the locomotive

bearing down upon Lee in the water

the jellied blue eye bearing down set in the midst of a furnaceface glowing redhot with the sound of the trainwhistle issuing in the long coupling scream from the black pit of the mouth

eeeeeeeeeeeeeeeeeeeeeeeeeeeeeeeeeeeeeeeeeeeeeeeeeeeeeeeeeeeeeee eeeeeeeeeeeeeeeeeeeeeeee

What manner of man is this that screams. I should like to know pre-cisely what Im doing. I swim. I put one arm in front of me. Then another. Still another. He is a madman in the water. He struggles in the straight-jacket of the Rocky River, of the churn. Hes caught. The closer I get to him the greater the risk of his murdering me. Hes brought in screeching. He thinks theres something in the sky that is focused on him, something that will kill him. If I touch him he will think me out of the sky and try to fight for his life. Ive got to get rid of him. But in order to do so Ive got to be close to him. Ive got to be in touch. It is only by being in touch that I can repel him. I cant turn back unless I ricochet back. I cant change my direction till he compels me to do so

now

now

now

Lee tangles, his lungs burning prickles, all his lungs little throbbing fingers slashed, air squirting out of them like blood, all his senses are running down the street, Lee tangles with the bobbing face's hair, indeterminate Medusasnakes, the gorgonhead, the hair wriggling under his fingers, his body buckling, sliding, skipping, squirming, cork upping and downing in the water, air and wet flexflungaling in his openjaw, not a depth knowing, not a topsand of a surface but a shifthacking of the slapping waters, the bobred face who the, what, object, gr

gra

GRAB a

gripa

GRABGRI

p

a THIS IS MEEEEEEEEEEEEEEEEEEE this is me

this is meeeeee

this is me

screams the drowning upon. Me. Lee. Me. Lee. Me. Lee, hahahaha-hahah the redface laughs I GOT I

got

got GOD yahhahhahhahyahgot god, thats, slidedown, cant GRAPPLE-GRAB slitherdown forearm

Lee feels the barnacles of the deadman's nails slashing down bicep and elbow

blood fanning

down forearm

and wrist

I want his hair, drag by his hair, back, bank, thats what, somebodys waiting, fifteen, twelve men, children, they can save

but redbloat with the final spasm of a spasm VISES Lee's wrist

holds

the spasm of the spasm locking upon itself, I wont give up the lock thats what, I wont give up the lock, its the lock that FORGETS ITS TURNING ON LEE'S BONE OF A WRIST

No. Impossible. Light thins, thickens to slate, all water, water blubbering inside Lee's mouth

And he sees the drowned man's scarlet face the single blinding blue freight of an eye turned on Lee through the thickening green water going down

slow elevator. To the Niagra, cant spell, to the Falls, at last descended upon him as the child descends to the bottom of the elevator's green shaft the mother is the dead man holding him in a grip of fatherice from the icy springs in the water slashing blood pumps of glassedges across his arms

So. Lee makes, descending, a tentative lunge. I got to get. Accidents survive, the fife of the dancing ant axes off the surf, I look up at myself as an eye looks upon its slate underbelly descending I look on myself I got to get off myself

chokenausead. Keep mouth closed. The lavender balloon inside his chest threatens to burst, though he wants to giggle, not now, not now, not now, the joke of being alive altogether surrounded by water deepening the green scum over the pond, heaving his neckmuscles this way and that, rearing his skull from side to side, setting a dynamite charge from his lungs to all points of his body, his legs kicking, thrashing, pumping, boiling, his spine bending double, triple, quadruple in the unutterable magic of divesting himself of his dragflesh, the man's spasmelectrode strapped around Lee's wrist, cutting off flow, Lee will unsocket himself from the socket of the blue dead eye staring him down staring him down staring him down hes got to kill him

kill him

the dead man does know who hes killing and if the dead man doesnt know then Lee cant know

and Lee can kill

can break the hold

can send the dead man to his death where he belongs murder him murder him, the water lancing his gums, the shore, the Rena, the mother, the air, the rock, he wont go insane, no, he wont go insane as to fall madly in love with green water, hes on the edge of the water's insanity, hes got to murder all the insane.

because theres bellyfeed on the shore, theres

THERES LEE

THERES LEE ON THE TOP OF THE WATER AND THERES LEE ON THE SHORE AND THERES LEE WALKING AND TALKING AND FUCKING AND SLEEPING AND RISING AGAIN IN THE MORNING YES THERES LEE AND

THERES ONLY LEE AND THERES NOTHING ELSE IN THE WHOLE WORLD BUT LEE AND LEE WANTS HIM AND LEES GOING TO HAVE HIM EVEN IF LEE HAS TO MURDER A DEAD MAN TO GET TO LEE

TOUCH ME NOT

TOUCH ME NOT

cant wait

not a moment

his lungs his grandfather his father are slipping away from him

STOMP ON ALL THE LIVING SO THAT LEE LIVE

I cant stand you touching me

Lees drowning

he watches himself. He sees. There it is. Hes a body. All the scenes are leaving. Quietly. Tiptoe in the water. Theyre going. Lee wont wait. Matter has too much to do. Matter will join other matter. It wont wait here. Not on your life. Matters got to move its fingers, matters got to dig toes in sand, matters got to have woman, matters got to curse, bless, weep, grieve. Matter must go from here. Matter judges the situation a matter for ridicule, but you can ridicule only up on the surface. You cant ridicule here in the depths.

Lee shrugs.

Thats all he does. But its large. His whole matter shrugs. The shrug says it impossible, it cant be.

Shrugs.

A gigantic shrug that lifts Lee out of the iron casing of the descending drowned dead man

and Lee sees the dead

man.

Silkily. The puffed red face. Inhuman face. Scarletscaled with the exit of terror when the face took its last

look

on its terror. I killed him, Lee thinks weary. As he floats up. Toward light, and

the dead man, silkily, like the last of all the gracefully created, his terrorface now averted for he shall not shame Lee living, facefirst away, the body in the beauty of its waterwheel oblique in the streaming ripple rippling down in the greendeep away from Lee, bid adown, bid adieun, at last unlimbering, slate as the surrounding undulance, gently shaken, all the dead body a ripple of slatehair upon the current, glimmerguttering down the slate oscillograph of the distance

but I

I cant forget his face. The red face and the blue bauble of the eye afright me, make me very afeard. For it is the surprise in the terror of the whole man clotted upon his face, as if, not as if, but all true as his body went down under, then, then all the parts of him, all the parts of the drowning man began to climb, up his legs, up his crotch, running up his ass, clambering up his spine as his body went down deeper, as all the compartments became flooded all the parts of him ran madly up and up and up, along his sternum, up his arms, through his airhole in his neck, to the top of his throat, each part of him crowded in panic through his mouth to the very top of his face, to his eyes, waving for Christ's sake, for the sake of one little part of me, take hold of me, lift me up

take hold, and lift me, were all frightened on the top of my face, my hands, all you living in the air, my hands beckon from my eyes, come quickly, quickly

for the tips of my fingers are slipping on the slippery round surfaces of my eyeballs

this I remember, Lee sweats in the night. This I will not forget.

Goodnight, grandfather. Goodnight, father. You have gone down with him. Lee goes to bed. No scene contracts. No scene expands as, Rocky River quite calm now, the turbulence drifted away, Lee swims languidly to the bank where the twelve men stand, the fifteen men wait. A languid grin inside Lee, curling the words, I can murder too, I too can murder. The red bloated face of the drowning man replaces in his dreams the face of his grandfather and father,

while at the front of the classroom in the Feltonville grammarschool the old female teacher, the hunched George Washington in white wig and wooden dentures, the green long shades rolled down to shut out the icy winter sunglare, raises her hand, then announces We will observe one minute of silence for the dead of the American wars. The whistle screams outside, stops. As the dead man goes gracefully down, the fifteen men and the twelve children bow their heads as the languid survivor swims toward the shore, Lee in the midst of the children, all gone mad as men, watching the man come to the shocked bowed heads of the children on the riverbank schoolroom, their hands folded on the stony desks listening to the music of the Philadelphia Orchestra, Stokowski conducting. Daniel Naroyan at last sitting calmly, panic subsided, the fire extinguished on Armistice Day, all Lee's fears amalgamated now in the languid drifting survival toward the riverbank, encompassed in a single scarlet bloated face. I accomplish the creation of a single dream of terror in the murder of one man, the ants of tiny clouds crawling across the one blue eye of the sky, and the whistle screams once more, terminating the minute of silence

leading Lee's eye, as he sits at the table in the rear of Horn and Hardart's with two other young men, to slant toward the aisle which runs the length of the food counters and the steam hissing from the coffee urn, suddenly hissing, as if at the appearance of a scarlet daub, a crimson blotch at the far end of the aisle near the revolvingdoor entrance and exit, the red gurgle becoming more pronounced as it expands in vibrating spheres up the aisle and Lee slowly tensing in the chair in his threadbare shitbrown doublebreasted suit, triangles of deep blue shadow from a day's growth of beard on either cheek, a thin tall torso of a boy with something like a turtle's neck scooting out from the shouldershell to hold in a concave scoop the big oblong of the skull, long from keel to superstructure and shallow through the beam, the jaw just short of a lantern. There are tilts and teeterings of at least a dozen empty cups and saucers on the table, coffee dregs at their bottoms rotting the crushed white slugs of cigarette stubs. There is a blob of something in green, of considerably lesser volume, skittishing beside the larger scarlet,

Sergeant Lee Emanuel.

Yes.

Serial Number 32866709.

Yes. In the modest onestorey brick building on Governors Island very close to the water Lee glances up at the officer addressing him and notices nothing more than the bright brass lozenge on the collar, the insignia of the Finance Department. The officer stands behind a wire cage counting out fresh crisp snowygreen currency. Musteringout pay. Travel pay. Allowances. There are men waiting in line behind Lee. There are men ahead of Lee who are walking through the bright oblong sunblocked door. Lee perks his ears, examines the dust motes falling aslant the sunblocked door ahead, runs his eyes down his khaki, hudgehudgehudges along his heart, slips a stealthy look around his bowel, squints in his belly, feels the toes in his shoes. There must be something unique lurking somewhere. But to this point, nothing. He conjures up certain names, as: Berlin, Stalingrad, Nagasaki, Hiroshima, Solomon Islands, Philippines, Coral Sea, Murmansk, Anzio, Tobruk, the Battle of the Bulge, Pearl Harbor when he crouches on the cot on the second storey of the barracks at Fort Knox and peers out at the slate ice landscape, the jagged ice hills, the iceclouds breathing frostily over the practice tank grounds in the late afternoon as a portentous voice silkily unburdens itself of a tale of treachery and infamy, Armistice Day silences bowing the heads of all the men in the barracks while the Japanese ambassador was in conference with the head of the United States State Department on methods of maintaining the peace a squadron of Japanese planes were only in for a year, were only in for a year but now the dusk deepens into death and no man knows when Mindanao, Corregidor from the fresh crisp snowgreen currency, but the names maintain their namehood and nothing more. It is a species of guilty lie for Lee to be thinking of the names at all, for he knows them only as names, but he experiences at this point none of the guilt, as if, indeed, even guilt is impermissible; as if, indeed, he must suffer from tranquillity, know only serenity, ICE NEVER FAILS

Serenity? Tranquillity? We go too far, perhaps. Dr Saul Reed, pediatricianpsychiatrist, leans forward in the cracked leather chair of the tiny livingroom of the Emanuels' sixroom groundfloor apartment at 229 Sullivan Street, a block from the New York University law library. Norma, Lee's secondwife, hunches on a hassock near the crackling fireplace in the winter evening. Nora Reed cups her saucerface in her hands, listening with her enthralled agony and glancing from time to time at Norma; the doctor's wife pictures a Marley Road livingroom in Philadelphia where Lee sits with his first wife, Rena. Flikker sits crunched in another corner under the single immense window. Norma sips slowly at her wine. Its true, Saul avers, in answer to Lee's objection, that an absolutely emotionless state is an impossibility, but there can be a minimal amount of emotion in the mentative process. And that, he stutters, inevitably indicates the neurotic state. The emotion is locked up, inhibited. When I say a minimal amount of emotion I mean minimal in the conscious sense. It means something is damned wrong

Damned wrong that Lee feels what he provisionally entitles serenity. He corrects himself. Theres quietude in him, apparently. He senses no anger, no hate, no love, no envy, not even the feeling that these have been evacuated. The sole feeling he has is a desire to feel something. And he is closer to it, there. A want to have a feeling to signalize his impending discharge from the Army of the United States. To signalize, to make salient and unique and special. But he can discover nothing within himself to so signalize in the quiet dimlit Finance office. The officer pushes the money due Lee through the wire cage and at the next counter a noncom hands Lee his papers, an honorable discharge from the Army of the United States for medical reasons, and a summary on another stiff piece of Lee's army record, the number of days absent without leave, the company punishment meted out, the day of induction, the serial number, the dates of serum and vaccine shots, the medical reason specified in the discharge, psychoneurosis, the number of years, months and days of service—four years, four years, four years, the medals awarded, the Good Conduct medal, the Victory medal, the Service medal for serving in the continental USA, the places of service, the Army Intelligence Test placement in Group 1, the rank attained, sergeant, the fingerprints. Then the noncom hands him the brass discharge button with its now notorious emblem thereon of the ruptured duck. Four years.

The draft board in the basement of the bank on the corner of Fifth Street and Wyoming Avenue.

The Armory and Link Cornwall.

The Pennsylvania Station at Broad and Market Streets. No, I dont want you down there to see me off, Rena

Camp Meade. Fort Knox. Fort Benning. Maneuvers in Carolina. The drowning. Randolph Field. Selfwinding automatic wristwatch bought in Gimbels in Philadelphia by his mother. Navigation. Telegraphy. Into the air, into the high blue yonder. East St. Louis. Rena's nosebleed all night. Washout. Garden City Army Air Field. Altus Army Air Field. Randolph Field. Fort Worth Army Air Field. The furlough in New York. Harry Ring's apartment. Governors Island

Four years. The farmhouse in Garden City where Rena and Lee live

Four years

Good luck, Mr Emanuel. Congratulations, youre a civilian, the noncom smiles.

Theres nothing more, Lee inquires. Because at Camp Meade the civilians are marched into a large barracks where an officer administers an oath to abide by the Articles of War, Repeat after me, repeat after me, their arms upraised, I do faithfully swear

Nothing more, the noncom says.

I can go, Lee says.

Thats right. Youre a civilian.

Lee grins uneasily, though no unease within, as though he must nevertheless show unease, then a jauntiness, then a relief. But none of these within.

And he walks through the door blocked by the sun into the crisp currency of the December air, down the curved path, around the curved street, along the neat, orderly, vinecovered buildings of the Army, toward the Hudson, to the ferry where he quizzically shows his discharge papers to two lumpy MPs who grin him on and he waits on the dock reading the quartzglitter on the great river, the angular thrusts of the ascending shafts of Manhattan in the sharp blue and purple shadowing of the December morning. Calmly he takes out a cigarette. Calmly he lights it, takes a long draw. Silently he records what he calls his rather banal mentation: but there are no martial bands; when we got off the train at Fort Knox a band was playing; there are no speeches now; theres no valedictory; theres no assemblage of men and an officer to bid us goodbye; nobody said goodbye; he couldnt find Major MacFarland, the army psychiatrist, to bid him goodbye—he was informed that the Major was on pass, there had been a remission of his dengue fever hed picked up in Burma with Merrills Marauders; he hadnt wanted Harry Ring to come pick him up; he could get across the Hudson by himself he told Harry; where are the four years in the Army of the United States; today is no different from the day preceding it; yesterday youre in the army, ten minutes ago you were in the army; now, at half past eleven youre not in the army; what is to be done now; Rena wants you to write plays, she will support you by her niteclub singing, you dont have to join your father in the Levi Coal Company; but there are no martial bands; theres no music, theres no ceremony marking the difference between now and ten minutes ago; what a shame; I want music, I want a speech, I want something official to mark this moment, I want to feel a surge of joy; I wonder where my brother is; the last I heard Clancys in Alaska with his second wife; I want to get home, to Philadelphia, to Rena, to my father and mother, to Esther Goldstein's kitchen where Rena can make me bacon and eggs because my mother wont have bacon in the house; there are no special flags waving; theres the usual American flag; Im not dead, Im not dead; I came through four years; I survived; Im out of the army; its here, Im done, I never thought it would ever ever ever be done; I wish I couldve known Anzio or the South Pacific or the London blitz but I really didnt want to, I mightve gotten killed; six million Jews are dead, I didnt help them but I feel no remorse; the wars over; where is the war over; where is the peace over; why isnt there some music?

The GENERAL CLAYTON, engines reversed, ferries into the keystone-shaped berth Sy Tarassoffs in New York with his wife Nina, the barnacle scars fanning down his arm, in Provincetown Harbor the wake from the great Boston ferry nearly capsizes the canoe, Ninad like to capsize Lee, a letter he writes Danny The woman is gross, vulgar, middleclass, raucous, its impossible to understand why Sy ever married her, I predict their marriage wont last beyond in the gloomy Old York Road mansion Naroyan proudly passing around to a circle of friends the gems he calls of Lee's correspondence but quite by accident

really quite by accident Id no idea it was there the letter to me about Nina falls out just as shes reading another

quite by accident Harry Ring sniggers in the eastside apartment, slapping his thighs but you two ought to make up, you and Sy, I talked to him, he isnt furious with you anymore, sure Ninas a little hurt still, but what the hell tell him youre sorry, go ahead, besides, he adds slyly, I want some of Sy's watercolors he walks the heavy iron planking aboard the Clayton to the Manhattanpointed bow, emotionless, on his way to Staten Island to claim Rena's things, a few gowns, a hat box, effects Yeh she said she had to leave suddenly, said she had a pain in her side, might be her appendix she said the man says on the phone to the Emanuels' 75th St apartment at seven oclock of the sultry summer evening, and theres a telegram from Rena, dont worry, it says, dont worry about me, Ill be back Ill be

back towards the bow Lee strides through the convex innards of the General Clayton, the polished oak seats, the flysnotted windows, the ammoniacal mens room odors pendant on the hangdog innard air to the deck outside to the left of the parked cars, the hard wind scattering pellets of glitter over the whitecapped harbor, Lee bending elbows on the rail as the Clayton shoves into the Hudson, dashing the spray over her round humble chin Ive never been afraid of the water since my father tossed me in the Atlantic when I was four and a half years of age and cried SWIM while he dogpaddled around me the only stroke he ever knew I love the water I love the water I love the water I love the water nothing but Lee and the water and then a red bloated face, bobbing

Looks up, Lee does. Theres emotion with the water. Disallowed, impermissible. Look up.

High up above the Empire State, above the Chrysler Building, are tiny choppedup clouds in a frozen cold chatter on the brilliantly clipped blue sky.

Quite by accident, Rena giggles over Danny's letter in the Garden City Kansas farmhouse.

I guess she hates me now, Lee tosses aside the newspaper

MOOOOOOOOOOOOOOOOOOOOOOOOOOOOOOOOOOOOOOOOOOOOOOOOOOOOO

Nelly mustve gotten out again, Rena goes to the springtime window. Theyll have to look for her in the neighboring pasture. There goes Mister Runnymede hippetyhop like a little gnome after Nellie the cow, Rena races to the door, I got to see, I got to see she cries in utter abandon to Lee, her breasts in the large creamcolored bandana rolling like little barrels around her chest, her sultrycolored midriff sinuously after her hips, her long powerful legs sponging her through the doorway

(From behind Lee tries to describe Rena to Rena, your legs resemble those of a little girl's. Not from the side. Not from the front. Where theyre sensuous, sensual, to which the rest of your body salaams. But from the rear . . .

Youre joking, Lee.

No. No Im not. Like a little girl's. You ought to see

Of course I cant, I

Thats right.

Like a little girl's?

Uhhuh. Oh, a girl say nine or ten or so. You know. Oned never suspect the front of you from looking at the backs of your legs.

Ah.

Its true.

She looks at him with a trembling brownblackeyed swerve of wide eyedness, brilliantly bare, the softlyhooked nose ducking slightly, the chin furthering shyly back, the hair the color of rotten oranges falling over one cheek, the brazen blessedness of her, the sultry chill of her. I like that, she says.

I love you, Lee says.

Yes I know

I love the backs of your legs that look like a little girls

All right.

Youre not irritated

Oh no, no. Why should I be irritated?

Youre a stoic.

You always call me a stoic)

Oh, shell get over it, Rena shrugs, returning to the livingroom. She loves you.

Lee staggers up from the armchair. What?

Sure she does. They got the cow back. Mrs Runnymedes bawling Mr Runnymede out. Nina told me she does.

When?

The first time she saw you at Sy's house

I was sorry for you the first time I met you Nina sits straight up her chair in her 19th St Studio between Broadway and Seventh Avenue, a district of garmentmakers' lofts, warehouses, garages. Coffee boils in an open battered pot on the tiny twoburner range over a packingcase. The wind creaks, stumbles and bumbles outside. A single bare overhead light glares on the cardtable where Nina eats her meals. In the rear a bed and a makeshift closet stuffed with expensive dresses. Toward the front near the lofty wide windows the newest canvas on a solid oak easel, a picture of a boy with a bird perched on his outstretched forefinger (I want that picture, you put it aside for me, Nina, Ill take it when I can pay for it. All right. You promise. Yes, I promise. Its a beautiful picture. Yes, I like it too, she shrills, her laughter hacking away). Against the wall huge stacks of canvasses (I think its a case of pure competition, Nina says, with Sy, that broke up our marriage. Two painters in the same family isnt any good. You think thats it, Lee says. Well, yes, part of it. Youre hedging). Because Rena told me she.

Told you what

Maybe I shouldnt ought to tell you.

Come on. Its all right now

Nina is worried, she frowns, painruts ridge her brow. Youre sure its all right now.

Yes. Yes

Well. She hesitates. Ah. Gee, Lee.

Oh, stop it

Well, as if shes forcing a defecation, well, gee, she told me she really didnt love you anymore, gee, God, I was so sorry for

The choppedup clouds resemble, just a little, white ants crawling very slowly across the blue sky. In December. In the start of winter

Even the atomic bomb. That should have an effect. The wind burns back Lee's cheeks, he feels his flesh in the icy wind beginning to flow behind him.

STATUE OF LIBERTY

CONSOLIDATED EDISON COMPANY

STATUE OF LIBERTY

The engines of the General Clayton roll long booms under his feet but the ferry doesnt pitch or roll; simply takes the slapping spray on the chin, pocking Lee's face

where we going now mommy

Mount Clemens. Did you like Niagra Falls

Misspelled, mother

I thought the waterd fall on top of us. What are you going to do in Mount Clemens

take the baths. For my joints

all of the olden people in Mt Clemens, rows of low columns supporting the hotel, the olden people sitting on the benches

why do olden people doze why do they want to be warmed

because theyre old and they dont feel so warm anymore and the sun helps them

they snore and spit runs down their chins

you musnt say that

the olden people dont see me

Stefanie, his adopted daughter, says its a picture about olden times

Stefanie youve got ants all over you, Norma protests in the California kitchen

Punchy the cat was sitting in them, Stefanie patiently explains

The white ants are far above the water, Lee muses. They wont drown. The fife of the dancing ants axes off the surf. In the matter of a specific moment, here aboard the ferry, four years in the Army of the United

States is a total deception. It may have occurred. It may not have. Keep me simple on the clear sunny day. I may have been a soldier, I may have not. One really does not know now and, unless discharge from the army is in itself a momentous experience for some reason, then leaving the military is a mild matter entirely. Nobody at last tried to prevent me from going. Nobody criticized me for going. Nobody thought it ridiculous. There was no hitch. But I wanted to be praised. I wanted a fanfare. I wanted gratitude to be expressed. But nobody seemed to care that I was leaving. Why should anyone. Millions of men are resuming civilian status. The matter of the past in a specific moment is incalculable; therefore, unbearable

The fatuous face of the Statue of Liberty. Im ashamed of it, the silly torch, I dont feel a

Little people walk on the paths around it. A bell buoy clangs. But there should be some reference in my mind to the atomic bomb. Lee lays his wrists against the cold rail, ICE NEVER FAILS, the Fairmount Park freshet slashes his wrist, the nerves are suicides in that circumscribed area, his cousin Charlotte crouches on the runningboard, Not anymore, dont, Lee, dont, dont, Rena swallows a dozen sleeping pills, Tess Rubens of the recessed nipples lays herself out on the bed in the empty Atlantic City cottage, were checking to see if its ready for summer she says, but you dont have a condom she says, Ill come outside, Lee says, youre sure you dont mind whats happening to Rena in Philadelphia she says, I cant let it matter he says, Ill just take off my panties she says, Ive lost an awful lot of weight in Kansas Rena says, you must be a lot happier here Lee says, if only I didnt have to go to the base every morning

in the ancient arthritic bus leaving the depot of Garden City at seven in the morning the gray snow huddled against the main streets stores huddled against the sleepy passengers' faces huddled against the dawn in the crowded bus with the soldiers and the female personnel wives girls of the town working at the base the thin twolane highway through the whitened wheatfields of Kansas on either side flat as the eye can see but no eye wants go see the seats are all taken huddled within huddledness the men and women standing in the aisle huddled one against the other in the slatedumb dark Lee standing and pitching and swaying against a female what female thered been a glimpse of a pretty face and a figure bundled in a huddle of wool and Lee bundled in a huddle of greatcoat nevertheless and notwithstanding her rump through his graylidded eyes and the graylidden dawning in the cold huddled through and next to their skins he rubs with the excuse of the bus's sway his prick through the great coat against her rump in her furcoat as his prick hardens asserts in the rumple and rumble and rock and rut of the bus from side of the road to the side of the road Lee staging a yawn but feeling a yawn staging a sleep but feeling authentic sleep as his prick sleepily nudges nuzzles thrusts against the faint separation of her buttocks in her furcoat as he feels her sleepy huddled return response more thrust than the bus permits her this the huddle of her preferred thrust back knowing in the crowdedness and the sleepiness and the huddledness that nobody will know and fooling themselves in the staging that neither of them need ever know whoever they are wherever they are he feels her squirm against him her lift and her drop as the bus clatters and clumps and hudgehudge hudges along he butts her and she butts him back he butts her and she butts him back done with a vengeance and an anger in a languor of the cold huddled snowmorning

if only you werent so angry Rena says, get the hell out of the breakfast room Dave says I got to study for my exams, Lee leaves, slumping, brotherslashed and humbled

The atomic bomb. Oh. Of course, insignificant, really.

Because we are the bomb. Therefore we shrug at the Hiroshima explosion, really. The point is that instant by instant a single human network is the vessel of an infinite number of cellular explosions, coordinatively contained, a coordination of energy so huge that an ecumenical explosion of atomic bombs is a minuscule achievement in the face of the human achievement, the achievement of the little ants flying, so that we are not really impressed, nor are we really afraid. This is the first night in Horn and Hardarts as the scarlet volumes approach him that the ringworm itching in his groin does not seem to affect him. The aircraft carrier the USS LEXINGTON in mild majesty moves down the Hudson, the flight deck a gray vast plane against the blue waters and the blue sky

NORTH PHILADELPHIA STATION ALL OUT NORTH PHILADELPHIA

Lugging his overloaded flightbag at shouldertilt down the ramp Lee crippleraces toward the exit to burst through the sunblocked entrance

JOHNNY WALKER

SCHENLEYS

IN PHILADELPHIA EVERYBODY READS THE BULLETIN

Rena's head, grinning, pops out of the front seat. Her brother Herb, in the drivers seat, turns toward Lee, grinning. In the back seat, Frances, Herb's wife, grinning. Esther, Rena's mother, grinning. Lee shoves in besides Rena, kissing her, grinning

WELL HOW DOES IT FEEL TO BE OUT HERB DEAFENS THE EARLY AFTERNOON BRIGHT SUNNY AIR

Rena and Lee look at each other, grinning

The scarlet volumes turn from the coffee counter to peer for a moment, simply a moment, only a moment, carefully a moment at the ganglylegged doublebreastedsuited Lee slumped in his chair at the Horn and Hardart table, and Lee a thousand times in a single moment reviews how the scarlet volumes begin at one end of the aisle, small, dim, a daub, and expand as they saunter, bending over the fruit counter, straighten, proceed a few steps, larger now, bend again at the sandwich counter. In two and a half years he will be drafted into the army. The reservists have already been called up. Germanys at war with England. Lee's rear eyes watch his blood on a pool on the ground, the rear eyes of his childhood watch it congeal and crack into tiny insects as the scarlet volumes begin to billow up the cafeteria aisle.

I

black ants and red ants

After the concert at the Academy of Music a half a block southwest of Horn and Hardarts at approximately tenfortyfive in the evening the tophatted whiteshirted tuxedoed and eveninggowned boxholders stray through the faded wooden doors. Appear in nonchalant witnessing upon the topmost steps of the main Academy entrance. A cane. A tiara topping the brilliant excavations of an aged face. A cane at the imperious angle. We who are summoned are about to summon. Velvet hudges the cinammon steps. An iron roof over the pavement, supported by slender posts, affords some intervention against whatever inclemency may be present or foreboding. To right and to left posters behind glass faces continue to announce THE PHILADELPHIA ORCHESTRA BACH PASSACAGLIA AND FUGUE IN C MINOR BEETHOVEN SYMPHONY NUMBER 8 INTERMISSION DEBUSSY AFTERNOON OF A FAUN WAGNER PRELUDE AND LOVEDEATH FROM TRISTAN UND ISOLDE LEOPOLD STOKOWSKI CONDUCTING. A slender post of light ripples up a tophat. We who are about to ascend, descend. The chauffeur towers over the limousine. A lady bends faintly, her escort has a deeper bow before ensconce as the slabfaced cop whistles and bellows at Locust and Broad for the next limousine to curve from Locust south on Broad, pausing before the Academy to spring a chauffeur and the next corsage sniffing up the skirt to avoid entanglement, and the lowering cane, the glittering black traffic north and south on Broad massed in temporary abandonment to the outpour while the numberwriters and the sportsmen pick their teeth watching from the vantage of LEW TENDLERS on the south side of Broad Street across the street as the galleryites politely storm from the side entrances along Locust Street, Link Cornwall in scarletlined black cape dribbling cloacae into the ear of a rakish dowager LEE YOU DARLING WHATEVER ARE YOU DOING ON LOCUST WITH THE CANAILLE he shrieks at the dodging sixfooter digging at his ear across Broad Street

through the revolving door of Horn and Hardarts whitefaced among the darker buildings on either side

the freshlyshaven light in the interior, square tables and redrumped chairs, gray steam curling from the food counter, the waterdispenser at the center of the wall on the right as you enter, the empty clean glasses bottomside up along the vertical nickel grillework carrying off any errant moisture, two coldwater faucets ready for the patron, the busboy traying the dirty glasses behind the dispenser, the front of the cafeteria already filled but the rear beyond the checker a woman of elephantine wads sitting with a bright metal puncher to bite the slim pasteboard printed with numbers graded from five cents to a dollar in multiples of five, the corseted wads of the checker punched by bright green eyes in a highrouged wads pumped up from cheekbone and chinbone and forehead as they scurry from one food item on the tray to the other, chicken ala king, apple dumpling, grilled cheese, coffee BITE and pass on NEXT, BITE, PASS ON, NEXT, BITE to the still empty rear, sanctorum of students, artists, bums

YEH CLIFFORD ODETS USED TO COME IN HERE EVERY NIGHT AND ARGUE WITH THE OLD CONTRIBUTORS TO TRANSITION THE MERITS OF THE BEETHOVEN QUARTETS AS AGAINST THE ART OF THE FUGUE

Got room, Jay. Sure, Lee. Jay the equilateral trianglefaced writer of avantgarde ballet plots

students, artists, bums, teachers, lifeclass models, Philadelphia Bohemia on display, night after night they come beginning approximately at tenthirty and sitting over coffee till one antemeridian, closing time

Maurie Rosens my name, Lee, I met you once over at Naroyan's front porch

Sure, sure, sit down, what are you doing.

Jewelers apprentice

Well

Lee look over this new ballet story I devised, based on the Minotaur myth

Shoulders twist, mouths cup, forearms stack up a curve

Waitll I get another cup of coffee, Lee mumbles and, ambling back, sprawling once again, the world is all at once in a vise when the eye slips over the handrail running the length of the foodcounter

I

black ants and red ants the Rouaultblackoutlined scarlet volumes of the girl at the far end. No hurry. With the greendress shorter girl at her side she ascends the Lee ramp. A tray. The smile grows clearer on the unbrassiered full mouth, the red in the freshlyshaven wintertime, the ventilation vent at the rear wall of the cafeteria sloughing off pelts of heat in humming excision. And at the coffeeurn the tall scarletsilkened girl urges back the shoulderlength hair of the color of rotten oranges from the sallowcream structure of the face in sheerest film and careens her eyes upon the maroonbrown glistens in Lee's. She has heuristic with the hip, brawnbreasted and something of a whip around her waist

Who is she, Jay

I dont know

Maurie?

Never seen her before

We will brood with the fullest most contained lunge of the vision upon the girl

Shes new in the Heel, Lee

Look at her. Look at her. Look at her, the sensual prespring of the girl in the scarlet dress. I love her, I want her, this is my girl, the forever girl, the endless girl, the neverbefore girl, I will have no other girls before thee at coffeeurn, at the head of a queue, just before the fatwadded checker with the metal puncher in her hands, the girl is here, Ive done nothing, simply sat at a table the old words crawl under the traditional triumphal arch erected as he sits not far from the food, the coffee, the meatballs, the spaghetti, the mashed potatoes, the green peas, the lentil soup, the chicken soup, the marmalade and the butter, the spongecake and the artichokes the ants carry in little bits along the path as the child broodwatches, the little bits painstakingly collected into a crimson mound with sallow big tits upon it, with heuristic whanging hips upon it, with slopeshoulders and yawning longlimbs upon it for the child to circle the long neck of her, to pull himself up the hanging rottenorange hair of her, nobody else will talk with her, I shall be the only soul in the world to talk to her now once I talk with her, Jay wont be able to mutter a word that she will hear, she wont be able to glance at anyone else in the cafeteria, I will take her, I will fix her upon me, there wont be a syllable of silence once shes by my side, there wont be the sense of any other matter in the world once I walk by her, take her arm, I will fend off all particles of quanta, nobody else shall be able to ask her a question, I shall have all questions, answers, interludes, commentaries, marginalia, epigrams, preludes upon my tongue at all times for each moment, for as long as she stays in here, till she goes out the door where I shall be, I shall insure my presence till she is once again alone, tonight, and tomorrow night and for all nights and days that shall come, I will be jealous of every point of time adjacent to her tonight, I shall repulse all comers, all contestants, if there be anyone who essays a sentence toward her I shall interrupt with a dissertation, I shall blind and fascinate and shut out any who dare compete, there shall be no competition because this girl is mine, is mine, is mine, I want her, I want to fuck her, I want to know the hair in her crotch, I want to goggle her nipples I

hes extraordinarily light, extraordinarily astonished

because, this is the girl of his beauty. Behold her, for he is beholden

Why dont you say something to her, Lee, Maurie urges. Before you lose her, the little jewelers apprentice crouches in his shoulders, squeezed thin in his blue serge, his black hair pasted back from his high bubbly forehead, the scarlet girl passing, a whiff of her mouth over her shoulder, her splendid buttocks tautening the dress, her green friend giggling

I will, I will, Lee grumbles, not looking, averting himself in stupid pride, sputtering fear

Hey look theyre sitting down over there near the wall.

So

So what do you think. Why dont you go over and introduce yourself, Lee?

I will, I will.

Dont you want to

Sure. I will, I will. The prospect a near catastrophe. The resolution at effort a physical impossibility.

Somebody elsell pick them up. They obviously want to be picked up, the two of them. Theyve come in for that. And the one in red is obviously attracted to you, Lee.

Obviously, obviously. Uhhuh, Lee mutters. Ill go over in due time.

It might be too late. What do you say. Want me to go over and invite them to the table

Lee fumbles with himself in the chair, barely managing the words, barely articulate.

Well, should I? the jewelers apprentice says.

All right, go

Maurie smarts his thin shoulders semiarc by semiarc to the table at the wall, bends over, says a few words, the girls grin in leaping acquiescence, rise and stand at Lee's table. Lee doesnt rise, merely sits, his body astonished, weightless as Maurie makes the introductions, the girl in scarlet instantly sitting at Lee's left, the girl of his beauty, he is beholden to her, therefore behold her as Lee beholds her, holding himself over her, holding his head over her, the words beginning to niagara from his mouth, the light tons of them, the mastodonic spray of them, he over them while at the bottom of the girl peering upward, closer upward, the face of her floating up from the ground, from the table surface where there had been bits before, little crawling things in the cafeteria, little odds and ends of girls, snips and snatches of them, Lee virgin to them, watching them being borne elsewhere so that now in the spring of a wintertime they are instantly an aggregate, in a body all one and effortlessly ascending upon Lee's own aircurrents so that he understands that all at once his virginity is numb and dumb and done, that while it remains still the very fantasy of a fact it is for the first time a reality of imagination and terminated once and for all because the girl has sprung up the aisle and he is sprung in vivid encirclement about her, she the tensility of his metallurge, she the burst not only exterior to him but interior, red red red the color of my truelove's spring

she the freshet on the heart's exposed wrist, that he in a wooden almost thrustaway mystery permits a nodding acquaintance, the jewelers apprentice, to bring into being

the gracious fallaway of the streaked chestnut brasscolored hair from the forehead's fine expanse he streaks his eye across. Black eyebrows, thickbodied at their spacebetween source, taper to a spiny glaze and challenge in their dark the undulant churn of the dullgold maroonglinted headhair. Her eyes in their stark glossed mahogany are acute startling blurs on their fleshwhite socketdomes catching the sprints of flarebits from the hair and reflecting the old settingsun paled color of her browskin. The high cheekbones ameliorate the faintlyhumped nose that gives her profile from one side the witchhandhag hover, from the other side the haughty spur. Her chin as the hair from her forehead falls away reluctantly. The one profile is ugly, the other arrogant; in fullface a sallowswart enchantment, the skin flawless in texture with the underground luminosity the Renaissance masters made fluent under their heaps of color; not a wart, not a blemish, not an excrescence in the expanse of forehead, cheekbone, chin, and the throat as though ancient and inexplicably renewable cream flows over windpipe and the remote wimple of the pulse while the highnecked scarlet frock slurs over and between the greekorthodox spiralminarets of her breasts and the sabresumptuous legs delta into heuristic hip and the tidal rise and fall of the crimsonclad belly, the naked woman waiting at the bottom of the girl, the bellytitted woman patient at the teartassels of the dark eyes, the luminous scarlet acidwoman under the reddressed girl and the ivoryfleshed chit, menstrualred under the cream of her, the sparks of Levi's horse's hooves sulfuric against the dusky haze of an ancient land of her, the crimson of the setting sun underneath her on her eastern spiretits, the devil astride her in the galloping fear of Levilee and Rachelee but the boy spongespurring on toward the wallowred in the blackening town, all the freshlyshaven light of the cafeteria pouring away from the girl as the sweatridden Lee reins himself short before her, glowering on the massed chords of her rottenorangecolored hair, the flawless dawnduskiness of her flesh, the tender springblack of her eyes before which the clattering sparkspitting hooves rear and rend, the haggy witchlike beauty of the girl clawing like barnaclesicicles across his testicles and heart, the death of a drowned man silverygray and gliding across her sinuousness in the tranquiltreacherous currents as Lee ascends to the surface of her, drawing the deep summerair of the girl next to his nosetongue of flowers decaying and cumbrous wings lifting, fresh water and salt, scarlet and cream, tension of the girl that does not venture a millimetre away from the boy, clogged by his coarse black curls, by the slimness of the boy long and swearing like a man at the shoulders, lechered by the ruddy fingers of him slender on cigarette and coffeecup and the fingers of his eyebrows lithe and thick above dense blackeye and broad straight nose, the two faces of the girl and the boy as upon rubber stone, already in clotted, yet wingbeating source and end upon each other, whirring and carcassed, slabbed and propellant she is the greasy glory, contaminated queen, hoot and adoration, expanding and contracting before the lad, weighty and buoyant, ponderous and feathersome, dream and consumed saturation

shes alive and shes dead shes dead and alive

the scarlet entombment within flowing cream. He rises with her.

Rises.

The crawling itching ants inside his groin coalesce, and in the wonder of his infancy with the girl all living creatures acrawl on the ground are lofted in one early love:

Rena.

the fife of the dancing ant axes off the surf ICE NEVER F

ACKNOWLEDGMENTS

Profound thanks are extended to the following for their generous financial support which helped to defray some of this book's production costs:

Bryan M. Acomb, Kevin Adams, Reuben Andrews, Matt Armstrong, Tara Circus Barnes, Cameron Bennett, Matthew Boe, Brian R. Boisvert, Ian Braddy, Anthony Brown, Matt Bucher, Aldrin Camba, Stanley Chau, Scott Chiddister, Natasha R. Chisdes, Drake Clapp, Seth Coblentz, C. Colla, Joshua Lee Cooper, Michael Corkery, Michael Ducker, John Feins, Nathan Friedman, Nathan "N.R." Gaddis, James & Savannah Galliher, Martin Georgi, GmarkC, Linda Gonzales & Philip Shalanca, B. F. Gordon Jr., Rob Hannah, E. G. C. Hemming, Frank S. Hestvik, Adam Hetherington, Griffin Irvine, Isaac Hoff, Per Kristian Hoff, Erik T. Johnson, Haya K., Handsome Ryan Kennedy, Larry Kerschner, Tom Kiefer, Asha Kodah, Yevgeny Kopman, Nathan Kouri, Tim Ledbetter, David McLean, Sidney McMahon, Kirby Miller, Mark S. Mitchell, Ronald Morton, Geoffrey Moses, Gregory Moses, Sidney Orr (Gil Orlovitz's nephew), Michael O'Shaughnessy, Nick Oxford, nelfalot, Marshall W. Parks, Ry Pickard, B. A. Pinter, Poems-For-All, Pedro Ponce, Philipp Potocki, Nickolas Promitzer, Borys Pugacz-Muraszkiewicz, Michael J. Richmond, Matthew J. Rogers, Evan Robertson, William Robertson, Anuj Rudhar, Dieso Sad, George Salis, Frank V. Saltarelli, Christopher Sartisohn, Serpentmoon, Connor Shirley, Matt Stephenson, Sean Stewart, Mathias Stroers, James Teller, Desiree Troy, Daniel Vallejo, Cato Vandrare, Ryan Vivian, Jack Waters, Geoff Wilt, Michael Zhuang

Rick Schober
Publisher
Tough Poets Press

CPSIA information can be obtained
at www.ICGtesting.com
Printed in the USA
LVHW050859150419
614196LV00015B/445